PRAISE FO...

Jennifer Probst

"Achingly romantic, touching, realistic, and just plain beautiful."
—*New York Times* bestselling author Katy Evans

"Tender and heartwarming."
—#1 national bestselling author Marina Adair

"Beautiful . . . and so well written! Highly recommend!"
—*New York Times* bestselling author Emma Chase

"Jennifer Probst pens a charming, romantic tale destined to steal your heart."   —*New York Times* bestselling author Lori Wilde

"Probst tugs at the heartstrings."   —*Publishers Weekly*

"I never wanted this story to end! Jennifer Probst has a knack for writing characters I truly care about—I want these people as *my* friends!"
—*New York Times* bestselling author Alice Clayton

"For a . . . fun-filled, warmhearted read, look no further than Jennifer Probst!"   —*New York Times* bestselling author Jill Shalvis

"Jennifer Probst never fails to delight."
—*New York Times* bestselling author Lauren Layne

TITLES BY
Jennifer Probst

THE SUNSHINE SISTERS SERIES

Love on Beach Avenue

Temptation on Ocean Drive

STAY SERIES

The Start of Something Good

A Brand New Ending

All Roads Lead to You

Something Just Like This

Begin Again

BILLIONAIRE BUILDERS SERIES

Everywhere and Every Way

Any Time, Any Place

Somehow, Some Way

All or Nothing at All

SEARCHING FOR . . . SERIES

Searching for Someday

Searching for Perfect

Searching for Beautiful

Searching for Always

Searching for You

Searching for Mine

Searching for Disaster

MARRIAGE TO
A BILLIONAIRE SERIES

The Marriage Bargain

The Marriage Trap

The Marriage Mistake

The Book of Spells

The Marriage Merger

The Marriage Arrangement

NONFICTION

Write Naked

OUR ITALIAN SUMMER

JENNIFER PROBST

BERKLEY

New York

BERKLEY
An imprint of Penguin Random House LLC
penguinrandomhouse.com

Copyright © 2021 by Triple J Publishing Inc.
Readers Guide copyright © 2021 by Triple J Publishing Inc.
Penguin Random House supports copyright. Copyright fuels creativity,
encourages diverse voices, promotes free speech, and creates a vibrant
culture. Thank you for buying an authorized edition of this book and for
complying with copyright laws by not reproducing, scanning, or distributing
any part of it in any form without permission. You are supporting writers
and allowing Penguin Random House to continue to
publish books for every reader.

BERKLEY and the BERKLEY & B colophon
are registered trademarks of Penguin Random House LLC.

Library of Congress Cataloging-in-Publication Data

Names: Probst, Jennifer, author.
Title: Our Italian summer / Jennifer Probst.
Description: First edition. | New York: Berkley, 2021.
Identifiers: LCCN 2020025342 (print) | LCCN 2020025343 (ebook) |
ISBN 9780593098462 (trade paperback) | ISBN 9780593098479 (ebook)
Subjects: LCSH: Domestic fiction. | GSAFD: Love stories.
Classification: LCC PS3616.R624 O87 2021 (print) | LCC PS3616.R624
(ebook) | DDC 813/.6—dc23
LC record available at https://lccn.loc.gov/2020025342
LC ebook record available at https://lccn.loc.gov/2020025343

First Edition: January 2021

Printed in the United States of America
1 3 5 7 9 10 8 6 4 2

Cover image by Andrea Comi / Getty Images
Cover design by Sarah Oberrender

This is a work of fiction. Names, characters, places, and incidents either are
the product of the author's imagination or are used fictitiously,
and any resemblance to actual persons, living or dead, business
establishments, events, or locales is entirely coincidental.

This book is dedicated to my mom, my aunt Rosemary, and my niece Taylor. I learned so much about myself on our epic trip to Italy. Thank you for showing me how much love and family mean in this life. I tried to keep our secrets, but some may have spilled out for the good of the story.

Don't worry—I never told WHO.

And in memory of my grandmother. I still remember sipping coffee with you in the kitchen while you tried to teach me how to speak Italian. You asked me to do two things: study Italian in school, and one day visit your homeland. I'm so happy I did both—you were always there with us in spirit during our trip.

Finally, for those who dream of big adventures, I wish you the wings you need in order to jump and take a risk.

Love is usually waiting.

Italy is a dream that keeps returning for the rest of your life. —ANNA AKHMATOVA

The journey not the arrival matters. —UNKNOWN

OUR ITALIAN SUMMER

CHAPTER ONE

FRANCESCA

"No, I SAID the deadline is Wednesday. That gives you two days to give me a decent hook or I'm pulling you off the account."

I ignored the glint of resentment in the young man's green eyes, wondering if he thought his charm and good looks trumped talent. In many places, they did. But not in my company.

I gave him credit for smothering the emotion immediately and forcing a smile. "Got it. I'll get it done."

I nodded. "I know you will."

He left my office with his shoulders squared, and I wondered what would eventually triumph—pride or the drive for success. He was young and had promise, so I hoped the latter for him. Pride was good in some cases, but working on a team to retain high-powered advertising accounts required the ability to do what it took, whether it was working with someone you didn't care for or swallowing the innate instinct to push back at the boss you hated.

Of course, he didn't hate me. At least not yet. It was hard to take orders from a woman who was blind to looks, charisma, or flattery. I'd learned that lesson early—and ran my F&F Advertising with a ruthless efficiency and cold-mannered sharpness that made me one of the best in the business. I'd even managed to snag a spot on the Top Ten Women to Watch in Business list from *Fortune* magazine.

Too bad I had no time to enjoy it.

I glanced at my watch, my mind furiously clicking over the day's crammed schedule. I'd have to work late again, but it'd be worth it once I nailed this new account. I headed to the conference room for a meeting with my team, my sensible low-heeled shoes clicking on the hardwood floor. Layla and Kate were already perched at the polished table, laptops fired up and endless papers strewn around.

"Morning, boss," Kate said, motioning toward the chair next to her. "Figured we'd be eating lunch in again, so I had Jessica get your usual."

"Thanks." I took a sip of my Voss water as I sat beside them. I lived on water and grilled chicken salads, which was the easiest fuel to shove into my body on limited time. "Where's Adam?"

"Running late," Layla said, shooting me a smile. "But I don't think we need him for the brainstorming session. Better to get his feedback on the social media after we have a few solid concepts."

"True. He didn't look too thrilled with our new product."

Kate quirked a brow. "He's been begging to sell something sexier than kids' lemonade."

Layla snorted. "I told him anyone can sell sex—it's not even a challenge. If he makes this work, he's a genius."

I laughed. "You always did know how to motivate him, Layla."

My valued art director preened. "Plenty of practice in the ranks of hell. At least it was good for something."

Layla had graduated at the top of her class and planned to take Manhattan by storm. Unfortunately, like me, she ended up with a slew of crap jobs, and being a black woman in the industry meant encountering prejudices to overcome. We'd worked together for a few years before I ventured out to create my own company, and I knew she'd be the perfect art director for F&F Advertising.

I trusted her with both my business and my personal shit. It was the best decision I ever made.

Kate was my advertising manager and my other right hand. She wore tailored designer suits, and her blond hair was pulled back tight in a chignon, emphasizing her classic bone structure. I had to admit, when I first met Kate, I thought she was too beautiful and quiet to be successful in such a cutthroat business, but she soon proved me wrong, and now I never discriminate based on looks. I made sure I hired a diverse, multicultural team, treated them like royalty, and offered enough incentives for promotion. It proved a good move, since I had low turnover and a core of hard-won talent.

Lately, I'd been thinking of offering them both a full partnership. My little boutique company was finally on the verge of exploding, and I needed people I trusted by my side. I had been intent on not bringing in partners, but now I saw that if I wanted to really grow, it was time I took the leap. Plus, I considered these women friends. They'd proven their loyalty, and we worked well together.

But that tiny sliver of doubt still crept through me. I'd gotten here by relying on my own drive, talent, and gut instincts to give clients what they need, twenty-four seven. I was the final say on everything for my company. Giving up that type of control made my skin prickle, like I was about to break out into hives. I'd heard horror stories of being pushed out by once-trusted partners and overruled on important decisions by lack of majority. What if Kate and Layla decided to team up and I found myself the odd woman out? Power sometimes had a funny effect on relationships. Did I really want to take such a chance? Even with these women I trusted and called friends?

I needed more time to think it through. Until then, I'd just push forward.

I shook my head and refocused. "Let's get to work. We only have two weeks until the presentation. I've been looking over all the reports from the research department and there's a few things we need to zone in on."

Layla jumped in. "Lexi's Lemonade is organic. That's the main buzzword."

"Exactly. Statistics show kids drive popular drink sales by pushing their parents to buy. We need to find a way to bridge the gap and get the children to beg mom to buy it."

"And the moms need to feel good about giving in," Kate added.

I brought up a picture of the label on my screen and tapped it with my fingernail. "Packaging is huge. The recycled box is earth-friendly and colorful. It needs to compete on the shelves with Capri Sun, Honest Kids, and the endless others. We need to find a unique inroad."

"At least it tastes good," Layla said. She pursed her red-painted lips. "Can you believe Kool-Aid still sells a shitload? Man, I loved that stuff growing up. And what a mascot. Genius."

"Hmm, but I don't think we want a mascot for this product," I said. "We need to gain children's attention with the ad, then slam it home that there's low sugar and no preservatives. The double hook."

"Shock value?" Layla threw out.

I nodded. "Possible, but not too much. I think funny."

Kate cocked her head. "Kids nowadays are immune to shock value with YouTube and video games. I agree, funny may be the way to go."

Layla groaned and opened up her email. "I'll get Sarah started on kids' comedy and what generates the most sales."

"Good, let's start throwing everything in the pot for possible scenarios," I said. The rush of adrenaline warmed my blood as the challenge of a new creative account settled in. This was what I lived for, the elusive hunt for the perfect hook to please a client and sell the product. It never got old.

We started brainstorming and my phone vibrated. Glancing quickly at the screen, I noticed my mother had called twice without leaving a voice mail. I held back a groan. Typical. If I didn't pick up, she just kept calling and refused to leave a message. Soon, a text came through.

Frannie, please call me. I have an important question.

Impatience flickered. She was always calling me with endless questions, from how to work the television remote to what movie to rent at Redbox to whether I'd read the latest article about coconut oil healing all ailments. Once, she'd called half a dozen times to tell me she had a thirty percent coupon at Kohl's and didn't want it to expire.

She'd never really respected my work or how far I'd come, still treating me like I had a disposable job that allowed me to leave when I wanted, relax on weekends, or delegate my work when I wished. Her constant refrains echoed through my mind.

I don't understand. Aren't you the boss? Why can't you take some time off?

I grabbed my phone and typed out a text. Busy now. Call you later.

I got back to work and shortly thereafter Adam came in. His curly brown hair was a bit mussed, and sweat gleamed on his forehead. "We have a problem," he announced, crashing down into the chair.

"You decided you're too fancy to work on branding Lexi's Lemonade," Layla teased, used to Adam's dramatics. The man was a bit over-the-top but a genius when it came to creating click-worthy social media campaigns.

"No. The IG ad for Dallas Jeans is tanking." He slid his iPad down the table with it opened to the screen. "Consumers hate it. We need a rebrand."

My heart rate rammed into a full gallop. I had no time for any failures that weren't scheduled. "It's still brand-new," I said, glancing down at the ad. "Maybe we need some organic growth first."

Adam shook his head. "Not with this. It's only going to get worse. I have a few suggestions on what to tweak, Frannie. I know you're busy so I can work with Layla and get it handled."

"No problem," Layla said. "I can make the time."

I hesitated. I was already overworked and overscheduled. I should just let Adam and Layla take care of it, but the Dallas Jeans ad was something I'd helped create. If it bombed, I needed to be involved in fixing it. "No, I can work with you."

Kate blinked. "What about Lexi's Lemonade? We don't want to get behind. It may be better to let them handle it, Frannie."

I squared my shoulders. "I know the client best, including Perry's preferences. I'll stay late a few nights and knock it out."

Kate and Layla shared a glance but held their tongues. They'd been pushing for more control, advising me to hire more people and to work lead on fewer clients. I knew they were trying to help and that they craved more responsibility, but I still had an uneasy feeling that if I stepped back too much, they'd eventually decide they didn't need me.

I tamped down on the tiny flicker of fear coursing through my bloodstream. That annoying, buzzing voice whispering the million ways I could fail. My entire reputation was based on running F&F Advertising and thriving at every level. I'd finally managed to secure some national-brand clients and needed to show they'd made the right decision in placing their dollars with a smaller firm.

Why did it feel like the entire world was waiting for me to fail? Successful women were still looked upon as dangerous, and one big mistake was gleefully gossiped about, with news of it spreading like wildfire.

I cleared my throat and took a deep breath. "Now, let's get to work," I said firmly.

They didn't protest.

Hours later, I collapsed in my office and buzzed Jessica. "Any messages?" I asked.

She rattled off a few I could put off until tomorrow. "Your mother called twice. Said you'd promised to call her back."

I groaned, rubbing my temples. "I forgot, thanks. Go on home. Thanks for staying."

"No problem. Have a good night, Frannie."

My stomach growled. I reached inside my desk drawer and nibbled on a Kind bar. Better get it over with. I dialed my mom's number.

"Hi, Mom. Everything okay?"

"You never called me back." Her voice held a slight sting designed to instill guilt. It worked. "You weren't at Allegra's track meet."

Shit.

My daughter's schedule was as jam-packed as mine, with tennis matches and races across the county. I'd missed the last few and swore I'd be there for the invitational. Her time was stellar and she had a good chance at getting a scholarship for both her running and her grades. This meet had been key. "I'm sorry," I said with a sigh. "We had a crisis here at work, and I literally just got to my office. Why didn't she call or text me?"

"Because she wanted you to remember on your own."

The whiplash of guilt stung deeper. Another test I'd failed. How could I be a rock star at my job and such a loser at home? "What was her time?"

"I forgot but I wrote it down for you. She beat her record in the eight hundred and got a medal for first in the fifteen hundred."

Pride flashed through me. "That's amazing. Is she there with you?"

"No, she went home on her own. But I wanted to invite you both to dinner this week. Allegra wants to try out a new dish and we've had no family time together. How about Wednesday?"

I closed my eyes, resenting the requests she threw at me. She had nothing on her schedule and assumed I should jump at any invitation. "I can't, Mom. I've got a hell of a week coming up with this new campaign, and I need to work late."

An impatient sigh huffed over the line. My nerves prickled with annoyance. "Again? This is a difficult year for Allegra, and she needs you home, at least for dinner. Plus, I can't freeze the grass-fed beef since it's been in the refrigerator and I got it specifically for you. It's expensive."

"Then make it for yourself, Mom. It has less hormones so it's better for your health."

Mom snorted. "I'm too old to care what I eat anymore. Why can't you come home and eat like a normal person, then go back to the office? At least we'll have some time with you."

I ground my teeth, remembered my last dentist appointment, and tried to relax my jaw. My mother had spent her entire life catering to Dad and me, creating domestic chores like a lifeline. And though she always said aloud that she was proud of my success, deep down I wondered. Instead of trying to support me through my struggles as a single mother, she turned to her skills as a master guilt-trip artist and exposed all my own crippling doubts. Did she resent my choice to become a career woman? To raise Allegra without a father figure? Or did she wonder what type of life she would've had if she'd embraced more than the four walls of her home?

I'd never know. We rarely got into deep conversations. It was easier to stick to mundane topics and trick ourselves into believing we had a connection—the sacred mother-daughter bond that movies love to exploit in sickening, shallow sweetness. I preferred the truth, even though it sometimes tasted bitter.

"I just can't. I have endless things to do and little time."

"One day you may find there's no time left, Francesca. And that you gave work more power over you than it should have."

It always came back to this—I'd never win, no matter what I did or how hard I tried. We viewed the world differently, and she had no interest in trying to understand me. For too many years, I had longed for an acceptance that never came, until I swore I'd stop looking for her approval. The hurt that sprouted from my mother's words was more humiliating than anything.

And still I couldn't stop leaping to my own defense. "I'm sorry if I own and run a profitable, successful company and can't get home for dinner. I'm sorry I'm such a disappointment to your high standards."

"Stop using that tone and putting words in my mouth!"

Oh God, we were going to fight again. And it would take up too much energy and precious time. I drew in a deep breath and focused on keeping calm. "Do you want me to text Allegra and see if she can join you for dinner? I was going to tell her she can invite friends over and order pizza, but maybe she'd like to visit."

I tried to ignore the disappointment in her tone, reminding

myself she didn't have a million balls in the air to juggle other than dinner. "I'll text her. You're busy."

I managed to hold my tongue. "Thanks."

"What about Sunday? Surely you have a few hours to be with us on the Lord's day. There's something I need to discuss with you and it's important."

I hadn't been to church since I was fourteen, when I finally declared my independence and refused to go anymore. "Fine, I'll come Sunday."

"Good. Make sure you congratulate Allegra when you see her. She worked hard for that trophy."

The direct hit caused me to wince. She acted like I didn't know how to treat my own daughter. "Of course."

We said goodbye and hung up.

I sagged over my desk. Tension knotted my stomach and squeezed my lungs, compressing my breath. No, I would not allow this to happen again. The last attack must have been a freak occurrence. Too much stress, too little sleep, too many cups of coffee. I had a thousand excuses for the crippling anxiety that had washed through my body last week and driven me to my knees, fighting for breath. Thank God it had happened when I was alone in my office, where it would remain a secret. But even now, just the thought of another breakdown clenched my muscles in fear.

I closed my eyes, fighting to slow my rapid heartbeat. For a few frantic moments I couldn't breathe, and I tried not to lose it, but then the air hit my lungs and I gulped it down gratefully.

What was happening to me lately? I'd always thrived in stressful situations, but maybe the Lexi's Lemonade account was bothering me more than I thought. Maybe after I put in the necessary hours and secured the campaign, I'd stop having these ridiculous attacks.

Yes, I'd just control it for now. Lately my nights were spent staring up at the ceiling and worrying. My body had begun to rebel, and I had no time for it. Next month, I'd see a doctor and get fixed up. It would all be fine.

I grabbed a bottle of water and took a few sips while my mother's words still churned in my brain. She'd be the first one to crow *I told you so* if she knew about my anxiety attacks and would probably cite my refusal to spend time on my health and appearance as the cause instead of old-fashioned work.

Even at seventy-five, my mother was beautiful, with firm, smooth skin in a gorgeous olive color; thick hair that had once been coal black but had turned to gray; and a trim, lean build that never seemed to thicken, even with her advanced years. She took pride in her appearance and was always tugging at my hair or begging me to wear makeup.

I'd inherited none of my mother's fine traits. My hair was pin straight and limp, so I'd begun wearing it short, with a shaggy, fashionable cut. Even my attempts at highlighting failed at coaxing the dirty-blond strands to sparkle, but I invested in a top-notch stylist so at least the color had some range. My eyes were plain brown. Not brown with gold specks, or an inky depth to give them more mystery. Just mud brown.

Mostly, I didn't care. I realized early on that not having my mother's beauty was an advantage. I had good skin and bone structure, thank God, enough to achieve a passable pretty. Since I was average height and weight, not too curvy or too skinny, I was able to dress in a wide variety of ways depending on the person I chose to reflect. I wasn't beautiful enough to cause men concern or women jealousy, and not unattractive enough to feel awkward. I built on my advantages young, learning what to accent and what to tone down, from my wardrobe to my speech, until I'd perfected the look of a female executive going places.

Marriage had never been on my radar, not when meaningful, exciting work, money, and travel were at stake.

Dad would have understood. Would have cheered from the sidelines to see his only daughter reach the pinnacle of success in this cutthroat business. He'd always been driven to succeed like me and spent most of his hours building his own business. Dad moved from general construction to building homes, until he'd created a small team and cultivated a stellar reputation. He used to tell me to stay on budget and stay on time and clients would pour in.

Mom consistently complained about Dad's absence and long work hours, but she was the only one who didn't understand. I knew he wanted to give me better opportunities. He introduced me to a glimpse of a world with no borders if I was smart enough and driven enough to leap for it. He used to tell me I was just like him—born with stars in my eyes and wandering feet, always looking for more. He never tried to curb my dreams or make me feel like I wanted too much. He understood.

God, I missed him. His death was a bitter loss I still lingered on, especially late at night when there was no one there to soothe the doubts. The heart attack had taken him hard and fast, but the worst of the grief was the knowledge that he'd never been able to hold his granddaughter. He would've doted on Allegra.

The thought made me reach for my phone to call my daughter.

When she didn't answer, I knew she was mad at me.

I'd broken another promise.

The familiar guilt slammed through me, but I took the punch like a seasoned boxer, already comfortable with the thousands of ways I'd failed at being a mother. It was so much easier when she was a baby. Sure, the lack of sleep and endless exhaustion sucked, but coming home to her precious giggles and obvious adoration made up for all of it. I was able to give her what she needed most of the time. A bottle. A blanket. Changing her diaper. Playing. Food. It was like a checklist to follow that guaranteed a high degree of success and boundless love.

Now?

I couldn't remember the last time she hadn't looked at me with utter naked resentment. As if I'd personally done everything I could to ruin her life. No matter what I tried—discipline, being her friend, ignoring her dark moods, offering advice—it was all wrong. And not just a little. Every day my failure was evident in her venom-dripping voice or the cold judgment in her big brown eyes, which had once offered reverence.

She'd always been extremely close with my mother and liked to visit or cook dinner over there. Maybe some extra time with my mother was good for Allegra, especially since I'd been working so much lately. Allegra wouldn't be pressured or pushed or grilled—my mother didn't believe in that. At least, not for her granddaughter. She loved to fuss and spoil and pamper, and Allegra adored every moment.

I had to stop worrying about everything so much. I was in a good place, and it had happened under my own drive, discipline, and hard work. Allegra would eventually see all my successes and be proud when she got older. Looking back, she'd finally realize she had more opportunities to make a difference in the world because I pushed both of us.

I refused to have regrets about my choices.

And I refused to fail.

CHAPTER TWO

ALLEGRA

I STOOD OUTSIDE Riverview Academy High School next to my two closest friends, Bonnie and Claire. Dressed in our ridiculous uniform of short skirts and blouses, I savored the fresh air before we had to go back inside for the next period. I only had one break in the late morning.

"Are we meeting at the party after the track meet Friday night?" Bonnie asked, reapplying her red lipstick as she checked her reflection in the tiny mirror. " 'Cause new guy is gonna be there and he's H-O-T."

Claire flicked her perfect blond hair behind her shoulder. "He's not that hot," she declared. "He's definitely no athlete. Maybe he'd be better off with Allegra. She's always liked the brainiacs."

"He was already talking to Debbie the slut," Bonnie said. "You know how she likes to do the new ones before anyone else gets their pick."

"Allegra is much prettier and has class," Claire pointed out. "You should make a move. Guys adore it when girls ask them out."

"You've never asked a guy out," Bonnie squealed.

Claire rolled her eyes. "I'm waiting for the right one. Hey, did you check out the new Gucci dress that just got released from the runway? I already asked my mom to get it for prom."

"You didn't! Bitch—my mother never lets me wear what I

want. Your and Allegra's moms are the coolest. I'll get stuck with last year's Vera Wang. What are you wearing, Allegra?"

I was already bored out of my mind with the conversation. Once again, I had the strange feeling of being outside my body, not meant to be trapped in a tiny, rich town. But as usual, I cranked to autopilot and answered. "Not sure. I'll figure it out later."

"Well, don't wait too long or Claire will buy all the good stuff. Hey, who's that?"

I watched as the faded black Dodge sports car pulled up to the school and idled right in front of us. A girl with shocking-pink hair and a nose ring stuck her head out the window. She flicked a gaze over all the pretentious outfits and brown loafers and long wavy hair because God forbid any girl wears a short cut.

Oh my God. I knew her. It was Freda.

I'd met her at the party I'd begged my friends to crash a week ago. It'd been a mix of people from various high schools and usually not our scene, but I was dying to do something different. I loved her pink hair, ripped jeans, and cool shoulder tat of a bleeding rose. I figured she'd be a bitch, but we'd actually talked for a while. She introduced me to David and Connor, her two friends, and they seemed really cool. They went to the public high school a few blocks away from Riverview. We got into some good conversations before my friends came looking for me, demanding we leave because of the trashy crowd. I'd apologized but figured they were done with me after such a crappy comment.

"Hey," she greeted me, ignoring my friends. "Whatcha doing?"

Bonnie and Claire stared in shocked silence. For the first time in a while, excitement pumped through my veins. "Waiting to go back inside."

"We're bouncing for the rest of the day. Wanna come?"

I looked at her as she waited for my answer. Connor leaned over from the driver's seat and motioned me in with a grin. "Come on, rich girl. Come play with us."

I didn't take offense. Ignoring Bonnie's gasp, I hitched my backpack tighter over my shoulder and made my decision. "I'm going to go with them. Cover me. If anyone asks, I went home with a stomachache."

Claire's mouth fell open. "Are you kidding me?" she hissed. "You can't go with them. You'll get raped or kidnapped or something. They're scum!"

Coldness trickled down my spine. I'd known Claire for years now, grew up with her, and liked her a bit less every day that passed. She'd always been the leader of the school, and everyone was jealous of my place beside her. But underneath, I knew Claire was plain mean. "I'll be fine. Call you later."

"Allegra!"

The car door opened and I jumped in the back seat. Connor gave a loud whoop and pulled out of the lot, leaving my friends gaping at the curb. A thrill raced through me as I leaned back and looked at David, the third in the crew. "Hey," I greeted him.

"Hey," he said back.

We settled into silence as the Foo Fighters blared and everyone lit up cigarettes.

With their piercings and tats, they didn't fit in with any of my current friends. I bet they weren't in track or tennis or swimming, or anything else that stunk of conformity. I needed that today. Sure, I was probably being reckless going off with people I didn't know. They might sleep around and do drugs and not care about grades or planning for the future. But, hell, they were real. And I wanted that so bad, I was starting not to care about the consequences.

"Want one?" Freda asked, tapping out a Marlboro Light.

All I could think of was those horrible TV commercials showing people with one lung or cutout vocal cords because of smoking. My mother's droning voice kept replaying in my head in a mantra of nonsense words like *stupid, cancer,* and *ruin your life*. I squeezed my eyes shut and pushed it all to the side.

"Sure." Heart beating at a ridiculous rhythm, I took the cigarette and Freda showed me how to inhale without mocking me. After a few coughs, I finally got it. I let the smoke settle, then blew it out, not liking it too much but feeling good about doing something my mother would hate. With every puff, her voice grew dimmer.

"Where to?" Connor called out, managing to drive, text, and smoke at the same time. He had long black shaggy hair, a pointy chin, and a wardrobe of black T-shirts and jeans. He was sexy in a rough, disheveled sort of way and I couldn't decide if I liked him or not. At first I thought he and Freda were hooking up, but now I knew they didn't believe in boyfriend-girlfriend stuff. Thank God. I couldn't handle any more bullshit politics on who was with who, and who was cool to hang with and who wasn't. After Ryan Thomas, straight-A student and track star, tried to shove his hands under my skirt at Bonnie's house, I was done with trying to be seen with the right crowd. Even worse, when I tried to tell Bonnie and Claire what he'd done, they'd actually berated me for not wanting him, taunting me with my virgin card. Like I'd ever give it up to an asshole.

"My dad's gone this week. We can go to my house," David said. I studied David, taking in his messy brown hair, his dark eyes, and the scar that ran down half of his right cheek. He was the quietest one, taking things in before deciding to speak, but his body language was jerky, as if he was always nervous about what he might encounter.

We drove for a while, then pulled into a house that looked

like it needed some TLC. The lot had sprung up with weeds, and the porch seemed to sag. The color was muddy brown with some shingles missing, but I already liked it better than my own house. Sometimes, I felt like I lived in a museum, with furniture I couldn't sit on. The floors were too bare and the ceilings too high, and I was too damn lonely on a regular basis. I'd take a house well lived in anytime.

We walked inside, straight into a living room with dirty beige carpeting and a large chocolate suede couch. A beat-up leather ottoman and a coffee table were the only other furniture besides a few basic lamps and a large-screen TV. The house smelled like coffee, cigarettes, and bacon. I spotted a small kitchenette ahead and a few doors down a short hallway. The walls were covered with various framed record stuff that looked like they were some type of important awards.

Dave headed to the kitchen and came back with a bottle of vodka and a pint of OJ. Freda brought in a few glasses and we all took a seat on the couch. More cigarettes came out while Freda poured hefty servings of liquid breakfast. I put up my feet and sipped tentatively at my vodka. I'd had vodka and rum before, but never this early, and never this much.

Freda took a sip, put her feet up, and tossed me a grin. "Now, this is what life is about," she declared. "I mean, what the hell are we ever going to use algebra for? And who cares if we know who the thirty-ninth president is? I can't wait to start working full-time and really live."

Connor hooked his foot over his knee and nodded. "Yeah, you can learn more about the world by actually reading books on your own and talking to people. Politics is shit. The environment is killing us. People are greedy assholes. Might as well find some pleasure in your own way."

David tapped his fingers on the edge of the couch, drinking in silence. I turned my gaze to him automatically, wondering why he kind of fascinated me. He seemed to have some deep thoughts but he didn't throw them out there like Freda and Connor.

"Allegra, what do you want to do when you're sprung from prison? Join the country club? Have a bunch of babies and marry a rich guy?" Freda asked.

I shrugged, not taking offense at her question. It kind of made sense. They saw me as different from them and they still hadn't figured me out. Neither had I. "I don't know. My mom is really strict about my grades. Always pushing college and career goals, like if I end up falling in love and wanting babies before I'm twenty-two, she'd lose her shit and think I'm a loser. Why can't I make my own decisions about what I want?"

Freda rolled her eyes. "I get it. They want you to be exactly like them—some sort of mini robot—but not do any of the bad stuff they used to when they were younger. They want you to live the lives they never got to."

I jerked back. I'd never thought about it, but it was a smart observation. My mom used to tell me she dreamed of giving me opportunities she never had, but if she was never around to do anything with me, then who cares? She hadn't even had time to fall in love and get married. She was actually proud of me not having a real dad. Being born by artificial insemination—via some random dude from a damn catalogue—sucked. It was humiliating and weird, and she'd taken away my right to have a father—or at least grieve not having a father who's around.

"Is that how your mom is?" I asked Freda, taking a drag on the cigarette. My throat burned but I was beginning to like it.

"Yep. She used to be some big deal at a bank. Talked about

Wall Street and stuff, but quit to have kids. Now she's miserable and wants me to be this financial wiz." Freda shook her head and laughed. "She's cray-cray."

"Same thing at my house," Connor said. "Endless state tests and college admissions coming up soon. My dad thinks I'm something I'm not. I don't intend to be trapped in some dead-end job with no vacay just for a paycheck. Fuck that."

"What are you going to do?" I asked curiously.

"Nothing. Live. Figure things out. I always thought working on a yacht or cruise ship would be cool. Heard it was good money."

Freda cackled. "You want to travel and go on vacation, not be the hired help."

"Whatever."

I turned to David. "How about you? Are you close with your parents?"

David stared back at me for a while, no expression on his face. "What kid is close to their parent?" he mocked.

"David's dad was a famous musician," Freda said. "He doesn't want David to follow in his footsteps. He was on the road most of the time and his wife died a while ago, so he felt guilty and now tries to save his son from the same type of future. All hail drugs, sex, and rock and roll."

David shot her an annoyed look. "Thanks for sharing my life story."

Freda grinned. "Welcome."

Now all those framed records on the wall made sense. "Are you a musician?"

For one moment, something glinted in his brown eyes, an emotion I couldn't name. "I play guitar," he said reluctantly. "Write some songs. No big deal."

"Bullshit," Connor said. "You're talented, dude. Been telling you that a long time."

David shrugged. "Nowhere to play in this town. Once I save enough money, I'm out of here."

"That's our plan for the summer," Freda said. "Connor's got an RV from his dad, so we're gonna hit the road. Check out some artsy towns or maybe even the city. David will play at some clubs, and maybe I'll do some poetry readings."

"You write?" I asked in surprise. She looked more like the rocker type.

"Yep, been writing since I was young. Just nobody interesting enough to share my shit with."

Connor snorted. "We're right here. Are you trying to insult us?"

She rolled her eyes. "You two don't count." Suddenly, she swung her head around and pointed at me. "Hey, why don't you come with us? Then I won't be stuck alone with two stinky men in an RV."

My eyes widened in surprise. I barely knew them, yet they were inviting me on a summer road trip. Trying to act cool before the guys rejected me, I shrugged. "Thanks, but I'm sure it'd be too many people."

David narrowed his gaze. "There's enough room. If you want to come."

"I don't mind," Connor said. "The more the merrier."

"See? Come on, what else you gonna do this summer? Get a crappy job? Study? Hang out at the country club?" Freda asked. "This may be your only opportunity to see what's out there on your own terms. Unless you think your mom would freak and not let you."

I was going to be eighteen this summer—heading into my senior year—and I had no fucking clue who I was. I didn't know what college I wanted to go to, what I wanted to be, or even what would make me happy. Sure, I had good grades and a solid

SAT score, and with my mom's connections, I'd have a decent pick of colleges. But just because I was smart didn't mean I knew what I wanted to study. I wished I felt free to make my own choices without pressure.

The only thing I truly loved was cooking. I loved creating new dishes and learning about how the ingredients in a dish worked together. Nonni had taught me how to make fresh pasta, bread, and gravy from scratch, but every time I brought up the idea of pursuing cooking as a career, Mom freaked out. She'd wrinkle her nose and tell me I had no idea what I was talking about. She thought the industry was below me and I was meant for great things. Like being the CEO of my own business, locked in an office, making money to keep myself trapped by buying more things.

She expected me to attend some top-notch college and fall in line. The thought of being on my own this summer zinged through my blood like a burst of fizzy soda. I'd always done everything my mother had asked. In June, I'd be eighteen and legally an adult. Could she really stop me? My thoughts whirled and I suddenly knew I'd do it. For the first time, I was going to do what I wanted.

I felt more comfortable with this group than I had in a long time. With my friends, I felt pressured to be someone else to fit in with the crowd. With my mom, I felt ignored, caught up in some weird ideal she imagined me to be. Maybe it was finally time I made my own decisions.

"Sure, why not?"

Freda gave a whoop. "Well, I think it's time we kicked this party up a notch," Connor announced, slapping his hands together. "Is it still in the same place?"

David nodded. Suddenly, he turned to me. "Do you smoke weed?"

I'd only done it a handful of times, always scared if I smoked too much it'd wig me out, but the idea of not thinking was too tempting. My mind was always jumping around, worrying about stuff, and I wanted to chill for a while. Most of my friends' moms took Xanax or Valium, and Bonnie and Claire stole the meds on a regular basis and got giggly or sleepy or buzzed. Their parents were hypocritical—screaming how their kids shouldn't do drugs when they couldn't start a day without the power of a little white pill.

"I've done it a few times," I admitted.

David's gaze held mine. "You don't have to smoke if you don't want to."

Something in my chest relaxed. My own friends liked to pressure me, either to cheat on a test or give Ryan Thomas a blow job because it was no big deal, but here I was with people who didn't care what I chose to do or not do.

I smiled at him. "I want to."

"You're okay with blowing off the rest of the day?"

I had track practice after school. I had a quiz in English fifth period. My mom would freak if the school called, and my friends would be pissed because I'd screw my team and anger my coach, but I didn't care. A thrill coursed through me, as if I felt more alive. I'd promised Nonni I'd go over for dinner, but I'd make sure I had plenty of time to come down off any high. "Yeah, I'm good."

Freda gave me a thumbs-up sign, and Connor came back with the bong and a sandwich bag full of weed and set them on the beat-up ottoman. Freda started talking about the places we'd go and the things we'd do this summer, and David put on some music, and for a while, everything was really, really good.

CHAPTER THREE

SOPHIA

ONE HAND PRESSED to my stomach, I tried not to wince at the achy, bloated bubble of pain hidden there. It had been growing worse, enough that the antacids and bland food weren't helping any longer. I figured it was a bladder infection, but the sulfur pills hadn't worked either. I thought of my doctor and how she'd schedule a multitude of tests, both to be sure and to get the extra fees. She'd already mentioned an endoscopy as the next step. I'd lived my whole life in relatively good health, and with each decade, the breakdown of flesh and bones and blood became more apparent. My habits of denial and my drive to believe I was still young had finally shattered under not only the consistent, nagging pain, but also the gut instinct that I was really sick, which I tried to bury even deeper.

How sick, I didn't know yet. Maybe I didn't want to. At seventy-five, I could still choose treatment options, or I might be reverting to my dramatic ways and it was only an ulcer. I wondered if other older women felt this way—trapped in an aging body yet stuck with a mind still full of possibilities. It was a bitter contradiction. But what really made me grieve was the lack of people with whom I could truly discuss this phenomenon.

Most of my friends didn't like lapsing into philosophical discussions of death—of either the body or the mind or the younger self. They were content with chatting about ailments and medicine and faith-inspired images of heaven, sort of like the Rainbow Bridge for animals. And though I personally couldn't wait to greet my beagle, Bagel, or my husband, whom I missed with every breath, I wasn't ready to test the theory.

No, I liked Earth here just fine.

Especially with the work that still had to be done.

I glanced at my iPhone, still wishing for the old-fashioned phones with real buttons to press and the inability to text a few words to anyone in the world, who could make any inference they wished because they couldn't hear the inflection in your voice. The warm April weather was a gift in a season when Mother Nature usually had PMS and couldn't decide whether to whack us with snow, rain, or an eighty-degree day. I needed to think about things and figure out what I was going to do. Best to go to the garden, where I could do useful work at the same time.

I took my time, putting on the red floral apron I liked to use because it had four pockets and snapped easily in the front. My wide-brimmed straw hat hung from the peg at the back door. I filled up my water bottle and walked through the small, sunny yellow kitchen and out the screen door that squeaked when it shut. A covered box I kept on a bench held my dirt-encrusted tools, with rubber handles and wide grips. I found that after a few hours, my hands cramped from my arthritis and my tangled fingers bent oddly at the knuckles, giving me a shiver of horror when I glanced down or studied them. Sometimes, pieces of my body seemed not to belong to me any longer, as if they'd suddenly appeared on me, kidnapping my normal appendages for ransom. The worst was when I took a shower and caught a glance of myself naked. I'd stand and look at my flabby flesh, which had once been firm and golden, distaste in my gaze as I took in my sagging breasts and soft, wrinkled stomach. I used to pride myself on keeping trim, painting my toes, and shaving every day, but after Jack passed, it seemed less important.

I tugged on my gardening gloves, filled up the cornflower blue watering can, and dragged my stuff over to the square patches of dirt filled with little green leaves sprouting up and an occasional shock of color. Slowly, with methodical movements, I lowered my knees onto the twin cushions and began checking all the plants and herbs. The sun warmed my back through the cotton fabric, and the gorgeous rush of spring noises filled my ears. The wind in the trees, the scrabble of a squirrel, the shriek of a bird, the flutter of wings in the air, all combined to put me in that hypnotic state I craved because it seemed to be the only time my thoughts were clear. I didn't sleep much anymore. I mourned the times I'd believed sleep was something I'd own forever—a precious commodity I always wanted more of when Frannie was young and Bagel craved a six a.m. potty break. I'd lie there on the fluffy pillow, stretch out, and dream of the day when I'd get a good nine or ten hours. I'd do anything to get that ability to sleep back, but it disappeared with all the other good stuff.

I dug in the dirt, snipped weeds, and began prepping the soil for my new additions of green beans. The pink gnome Frannie had given me when she was in second grade stared grumpily at me like an old friend. Bagel used to growl and bark at him, as if afraid he'd turn real, and a pang for my dog hit me in the gut, surprising me with its violence. He was a good dog, with a crooked ear and a goofy grin that made me smile. After Frannie left, he used to follow me from room to room, as if sensing I was the only person left to take care of him. Grief was funny that way. The moment you thought you'd beaten it, or at least made peace, it bashed you on the head during a warm sunny afternoon in your garden when you weren't expecting it, then watched you bleed.

I worked for a while with no important thoughts other than getting ingredients prepped for dinner with Allegra and wondering whether *Dancing with the Stars* was on tonight—I always got my days mixed up—until my mind was strong enough to begin dealing with bigger problems.

My girls were in trouble.

I sensed it, just like I sensed something rotten growing inside me. After the conversation with Frannie, I realized I had expressed myself poorly again. I always thought birthing children would give me some type of wisdom to guide me. It didn't, of course. Motherhood was a complicated maze of disappointments and failures, peppered with the occasional wave of pure love that made it all worth it.

How could she believe I wasn't proud of her accomplishments? Was it wrong to worry that she'd dedicated her days to the pursuit of success and that she'd regret not making enough time for her daughter? I wasn't judging. I wanted her to have it all. The last time I saw her, she seemed high-strung and nervous. Her actions were jerky and unfocused, as if she was afraid of something. Was losing control or admitting she was human so hard for her? What if all that stress was beginning to affect her body?

God knows, Jack had suffered the same. His love for his job had eventually torn apart his body until he was ripped away from us far too soon. My worries for my daughter were completely valid. She was following right in his footsteps.

Then there was Allegra. My sweet Allegra, who looked at her mother with the same type of resentment I remember in my own daughter—a youthful arrogance that was probably needed in order to carve out an independent life. I was lucky my granddaughter and I were close, that she actually liked spending time with me. But lately, I sensed a simmering anger wrapped in disdain growing toward her mother. Frannie laughed it off as teenage angst, but I knew it ran deeper. Maybe that was what also kept me up at night, staring at the ceiling while I waited for dawn, hoping I wouldn't die before I was able to help fix their relationship.

Always so melodramatic, the familiar rough voice whispered in my ear. *You can't fix everything, my love. Life doesn't work like that.*

My skin prickled but I kept my attention on the dirt sifting through my gloved fingers. I'd learned not to question the voice, or the solid sense of his presence beside me. Jack always liked to surprise me, whether it was presenting me with a bouquet of fresh wildflowers he'd picked on a high hill on his way home from work, or whisking us out for an expensive late-night supper where he'd set up dozens of candles or a musical serenade. It would make sense that he liked to jump out at me when I least expected it.

I shot back my answer.

Yes, I can. Our daughter is in trouble. I need to do something.

The image of his face danced in my memory. Laughing blue eyes, crinkled at the corners, with rounded cheeks and a mouth that loved to smile. Thick dark hair that turned to a premature yet beautiful white, crowning his head in Einstein glory. He worked so hard at his job nonstop, up until the day the heart attack struck. How long I'd begged for him to retire, but he'd thought we had plenty of time. Another cruel joke life played on you. Taking away the only person who could make aging bearable.

I'm sorry, my love. I didn't know. I would've taken you to Italy on the tour of a lifetime, like I promised so many times.

I grunted, but how could I be mad at his ghost? I'd longed to travel to my parents' homeland for years. It was always the big trip that would happen one day—when Frannie grew older; when we had more money; when work eased enough to take a long vacation. It never happened. I was left with the strains of Frank Sinatra in my kitchen, making homemade pasta and dreaming of the rolling Tuscan hills I ached to see. I wanted my feet on the same ground my mother had walked and to hear the lilt of Italian drifting in the air. One day. Always one day . . .

The thought was so fragile, so delicate; it brushed my mind like gossamer wings. As I covered the seeds with fresh dirt, making sure to turn and dampen the soil, the possibility began to form and take shape.

I paused, gazing down at a small worm frantically trying to dig back into the moist darkness of home. And I was suddenly struck by an innate instinct of what I needed to do.

I would take my family to Italy.

I could go this summer. It'd be Allegra's last opportunity before college, and a birthday celebration. Frannie hadn't taken a vacation in years. We'd have time to bond as a family and rediscover one another.

The trowel fell from my grip. Excitement unfurled in my belly, and for the first time in a while, I felt brilliantly alive. I'd probably have a hard time convincing Frannie. She worked nonstop on her deals, chasing the next one with a furious intent that left no room for any other type of pleasure. As for Allegra, maybe she'd be excited to try something new. An adventure. A way to escape.

The thoughts churned in my mind, the details still blurry, but I already knew I'd made my decision. I would make this happen. A summer filled with the possibility of change—which we all desperately needed. The backdrop of a beautiful country and a foreign culture would be enough to push us all together again. Remind them all that roots and blood and family were everything.

Some things can't be fixed with a different location, my love. Remember that.

Another ripple of pain wove its way through my gut, almost in warning. I pressed a dirty palm against my apron. *But time can. And I can give us all that. For now.*

You need to go to the doctor.

Can ghosts worry? I smiled at the thought, his presence pulsing around me. I had figured spirits brought cold, from all the movies I'd seen, but Jack was always like warm sunshine wrapping around me.

I will. Right after the trip. I promise.

I didn't want anything used as an excuse not to go, including my health. I waited to see if he'd yell or scold me, but the air seemed to let loose a breath like a shrinking balloon, and I knew he was gone.

I'd never planned a big trip before, but maybe I'd go to an old-fashioned travel agent instead of surfing sites on the computer and ending up confused. I'd talk to a real person and explain I wanted it to be a surprise. There had to be a way to convince them what an opportunity this would be.

Sunday. At dinner. I'd make sure they both came—I'd been wanting to cook that turkey in the freezer for a while—and I'd break the news. Maybe I could even get some of those pretty brochures. A tour would be perfect. We'd be safe with a guide and get to see multiple cities. Though I would love to stay in Tuscany for a while and soak in the local flavor. Maybe I could combine a tour with a short stay.

Suddenly, I didn't want to garden anymore. An adrenaline rush skated through my blood, giving me extra energy I hadn't experienced in a while, even when I was on those super-energy organic vitamins Francesca swore by. I quickly packed up my tools, jumping up from the ground instead of slowly unfolding my old body, enjoying the bounce in my step. I had a new purpose, bigger than the threat of illness or worry about convincing my girls to accompany me overseas.

This could be the most important trip of a lifetime.

I walked inside and began making a list of all the things I needed to accomplish.

CHAPTER FOUR

Allegra

Nonni's house always gave me a cozy, safe feeling I thought was missing in my own. Mom loved the color white, so at home everything was neutral and looked like fresh snow—pristine and clean and untouched. Even though my room had a pretty pink chandelier, fancy furniture, and a queen-size bed with black raspberry satin sheets, it felt like too much space. Nonni's house was like being wrapped up in a tight hug. She preferred colors like brown, gold, and deep red, always citing white as showing the dirt too easily. There were thick carpets and lived-in furniture that cushioned my butt when I sat. The kitchen was always filled with amazing smells like tangy garlic, fresh tomatoes, sweet basil, and citrusy lemon. The oak table was round so everyone felt close. The best part was the clutter. It was clean—I could tell from the lemon furniture polish scent, and there were never any crumbs on the counters or dust—but there was interesting stuff. Endless pictures crammed into every inch of space on the tables, paintings of beautiful Italian landscapes on the walls, books and magazines with thick, glossy pages stacked up. Yards of colorful yarn with crochet needles and half-knit projects of afghans and pillows littered the living room. Knick-knacks of shot glasses, heavy glass ashtrays, scented candles, mini statues of the Virgin Mary and St. Francis, and mementos from my mom's childhood, from twisted pottery to macaroni art for Girl Scouts, filled the shelves.

I always loved picking through them and hearing my grandmother's stories about each item. It was a nice reminder that once Mom was a child, too, and not always perfect.

I watched Nonni get up to retrieve more lemonade before I could get it myself—she was always able to anticipate every need of mine before me—and took in her wince of pain. She rubbed her stomach and plucked the pitcher of freshly squeezed juice, laying it on the table.

"Nonni, are you okay? Did you hurt yourself?"

She looked startled, then smiled and shook her head. "No, just a bit of indigestion. I made a pot of that escargot and bean soup I used to love, but beans don't agree with me anymore." She made a face. "Gives me gas."

I laughed. "Can't be as bad as sitting next to Curt in English class. He farts so bad the teacher needs to open the windows. Even in winter."

She laughed, too, and poured me a cup. "How are your classes going? Are you ready for finals?"

I shoveled in a forkful of salad, making sure I snagged a green olive. The tangy oil and vinegar with just the right amount of salt and seasoning was my favorite. "I think so. Just not sure about the Regents in Italian. I suck at foreign languages."

She clucked her tongue but her brown eyes were warm. "Silly girl. You were born to speak the language of our ancestors, but you are learning the proper way. I spoke some of the rough dialect of Naples from my mother. It's not the same."

"Yeah, but they make me do all these conjugations and stupid stuff. I'm never going to write a book in Italian. I just want to speak it so one day I can go to Italy."

She cocked her head and studied me like I'd said something interesting. "Would you like that? To take a trip to Italy?"

I ate more salad and nodded. "Sure. Maybe on my honeymoon or something. How come you never went?"

Her face softened into a wistful expression. For a moment, it made me sad, wondering what types of regrets my grandmother might have. But she always told me she loved her life, even though she missed Pop Pop. Funny, I watched my mother run around trying to rule the world and wondered if she was even happy. With Nonni, she lived more simply and seemed more satisfied. I hated the way my mom rolled her eyes at the stuff Nonni said, like she was making fun of my grandmother because she didn't run a big business. Like that should equal a person's worth.

"Time goes fast," she said with a sigh. "I always wanted to go with Pop Pop and your mom, but I blinked and she was grown up and not interested in traveling with us anymore. We always felt like there'd be time next year."

"I'm sorry," I said, reaching out to squeeze her hand. It looked delicate and frail, but she squeezed back hard.

"Don't worry about me—I've had my time. Your final track race is Friday, right?"

I nodded. "Coach said we can bring stuff for a party afterward."

"I'll make chocolate chip cookies for the team," she said firmly. "You did so well, Allegra. You broke your own record from fall! Would you want to run on a scholarship?"

Pride shot through me. I hated tennis, but running gave me a sense of freedom, plus I could do it mostly alone. But the idea of owing a college all my extra time to run on a team, and dealing with my mother's pressure, wasn't a great incentive. Once again, the confusion of what was going to happen next year rushed through me. "I like running, but I don't think enough to go after a scholarship."

As if she sensed my frustration, she waved a hand in the air. "Then don't. You're a smart girl, and you'll figure it out. Don't pressure yourself by thinking you need to know everything before you turn eighteen."

"Mom does," I muttered. "You know she keeps a running spreadsheet of my grades so she always knows my current GPA? I wish she'd chill out."

Sympathy glowed in her eyes. "Your mother's worried about you. You're at a difficult age, and she doesn't want you to make any mistakes. I'm sure she's doing the best she can."

I thought of my decision to join my new friends this summer and how Mom would lose it. Somehow, I had to convince her I just wanted to have an experience on my own. God knows, she'd probably be MIA the entire time anyway, leaving me bored and stranded for two months. "If she was worried, she'd be home more. Or at my track meets if she's so hot on me getting a scholarship. All she cares about is her job."

I hated the worry etched in my grandmother's frown, but I was tired of pretending. When I was with my mom, there was nothing left to say other than all the surface subjects a stranger would ask about. The worst part? I'd spent too much time mad at her, or sad, trying desperately to gain her attention. Now I kept telling myself I didn't care and it was her loss. Soon I'd be in college and living my own life. I needed to concentrate on the future.

"She's so much like your grandfather," Nonni finally said. "I remember he used to believe working nonstop meant he was taking care of the family. That's how he knew how to show love. It took a while for him to realize we wanted his attention and time more than nice things."

I wish I'd known Pop Pop, but he died before I was born. I liked the way my grandmother spoke about him, with love still in her eyes and her voice soft. I dreamed of loving another person that deeply, for so long. I noticed Nonni rubbing her belly again, so I switched the subject. I hated upsetting her. "It's okay, I'm just stressed and have a lot on my mind."

Her face softened. She was beautiful, with her thick gray hair and almond-shaped brown eyes. It was cool she still loved wearing makeup and pink lipstick and a hint of perfume that always smelled like lilacs and not that yucky old-lady smell like mothballs. "I know, sweet girl. But I have a surprise I wanted to talk to you and Mom about on Sunday. Maybe it will help."

"What kind of surprise?"

"I want to tell you together," she said, folding her hands on the table. "I'm sure your mom's big presentation will be over soon, and we'll spend the afternoon together. Maybe even go see a movie."

"Horror?"

She sighed, pretending to think about it. "No nudity. But some blood is okay."

I laughed, wondering what the surprise was. "Okay, I can wait. But Mom will never come. She had to walk out on *Toy Story 4* for a client, so I don't invite her anymore. Want to play pinochle?"

Nonni pursed her lips as if she wanted to defend Mom but then fell silent.

Good. Maybe she'd finally run out of excuses.

Cards were revered with Nonni, and I'd learned young how to play lots of games, from poker and war to bridge, but pinochle was my favorite. I wished I could tell her my plans for the summer, but I suspected it would be better if I let them both know later on, after I nailed my Regents and proved I was responsible. Maybe then Nonni would back me up if I could help her understand.

She nodded. "Yes, I'll get the ice cream."

"I thought you had indigestion."

She gave a big smile. "And what do I say is a cure for that?"

I laughed, shaking my head. "*Finocchio* and ice cream."

"Let's go straight to the ice cream. I have bananas to make sundaes." I helped her clean the table, and she spread out all the toppings so we could make our own. I grabbed sprinkles and crushed Oreos, and she heated up the caramel and fudge, and we stuffed them in the tall parfait glasses she kept just for sundaes. Michael Bublé crooned from Alexa's speakers—I'd finally taught her how to use it—and we ate and played cards and chatted as it got dark. I savored the peaceful feeling being around my grandmother always brought, and for a little while, I was able to forget about everything else.

CHAPTER FIVE

Francesca

"What's new in your schedule this week?" I asked, trying to break the awkward silence in the car. I was inundated with work, needed to go shopping to get Allegra new running sneakers, and craved a hot bubble bath rather than a quick shower, but I swore I wouldn't break my promise for this Sunday dinner. Besides, I was looking forward to spending time with Allegra, but so far, all my questions had been met with one-word answers.

"Not much."

I let out an annoyed breath. "Maybe you can give me a bit more than that?" I suggested, trying to keep my voice calm. "Is there something bothering you? You've been quiet."

She turned from the window and shot me a look. "No. Everything's fine. I'm just tired."

"You slept till eleven," I pointed out.

Her chin jerked and I knew I'd irritated her again. Breathing seemed to irritate her lately. "I stayed up late finishing my essay."

"That's great, honey, good for you." I knew her honors class was difficult and she struggled for those As. "Hey, I was talking to Connie and she said they have an opening at her husband's law firm for the summer. It's part-time, but it would look fantastic on your applications. I told her to hold it until I spoke with you."

"No, thanks. I'll pass."

I pressed my lips together and kept my tone bright. "Maybe you can think about it. You'll still have plenty of time to yourself, and they offer decent pay. I know you mentioned law before, so this may be a good way to see if you like it. I found I loved advertising during my own internship."

"Yep, you told me a million times," she muttered under her breath.

I hated the disappointment that cut through me. Rationally, I knew this was a difficult age, but my patience was beginning to wear thin. "Okay, you can lose the attitude. I'm only trying to help. Summer is a month away and all the good jobs and opportunities will be gone."

"I don't want to be a lawyer, okay? I actually wanted to talk to you about something. A different plan for the summer."

I perked up, relieved that at least she'd been thinking about it. I couldn't have her hanging around with endless free time while I worked nonstop. I definitely planned on taking a few long weekends with her, maybe at the Jersey Shore, but she needed to have some responsibility at this point. "What is it?"

She hesitated and shook her head when I pulled into my mother's driveway. "I'll tell you tonight after dinner."

"Oh, I'm intrigued."

She jumped out of the car without another word, and I clamped down on another sigh. When I walked inside, Allegra had already settled into the kitchen, chattering with my mother with an enthusiasm I never got to see. I felt bad about the sharp zing of resentment but buried it quickly. Of course she wouldn't have any issues with her grandmother. Mom had watched her regularly since she was young and loved being involved in every detail of her life. She also spoiled her rotten, I reminded myself.

"Hi, Mom," I greeted her, kissing her on the cheek. She wore a bright-red floral apron and matching lipstick and smelled of sugar and lemons. Her hug was extra-tight and the flare of guilt hit again. I had to be better. Yes, I got frustrated with the constant judgments, but I was sure she was lonely without Dad. After I scored this account, I was slowing down. "Smells good."

"Nonni, can I do the mashed potatoes?"

"Of course—they're already peeled. The fresh chives are in the herb drawer." She wiped her hands on a faded towel and smiled. I noticed the lines around her eyes had deepened, and she looked more tired than usual. "How are you today? Here, take some bread. Do you want some wine?"

My mother fussed about, putting out thick slices of Italian bread and pouring a glass of Bolla. I was used to it and let her do it without protest. First, it was nice feeling taken care of, and she'd told me numerous times she enjoyed feeding me, bringing back all the years of Sunday dinners spent at the table with my father, playing cards and Scrabble while the football or baseball game blared on the television. She'd been disappointed in my complete rejection of cooking—no matter how many times she tried to teach me, I hated it. At least Allegra seemed to bloom under her instruction. I sipped my wine and watched my daughter doctor the potatoes with an expert ease, moving around the kitchen with my mother like a trained dancer. Funny, she never wanted to cook at home or experiment with meals. It seemed the act of cooking gave her a sense of excitement only here.

"How's the new account going?" my mother asked, peeking at the turkey and basting it a few more times while she watched the juices drip down the crispy skin.

"I pitch next week. If I get it, the brand has the potential to go national and bring in some bigger clients. It can change everything."

She frowned, but she was focused on the meat, slicing off a piece and giving it a taste test. "I thought F&F was already profitable. You were written up in that magazine. Allegra, taste this, does it need more salt?"

"Yes, but even though the company's grown, it only takes a few lost accounts to crash back down. I'm always looking to increase the company's profits, Mom. Growth is everything, and one mistake can be critical with all the competition in this market."

"It's good," Allegra said, nodding. My mother's face lit up, and she powered up the electric knife, expertly slicing thick white pieces and separating the dark. The mixer roared, pausing only so Allegra could swipe a taste, her face screwed up in concentration as she sifted through the flavors on her tongue to decide if it was good enough. I watched them focus on their tasks with a strange sort of distance, feeling oddly out of place as I drank my wine and relaxed at the table, talking of a world they didn't seem to care about. The longing for my dad cut deep. He knew the sacrifices it took to maintain a successful business.

Sure, he'd been gone a lot, but when he was with us, his focus was complete. He'd play tickle monster and read endless books and take me out for ice cream. I remembered lingering for hours at the dinner table, watching him drink little cups of black espresso and talking about fascinating subjects. He'd taught me so much about the ins and outs of running a business: how to figure out invaluable information by reading a person and their tells; how to redirect a dialogue and create trust; how to upsell once the client was hooked. Without some type of connection, failure was imminent. I'd soaked up his lessons and vowed to be just like him one day.

And I was.

After he died, we'd been able to sell the business to his partner and set Mom up with a nice cushion, especially since she had no social security. He'd done everything to take care of his family. Had he experienced the same distance with my mom when he spoke about work?

I'd never know.

Soon, all the food was prepped and on the table. We passed around bowls of fresh peas, potatoes, turkey, and cranberry sauce. I'd avoided the bread—always ruthless with limiting carbs—but took a healthy portion of Allegra's potatoes, surprised at the creamy texture and flavor, which were restaurant quality. "Honey, these are really good," I said. My daughter's flushed cheeks were an even bigger surprise, and she ducked her head quickly as if hiding her pleasure at my comment. My heart squeezed. Had I not been acknowledging her enough? I always told her she was smart and could do anything she put her mind to, but she usually rolled her eyes or made some snide comment that cut off my praise.

"Thanks. Nonni knows all the tricks. She's teaching me how to make lasagna next."

My mother laughed. "That will be easy compared to the Easter pie. Remember that fiasco?"

My daughter laughed with her. "That was harder than a Regents test! Mom, have you ever made it before?"

I shook my head. "I couldn't get her into the kitchen unless I bribed her," Mom said with a snort.

"It's insane! There's like a thousand steps, and four kinds of meat, and the layering process is a math equation."

"But worth it, right?" Mom asked.

"So worth it. I wish we could make them year-round instead of only at Easter," Allegra said.

"Are you kidding? After I make even one of those I need a nap."

I smiled, enjoying the pleasure on their faces, even as the tiny bite of jealousy at their closeness reared up. I smothered it quickly, embarrassed. I was thrilled Allegra loved her grandmother so much, especially since she never got to spend time with Dad.

"Now, I wanted to talk to you both about an idea I had for this summer," my mother announced. She met my gaze with an odd intensity, her brown eyes shining with a mixture of excitement and pleading. "But you need to hear me out first."

Probably a knitting or cooking class she wanted us to all do together, I figured, indulging in another spoonful of potatoes. "Sure, what is it?"

"I've been doing a lot of thinking lately. I'm getting older, and one day, I may not be able to get around as well. Allegra will be going off to college, maybe working a summer job, and I feel like since your business has been growing, you haven't had time to slow down at all. I've always dreamed of going to Italy to see where your great-grandmother was born. So, I contacted a travel agent and worked out a trip for us to take together. This summer."

Shock barreled through me. I figured Allegra might be jumping up and down, but pure distress shone from her face as she stared at my mother. "You want us to go to Italy?" I asked. "All of us?"

"Yes! We need to take some time as a family before everything changes. Summer is the perfect time—you'll be done with your new client, and Allegra will be off, and I'm treating for the whole thing. I socked away some extra money from your father's life insurance. And look at the information I have." She jumped up from the chair and withdrew a catalogue and folder from the junk drawer. "We can combine a tour along with a villa rental in Tuscany! For the first three weeks, we'll see Rome and Florence and Venice, and all the other amazing cities, and then we'll stay at an actual vineyard. There's even a lake for Allegra." She shoved a bunch of glossy brochures at us, the covers filled with sprawling houses surrounded by lush green hills and trees. "I'll take care of everything—we can leave the first week of July and return early August."

My fingers closed around the sleek paper, but already I was trying to think of the best way to phrase my rejection. Sure, I wanted to visit Italy—who didn't? But not for a month on an extended tour. If I did score the Lexi's Lemonade account, I'd be buckled down overseeing every aspect of the campaign for most of the summer, plus the demands of my other clients.

Plus, I couldn't handle being with my mother for that long.

I opened my mouth to gently raise all my objections, but Allegra was already speaking. "Nonni, I'm so sorry. I can't do Italy this year. I-I made some other plans for the summer."

My mother's face fell. She blinked, glancing down at the line of brochures in confusion. "I think your mom would agree you don't have to get a job right now. And it will be an early graduation present!"

Allegra chewed at her lip and touched my mother's shoulder. "It sounds amazing, and I do want to go one day, just not now. Maybe next year before college?" she suggested. "We can have more time to plan."

"Allegra's right, Mom," I said quietly. "I think this is really sweet, but there's so much going on, it just won't work. Definitely next summer. In fact, I'll help you plan it—we'll do a two-week tour and see all the highlights, including Naples. Okay?"

Her shoulders drooped. I was ready for a full-on guilt trip, but she raised her chin, staring at me with a fierce determination I rarely experienced. "No," she said firmly. "It's not okay. It has to happen now or it won't happen at all." She grew tense with frustration, and her breath came faster. "Don't you see it's important? We all need this trip. We've mentioned doing something like this for years, and if we don't grab the opportunity and make the time, we won't get another chance." Grief flashed briefly in her eyes. "It goes too fast. A trip like this will give us memories for the rest of our lives. It can be an entire turning point, don't you see?"

"Mom, calm down. You have to understand Allegra and I have a lot of responsibilities. And though it sounds amazing, we can't just be ready to take a month off. Allegra starts track in August, and I own a business. I could never get all that time off."

"Nonni, I'm sorry," Allegra said. "Don't get upset. I know you want to see Naples. Maybe spring break? Or Christmas break if you don't want to wait?"

I nodded. "Absolutely. Here, can I take these brochures home and look at them? I'll check our schedules and see what we come up with."

My mother had always been the calm one in the household, a quiet, stable presence. She rarely lost her temper, even with her Italian genes, and Dad used to joke about her good nature as the trait that held the seams together. But right now, she looked at me with a deep betrayal, like I'd done something terrible rather than say no to a European vacation with no forewarning.

"Sure," she said. Her voice fell flat. "Let me know what you think. I better clean up."

My daughter and I shared worried glances, but for the first time in a while, I didn't know what to do. Maybe Mom was lonely and needed to get out of her house or have something big to look forward to. She'd never acted like this, as if a trip was a make or break for her happiness.

I jumped up to help, and we cleared the table and did the dishes. Allegra kept up steady chatter, but I could tell my mother had locked herself away somewhere, even though she nodded and smiled on cue. We had a quick dessert and then we left. I hugged my mother and tried my best to console her. "Mom, get some rest; you're tired. I promise we'll work something out."

"We need this trip together, Frannie," she said, gripping my arm. "It's more important than you realize."

Her words rang in my head on the drive back. My daughter kept her usual silence until we were halfway home. "Mom, you think Nonni is okay? She's not sick, is she?"

"No, honey, I always keep up-to-date with her doctor's appointments. Maybe we can try to squeeze in a weekend and take her somewhere."

"Okay."

"I'm a little surprised at your reaction, though. Figured a trip to Italy would be a dream, especially with you being such an art lover. What do you have planned that you'd rather do? You wanted to talk to me about your summer plans, right?"

She shifted in the seat. "My friends and I want to do a little cross-country driving. Explore some new places, you know?"

"Bonnie and Claire?"

"No, some friends I recently met. One is a musician, and another writes poetry. They want to book some performances in different clubs and I want to go with them."

Already, the scenario didn't sound completely truthful. I could tell by her forced-casual tone that she was trying to phrase it so I'd think it wasn't a big deal. Also, her fingers twisted in her telltale gesture that said she was stretching the truth. God, I was tired. I had crap to do when I got home, and I wasn't up for another round in the ring. I tried to keep my voice nonthreatening. "Who are your new friends?"

She hesitated. *Bingo.* "Freda, David, and Connor."

"Two boys? You've never mentioned any male friends before."

"Because I thought I only had to provide you a spreadsheet with my grades, not my friends." The resentment leaked in even though she was still trying to be civil. "It's no big deal."

"For you, it's not. Where are you going? Staying? Who's driving?"

"The whole point is not to have exact plans. We want to head upstate to a few towns, and Connor's dad has an RV we'll use so we don't have to worry about hotels."

I wanted to laugh at her idea that I'd even pretend to let her go, but I needed to save the big *no* for later, when I was more prepared. "An RV? That's not safe, honey. And I know it sounds glamorous, like some cool movie, but it doesn't work that way. You'd need to schedule sites to park, and the plumbing could get backed up, and what if you break down? I don't think you've thought this through. Do I know them from your school? Who are their parents?"

A smothered groan hit my ears. I could feel the hot burn of her stare as I concentrated on the road. "Mom, they're not part of your fancy country club, okay? They're just regular people who are interesting and creative and want to experience new things—not pretend this crappy world full of pretentious people is all I have to look forward to."

I tamped down my own temper. "Sorry, I didn't realize working hard to have a decent life was pretentious or wrong."

"You never listen. And if I have to hear one more time about everything you've given me, I'm going to die."

"Maybe if I hear you complaining about everything you have one more time, I'll die."

That cost me. The tension in the car cranked up and the temperature dropped. Why was I always snatching the bait? But, damn, she pissed me off.

"Forget it. I'm going to be eighteen this summer anyway."

I raised my brow. "And what is that supposed to mean?"

She shrugged. "I can do what I want at eighteen. I can vote. Make my own decisions. You can't stop me."

I couldn't halt my strangled laugh, even though I tried. "Oh, yes, I can. You live in my house, under my rules, and you're not going anywhere in an RV with some strange kids. I'd need to meet them, talk to their parents, get a detailed itinerary, check out places, make sure the campgrounds are safe. Maybe if we go over it all and you check your attitude, we can talk about it."

She pressed her hands against her temples and shook her head back and forth like she was having a breakdown. "I can't stand it anymore! Isn't there anything in your life you don't plan? Was there even one time you did something exciting or different or adventurous? God, I'll die if I ever end up like you!"

I was always the bad guy. Sometimes I wondered, if there was a father figure around, would things be different? Or would she still hate me because I was her mother? "Don't talk to me like that. I don't deserve it. There's not a mother in the world who'd allow you to take off. And if your so-called friends are doing it, I bet they have parents who don't care. Consider yourself lucky."

I pulled into the driveway and shut off the engine. The silence was explosive. I waited for her to rush out, scream, or come up with some more vicious verbal attacks, but she just turned her head and looked at me for a while. For a few shocking seconds, she reminded me of my mother, that same yearning and grief in her beautiful dark eyes, where once there had been love and trust and joy.

"Sure, you care, Mom. But not the way you think. Not about the stuff that's most important."

She opened the door and ran out before I had a chance to answer.

I sat in the car, in the dark, and watched as rain began to drizzle down on the windshield. I watched the running rivulets trickle in wiggly waves and wondered what she meant.

"I care about you," I whispered.

But there was no one there to hear me.

CHAPTER SIX

ALLEGRA

"ARE WE READY to party?"

Freda waved her hands in the air, scrunched up tight next to me in the back seat of the car. Connor shouted in agreement, pumping up the music, and blew out a steady vape stream. I liked that a lot better than the cigarettes so had gratefully switched. It didn't give me that unpleasant burn in the back of my throat and went into my lungs smoothly, with the flavor of mocha.

We pulled into a house where a bunch of cars were already parked, and kids packed the grounds, drinking and smoking, while a small bonfire crackled with welcoming warmth. "Let's go, ladies," Connor said, climbing out and opening the door. We headed in, and I stuck tight with Freda. I'd told my mom I was studying at Bonnie's tonight, and she never bothered to check up. The past week had been better than the entire year. My new friends had no qualms about breaking rules and searching out fun. For the first time in ages, my insides felt lighter, but that good feeling was still mixed with a shred of worry I couldn't seem to shake. This wasn't my normal life. I was a rule follower and felt as if for the last few years I'd lived in a fake, shallow tunnel, just existing. I didn't seem to fit—with either the popular crowd or the athletes or the nerds. With Freda, David, and Connor, I finally felt heard. They listened to my opinions, and we had endless discussions about life and embraced the hard stuff rather than pretending it didn't exist. And even though Mom had said no to my summer proposal, I wasn't done. I'd just decided to back off and go ahead with my own plans. After all, I already had money stashed away in cash and didn't need to get into my savings account. I even had a credit card in my own name, for emergencies. There were options, but I was still hopeful I could convince Mom to let me go without a war.

We went inside and popped open some beers, and Freda introduced me around. Most of the kids were from the public school and seemed cool. I drank the beer and hung back for a while, taking in the groups and who was hooking up with whom. There were a few hot guys, but I kept glancing over at David, keeping him in my peripheral vision. He didn't move around a lot or look interested in any specific girls. I liked the quiet calm settling around him, as he hooked his ankle over his knee, sprawled back on the couch while he talked to some guy friends. His hair fell messily over his brows. I had the weirdest urge to brush it back.

Keeping my eyes on the time, I let Freda know I needed a ride back to my car by ten or my mom might start texting. She usually didn't bother me unless it got too late—then I'd suddenly get a bunch of calls or a stream of texts like she'd gone into a panic. It was better to be one step ahead of her.

I went upstairs to use the bathroom, taking a few minutes to fuss with my hair. I'd worn it down today instead of in its usual ponytail. I liked the thick waves and the color, but I hated blinking the strands out of my eyes or pulling them from my mouth, so it was easier to tie it back, especially with track. But now I liked the way it covered some of the harsh angles of my face. My nose was too big, and my eyes too wide apart, and of course I'd gotten a zit on my forehead again, just like a stupid beacon flashing a signal of my awkwardness. Still, I knew I wasn't ugly. Just not beautiful or memorable.

The door stuck, so I banged it open with a crash, then stopped short.

"Hey."

David leaned against the wall, obviously waiting for the bathroom. My ears grew hot so I gave a casual smile. "Hey. Sorry if I took too long."

He smiled back and I wished I could make him smile like that more often. He lost his broody edge and it made him more approachable. "Nah, I was actually up here looking for you. Want to hang out a bit?"

My heart beat crazily in my chest. "Sure. Where?"

He pointed to one of the bedroom doors. "Here's good." He walked in and I took a deep breath and followed. Through the thin wall, I heard moans and banging and realized someone was screwing next door. I tried to play it cool, but my skin was burning and I hoped I didn't look all flushed and red. So. Embarrassing.

David rolled his eyes at the crude sounds but didn't seem bothered. "You really gonna come with us this summer?" he asked, taking out his vape pipe and lighting up.

I stiffened. Did he want me to? I couldn't read his expression, so I shrugged. "Sure. Still trying to convince my mom, though. She's afraid traveling the country in an RV isn't a great idea."

"Probably isn't, but that's why it'll be epic. What if she says no?"

I hesitated. "Not sure. I may do it anyway."

He smiled again, nodding like he approved. "Cool. You ever sing?"

"You mean like karaoke?"

"Anything. I'm looking to play guitar, but it's helpful to have a decent singer. Freda's awful."

I laughed. "I could tell just from our car rides."

On cue, a groan rose from the other room. Then a girl's voice. "Yeah, baby, yeah!"

I ducked my head, trying to pretend I didn't care, but he must've known because he grabbed his phone and began playing music to drown out the noises. "Better?"

I nodded. "Thanks."

"So, would you consider singing with me if we get a gig?"

I considered, wondering if I could be brave enough to do that onstage in public. "What if I suck?"

"Then you get fired, or we only play at clubs where everyone's already drunk."

We both laughed, and I relaxed. "Sure, I'd give it a try."

"Cool, let's do it now." He scrolled through his phone, and the song "Without Me" by Halsey came on. "You know this?"

I blinked. "Yeah."

"Okay, sing."

I twisted my fingers together, shifting my weight. "Now?"

"Why not? It's just us."

Which made it worse, I thought to myself. I got ready to tell him it wasn't a good time, that I was too tipsy or something, but his gaze met mine in a bit of a challenge and I opened my mouth and began to sing. I didn't try to hit any high notes, just gave him the basic middle strains. I kept my chin up and pretended we were in some smoky bar and I had this one moment to impress him. I had a decent singing voice, but other than chorus, I'd never tried to sing in front of someone. Finally, I stopped, curious to see what he was going to say.

"You're good." Warmth rushed through me. "You got the job."

"Singing for my supper," I teased.

He didn't tease me back. His expression changed, the room got tight with tension, and my stomach dropped. Then he walked slowly over to me until he was super close. His breath smelled like mocha and smoke, and his eyes were dark and serious, and then he was leaning his head over and he kissed me.

I'd only been kissed a few times before, on a dare or because I was desperate to see why everyone thought it was a big deal. Mostly, they were sloppy and wet with tongue and awkward fumbling that turned me off.

But this was nice. He didn't try to grope or shove his tongue in my mouth. Just kissed me with a firm pressure, as if testing me out. When I tentatively opened my lips wider, he finally held me, and his grip was firm and strong, so I let him take it further. It didn't take long for his palm to cup my breast, and though it felt good, my brain began to churn, and suddenly the bed in back of him seemed too big and overwhelming, like it was taunting me.

I pulled back, unsure why I'd changed my mind, then panicked when I realized we were alone in a bedroom at a party where I didn't know anyone. I'd seen my share of Lifetime movies where girls got raped at strangers' houses and no one ever backed them up. I was just about to push him away hard and run, but he stepped right back on his own, staring at me with a surprisingly intent and sober gaze. "What's wrong?"

"I just—I'm not ready for that. Yet." My cheeks burned. My virginity had never bothered me before, but I figured he'd laugh or make a teasing remark.

Instead, he nodded and sat on the edge of the bed. "That's cool."

I relaxed, twisting my fingers. "You think?"

"Yeah. You should be able to do stuff on your own terms. I guess most people I know aren't like you."

"I'm not a prude or anything," I rushed to say.

"I know. I like that you're different. Most of my friends need sex and drugs to cope with shit, you know?"

I cocked my head, fascinated by his deep, thoughtful voice and the way he looked at me. "Like what?"

"Pain. Too much fucking pain."

The darkness was back, shadowing his face. I didn't know what he was thinking about, but it was bad. I wanted to go and take his hand, but I felt frozen, not sure what to do. He got up and pocketed his phone, then motioned toward the door. "We better get downstairs. Freda will probably be looking for you."

"Yeah."

I followed him out, my emotions sharp and jagged like cut glass. The rest of the night was good and we climbed back in the car at exactly ten thirty to get me back by eleven. I sang along with Freda, and Connor passed around a joint, and it was pretty much perfect until the cop pulled us over for speeding.

I figured we still had a shot, but he smelled the weed and found the bag stashed in the glove compartment.

Everything turned bad from there.

CHAPTER SEVEN

FRANCESCA

I'M NOT SURE when I realized I wasn't like other girls. I never got giggly over boys or spent endless hours dreaming about Tim Collins—the hot jock the entire school adored—asking me to prom. I only remember trying hard to care about all the things my friends did, like makeup and kissing and being noticed by the popular crowd. But even back then, I think I realized I was missing some type of gene that made me feel romantic love. I didn't understand romance novels, poetry, or chick flicks, and was more interested in those underdog movies like *Cool Runnings* or *Rocky* or even *Wall Street* (I loved Gordon Gekko and think he got a bad rap).

I never knew advertising was a thing until I scored an internship at a Manhattan firm for the summer in between semesters for business credit. I was pretty much an errand girl, getting lattes and lunch, copying and filing, but one day I was able to witness a high-level meeting with a team pitching a potential client to sell a new cereal to the marketplace. I knew immediately I wanted to experience that rush of adrenaline. I loved the concept of finding the right hook to sell a product. It was a perfect combination of statistics and research, driven by forcing the brain to think outside the box for creativity.

The creative director in the meeting was a sharply dressed male, handsome and charismatic, but it was the woman next to him who fascinated me. Her power suit and tight bun gave off a cool capability I craved to duplicate, and it was obvious she was the one who knew the most about the project. The man was the face of the company. She was the brains, evident in the way she answered the client's endless questions while the supposed lead pretended he was allowing her to speak on his behalf.

I realized then that it was a boys' club I'd have to break into. I didn't just want to be her.

I wanted to be more. I wanted the man's job. I refused to let any man try to steal my power. So, at twenty years old, I made myself a promise to learn everything about the business world and advertising. I swore I'd run my own company one day, on my terms.

I learned everything from the big power agencies, then moved north to avoid the major competition and opened my own place. I marketed it as a boutique alternative for clients who wanted to be treated like the national brands but didn't have the big dollars. I drained my savings to invest in marketing and publicity, creating my own ads for my business, and my client base doubled within the first year.

Life was pretty much perfect. I was a young woman with a burgeoning business, finally making money. But I hadn't counted on a strange twist that occurred when I turned twenty-eight. My valued assistant at the time, Sierra, had become pregnant. Yes, I was thrilled for her, but more concerned about how I'd plug the gap in my busy schedule for the three months she'd be on maternity leave. When she came into the office to show off her new daughter, I handed her an elegantly wrapped present, resigned to cooing and fussing over a newborn who couldn't do anything but poop and sleep. Then she'd expertly slid the baby into my arms.

I looked down at the infant's wrinkly face and pink skin; the way her tiny fingers curled into a fist and tried to push into her rooting mouth; the crease of a frown between her tightly closed eyes; the wriggly body squeezed into a white onesie printed with

happy colorful butterflies; the smell of powder, soap, and inno-
cence drifting to my nostrils. My insides suddenly stilled. Time
became a flowing, liquid thing that made no sense as I stared,
fascinated, at the magnificent creature in my arms. And as if
right on cue to the perfect stimulus, my biological clock burst to
life in stunning, vicious Technicolor.

For the first time, I craved something I couldn't do on my
own. This was nothing hard work, perseverance, and effort could
accomplish. I spent an entire year obsessed with babies and pregnancy and the hidden life of motherhood I'd never cared to explore before. After researching every angle and option, I decided
to attack my intense need for a baby like I had everything else.

I set a time limit of thirty. If I hadn't met a man whom I
envisioned a future with, I'd have the baby on my own. Freezing
my eggs was a valid option, but I couldn't imagine waiting too
much longer to get pregnant. I refused to be one of those mothers who were too old to keep up with an infant and gray-haired
by prom time. Already, biology was against me, favoring healthy
pregnancies at a younger age. Maybe I wouldn't have the traditional route the world believed in, but I knew I'd be a good
mother, and my future son or daughter would have enough love
from me to equal a dual set of parents.

The process suited my nature. I was able to pick out the father by doing meticulous research to find the best traits and
advantages for my future baby. I became pregnant immediately
and embraced every change in my body, relishing the growing
life inside me that would give me new purpose.

When Allegra was born, I learned a valuable lesson. Books and
research and intellectual knowledge meant nothing compared to
the type of all-consuming, massive love I'd been capable of. The
moment she was put on my stomach and our gazes met, I realized
I'd reached an almost dangerous precipice. Nothing was more

important than my daughter. The violent, ferocious need to protect and cherish my precious baby rocked and tore my stable world apart. My entire body trembled and shook when I held her, and for the first time, a crippling fear shot through my system, draining away my egotistical belief that I'd be able to control things. I was helpless and vulnerable to the cruel fates, no longer locked in my Rapunzel tower of confidence and capability.

And the voice inside me whispered, tormenting me with words that stung like a nest of wasps.

You made a mistake. This time, you'll fail. You'll never be enough for her.

And I cried, my head bowed over her perfect, precious face, and swore in that hospital bed I wouldn't let her down.

I blinked, the distant memories slowly fading away. My surroundings took hold and I walked over to the French doors that led to the patio.

My daughter had been arrested for drugs.

I pressed my palms against the cool panes of glass and stared outside. The gardens were in full bloom, opening up to the spring sun with a hungry thirst to be reborn. I'd never had the inclination or patience to involve myself in gardening like my mother, preferring to hire out and enjoy the cultivated, clipped blooms after they'd been weeded and pruned and watered. As I stared at my pristine gardens, I wondered if I'd made a mistake yet again, like I had with my daughter. It had been easier to shroud myself within the safety of work and farm out the hard stuff to experts rather than diving into the mess. Maybe the dirt, thorns, and weeds were required to be dealt with before I'd be able to appreciate any future beauty. Maybe if I didn't do it myself, I was just a fraud, like that man I'd observed long ago in that ad agency, his success only a pale imitation, hidden behind ego and a partner who'd done the actual work.

Dear God, what was I going to do?

I pushed away from the all-seeing windows and made my way into the kitchen. The cold gleam of stainless steel, black-and-white tile, and marble countertops usually soothed me, but right now I felt only emptiness as I poured myself a glass of Chardonnay and sat down on a high-backed white leather chair.

I'd failed in the worst way possible. My daughter was smoking pot behind my back. Her name could appear in tomorrow's paper—not to boast of an academic scholarship, but included on the local police blotter. All the hard work to get her poised for a successful college career tipped precariously toward disaster. But even the threat of community humiliation, academic discipline, or loss of opportunities meant nothing next to the knowledge that Allegra was in trouble.

Oh, I knew most mothers never believed their children could be doing drugs, drinking in the basement, or having sex without their knowledge. We figured we knew our kids. They'd grown in our bellies and were ripped out of our bodies. We watched every single moment of their life unfold in front of us. We bathed them, cleaned their poop, and introduced them to the world on our terms. But it meant nothing now.

How did so many years of preparation and worry and love mean so little? She was making her own choices and going down a disastrous road. These new friends of hers smoked pot and skipped school. Did she actually believe I'd allow her to travel cross-country in a broken-down RV with delinquent strangers? This was the group she chose to hang out with?

Not on my watch. I'd die before I let her go.

My fingers trembled around the stem of the glass. Instead of being contrite and crying as she begged for forgiveness, she'd blamed me. Where had the hate come from? We hadn't even had a blowout fight in the past year. I deliberately backed off to allow her space to grow and find her own way. Tried to give her privacy instead of being one of those pushy, nosy moms.

Look what that had done. She'd gotten worse with the freedom and now I had to get a handle on it.

I rubbed my temples, head throbbing, and downed the glass of wine. I had to deal with this presentation tomorrow and then I'd handle Allegra. Once I snagged the account, I'd take some time off and concentrate on what she needed and how I could fix this. Maybe get her a therapist. I'd mentioned one to her before, but she'd scowled at my suggestion and refused. This time, I'd insist. Did she need antianxiety drugs? Was peer pressure getting to her?

The questions whirled through my overtaxed brain.

Just one more lousy day until it was time to dazzle and close a big win for my team.

I could do it.

I headed up to bed.

THE NEXT MORNING, my team gathered in the war room to go over last-minute details before the presentation. I'd dressed in my favorite lucky suit—a smart, sleek black pin-striped Michael Kors number that both was stylish and projected confidence. Kate looked polished in slate gray, the feminine ruffles on her blouse a delicate touch by Vera Wang. And Layla sported a Donna Karan pantsuit in rich cream, her dark skin a gorgeous sheen against the pearl. Adam exuded enthusiastic energy and was dressed in a classic Calvin Klein with a narrow cut in a muted navy with a red tie.

I sipped some water, forgoing my usual coffee, and tried to get into the zone. I was much more nervous than normal—my heart beating at a more rapid pace than I was used to—and I needed to reflect a calm, competent demeanor. I shouldn't be worried. My pitch was razor sharp.

Kate sipped her espresso, her blue gaze shredding through the proposal to double-check for accuracy. "We have lunch reservations at Anthony's right after the meeting," she said in her low voice.

"Good." I dragged in a deep breath and swore that after I nailed this, I'd begin taking regular yoga classes. I hoped I didn't start to sweat and thanked God for jackets. "We got this. We've practiced nonstop, our video campaign is brilliant, and we have a chance to go viral on IG."

"As long as Alan isn't a conservative," Layla pointed out. "He has the capacity to kill it."

"He'd get outvoted," I said firmly. "Lexi would rather go with a daring campaign than boring. Plus, humor sells."

"True," Kate said, nodding.

Finally, my assistant called to let me know the clients were here. Showtime.

I slipped into charm mode and soon had settled everyone in the conference room. Lexi's Lemonade was the brainchild of Lexi Hutchinson, who'd become obsessed with the juice-drink culture when her own kids became addicted to sugary sports drinks. I liked her immediately because she wasn't pretentious and she wanted to find the right niche to sell to and get the brand national attention. Right now, she was in local supermarkets from a grassroots endeavor that had exploded.

Alan, dressed in a conservative black suit, was bald, proper, the numbers guy. Johanna was the head of marketing, a fierce redhead who'd challenged me to think big or forget the whole thing. I wanted to impress her the most.

Once coffee had been poured, pastries grabbed, and the anticipatory hush settled, I launched into my intro, moving confidently into the multiple reasons F&F Advertising was the perfect fit, and what we could do for Lexi's Lemonade.

Kate and Layla stepped in at crucial points to discuss the

budget figures and research demographics, which Alan seemed to appreciate; then Adam transitioned smoothly into our social media campaign. I'd gone with live video rather than graphics to achieve the full effect and had dropped a substantial amount in a gamble that I'd get the account if I spared no expense.

As Adam finished up, I began to notice my nerves tighten and stretch under my skin and my lungs constrict around my breath. I took a sip of water and kept my smile firmly in place. My palms grew damp around the bottle, and I silently prayed Adam would hurry. Once I began speaking, I knew I'd be fine. I was having the strangest performance anxiety, which I'd never experienced before. And unfortunately, the more I tried to relax, the harder it became to breathe.

Thankfully, I heard my cue and stepped front and center. The television behind me geared up with the video.

"Thanks to Kate and Layla for their presentations. And Adam, for his fresh outlook on social media. Personally, I took his advice and gave my own IG account a nice face-lift and I'm proud to report Kylie is now a follower. My teenage daughter was quite impressed."

They laughed on cue.

I tried to swallow, but there was a giant lump in my throat that wouldn't budge. I tucked my hands behind my back so no one could notice the shaking.

"The most important thing the public is looking for in a good commercial is the hook. Attention is almost impossible to keep, so we combined the hook with humor and enough mystery to keep them to the very end. It's also extremely watchable over and over again, which allows Lexi's Lemonade to always be in the forefront of children's minds. I'm proud to show you this original production that will make both kids and mothers laugh."

My vision blurred, then steadied. I could feel a trickle of

sweat slide down from my armpits. I gritted my teeth and fought my body with everything I had, desperate to close the deal, lock myself in the bathroom, and then lose my shit.

"Instead of graphics, we produced our own commercial to give you an idea of what it will look like on the screen. And without further ado, I'll let the work speak for itself. We call this commercial 'Wishes Do Come True.' Enjoy."

Kate pressed the remote and the video began playing.

I knew every second of every frame, every movement and detail. With the lights dimmed, I blinked and tried desperately to focus on the screen, tamping down on the tendrils of panic beginning to hit at the realization that something very bad was happening to me.

In my mind, the commercial unfolded. The little girl running through an intricate maze of vivid colors. Stumbling across a genie lamp and giving it a few rubs. The genie exploding from the bottle, half human, half dog, drawn painstakingly by one of the most talented graphic artists in the industry, who happened to be a friend of mine. "What are your three wishes?" the odd monster boomed to the little girl.

A horrible, slicing pain squeezed tight around my heart. My breath felt strangled, and I began gasping, desperate to get air. The pictures kept flickering across the screen.

The little girl does a happy dance and flashes a gap-toothed smile. "I wish for a box of Lexi's Lemonade!" she shouts to the genie.

Immediately, a puff of pink smoke swirls and the familiar box of juice is in the girl's hands. "Wish granted. What is your second wish?"

"I wish for a box of Lexi's Lemonade!" she says again.

The genie frowns, then nods. A puff of blue smoke appears along with another box.

I tried to suck in a breath but there was no air. I was dying. I was having a heart attack right in front of my clients, and there was nothing I could do about it. A vision of Allegra swam past me, and my hands fisted in helpless fear as I began to crumble to the ground, trying to shout for help.

"Wish granted. What is your third wish?" the genie asked.

"I wish for a box of Lexi's Lemonade!" the girl yells.

A puff of glittery silver smoke, and then the lemonade is in her hand. The girl hugs all three boxes to her, beaming.

"Your wishes are granted," the genie announced.

"Thank you, genie. Boy, I wish I had one more wish left. I'd wish for a lifetime supply of Lexi's Lemonade!"

The genie shook his head in obvious confusion, then shrugged. "Before I go back in my lamp, do you think I can have one? I don't want to wait another ten thousand years to taste Lexi's Lemonade."

"Sure!" The little girl gives the genie one of her boxes and they both drink.

The words pop on the screen in huge neon glitter letters.

Lexi's Lemonade—Make All Your Wishes Come True!
Good for Moms Too—100% Organic and Packed in the World's First Recyclable Boxes!

With a pain wracking my chest, my lungs unable to draw in any air, I hit the floor as dim shouts seemed to come from far away. I clawed for focus, but my vision blurred and the room did a drunken spin. The words got stuck in my throat and refused to emerge. In those final moments before I lost consciousness, one thought repeated over and over.

I should have brought the meeting to a close earlier.

CHAPTER EIGHT

SOPHIA

THE DAY MY husband died, I won two thousand dollars.

I was with my church friend, Kathy Burke, and she had talked me into heading over to bingo after Saturday mass. Jack had said he wasn't feeling well and was going to stay home, and I didn't give it much thought. I remember telling him I wasn't sure if I was going to bingo and did he want me to check in, but he said no, if I didn't come home by six, he'd put in the leftover chicken and take care of himself.

The mass was long because Father Bill was dealing with some drama from the fallout of the church mergers, and some of the congregation had a bee in their bonnet about mass times getting cut. After he addressed the issues, he went into a detailed sermon on forgiveness (probably directed at the specific people who'd been giving him a hard time), and then the birthday blessings came up, and by the time I'd shaken Father Bill's hand, I just wanted to go home and watch a movie with Jack.

But Kathy was insistent, so I told her I'd go for a short time. The event ended up being more fun than I'd expected. A group of friends flocked over, and we had a whole table to ourselves, and they even served some wine, which was rare. The time flew, and I ended up winning the final game of the night, which was the big jackpot.

I couldn't believe it. I'd never won anything in my life. And two thousand dollars was a huge amount of money for us at the time. I remember how excited I was to tell Jack. I decided not to text or call but to surprise him when I got home. We'd make plans to go out to a fancy dinner with Francesca to celebrate. I drove home singing to Justin Timberlake, who seemed like such a nice boy with an amazing voice, and was surprised when I walked in and saw there were no dishes in the sink and the television wasn't on. Jack had never washed a dish in his life and I didn't expect him to start now, so that meant he hadn't eaten dinner. Had he gone to bed already?

I walked up the stairs and found him dead on the carpeted floor of our bedroom.

Nothing was out of place. No phone by his side to call 911. He was dressed in his normal outfit of loose khaki pants and a white shirt. His face didn't reflect any distress or regret or pain. It was just smooth and expressionless.

And gone.

Jack was no longer in there. The body had been just a shell after all. And as I called 911 and felt the hysterics begin deep in my bones, the full horror unfolding over losing the man I'd been with for my entire life, I wondered, if I hadn't stayed for bingo, would he still be alive?

I never told Frannie about the money or being at bingo. I donated the funds back to the church and buried the knowledge deep. But right now, walking into the hospital to see my daughter, I couldn't stop wondering whether one bad decision can wreck the rest of one's life. If I'd come home from mass, maybe I could have saved my husband, and then maybe Frannie wouldn't have collapsed at forty-eight years old.

Men plan and God laughs, the familiar voice whispered. *Why are you still obsessing about that? You should have never donated the damn money. You could have used it.*

Shush, I told Jack, hurrying my steps to the nurse's desk. *It was blood money. I didn't want it.*

You've been watching too many old movies on TCM. It was from church bingo and it wasn't your fault.

I had no time to converse with my dead husband right now. Instead, I gave them my name, and they told me floor four, and I got off and made my way to the nurses' station. I tried to remain strong for my daughter's sake.

Dear God, let her be okay. If I lose her, I won't be able to cope.

My voice shook but at least it worked. "Francesca Ferrari. She's my daughter."

The nurse smiled and gestured down the hall. "Room 404. The doctor will be there shortly."

"Thank you."

They'd told me she was out of danger, but that was all I knew. I walked in and she was propped up in bed with some pillows behind her, eyes closed. I stopped at the edge of the bed, trying hard not to cry. She looked so fragile. None of her usual strength and force radiated from her figure. Even when she was young, she'd run from place to place with a determined focus to conquer every task. "Frannie?" I said softly.

Her eyes flew open. "Mom." She shook her head, a self-conscious smile curving her lips. "I had an incident."

I sighed and sat down, my hand automatically reaching for hers as I reassured myself she was okay. She accepted my embrace, her fingers curling around mine, and for a moment I remembered when she was young and used to hold my hand for guidance, her warm flesh a comfort and guiding light for every second of my day. Now I grabbed any crumbs my daughter would give me and was grateful.

I never realized motherhood could be so awfully lonely.

"What happened, sweetheart? What did the doctors say?"

"I was positive it was a heart attack. I never felt like that before—like I couldn't breathe, and with this intense pain in my chest. It was awful. I collapsed at my meeting. They did a whole bunch of tests, but I feel fine now. The doctor said he'd be here to give me the results soon."

I nodded, covering up the raw fear by rationalizing that if it was something serious, it could be fixed. Medicine was amazing nowadays, and she was young. "Okay. What about Allegra? Should I call her?"

"No!" She glared, showing some of her familiar spunk. "I don't want her to know anything until I hear what the doctors say. There's no need for her to panic and miss school."

"Okay. Have you had any of these symptoms before? When was your last physical?"

She glanced away and dropped my hand. I'd already lost her. Irritation glimmered in her brown eyes. "Yes—I go every year, and everything was fine. I've had some anxiety issues lately, but I figured it was just the stress of this new account."

I held my tongue, even though I shook with the need to scold her for being so blasé about her health. "It could be premenopausal," I suggested. "I had a hard time around fifty. Night sweats and emotional breakdowns. I ended up going on hormones for a while."

She seemed thoughtful, and I felt ridiculously proud of myself. "That makes sense. Maybe I'll go to one of those Chinese practitioners that use herbs and holistic medicine."

I didn't like the idea of not using a medical doctor but, again, kept silent. She let me fuss a bit and comfort her, and then the doctor came in.

Immediately, I relaxed. He came into the room with a confidence that screamed, *I can fix you!* He paused in the doorway to clean his hands, which gave me time to study him. He even looked the part—tall, with thick dark hair and a strong face. He wore trendy glasses and his white coat was clean and starched. He seemed old enough to have treated plenty of patients to know what he was doing. He smiled, flashing perfect white teeth, and greeted us in a booming voice. Even better was his ringless finger. Francesca would be a perfect fit for him.

"I'm Dr. Hollingsworth," he said, reaching out to shake my hand.

"I'm Sophia," I said, boldly gazing into his bright blue eyes. "Frannie's mother."

"Good to meet you. And how is our patient doing?" He reached over and did a quick check on Frannie's vitals. I noticed my daughter tense when he drew near. Was she attracted to him? I always knew she needed a strong man in her life, one with a respectable career to challenge her.

"Better," she responded with a smile.

"Good. We have the results of the tests back and I have good news. There was no heart attack."

My muscles practically collapsed with relief. "Oh, thank God."

"What caused the breakdown?" Frannie asked. "It felt like one."

He nodded, a frown creasing his brow. "I understand. What you experienced was a classic panic attack. Very commonly mistaken for a heart attack due to the intense bodily reactions. Have you had one of these before?"

Frannie blinked, averting her gaze. "No. Well, I've been having some breathing problems, but I knew it was stress. I never collapsed."

Shock barreled through me. Dear God, it was happening all over again. I'd watched my husband suffer for years to control his panic attacks, but I never thought Frannie would have the same problem. Somehow, I'd believed she was different.

The doctor continued. "It's a scary experience. Most of my patients who experience these attacks are under a good deal of stress or going through a big change. Divorce, death in the family, new job, et cetera."

"What can I do? I never want to go through something like that again. It happened in front of my clients."

Sympathy emanated from his blue eyes. "Unfortunately, there's no cure for panic attacks. I'd suggest seeing a therapist who can give you coping tools or prescribe antianxiety medication. Many of my patients have changed their diet or used exercise to help manage the stress. I'd be happy to give you a referral to a therapist who specializes in anxiety. But your blood results came back perfect. You're in wonderful health, so there's no need to be concerned. Do you have any questions for me?"

Frannie stared back at him, an array of raw emotions flickering across her face. I noticed the fear the most. The idea that my strong daughter couldn't control her body would torture her. I knew she'd punish herself, thinking the breakdown was weakness.

Just like Jack.

"I don't think so," she said slowly.

He nodded. "Feel free to contact me anytime. I'll give you the referral."

I had to interrupt. "Doctor, do you think taking some time off has an effect on stress?"

"Do you have a stressful job, Frannie?"

"Yes, I own an advertising business."

He cocked his head with interest. "Impressive. Do you know before I decided on premed, I worked at an ad firm for a while. I was a bit lost in my youth and tried a few different paths before deciding to commit," he said wryly.

"Which one?" Frannie asked.

"Duke and Liebowitz."

She lit up. "Yes! I was over at Emerson Advertising."

"Our competitors." His laugh was deep and rich. I kept quiet, hoping their conversation would keep going. "I'll have to check out your website. Do you enjoy the work?"

"Yes, when I'm not collapsing in front of my new client."

He laughed again. "Just remember it's quite common and completely treatable. And to answer your mother, yes. Taking some time off may be just what you need to reset, if you can manage. I certainly know about demanding work schedules, but health should come first."

Frannie thanked him, and he gave her a kind smile, but when he turned to leave and she hadn't said anything else, I jumped in. "Could we have your card, Doctor?"

"Of course." He plucked one out of his pocket and handed it to me. "Please call me if there are any issues."

I noticed he gave Frannie a pointed look, but then he quickly exited the room and I had no time to stall him. I'd save the matchmaking for later. Right now, I had to convince my daughter it was time to take a vacation. It hadn't worked with her father, but this time, I wouldn't take no for an answer.

"I think you should make the therapist appointment."

She gave a sigh and rubbed her temples. The stress was back in her face and the doctor had just left. "Yeah, I know. I'll look into that. But I think there was something else contributing to this whole attack."

My own heart started pounding crazily at my daughter's expression. "What is it?"

Slowly, she told me all about Allegra. The drugs. The police. Her idea of taking off with these hooligans for the summer. Not my sweet Allegra. This wasn't like her at all—I'd known she felt lost, but I'd never imagined her making such bad decisions.

Were things worse than I'd thought? I pressed my fingers to my mouth and tried to regain my composure.

"Will she have a record? Does she have to appear in court? What's going to happen to her?"

"Right now, she has to appear before the judge. I'll hire a lawyer, but she didn't have any weed on her and wasn't high at the time, so that may help. Of course, the driver was, which makes it a hell of a lot worse."

"She could have been killed." The words lay flat and lifeless between us.

Frustration sparked from her. "I expected some teen-rebellion stuff, but nothing like this. I don't know, I was probably naïve to think she wouldn't try pot, but getting in the car with a driver who's high? What else has she been doing that I don't know about? I left a message at her school and I contacted Bonnie's and Claire's mothers to see if they know anything. She's just so angry."

"Frannie, listen to me. I know you said it was impossible, but I think an Italy trip is exactly what this family needs. You can get Allegra away from those kids for the summer. You can get a well-needed rest. And I'll get to spend time with you—quality time, in a beautiful place that's your heritage."

"I don't know. I have to call the office ASAP, Mom."

My mouth fell open. "You're worried about the office after this? Do you see how out of control things are getting? For God's sakes, go home and rest. Talk to Allegra."

"I will. I have to get going."

I was losing her again. Already, her mind had shifted as she analyzed how she could force her body to behave, ignoring all the warning signs around her. Jack hadn't listened either. "Frannie, please," I begged. "Think about Italy. Do you want me to talk to Allegra?"

She shook her head, bopping around the room to gather her things. "No, I'll talk to her, Mom."

I opened my mouth, determined to make her listen, frightened that if I didn't get her to take a break from rushing through life toward the next goalpost, I could lose her. But it was already too late.

She'd rushed out of the room and left me behind.

She wasn't listening anyway.

CHAPTER NINE

FRANCESCA

"WHAT DO YOU mean they want me off the account? It's my company."

I stared in growing disbelief at Kate and Layla, who, after a long, drawn-out reunion consisting of me telling them the details of my panic attack and reassuring them I was fine, had reluctantly launched into an explanation of the status of the Lexi's Lemonade account. The chill began deep in my gut and spread outward, and the sick feeling of betrayal began to flicker.

It couldn't be. I trusted them. What were they talking about?

They shared a pointed glance, but it was Layla who took the lead. "Fran, please listen to me. It was an extremely stressful experience for everyone in the conference room. We were all terrified something serious had happened to you. When you called to let us know things were fine, we took them to lunch. Both Lexi and Alan agreed they loved the pitch, including the proposed commercial and social media launch. But they were also insistent they preferred us to be the leads."

"Why? Because I collapsed? It was one incident. Listen, I left a message with Lexi, and I'm sure I can make things right. I'll explain it was a fluke, tell them what the doctor said—I'll handle it."

Kate nibbled her bottom lip in her telltale sign of discomfort. "I'm sure you will. But I will say there's been a lot of gossip in the office. Talk about another incident during the launch meeting with the bakery bread account."

Dammit. I'd excused myself early, locking myself in my office until I'd calmed down. I didn't think anyone had noticed after I'd cited an emergency call that trumped the meeting. I should have known eyes were on me at all times.

My voice turned cold. "I guess people aren't working hard enough if they're gossiping over such ridiculousness. Nothing was wrong with me."

Layla nodded. "Okay, we believe you. We're on your side, Fran. We never promised them anything—when you talk to Lexi and Alan, you'll see we backed you up and cited our complete confidence in you. But it's more than work. We're both really worried about you."

"You're not the same," Kate said slowly. "Distracted, making silly errors in meetings. But watching you today, thinking you were going to die, we just think you need a break."

I gave a humorless laugh. "You want me to take a vacation, right? That way I can come back and find you tried to take over my company."

Kate's lips pressed into a thin line. "That was low," she said. "If you're even considering us for partners, there should be trust. We're not out to take anything away from you, Fran. We're here to bring you more success, but if you don't believe it, maybe I need to rethink my position here."

She stood up and walked out.

Layla gazed at me with a touch of sympathy. "I'm sure you'll fix it with Lexi. I just wanted to be clear about what was said. We're a team, Fran. You don't have to do everything alone all the time, you know."

She waited for me to answer, but I had nothing to say. She

ducked her head, then followed Kate out, shutting the door softly behind her.

My hands began to shake. I was losing control, and I didn't know what to do about it. Already, just thinking of Lexi yanking the account made my entire body clench and my heart beat faster. I thought of Allegra and how I should be calling to make sure she was at track practice and not with her new criminal friends. I thought of my mother, with her worried gaze and admonishments and the guilt I always felt in her presence. And I even thought of that doctor, who'd looked at me with kind eyes and a sexy smile, and I wondered what that strange flicker of recognition was, because it had been so long since I experienced any type of sexual spark, I didn't know how to deal with it, let alone flirt. And then all the thoughts jumbled up into one big roaring mess, making me want to lower my head in my hands and cry.

But I didn't.

I pulled myself together, sipped some water, took some breaths, and called Lexi again.

Hours later, I sat behind my desk and brought up the site for Italy tours.

Seemed as if I had no choice after all. We were going to Italy.

CHAPTER TEN

Allegra

I STEPPED OUT of the cab and stood on the curb, blinking away the fatigue that made me feel like I'd had too much to drink. The flight had seemed endless, starting with a delay, then long lines at customs. Our pickup never showed, so Mom had gone into her bitchy business mode, calling the tour director and complaining. I'd exchanged suffering glances with Nonni, but we'd just kept quiet and let her do her thing.

The driver unloaded the luggage and I studied the Hotel Artemide, which seemed more modern than I'd imagined. The multitiered building was squeezed on both sides by storefronts, lined up in a neat row on a narrow street. The road was packed with tiny cars touching one another's bumpers, and it was loud, like NYC. Lots of voices and beeping attacked my ears. Then again, Rome was a big city, and not rural like Tuscany, so I figured it'd be a different experience. Right now, all I wanted was something to eat, a bed, and a long nap.

I also didn't want to be here.

Bonnie and Claire thought I was nuts. I'd been busted for pot and rewarded with a trip to Italy. They didn't understand the real punishment was taking me away for the entire summer so Mom could act as my jailer, able to watch and examine my every move. Connor had gotten off with probation, and Freda and David ended up being released. Seemed like the judge didn't feel like putting a bunch of teenagers in jail for being stupid. Of course, Mom had to show up with a fancy-ass lawyer she didn't even need to argue my case, which got some eye rolls from Freda, and after a public scolding, I was mercifully let go.

The last two months had been hell. Mom almost lost that big account she'd been working on, and when I came home, she announced we were going to Italy with Nonni. No discussion. I flipped out, refusing to go, but she'd just looked at me with cold eyes, and I broke a bit inside. It seemed harder and harder to connect with her. It was as if she felt nothing and didn't care. I could have dealt with a temper tantrum, where she yelled and screamed at me—anything but that flat stare. She shrugged, said I had no choice, and went to bed. After that she checked up on me wherever I went, called my guidance counselor to make sure I skipped no classes, and contacted Bonnie's and Claire's parents when I spent the night at one of their houses. By the time I got on the plane for this supposed family-bonding trip, I already felt battered and pissed off.

God, I was tired of feeling like such a mess. But I didn't know how to feel any different.

We went into the lobby, decorated with shiny white floors, sparkly chandeliers, and wine-colored couches. A red-and-black painting of a woman in a fashionable hat took up one whole wall. There were a lot of mirrors and fancy gold accents everywhere. I was about to head over to the couch to wait while we got checked in, but a man dressed in a sleek black suit came right over.

"*Buongiorno.* Ferrari?"

I nodded. Mom stepped forward. "*Sì.* Do you know where our tour guide is?"

The man gave a smile that immediately made his face grow from okay to handsome. "I am your tour guide, *signora.* My name is Enzo, and I'll be your main contact these next three weeks. I'm very sorry about the mix-up at the airport and hope you can forgive me. I have your rooms all ready, and if you'd like to take a seat, I can explain the schedule."

I was impressed with his English and the way he apologized so nicely. It also seemed to take away Mom's anger at being forgotten, 'cause she nodded and he led us over to the cozy sitting area. He handed us each a bottle of water and I immediately guzzled mine down. I felt like a dried-out raisin.

"Now, we have Francesca, Sophia, and Allegra." His dark eyes filled with amusement. "Are you all Irish?"

I smiled, liking him immediately. I hated the idea of getting stuck with a tour guide who spouted off dry information and made me want to stab myself in the eyeball from boredom. Mom answered. "My grandparents are from Naples. This is my mother, Sophia, and my daughter, Allegra. I'm Francesca."

He directed his next question at me. "Are you excited about this trip, *signorina*? Not many get to experience visiting their family's roots."

I felt the pressure of my mother's gaze, as if mocking me. I ignored the twinge inside that I was getting used to burying, wondering about my genetic father and his family. "Yes. How many people will be on this tour with us?"

"Fifteen, including your family," he said. "We'll be having a welcome dinner right here at the hotel at six p.m. You can meet everyone and get to know one another. The rest of the day is free, so you can get something to eat, or rest. I'm here for anything you need. I'll get you folders that explain every detail of our itinerary. Tomorrow morning we'll meet in the lobby at nine a.m. to board the bus for our first site. There will be a simple breakfast of cappuccino and pastries provided in the restaurant. Do you have any questions for me before I get your room keys?"

"Is the restaurant open for lunch now? Or can we get room delivery?" Mom asked.

"Yes, either one. Let me get your keys."

He walked away and Mom leaned over. Her face still held a crease from the line of the pillow she'd laid her cheek on during the flight. "What do you want to do? Room service or grab something now?"

"Room service," Nonni and I said together.

"Okay. I think we all need a nap and a shower to feel human again. Mom, how are you feeling?"

Nonni smiled. "Good. Tired, but excited."

Enzo came back with two cards and handed them to my mother. "You have two rooms. One has two doubles and one has a queen."

"I'll stay with Nonni," I said.

A short silence settled. Everyone stared at me, but I pressed my lips together and didn't back down or say it didn't matter. Right now, I didn't want to be in the same room as my mother. If I stayed with Nonni, at least I'd get some breathing room. "That's not necessary," Nonni said, glancing back and forth between us. "Stay with your mother, honey."

"No, that's okay." Mom's voice was polite but cold. "You can look after your grandmother. Just remember she snores."

Enzo laughed, not seeming to sense the tension. "Go down this hall, take the elevators to the fourth floor. Your luggage was already brought up. I also included my cell phone number in case you need me."

"*Grazie,*" I said, liking the way the word sounded on my tongue, especially in Italy and not Italian class.

"*Prego.*"

He winked and walked away. We headed to the elevators, remaining quiet, and when we got to the rooms, Mom turned her back and began fiddling with the key card. "I'll check on you in a few hours. Let me know if you have any trouble with room service."

Guilt threatened, but I pushed it down. I had the right not to want to be in her room. The idea of strained conversation or fighting right now made my stomach hurt. So I nodded and went inside with Nonni.

"Nice room," I said, shutting the door. The two double beds held piles of pillows and I had an urge to crawl up on the mattress and fall dead asleep. There was a basic couch and a table with a small TV, but when I went to the window and pulled back the curtain, I gasped. "Nonni, come look."

She stood beside me. "How beautiful." She sighed and leaned against me so our shoulders were touching. The city spread out before us, all rough stone and jagged edges and dozens of shades of brown edged with green. I spotted the faint outline of the Duomo, and endless streets crisscrossing in an elaborate puzzle. Wrought-iron balconies filled with brightly colored flowers seemed to spring from every building. "It's like we stepped into a different world."

We enjoyed the view for a while, then decided to order. "I want the pizza," my grandmother declared. Her eyes glinted, and even though I knew she was tired from the trip, she seemed more excited than I've ever seen her before. "How different do you think it is from America?"

"I don't know, but I'm getting one too." I made the call and was relieved the person who answered spoke English, and they promised to have it up within thirty minutes.

"Allegra, you should have stayed with your mother."

I stiffened. "I will at the next hotel, okay? Right now, I just don't want to."

She gave a long sigh. "She has every right to be mad. It only takes one horrible mistake to ruin your life. Give your mom a break. She's going through a hard time too."

"Because she lost the lead on an account." I wondered if this Italy trip was because of her job or me. Not that it mattered. She'd made it clear it wasn't for Nonni.

"I want to look at this trip as a fresh start, for all of us. Is it silly to want the two people I love most to get along? Have some fun for a change?"

"No." I knew how important this was for my grandmother, and I swore I wouldn't act like a bitch. I'd try to take the opportunity and enjoy it with her. Maybe I'd even try harder with my mother. God knows, we were stuck with each other now for most of the summer. "But I don't trust you."

She frowned. "What do you mean?"

"I'm afraid you'll drink too much wine and end up dancing in the Trevi Fountain."

I loved her laugh and the way she hugged me, never afraid to show affection. "Or maybe I'll meet a handsome Rossano Brazzi and fall madly in love and never return home."

"Who's that?"

Her look of horror made me laugh. "You've never seen the movie *Summertime*? It was a love story with this handsome Italian actor and Katharine Hepburn set in Italy. Oh, I need to fix this. You poor thing—believing that men with oversize pants that sag are sexy. You have no idea of the sheer class and sexiness of my generation."

I thought of David, and his kiss, and the pot, and wondered if my grandmother was right.

Once the pizza was delivered, we ate it at the table. It was hot and cheesy with the perfect thin-type crust I loved, and after I finished the whole thing, my belly bulged and I crawled into the bed. "Nonni, I have to sleep."

I heard plates clink and clothes rustle, and smelled the soothing scent of lavender. She smoothed my hair back and placed a kiss on my forehead.

I drifted off, finally content.

CHAPTER ELEVEN

FRANCESCA

THE DINNER WAS held at a restaurant on the rooftop of our hotel. The elegant display of crisp white linens, sparkly china, and the stunning view of Rome spread out like a gift made me thankful I'd insisted on upgrading our tour. Mom had wanted to settle for a larger group and lower-class hotels, but I'd finally found a more boutique tour that catered to clients with top-rate lodging, meals, and experiences. A large rectangular table was set up and already a few of the tour members were sipping water and chatting. Immediately I cringed, since I'd hoped to snag a table alone with Mom and Allegra so we didn't have to socialize the first night. I knew it was a mixer, but we'd had a long travel day, and I was in the mood to enjoy a good meal without trying to get to know strangers.

Anxiety started to seize me, and I gritted my teeth, determined to ward off any type of attack. The plane ride had spiked the same type of panic, reminding me of that slow, torturous downfall at my office; reminding me of being out of control and helpless under the flighty impulses of my body. I shuddered out a breath and tried to focus on a relaxing dinner.

"Should we sit there?" my mother asked, pointing to the end where we'd only have to deal with people on one side. I nodded, quickly motioning for them to grab the seats before anyone else could. Allegra shot me a strange look but was thankfully silent as she plopped down.

The stout Italian waiter brought over a tray with bottles of red and white wine. "Mom, can I have a glass of wine?" Allegra asked.

"No," I said, still shaky over the pot incident. Didn't they say weed was a gateway drug? Had she also been getting drunk on school nights or weekends and I'd never even suspected?

My mother smiled with indulgence. "Oh, let her have just a few sips. We're in Italy and it's with dinner. Most families give their children wine young so they learn to drink it with meals as an accompaniment. Maybe if we didn't make it such a mystery, fewer kids would want to get drunk."

My mouth fell open. "Are you really questioning me on this? You never let me have wine."

She shrugged. "We weren't in Italy."

Allegra smothered a laugh, and I shook my head. It was nice to hear my daughter laugh. Maybe I needed to try to not make everything a battle between us. Better to keep the peace, and my mother could help chaperone. "Just a few sips," I warned.

"We'll do Pinot Grigio," my mother declared. "It's light and fruity."

While she initiated Allegra into the pleasures of adult beverages, I swept my gaze over the table. The chairs next to me were still vacant, and I counted nine people so far. I did a quick catalogue, making the initial assessments that had always served me well. A family of three—their son looked to be a bit older than Allegra. One older couple who looked around Mom's age. And two female friends in their late twenties who seemed carefree and excited for the adventure ahead.

I settled down. No one seemed to throw me off or give off bad energy. God knows, I didn't want to get stuck with a bunch of annoying people for three weeks. I murmured, *"Grazie,"* when the waiter slid the plate of prosciutto and melon, entangled delicately with a few sprigs of mint, in front of me. Thick, crusty loaves of Italian bread were set out in baskets, with olive oil and pepper drizzled on small plates. My fingers twitched with the need to taste, and I reached halfway toward the basket before snatching my hand back. There'd be more carbs to choose from later, and I'd need to be careful.

"Bread is life, *signora*," an amused, lilting voice echoed from behind me.

I turned around, startled. Our tour guide—was it Enzo?—stood before me, a half smile resting on his full lips. Was he judging me as one of those typical Americans who refuse good food in the name of thinness? I really wasn't like that, but I also knew if I gobbled up pasta, sweets, and bread for a month, I'd never fit into my designer suits again. Food had been delegated to sustenance, not pleasure, for a long time. "Too much life and I won't be able to zip up my pants after the tour," I quipped, softening my answer with a smile.

He laughed, and I was surprised at the rich sound, full of gusto and volume. I studied him with interest. I pegged him at about only five-seven, and his face held nondescript features that combined to make him easy to dismiss. He couldn't boast of a sharp jawline or high cheekbones or even a sexy goatee. His face was round, with a blunt nose, high forehead, and heavy brows. His hair was dark and curly, and his eyes were a rich brown, the color of melted chocolate. He wore tan pants, mustard-colored loafers, and a crisp button-down green shirt with oversize cuffs. His body seemed fit, but it wasn't as if he was busting out of his clothes with muscled biceps and rock-hard abs. The man was completely forgettable, and not my type. But there was something else that intrigued me—an energy that almost burst from him, an ease in the way he held himself and looked at me with a warm humor I rarely spotted in the male species unless they had a goal of seduction or gaining something they wanted. His scent rose to my nostrils, a delicious mix of musk, coffee, and rich spice that made me want to take a big whiff. His gaze met mine, and for one crazy moment, my cheeks began to heat in a blush.

"Then I will try not to tempt you too early in the tour," he said, opening his hands in the air. "But I must warn you about the bakeries. Especially Nonni's in Siena. One of my favorites."

I couldn't help but smile back. He wasn't mocking me but seemed to appreciate my dilemma. "Then I'll save up my calories for it."

"You won't have to. We'll be doing so much walking on this tour, carbs will become your new friend. You want to be sure you're not hungry and have comfortable shoes. It is the only way to enjoy Italy."

It was odd to speak with a man who tried to take care of me. Maybe it was part of the tour-guide training.

"*Buona sera*, Enzo," my mother said.

He directed his attention toward my family. "*Buona sera*. I hope you had a good rest and will enjoy dinner."

"I'm starving," Allegra said. "Is tomorrow the Vatican and Sistine Chapel?"

"*Sì*. I'll be going over some of the stops for the next few days after everyone eats."

"Would you like to join us?" I asked, motioning to the empty seat next to us.

He shook his head. "*Grazie*, but I shall be eating separately tonight and will return later." With a nod, he moved down to the next couple, chatting a bit and working the table like a pro. I wondered if he'd always been a guide or had previous business or sales experience in another field. What was the job market like in Italy?

My mother bent her head toward us. "He's very cute," she whispered.

Allegra laughed. "Go for it, Nonni. Maybe you'll have a big love affair in your homeland."

She pointed at me. "I was talking about your mom."

I refused to squirm like a teenager. "Don't be ridiculous. We're here to bond and see the sights, not crush on our tour guide. I'm sure he has a wife and children at home."

"No ring," my mother sang, her dark eyes glinting with mischief.

I sighed and concentrated on my appetizer. "Not interested," I said firmly.

"Mom, why don't you ever date?"

I jerked back under their suddenly intense, questioning stares. Surprise shot through me. My daughter rarely asked about my love life, or lack of it. I figured she'd be happier without a trail of men being paraded in and out of the house, and work was my full-time companion. It'd been just us against the world for so long, I never thought of even wanting to pursue a relationship. The few men who approached usually worked for me, and I didn't mix work with pleasure. The one time I'd said yes to a date with a colleague, I found out over dinner that he was married, and I left. I'd missed out on my filet mignon and ended up binging on a Dairy Queen Blizzard. "I'm always busy, honey," I said.

Was that worry glinting in her eyes? Or something deeper? She hesitated before seeming to pick at her words. "It's just that when I leave, you'll be alone. And all you do is . . . work." My mother's judging look only slammed home the discomfort that Allegra's words set off. I'd built a thriving business from nothing, and they both believed I sacrificed too much. When would a woman finally be respected for her drive and success rather than for how many heartbreaks she'd racked up? I'd managed to birth and raise my daughter with no man, yet it wasn't celebrated but pitied. I'd assumed my actions would show Allegra the path to freedom to experience all her power as a woman of this world. But all she managed to see was the lack of a husband. The injustice of such judgment roared through me, and I opened my mouth to launch into a speech defending my choices, but the last couple arrived at the table and interrupted us.

"I guess we're the last ones to arrive," the woman announced, reaching over to offer her hand. "Nice to meet you. I'm Dana and this is my husband, Steve." We introduced ourselves and I took a moment to study them.

Dana was dressed in a daffodil-yellow dress with red ankle boots. Her hair matched her shoes and was worn long and curly. Chunky colored bracelets clinked on her wrist, and a large purple stone swung in the V between her breasts. Her blue eyes snapped with a bright energy that hinted she was always ready for a party or an adventure. Her husband seemed more conservative, dressed in a white button-down shirt and jeans with a western-type belt buckle. His hair was gray and neatly trimmed, and he sported a smart mustache that reminded me of Sam Elliott. He towered over his petite wife, but his face was sun kissed and creased with laugh lines.

"When did y'all get in?" she asked, an obvious Texas drawl lilting her words.

"This morning," I answered. "We're still kind of jet-lagged."

"Our flight was delayed and we got here a few hours ago. I watched three movies on the plane, drank a bottle of Pinot Grigio, and haven't slept in forty-eight hours. I just hope I don't pass out while looking at the Sistine Chapel," Dana said, waving her wrist in the air as she attacked the bread basket with gusto. "Where are y'all from?"

"New York," my mother said. "This is my daughter and my granddaughter."

"How wonderful!" Dana said. "Three generations of women

touring Italy. I love it. Are you heading to college in the fall, Allegra?"

"Next year," she said.

Dana sighed. "Those were my favorite years. Learning new things, falling in love with a different boy each semester, and being full of passion for causes. I still remember marching for animal rights and chaining myself to the mailbox at the animal kill shelter we tried to shut down."

Allegra's eyes widened. "What happened?"

"They just pulled the mailbox out of the ground and threatened us with arrest. But now it's a no-kill, so we did make a difference."

The waiter glided by and placed a garden salad in front of us, then stocked up the bread basket again.

I dug into my salad, enjoying the flavorful dressing of garlic softened with oil, vinegar, and salt. Dana chattered on, informing us they were here for their tenth-anniversary celebration and that she owned a clothing boutique. She fell into a lively discussion with Allegra on saying no to black and embracing bold, seasonal colors, and I loved watching my daughter relax and enjoy an adult evening getting to know people. Maybe this wasn't such a bad idea after all. It was good for all of us to get away from our usual routine, stuck with the same people who shared our daily schedules.

"Do you both travel much?" I asked Steve, who remained quiet next to me.

"We try. I run a ranch, so it's hard to get time away," he explained in a gravelly voice. Yep, definitely like Sam Elliott. My mother perked up at the mention of a ranch. She had a weakness for the movie *The Horse Whisperer* with Robert Redford. Except that took place in Montana.

"A horse ranch?" she asked, cocking her head.

"Yes, ma'am. Been raising horses since I was young. Inherited the place when my parents passed."

Dana's ears perked up at the sound of her husband's voice. I wondered if she gave him much time to speak. "We even host guests who like to experience a working ranch as a vacation. You get to shadow Steve and eat all sorts of delicious food and go for rides. It's highly rated on TripAdvisor. Maybe one day you'd like to come visit!"

"It sounds so exciting," my mother said. "But I can only imagine how much work it takes to run a ranch."

"We have a ton of employees, but Steve likes to be involved with everything. I keep telling him to go to a part-time schedule, but he's stubborn."

My mother snorted. "My daughter is also a workaholic."

"Ah, what do you do?" Dana asked.

I bristled at the way Mom spoke about me but forced a smile. "Advertising. I own a company, so I understand the challenges. At least we love our work," I said brightly. "Too many people suffer through boring day jobs just to gain a pension. I think the world needs more passionate employees."

Steve nodded. "Agreed."

Dana spoke. "I love dressing women in new designs and watching them feel confident in their bodies. But too much of anything isn't good. That's why I insisted on a long trip for our anniversary, to take a breath. We've always dreamed of seeing Europe." She turned to Allegra. "How about you, honey? Are you like your mama? Ready to set the world on fire with your career?"

The words were obviously meant as a compliment, but my daughter's reaction made my heart stop. Distaste carved out the features of her face and she shook her head hard. "No."

She didn't explain any further. An awkward silence fell, and Dana and Steve shared a look. Allegra ducked her head, and I forced a breezy laugh, pretending it didn't bother me. "What daughter wants to be like her mom, right?"

Everyone chuckled. I avoided my own mother's gaze and steered the conversation back to Dana, where it was safe. I wasn't ready to showcase the cracks within my family on the first day of the tour. Another reason I'd wanted us to eat by ourselves, but at least Dana was entertaining, and it was obvious my daughter enjoyed her lighthearted dialogue.

We'd just finished the main course—a branzino with crisp green beans and roasted potatoes—when Enzo returned and stood at the front of the room. The chatter died down and everyone looked expectantly at the man who held their entire vacation within his grasp. He paused, letting the anticipation build, and finally spoke in his deep, lyrical voice.

"You are about to embark on the vacation of a lifetime."

Oh, he was good.

Low murmurs of approval rose in the room. I shifted in my seat and gave him my full attention. "Destino Tours is committed to showing you not only the beauty of Italy, but the hidden treasures most tour groups would never experience. We begin tomorrow with seeing the Vatican and the momentous Sistine Chapel by Michelangelo. There will be plenty of free time within our schedule to explore on your own, but before booking any extra excursions, come see me first. As in every big city, you must be aware of pickpockets and frauds."

A woman chimed in. "Should we carry our passports with us?"

"No, you should keep important travel papers locked in the hotel safe or secured in your luggage. Be careful of your wallets and purses within easy reach. You don't need to be afraid—just aware. From now on, I am at your disposal. I will be giving you all my cell phone number, and I'm on call twenty-four hours a day."

Okay, that was impressive. The poor man's phone was probably blowing up on a regular basis, and I'd say he didn't mean it, but there was a ring of sincerity laced in his tone.

"I've given everyone a detailed itinerary, so let me know if there are any questions. We meet at nine a.m. in the lobby to take the bus to the Vatican. Shoulders and knees must be covered, so bring a jacket with you if you're wearing a tank top."

"Why?" another woman called out.

"The churches are strict about proper clothing in a religious setting. We must respect the rules."

His tone brooked no disagreement. I was more impressed with each minute of his speech. He spoke excellent English. I'd never thought about how hard it would be to contain and please a large group of people with so many different views on what they wanted or needed.

He continued. "A breakfast buffet will be served in the restaurant. Now, I will be around if you have any private questions or concerns. If you will take out your phones, I will give you my number."

We all took them out and I added him as a contact. I didn't remember his last name, so I saved it under *Enzo Tour Guide*. Dana and Steve stood up. "We're going to head up early to catch up on sleep. It was so nice to meet you," Dana said.

"Same," I responded. "See you in the morning."

I pondered the fruit tart on my plate and settled on a few sips of precious coffee. It was strong and a touch bitter and absolutely perfect. "They were nice," my mother commented, forking up a piece of her dessert. "She's a hoot."

"She's cool," Allegra said. "I'd love to run a clothes shop."

I snorted. "Retail has awful hours and high turnover. You'd hate it," I said.

Immediately she stiffened. "Why do you have to ruin everything I mention?" she asked, her eyes burning with resentment. "Just because you don't like it doesn't mean I wouldn't."

I sighed. "I'm just telling you the truth. Lots of jobs seem glamorous from the outside, but you realize there's too many limitations or downfalls. I'm trying to help."

"You do it all the time. I told you I'm interested in cooking and would love to take classes, but you said to stay away from the restaurant business."

"Because it's a nightmare. You work nights, weekends, and odd hours. The pay is terrible, and it's competitive."

"I don't care. I'm tired of you crapping on all the things I'm interested in."

"Allegra, language," my mother scolded. "Your mother is only trying to help. Just let her know when she's doing something to upset you and you can work it out."

"Forgive me for trying to teach you a few things about life," I said, tired of always being the bad guy. "When you declared you'd be a Broadway dancer and you couldn't even get through your first recital, did you want me to give you false expectations? Or how about when you said being a vet was your calling but you pass out at the sight of a needle? There are endless numbers of jobs you'd excel at. I'd be happy to help you explore them, or get internships, or make phone calls to my contacts. Whatever you want."

"Forget it. You don't understand. I'm tired." She turned toward my mother. "I want to go to bed. Can I have the key?"

My mother glanced at me, obviously torn between the both of us and whose side to take. Our first night in Italy and we couldn't get through a dinner without fighting. I pushed my chair away from the table. "It's okay, I'm going to bed too. I'll see you both in the morning for breakfast. Text me if you need anything."

Mom looked like she was about to say something, then thought better of it. I remembered when things fell apart when I was young, her advice to fix any problems revolved around two sacred things.

Feed me.

Make me go to bed early.

If only things were that easy.

I spun on my heel, took the elevator to the ground floor, and headed toward the exit. I needed some fresh air and to take a breath. I had to get in the right headspace, and feeling consistently frustrated at Allegra wasn't helping.

I smiled at a few of the staff, then pushed through the double doors onto the sidewalk. The main street of Via Nazionale was lively and packed, with crowds meandering in and out of the shops, laughing, and talking in Italian. Darkness only accented the landscape, with the buildings lit up and the earthy smells of the city drifting to my nostrils. Cars beeped and zigzagged down the road. I ducked into a darkened doorway, seeking a few minutes of solace. Tipping my head up toward the midnight sky, I prayed this trip would give me back the balance in my life I'd been missing.

The sweet scent of smoke hit me before the voice did.

"Did you at least have the pasta?"

I whirled my head around. Our tour guide stood a few inches away. Had he followed me? Legs crossed at the ankles, back resting against the building, he gave me a lazy smile while he inhaled from the cigarette clasped in his elegant hand. Odd, but I always checked out a man's hands first. There was something about the firm strength, the tapered fingers, the sinewy wrists, that fascinated me. Maybe it was all the things a man could do with good hands—from fixing a car or leaky pipe to cradling and protecting a baby to stroking a woman straight into orgasm.

Maybe I was just crazy.

"Yep. My willpower didn't extend that far tonight."

"Italy is about pleasure. Not willpower."

I lifted a brow at the intimate comment. His tongue practically sang the word *pleasure*. I ignored the slight dip of my stomach as he said it. Now I knew what the game was. Maybe he wasn't married and he enjoyed delving into affairs with the tourists. My back straightened; I was angry he figured I'd be such an easy target. "Too many pleasurable things are bad for you."

He grinned, flicking an ash on the sidewalk. "Americans," he murmured. "So very focused on what is good and bad."

"Italians. So quick to dismiss heart attacks and cancer for the lure of a meal or a smoke."

He laughed then, loud and long. Again, he caught me off guard with the ability not to take himself seriously. "*Mi dispiace*, perhaps you are right. Though now I only indulge in one cigarette per day, after dinner."

I frowned. "Statistics show even one cigarette raises your odds of getting lung cancer just as much as a regular smoker. You need to give your body space and time to clean itself out."

He smiled at me, and I could tell he didn't really care. "I believe you. But to cut out all the things I enjoy in this world for a future statistic? I'd rather take a gamble. Sweets, wine, carbs, cigarettes—they all make me happy. Is that wrong?"

I studied him to make sure he wasn't mocking me, but he looked serious. I considered the question. "No. But if we indulged in everything we wanted, the world would be a chaotic, greedy, lawless pit of debauchery."

He gave a long sigh, pulled on the cigarette one last time, and threw the butt on the ground. He crushed it with the heel of his shoe and turned to face me. "But it could be fun for a while."

He teased out a laugh from me. Oh, he was a charmer. I'd just need to make sure he respected the boundaries and knew I wasn't here for a fling during my tour. "I'm more goal oriented. If you think long-term, it becomes easier to stifle those temporary urges for the greater good."

"How delightful." His dark gaze met mine, shredded past my usual barriers, and he looked intently at me. "You believe in the greater good?"

I blinked. "Of course. Doesn't everyone?"

"I don't think so. Most would prefer to disregard consequences."

"Like you smoking one cigarette even though it may give you cancer?"

"Or other things."

His voice reminded me of soft, rich velvet. I shivered in the warm air. It'd been a while since a man seemed interested, but I hadn't expected to feel so off-kilter because of his innuendos. Were all Italian men flirty? Or was he trying to come on to me? And if not, how embarrassing if I said something. But the conversation already seemed intimate, so I did anyway. "My daughter and mother are on this trip."

He quirked a brow, probably at the sudden change of subject. "I know. I think it's wonderful to experience a trip like this with family."

"I'm just saying it's not like I'm alone and free to engage in all sorts of pleasures that have consequences."

His eyes widened, and then he grinned, shaking his head. "I think I gave you the wrong impression. I'd never make any of my tourists feel uncomfortable. I saw you rush out a little upset and wanted to make sure you were okay. Plus, I enjoyed your wit and I like to tease. Please accept my apology."

His words seemed sincere, and I was grateful for the darkness that hid my hot cheeks. The compliment meant more than the insult of rejecting me, or at least, his rejection of my rejection. "No worries," I said. "I'm perfectly fine. I think I'm overly sensitive and read too many things about Italian men being forward. I just didn't want you to get the wrong impression."

He gave a slight bow of his head. "Understood. And you are right. Italian men are forward, but I have been a guide for over ten years and would never break the rules. You are safe with me, *signora*. I promise."

I opened my mouth to tell him I wasn't worried and that I enjoyed talking to him too, but he was already stepping back from the shadows and into the light.

"*Buona sera*. I will see you in the morning."

He disappeared.

I groaned. *Well done, Frannie.* I managed to scare off our tour guide by insinuating that he wanted to seduce me, and all he was talking about was some damn pastries and cigarettes. Not dating was becoming a serious disadvantage. I didn't know how to talk to men anymore. I was so focused on not getting involved with any men at work, I ended up cutting myself off from all of them. And now I didn't even know how to be comfortable around a man who wasn't an employee or a client.

Depressed, I trudged back inside and went up to my room. It was a good thing I had an entire month ahead of me to figure things out. To heal my relationship with Allegra and get closer to my mother. To stop feeling so much anxiety about what I couldn't control. To live a happier, more stress-free life.

I wasn't asking for much, right?

CHAPTER TWELVE

ALLEGRA

THE VATICAN WASN'T what I expected.

I followed the crowd and partially listened to the tour guide trying to educate me on every aspect of St. Peter's Basilica. I appreciated a good teacher just like any student, but I almost wished she'd remain silent so I could soak it all in. Everything felt . . . overwhelming. Like there was so much beauty and opulence and space and color, my senses went into overload. All of this seemed to contradict the hushed silence of the church, where people knelt praying at marble statues and held rosary beads with heads tilted up toward the sky, as if they knew someone was listening.

I tuned out the words droning in my ear and slowly pivoted to take it all in. Sure, I've seen pictures of Italy and its treasures, but experiencing the power in such a holy place made me feel strange things. I wasn't religious; Mom had me baptized but, to my grandmother's distress, had pulled me out of Sunday school before communion because of the church scandals that blew up about rampant sexual abuse. I remember watching Nonni fight in furious whispers with my mom, begging her to give me something to fall back on in a crazy world. Mom still refused, but I'd grown up with Nonni sneaking in Bible stories and teaching me how to say the Our Father and the Hail Mary. But I didn't know much more than that.

My gaze took in the richly painted walls depicting religious scenes, the massive altar with its bronze canopy rising toward the dome, the numerous columns of marble framing the aisles, and I breathed in the faint scent of incense lingering in the air. The guide finally gave us time to explore on our own, so I motioned to my mom that I was heading back toward the *Pietà*. The sculpture seemed to pull me, and I wanted more than the few seconds that we'd been previously given. I'd always been into art and loved to pore over thick coffee-table books that featured famous paintings from around the world. There was something about gazing at another person's view of the world through a painting and having the freedom as the onlooker to interpret that view. Italy held many masterpieces, and even though I was pissed about being dragged on this trip, I was secretly looking forward to indulging in my hobby.

My phone buzzed in my back pocket. I hesitated but slipped it out just to peek.

David.

How's Italy?

He'd been texting me casually since I left. At first, I didn't know if it was because he felt sorry I got busted and had to deal with my mom, or if he was actually interested in me. I was mixed-up. Part of me was still fascinated by his quiet, broody nature, but the other part would never forget his expression of loathing when he got picked up by that cop. He didn't seem scared or worried at all. Then again, his dad didn't seem to really care. David said he'd been told it was good to experiment as a creative artist but not get caught, so that had been the only thing that bothered his dad.

Would I ever fit in somewhere? My school friends seemed too uptight and fake. But Freda, David, and Connor were wild, and that bust had freaked me out. I wished I could just turn off my thoughts and do stuff that felt good at the time, but then look where that had gotten me.

I tucked my phone back in my pocket and planned to call him later.

I headed to the *Pietà* and eased my way right to the front. The tour guide had said it wasn't crowded today, so I took my time and studied the sculpture. I loved the way the marble sheen seemed so cold and perfect, yet I could see the actual folds in Mary's gown and Jesus's cloth. His legs seemed alive and gently muscled, with veins coursing under his skin. A warm sensation curled up from the base of my spine and tingled through my body. The expression on Mary's face, carved of grief and a simple purity of acceptance, haunted me.

"Incredible, isn't it?" a low voice murmured.

I turned my head. One of our group members stood next to me, staring at the sculpture with his own expression of awe and humbleness. I raked my gaze quickly over his figure. He was older than me by a few years. A ginger, but not cute like Prince Harry. His hair was short, with a cowlick rather than royal red curls. Pale skin with freckles. His eyes were a pretty, deep blue, but his face was a bit too round, his lips a bit too red, as if all the colors of his face were overly bright and contrasted with one another. He was tall and lean and wore jeans, a simple T-shirt, and sneakers. A silver type of medal hung from a chain around his neck. Definitely Irish—he spoke with a slight brogue, which was cool.

I nodded. "Yeah. I didn't think it would be this impressive in person. To be honest, the statue always seemed boring in the books they gave us in art class. I always preferred the paintings."

He grinned. His teeth were white and perfectly straight, like he'd worn braces for years. "Same here. Can you imagine being able to make a slab of marble feel human?" He sighed. "There's no great artists anymore. None like da Vinci or Michelangelo."

I frowned. "That's not fair. It was a different time. We treat creativity and art like a commodity nowadays. Our society doesn't value artists like they once did. There are fewer opportunities for apprenticeship and learning an art. Everyone needs to pay their bills."

I couldn't believe I'd burst out with something so nerdy with a stranger, but his face lit up. "Agreed. But even in the Renaissance, they needed to find wealthy patrons to finance them. Sometimes that meant giving up what they wanted to work on and pleasing the patron. Don't you think the same thing happens today? Rich people pocketing artists to finance what their vision is?"

I'd never really thought about it. "I guess. Kind of like the record companies who tell musicians they have to be a certain way in order to sell the music."

"Yes!"

"Like Lady Gaga in that movie *A Star Is Born*."

He frowned. "Like what?"

I laughed. "Never mind."

"I'm Ian."

He stuck out his hand and I almost snorted at the formal gesture. But I shook it anyway. "Allegra."

"Nice to meet you. I'm still learning everyone's names and stuff. Who are you with?"

"My mom and grandmother."

"Women's trip, huh? You guys celebrating?"

I thought of my mother's rage when she picked me up at the police station. "No, just a summer trip. How about you?"

"I'm with my parents. I graduated from college, so it's their gift to me."

I winced. "Congrats on graduation, but sorry you didn't get to hang with your friends. Probably would've been better, right?"

Confusion clouded his eyes. "No, I actually like my parents. They're cool."

Heat rushed to my cheeks. "Oh, sorry, I didn't mean it like that."

He laughed and touched my upper arm. "No, it's fine. I know a lot of people would agree with you. I don't know, maybe 'cause I'm an only child? I kind of grew up comfortable in their company. You have any brothers or sisters?"

I shook my head. "I wish."

"Yeah, me too. They say onlies are spoiled, but I think it's a crock. They were tougher on me 'cause I was the only one to practice parenting on."

I smiled at that, liking the way he said *crock* in his Irish accent. He might not be sexy or cool, but he was nice to talk to. God knows, I needed someone to hang with other than my mom and grandmother. "Truth. What did you study in school?"

"Psychology. You know, the degree similar to English literature? The one where every person you speak to gives you a look and says you'll never get a real job?"

"I think psych would be really interesting. And, yeah, I know what you mean. Why does everyone feel like they need to give an opinion on someone else's life?"

"Because they think age equals wisdom." He made a face. "Unfortunately, it usually does."

"Then you'll have to prove them wrong."

Surprise flickered over his features, and warmth infused his blue eyes. "Thanks, Allegra. Can I say how damn happy I am that there's someone else on this tour I can talk to? I love my parents, but even I can't do three weeks in their constant company."

Pleasure shimmered through me. "We'll rescue each other." I caught my mom waving at me from the corner of my eye and stifled a groan. "My mom needs me. I'll be right back."

"Take your time. I'm going to pray for a while near the altar."

I nodded. He was probably Catholic. It was nice he had beliefs and took the time to worship without anyone telling him to. I'd heard from my friends how they were guilted or pushed to go to church and how much they hated it. I watched him head down the massive aisle, his head bowed, his movements graceful and humble as he dropped to a knee before sliding into the pew and clasping his hands together.

A weird type of longing rose inside me, but I didn't know what to do with it, so I just walked over to my mother. Her brow creased in a frown that immediately prickled my annoyance. "I couldn't find you—I got nervous."

"Mom, we're in St. Peter's. I'm not going to get kidnapped. And I can't be expected to stay by your side this whole time. I'll go nuts."

She gave a tiny sigh. "Okay, you're right. There's just a massive amount of people here. I saw you talking to that boy. What's his name?"

"Ian. He's celebrating his college graduation with his parents."

A smile brightened her face. "How wonderful. It'd be nice for you to have a friend on the tour."

She was right, but hearing her suggest it only made me want to seek out an Italian bad boy on a bike. What was wrong with me? I thought of David's text and knew Mom would freak. I'd promised to stay away from him, Connor, and Freda, but a few texts back and forth wouldn't be a big deal. "Where's Nonni?"

"Lighting a candle for your grandfather."

"How come you never raised me Catholic or took me to church?"

The question popped out of my mouth and surprised us both. Guilt shone in my mother's eyes, then got buried. "Because I never got anything out of it. Nonni dragged me to church every Sunday, rain or shine, not caring about vacations or sleepovers. And I don't like the issues they push—the guilt, and not having women in the church—plus the sexual abuse scandals. I wanted you to grow up to make your own choices."

It made logical sense, but if you weren't given anything to start with, wasn't it harder to decide what worked and what didn't? "Nonni gets upset when we talk about it. She thinks I should receive communion and confirmation."

"I don't believe your soul should be dependent on rituals. But I do think church can be a safe haven to figure things out and be silent."

I pushed on. "But you still never took me, even once. Even to try it."

"I thought I was doing you a favor." Her tone hardened a bit. "You could've gone with Nonni anytime. You preferred sleeping in on Sundays."

"And you prefer work," I shot back. "Money over religion, huh?"

She jerked back, glaring, and once again that wall shot up between us. The wall of misunderstanding and unspoken resentments that kept growing higher. Mom seemed to realize it too, but before she could say something else, the tour guide interrupted.

"Do I have my group?" she chirped merrily. She was a chic young brunette dressed in slim black pants and a white silk top. "We will move on to visit the famous Sistine Chapel. We'll be passing through multiple corridors of exquisite paintings." She held a stuffed pink daisy mounted on top of a long pole, and she waved it back and forth. "Remember to follow the flower. There are no flash photos or talking once we enter the chapel, so I will tell you all about it as we walk. *Andiamo!*"

I glanced back and saw Ian flanked by his parents. My mother made a move to take my hand, but I pretended not to notice and linked my arm with my grandmother's. Nonni smiled and squeezed me with affection, her lined face lit up with pleasure. It was so easy to be around her. If only it could be like that with Mom.

Mom quickly turned and pretended to study a painting, but not before I saw the hurt expression she tried to hide.

On impulse, I went to reach for her hand, feeling bad, but she'd already walked ahead and refused to look back.

Whatever. It wouldn't have meant much to her anyway.

Later on, I jumped on Snapchat with David.

How's the road trip? I typed.

Chill. Managed to book a gig at small club tonight. Freda wanted to sing but I said no.

I put a laughing emoji in the text. At least let her hum backup.

Nah, after a few drinks she'll be hooking up and won't care. Having fun? How's your mom?

Still pissed but distracted with the tour. Gonna see how long till she bails on me and her crap about bonding time. She's never gone a whole day without work before.

Don't let her jail u while she works. She already ruined your summer. Push back.

Yeah, he was right. If she began missing stuff for calls or meetings, I'd make sure to do what I wanted. Truth. Saw the Vatican.

Was it as pompous as I imagine it? Gold and glory for fat old guys who pretend they're better than anyone else.

I hesitated at the venom in the text. Of course, most of my friends sneered at any established religion, and I never judged people's beliefs, but I remembered the way Ian knelt and prayed, as if humbled to be in God's home. Maybe the church was messed up but some people found comfort here, like Nonni. Right?

The art was sick. The Sistine Chapel was beautiful but I got a neck cramp looking up, and got smooshed between a bunch of strangers. Not what I expected.

It never is. Gotta go. Wish you were here. TTYL.

I sent another emoji and clicked off. He wished I was there. That was the second time he'd said it, so he probably meant it. I thought of him playing in clubs, getting high, and picking up girls, and of Ian, who said he liked his parents and who prayed in church.

David was right about one thing. Mom swore she was taking a real vacation. If she thought she could drag me to Italy and leave me with Nonni for the whole time, I'd show her how wrong she was.

I pocketed my phone and went to join my family on the bus.

CHAPTER THIRTEEN

FRANCESCA

I REMEMBER TAKING an art history class back in college and studying the Sistine Chapel for weeks on end, until I became tired of Michelangelo and his endless work of religious figures and naked muscled men in loincloths.

I got a C and I blamed it on that segment. But staring up at the familiar panels, my neck already cramping from the position, I experienced a shudder of recognition that tingled through my nerve endings and settled into my bones. The feeling of seeing greatness up close.

The soaring, colorful images squeezed together created an unending row of visual treats—a feast for the senses. Angels were not only people with wings but held fierce expressions that reflected basic human struggles, from envy to pride, and agony to joy. Cloaks rippled and flowed with delicate wrinkles. Fingers stretched out to grasp at God, and God judged and found man lacking. No inch of the ceiling remained untouched, and I felt locked into a small space of artistic vastness.

Cell phones vibrated. Occasional coughs, exhalations, and quiet murmurs and shuffled steps were the only sounds in the chamber. I soaked it all in, letting the experience overtake the nonstop chattering in my head, and in that brief moment of time, I touched a tiny piece of nothingness.

It was beautiful.

The reprieve lasted fifteen minutes. Soon after, we were ushered back outside, stripped of our earbuds and mini speaker attachments. We boarded the bus to get back to our hotel and spend the afternoon on our own. I took a seat in the front, but Allegra stuck with Mom and sat behind me. I glanced at my watch to calculate the time difference back in New York and estimated I'd need at least a few hours to work. Kate and Layla had been holding back on sending emails, but I knew they were trying to respect my vacation time. They'd agreed to keep me informed of every move on the Lexi's Lemonade account, even though they were both technically the leads.

The idea of all I was missing back at the office, especially after the panic attack, bothered me. I needed to be available to weigh in on decisions so I was still involved. I'd still have plenty of time for the tour and family time. A few hours per day was practically nothing.

Enzo stood in the front of the bus and raised his hands. Today he was dressed in a smart cream-colored suit in a light cotton material, with a bright blue T-shirt underneath. His shoes were a supple leather and his socks matched his shirt. A pair of dark sunglasses perched on top of his head amid thick brown curls. Italian men certainly knew how to dress.

"I hope everyone enjoyed the Vatican and Sistine chapel. Beautiful, *si*?"

Everyone shouted in agreement.

"We will get you back to the hotel so you can nap or go out to explore the city. I am here if you have questions on where to go or need recommendations. And tonight we will have dinner at a delicious local restaurant, so please be ready by six p.m. in the lobby."

I slipped my phone out and opened up my email program.

Enzo dropped into the seat beside me. "Are you posting your pics to Facebook?" he asked in his usual teasing manner.

Relief cut through me. Since last night, I'd been worried he'd be cold and businesslike after I accused him of hitting on me. But it seemed he was back to normal, and I was grateful. "No, I'll leave that to my daughter. I'm actually checking in at work."

"What do you do?"

"Advertising. I run my own company back in New York."

He nodded. "Ah, big responsibilities. Do you create commercials or print ads?"

"Both." I tried to concentrate, because his scent was all around me again. Why did he smell like fresh-baked cookies and rich chocolate? "We just scored a major account, so I'm trying to make sure everything is going smoothly."

"Then you must love it. It is good to love what you do."

"It is. Do you love being a tour guide?"

His face lit up. His features shifted and changed with each of his expressions, his dark brown eyes alive. "*Sì*. My father was a tour guide, and I learned from the best. I love teaching people about Italy."

"Is it hard to travel all the time? I imagine everyone misses you back home."

I hoped my question seemed low-key. I was kind of dying to know if he had a partner or kids back home, even though he wore no ring. "A bit hard for a serious relationship," he said thoughtfully, "but it is part of who I am. I'm gone for a month, then return for two, then back out again. So far, I haven't found the true love of my life who is meant for me, so there is no one to get back to except my dog."

His statements on true love threw me. Men didn't talk like that, so I wondered if he was being a bit mocking. "What breed?"

"An old-fashioned mutt. Her name is Sophia, for Sophia Loren—our most famous movie star."

I laughed. "I have to tell my mother she has a namesake. I'm sure your dog misses you when you're away. Who takes care of her?"

"My neighbor, who spoils her rotten. We share custody, so this makes Sophia happy. You must take care of your woman, no?"

His gaze met mine in that intense way again, but this time I didn't jump to conclusions. He was just a passionate guy who acted different than I was used to. "Yes. Or she craps all over you."

His hearty laugh made me smile. Most men I encountered were so serious, I rarely felt comfortable being silly. It was fun to be lighthearted. "This is true. Now, tell me what you want to see this afternoon. Can I be of any help?"

"My mother mentioned the Spanish Steps. Is there a nice place for lunch and some light shopping?"

"Ah, *sì*, I can text you a few suggestions. I advise you to avoid any restaurants where you cannot see the kitchen—this means the food is not fresh but frozen. And a few shop owners will give you good price if you pop in. May I text you?"

"Oh, that'd be great." I recited my number and he plugged it into his phone and began typing a short list. "Will we have time if we go a bit later? I wanted to work a few hours."

A frown furrowed his brow. "I'd say wait no more than an hour or you shall miss your afternoon. Free time is precious on such a busy tour. Many people tell me that is their favorite part of Rome."

"What?"

"Getting lost. You must get lost in each city to experience the true flavor. You agree?"

"No, I like to know where I'm going. That's why GPS was invented."

He sighed and gave a shake of his head. "Then there are no side-road adventures. I know your job is important, but take at least one detour today and let me know how it went tonight."

I hesitated. My first instinct fell to defensiveness. To explain that as a business owner I had responsibilities, and that detours usually ended up being a waste of precious time. But I bit back the words, not wanting to ruin the easy camaraderie, and nodded. "Maybe."

"Good." He stood up and walked up the aisle, chatting with the various groups about their upcoming afternoon. By the time we got back to the hotel, Mom and Allegra were in an upbeat mood. "Mom, I found a cool café on Yelp we can go to for lunch, and then Nonni wants to do the Spanish Steps and gelato. We'll have enough time, right?"

I thought my mother would be tired, but she looked animated. "I just need to change my shoes and I'm ready. We can shower before dinner."

I bit my lip just as my phone buzzed. I knew it was Layla or Kate, needing some input on a few items. "Umm, listen, I have to do a few quick things for work. I'm really sorry—I promise it won't take long. How about I meet you?"

Allegra's face fell. My mother's expression pleaded with me to change my mind. "Honey, it's only our first full day here! Can't you get back to them tonight after dinner?"

"We're on a deadline and I really need to check in. It won't take long . . . Listen, I'll take an Uber right to the Spanish Steps in an hour."

"But I'm starving," Allegra whined.

"Go eat without me. I'll grab a granola bar and make up for it with gelato at the plaza. Enzo said the cabs outside are trustworthy and most drivers speak English. Text me when you get there, okay?"

Regret and guilt twisted inside me, but I had to check in so I could relax for the rest of the day. There were too many balls flying in the air that I had to catch.

Allegra shrugged and turned away. "Whatever."

I winced, but my mother held her tongue, so I decided not to answer. We went up in the elevator together, and the moment I hit my room, I grabbed my laptop and a bottle of water and called Kate. "I have an hour," I said after we exchanged the normal pleasantries. "Bring me up to speed."

Her voice was crisp and assured. "I've implemented a focus group to test out some tweaks to the video campaign, and Layla is working with Adam on the social media sets. We're in good shape, Fran."

I should have been relieved, but my nerves pulled taut. I was used to being involved in every aspect for a new client. Yes, I hired good people, but I'd gotten to this point by having every decision run through me.

But they didn't want you, the voice whispered. *They wanted Kate and Layla.*

I smothered the mocking reminder. "Who's working on the brand-awareness proposal? Adam?"

Her tiny hesitation gave me what I needed to pounce. "I put Sarah in charge because she did such a great job with the DesignIt campaign, and Adam has a full load."

I quickly clicked through the Dropbox folders and scanned the outline. "Kate, didn't you take a look at this? It's thin and she's using the same technique used for fashion accessories. This is a totally different market. We need to target moms, kids, school groups, any type of outreach that revolves around organic juice. Have you seen how the Honest company branded themselves? It was brilliant."

"Jessica Alba was already a celebrity," Kate pointed out.

"Doesn't matter—it's all about getting the moms to think putting Lexi's Lemonade in their kids' lunch boxes is the right thing to do. That's our target."

"I'll talk to her and have her revise it."

"No need, I'm on it. I'll work on the new proposal, and let's set up a conference call with Sarah so she knows where she's missing the mark."

A hint of frustration interspersed her tone. "Fran, you're in Italy. We can deal with this."

"I'm sure you can, but there can't be any mistakes with this. I'll send you the revisions in a few. Anything else?"

"I have another meeting scheduled for tomorrow afternoon with the entire team."

"What time?"

"Noon."

I mentally calculated my schedule. I'd be at dinner, but maybe I could sneak in a quick update. "I'll call into the conference room around that time—pipe me in."

This time, Kate didn't protest. "You got it. Enjoy Rome."

"Thanks." I clicked off and began to pick apart Sarah's plan. The more I changed, the more I realized how much it was lacking. Print ads were still important, but it was all about television, the internet, and social media channels. Facebook still brought huge numbers if the ad was click-worthy, and Sarah's ideas weren't high-concept enough. I considered batting it back over to Adam even if he was overloaded, but at this point, it'd be better if I handled it myself.

The stress took hold, but it was mixed with a familiar sense of necessity. Finally, I could prove why I was in charge. Why I was good. Why I was successful. Work was the only place in life I felt like a rock star.

I got to work. Usually, I experienced a jolt of adrenaline when I tackled a problem, but my head throbbed with tension. I tried to breathe deep, but my lungs tightened up and it became harder to draw in air, and that's when I knew it was happening again.

The panic attack. God, no, not now, please . . .

The harder I tried to calm down and ward it off, the worse the anxiety and fear came at me, pummeling me like tiny fists, and I moaned, falling off the chair and curling myself into a tight ball as I fought for sanity.

My vision swam, and I clutched myself for comfort as I lost control of my body. My mind was pinging around like a tennis ball, a wild rush of thoughts and terrors all mixed up, and I surrendered to the madness. I had no idea how long I was lying there. Eventually, I crawled to my knees with shaky limbs, my skin damp with sticky sweat, and I gazed at the laptop and my consistently vibrating phone still lying on the desk and wondered if I would ever be okay again.

How had my safe place become my trigger?

I glanced at my watch. I'd been here for almost two hours, way past my promise to Allegra. I quickly brushed my teeth and washed my face, repairing my makeup, and switched my shirt out for a clean T. Grabbing my phone and bag, I texted Kate and let her know the new proposal would be sent over tonight. I'd finish it up after dinner.

My phone buzzed.

Done with lunch. Just got to the Spanish Steps. TTYL.

No smiley face. She was definitely angry. Muttering a curse, I headed out, intent on grabbing a cab and buying something fun and expensive for my daughter to make it up to her. The moment the elevator doors swished open, I was met with trouble.

"Fran! I've been looking for you but forgot to get your number!" Dana rushed over and hooked her arm through mine, her face wreathed in a smile. "Where are you going?"

I hesitated, looking past her to where Steve stood, giving me a polite nod. He was dressed in jeans and a button-down short-sleeve shirt and wore a Stetson hat. Dana had changed after the Vatican into a short summer dress with hot pink wildflowers and teetering matching spiked sandals. I winced at even the idea of the heels getting caught between the cobblestones. Next to Steve were Cherry and Laura, whom I'd met at breakfast this morning. They seemed nice, and easy to chat with, but definitely more low-key than Dana. Cherry was petite, with a cute pixie cut and big dark eyes. Laura was blond and wore her hair in a sleek bob. She was curvy and had a great smile, shown off in a peach-colored lipstick that complimented her fair skin. Both of them had on denim shorts and tank tops with flip-flops.

"Oh, I'm going to the Spanish Steps. My mom and daughter are meeting me there."

Dana gave a delighted squeal. "Perfect! That's exactly where we're all heading—let's share a cab and go together!"

I opened my mouth to frantically backpedal, but I didn't want to seem rude and Cherry began asking me questions about my thoughts on the Sistine Chapel, and before I knew what was happening, I was seated in a cab smooshed between Cherry and Dana and speeding away from the hotel.

During the ride, I found out that Cherry and Laura were a couple and celebrating their honeymoon. Cherry worked as a nurse and Laura was a lawyer for animal rights. They owned a farm in Nashville and claimed to know Luke Bryan. They had horses, cows, pigs, two alpacas, five dogs, and more cats than they could count. They'd bought an old farmhouse for pennies and spent two years fixing it up themselves. Even though I preferred not talking to anyone on vacation other than my family, I became fascinated by their story. I loved meeting people who were open and authentic and didn't make explanations for who they were. I'd gotten a ton of flack for having Allegra without a man in my life. People called me selfish and impatient. Once, I'd been at a bar with colleagues, and when I shared my story, a few of the wives got upset, telling me I was setting a bad example for young women who thought thirty was too old to wait for love. The discussion spiraled out of control, and after that, things were awkward between some of my employees. That was one of the last times I went out socializing with my coworkers. It was easier to avoid potential issues.

But Cherry and Laura didn't seem to care about anyone judging them, and I wondered if I had given up too easily on certain things, like defending my own choices.

We arrived and climbed out of the cab. I shot Allegra and Mom a text that I was there, then looked around and allowed the beautiful chaos of the square to settle around me. Multiple shops squeezed the sides of the cobblestone streets, and groups of people strolled around, eating gelato and taking in the sights. A huge fountain was centered in the middle, and my gaze lifted to the impressive row of steps that led up to the twin-towered church whose spires thrust into the air, framing the scene like a postcard.

The beauty was in the odd details. The zigzag play of steps leading to different tiers and terraces. The stripped-bare paint peeling from the buildings. The rough cobblestones and smooth, wet-looking steps. The elegance of the architecture, which revered sweeping curves and soaring domes. The bold, natural colors of terra cotta and mustard amid the blue waters of the

Fontana della Barcaccia and the white columns. The lone tree sprouting near the top of the steps and the vivid blooms of geraniums bursting from the sides. But most of all it was a matter of time. A vision slammed through me. Roman soldiers walking in their sandals on the very same ground, their dust-covered bodies weary from war, while they beheld the creative and natural beauty around them.

Italy was a gorgeous contradiction. A place where bloodshed and combat thrived and ruled, a location where the Colosseum was entertainment and death was common, yet a place where great art bloomed among the rubble. I stood for a few moments, taking in the scene and letting my mind touch on things I rarely thought about because I was trapped in my day-to-day activity.

"Let's get gelato and explore," Laura suggested as we gathered in a circle.

"I have to wait for Allegra. You guys go ahead and we'll catch up," I said.

"You sure? We can wait," Dana said.

I shook my head. "No, really, I'm going to poke around here a bit."

They finally agreed and I watched them stroll slowly out of sight. I glanced at my phone, but neither of them had texted back. Biting my lip, I decided to stay in the general area and enjoy my surroundings. A young couple kissed passionately by the fountain, and people snapped selfies from long sticks. Tour guides led their groups through the crowds, and sellers hawked their wares, from fresh roses to knockoff purses, hats, and cold bottles of water.

I was walking around the fountain, studying the details, when I saw Enzo ahead. He was with the elderly couple from our tour—I think their names were Mary and Ray—and he was smiling as he chatted, pointing down the road toward something. I studied him from a distance, noting his silky T-shirt in a cream color, and camel slacks with canvas shoes. His hair was thick and unruly, those curls blowing in the slight breeze. His hands moved animatedly as he spoke.

My gut gave a tiny lurch. This time, it had nothing to do with stress or panic, but was a tickle of awareness I rarely felt. Strange. Maybe it had something to do with the fact that he was in charge of us. An authority thing. Who knew? I still didn't think he was classically attractive, but his energy and personality drew me.

Not that it mattered. God knows, I'd shut him down full force and he hadn't even been flirting. It was still so embarrassing.

His gaze lifted and slammed into mine. I tried not to blush and hoped he didn't think I'd been staring, but he grinned and waved me over with such enthusiasm, I couldn't pretend not to see him.

"Hi," I said when I reached them. "Seems everyone's gathering at the steps today."

"As it should be," Enzo said. "The steps were used as a popular meeting place over the years. Imagine great philosophers and artists gathering to exchange ideas over cappuccino. I can set you up with a local guide if you'd like a tour, Francesca."

"Oh, no, thank you. I'm meeting Allegra and my mother here." I turned to the older couple. I pegged them for their mid-seventies. "I'm not sure if we officially met? I'm Fran."

We shook hands. "I'm Mary and this is my husband, Ray. We were just at the Trevi Fountain and met a few others from our group there, too. It's a good day to get in all of our exploring."

"It's a good thing we trained for this before we came," Ray said. "We made sure to hit the gym and walk a few miles per day. I refused to be the one lagging behind."

"You'll do better than me," I confided. "And my mother said the same thing. She began using those Jane Fonda DVDs that had been collecting dust."

"Oh, those are very in right now," Mary said seriously. "They call it vintage. Or retro. Makes me laugh that all the old stuff is now popular. My granddaughter saw *The Book Club* and had the nerve to ask who that cool actress was and was she in any other movies. But she did know about *Fifty Shades of Grey*."

Enzo cocked his head. "What's that?"

Mary and I shared a look and burst into laughter. "A popular book. It was actually very good."

"Would I like it?" Enzo asked.

Ray reached out and patted his arm. "It's not for us. But it's nice to see female writers finally getting the recognition they deserve."

Mary and Ray shared an intimate look and I choked back a laugh. Another surprise. How long had it been since I saw a longtime married couple actually still in love? Enzo seemed to be thinking the same thing, since he glanced at me with a twinkle in his eye and winked. I studied his face again, fascinated by my reaction to him. His nose was too blunt. His features were craggy and rough, and he was just my height. I had only dated tall men. Maybe I'd been too narrow-minded and shallow. It wasn't as if I was beautiful either. I was more used to men being attracted to my position of authority than my looks. Now here I was judging my tour guide for not matching the image in my head of the hot Italians with their practiced, sexy moves and dark, handsome faces.

We chatted for a while longer before Mary and Ray declared they were off to a late lunch. "Thank you for helping us out today," Mary said to Enzo. "I think we would have been overwhelmed alone."

"Visiting a foreign country where you don't speak the language is scary. I'm here to make sure you enjoy your trip. It's truly my pleasure. Don't forget if you have any trouble getting back to the hotel, call my cell. And go to one of those restaurants I recommended—they are good in price and have excellent food. Tell them Enzo sent you."

Ray clapped him on the shoulder. *"Grazie."*

"We'll see you tomorrow for the Colosseum," Mary said. "I can't wait."

They walked away and I faced him. "I didn't think you really worked during our free time. You need to have some type of break, right?"

His white teeth flashed. "Mary and Ray needed a little extra care. And, no, I consider myself working twenty-four seven. It's my job."

"That's very nice of you. And responsible."

"What can I help you with? Have you visited everything you wanted today?"

My phone remained silent in my hand. Where were they? Guilt hit again. I'd managed to miss most of our early afternoon and now I was getting worried. "I had to stay in the hotel and work, so I'm supposed to meet Allegra and my mother here. But they're not getting back to me."

He frowned. "I'll wait with you. If we don't hear back soon, I'll help you find them. Do not worry—I'm sure they just lost track of time. It's easy to do here."

I dragged in a breath. He was probably right. "I'll be fine. No need to waste your time babysitting me."

"Not a waste. I like spending time with you. Let me show you a few highlights."

His words caught me by surprise, but he was already leading me toward the steps, launching into an easy commentary. "This is an early baroque fountain created by Petro Bernini. It is called Fontana della Barcaccia, or Fountain of the Old Boat, because it looks like a sinking ship. There is a legend about a fishing boat being lost in a flood of the Tiber River, and it was carried to this spot."

"Was a lot of the art based on legends?" I asked curiously.

"The majority of art and sculpture during this period was based on religious tales and mythology. The greater and more colorful the story, the more the people embraced it."

"Makes sense. How many steps are there?"

"One hundred and thirty-eight."

"And why on earth aren't they called the Italian Steps?"

He laughed. "Ah, a bit confusing, no? This square was named after the Spanish embassy, so it was considered Spanish territory. Francesco de Sanctis was hired to build steps to link the Trinità dei Monti church and the seat of the Catholic Church together, called the Holy See. But guess who the church belonged to?"

"I'm guessing not the Italians, either?"

"No, the church was under the patronage of the French king. And they also planned to erect a statue of King Louis XIV at the top of the staircase, but thank God it never happened. The pope refused."

"So, this entire area once had three different countries involved."

"*Sì*. But we now claim it as ours, as it should be."

"Are you still pissed off as an Italian over the whole *Mona Lisa* debacle?"

A fierce frown creased his brow. "The *Mona Lisa* belongs to Italy."

I pressed my lips together. It seemed I'd found a sensitive

spot. "But the *Mona Lisa* is located in the Louvre and da Vinci died in France, not Italy."

He stopped walking, regarding me with serious concern. "Da Vinci is an Italian and it is where his heart truly is. We allow the Louvre to have this amazing painting because we are generous and neighborly, but it belongs to us. *Capisce?*"

Oh, this was hysterical. I tamped down my laugh and managed to nod. "I'm glad I learned the real truth."

"So am I." He pointed out the house to the right. "A fun fact for you. This is where the poet John Keats lived, which is now a museum."

"I always enjoyed his poetry."

"It has many memorabilia, so you may want to check it out while you are here." We began climbing the stairs and he shared a variety of facts. There was a richness to his voice like velvet, and a lyrical quality like music. I debated taking Italian lessons when I got home. I should have had Allegra teach me while she was learning it in school.

"Do you like McDonald's?"

I blinked at the question. "No."

His relief was palpable. "Good. They had the audacity to build a McDonald's here, which was met with a very large protest."

"Who won?"

"McDonald's, but many have boycotted. This actually started our own protest, which is now the Slow Food organization. There is no need for false food when you have the land and ocean to nourish your body. Many forget the real truth of food. The purpose."

"Not to die?" I teased.

He didn't smile back this time. Those dark eyes were filled

with intensity. "It is for the soul, not just the body. Feed it falsely and you will begin to lose yourself."

The sunbeams caught his face and in that fleeting moment he was beautiful. I'd read several books regarding the Mediterranean diet, keto, South Beach, and other smart ways of analyzing food intake and nutrition. Food as fuel for the soul was a familiar motto, spoken on cooking and morning talk shows in order to promote a product or lifestyle. But I'd never heard the philosophy uttered like a Bible verse, full of respect. It was like hearing something a thousand times, yet on the thousand and first, it made sense. I finally got it, standing in front of my tour guide in Rome.

He had no idea he'd suddenly shifted my thinking. All those times food was shoved in my mouth as a resented requirement of either good health or weight loss, each time I rushed through a drive-through and congratulated myself on eating a limp, dressing-free salad, I had been false. Even my junk-food choices were picked without care or concern. I thought of how many times Allegra mentioned cooking with my mother, and how I viewed it as a traditional block to a woman's freedom, thinking my job was to push her to be more like me.

Maybe I'd been wrong.

Enzo continued talking, ignorant of the sudden spin of my thoughts over his last statement. We climbed to the top and leaned over the rail to study the square spread out before us. The view, like many historic spots, was worth the climb. Looking down at anything usually gave me a sense of power and accomplishment. Right now, I felt more connected to the people milling around the square, as if there were no differences between us. As if we had all shared the view and claimed our power together.

Our shoulders brushed against each other and I didn't move.

The light scent of his cologne drifted in the air and tickled my nose, a scent of familiarity, like I'd smelled it many times before, almost like a dim memory I couldn't place.

"Did you finish your work?" he asked.

I sighed, resting my elbows on the ledge. "No, but I can finish tonight. I think that's why Allegra isn't texting me back. She's mad."

He didn't respond for a bit, like he was thinking about what to say. "Children don't realize our responsibilities. And I think the mother-daughter relationship is the most complicated of all."

"How do you know?"

"Because I have four sisters."

I gasped. "Four! Are you kidding me? How did you survive?"

His grin was back. "Well, I never got the bathroom, but my mama treated me like a king. And though they drove me nuts, they spoiled me. I'm the baby."

I began to laugh. "Typical. You're a mama's boy."

He shrugged. "I am proud of this. She taught me all the important things."

"Like what?"

"How to cook the perfect pasta and gravy. How to romance a woman. When to fight and make my stand, and when to run."

"And your father? Was he hard on you and easy with the girls?"

A shadow flickered over his face. "My father died when I was seven."

"I'm so sorry." I touched his arm, then quickly drew back. "My dad died when I was in my late twenties and I still can't seem to stop grieving."

"Our parents make us feel valid. They are the ones who saw everything of who we really are and loved us anyway. Losing them is like losing a limb, no?"

"Yes." Allegra had missed out on having a grandfather, and it still tore me apart. And for a long time, Mom was completely lost, like she had no compass. Her granddaughter had brought her back to life. Even though she'd disapproved of my choice to get pregnant alone, Allegra gave her new hope. "Are you all close?" I asked.

He nodded. "Very. When I am not on tour, I see my mama and sisters every Sunday. I have two nieces and a nephew so far."

"That's so nice. Where do you live?"

"A tiny town you've never heard of. It's called Lucca, which is in the Tuscany region."

I blinked and shook my head. "Are you kidding me?"

"I'm not sure what you mean."

"We rented a villa half an hour from Lucca. I got it on Vrbo—it's an old farmhouse."

Shock filled his dark eyes. "Do you know the exact location?"

"It overlooks the town of Borgo a Mozzano, I think? It used to be a chestnut farm. It looks like a beautiful property with a terrace, and views, and even a lake. We can walk into town for the market. We're heading there for a week after the tour."

"You picked a charming spot. And if you want, I'd be happy to show you around or give you any information since I will be there after the tour, too."

Our gazes suddenly locked. My chest tightened and I got caught up in the rich dark brown of his eyes, framed with a perfect ring of gold to give his stare a deep intensity. I liked the thought of spending time with him at our villa. I liked it a bit too much, which confused me. I stepped back casually. How I hated acting like a schoolgirl, when I was a grown woman. But I was beginning to realize it had been a long time since I'd talked to a man at length without a particular goal in mind. And, damn, why was his scent so mouthwatering? I needed to find out what type of cologne or lotion this man was using. "Thank you. I think that will be really helpful." I cleared my throat. "My mom insisted on something simple and rural so we can spend quality time together. I think she's hoping there's no internet."

A smile tugged at the corners of his mouth. "Could you last?"

"Maybe. I think my daughter would be the first to go mental." The thought of Allegra made me check my phone again, even though it hadn't buzzed. "I'm starting to get worried."

"Then let's go find her. I'm very good at tracking people down in a crowd. Tour Management 101."

He reached out as if to take my hand in a natural manner, then pulled back, as if realizing he'd made a grievous error. I wondered if his hands were rough or smooth, and if they'd grip my fingers with a firm grip or light caress. I wondered if I'd ever find out.

"Mom!"

My daughter's voice rang across the square and filled me with sheer relief. I turned and Allegra was racing over, her hand linked with my mother's. They were both laughing, and the joy and strength of their connection hit me full force. I'd never felt such a bond with my mother. It was as if my father had sucked up all my attention and emotion, and when he passed, all of that went straight into Allegra. Enzo stepped a few paces back to give them room as they reached us.

"I was so worried," I said. "You didn't answer my calls or texts, so Enzo and I were going to try and find you. Are you both okay?"

"I'm so sorry, Fran," my mother said. "We lost track of time and you know I rarely check my phone. I feel terrible you had to contact Enzo."

"No, I was here already, Sophia," he said smoothly. "It was no problem. I told your daughter how the charms of Rome can make you forget time."

Allegra's face lost its lightness and grew cold. "You said an hour. It's been three, so we figured you weren't coming anyway."

I thought of my crippling panic attack and held my tongue. "Sorry, I ran into some trouble and had to fix it. How was lunch?"

"Really good. We had pizzas, and they have this incredible soft drink like cola, but it's a touch bitter and has this cherry taste that's so good. I forgot what it was called . . ." Allegra trailed off.

"Chinotto," Enzo said. "A treat for the summer months and refreshing, right?"

"Yes, I loved it. And then we walked over here and the funniest thing happened—Nonni, do you want to tell the story?"

Sweat gleamed on my mother's brow and her T-shirt clung to her flushed skin. "Mom, do you need water? I brought an extra bottle." Guilt flicked through me. I should have been watching her more closely and not given the job to Allegra. At Mom's age, she had to be careful of the heat and physical exertion.

She waved a hand in the air. "I'm fine. More than fine, I guess." The words made Allegra burst into giggles. "We were getting some gelato and standing in line, and this man kept looking over at us. Of course, I knew he was gaga over Allegra even though he was too old for her."

"He was sexy," Allegra added with a mischievous wink. "Right, Nonni?"

"Oh, shush, he was average. But I was getting a bit concerned when he began to follow us down the street, and every time I looked back, he stared at us. He wasn't even trying to hide. So, I lost my temper."

Allegra jumped in. "Nonni suddenly turns around and says, 'What are you staring at? Don't you know that's rude?' and he starts apologizing and says he was struck by beauty and he didn't know what to do so he decided to follow us, and Nonni starts telling him he shouldn't be trailing after young girls because it's

wrong, and he said, 'But, *signora*, it is you I'm interested in!'
And then Nonni got all red and started stuttering—"

"I did not stutter! I was just surprised. My goodness, he was
much younger than me!"

"Well, you guys were adorable, and then he asked for Nonni's number and said he would love to take her to dinner!"

My eyes widened and I began laughing with them. "Mom,
you're getting more play than either of us," I teased. "I think it's
those hot shoes."

Her sensible, thick-soled nude loafers had been a target of
insults from me and Allegra, as we'd tried to cajole my mother
into wearing regular padded sandals. "Very funny," my mother
said. "Don't come crying to me when you all have blisters or slip
and fall."

"Did you say yes to dinner?" Enzo asked, his brow arched.

"Oh, goodness no. I told him I was on a tour and would be
leaving Rome in a few days."

Allegra sighed. "I told her to go. He seemed very nice."

My mother looked horrified. "I don't even know him! Besides, I'm here to spend time with my family—not gallivant
with strange men."

"I think it's awesome," my daughter said with twinkling
eyes. "I hope I'm just like you when I'm older."

I knew the comment was innocent, but it still stung. I'd always been proud to show my daughter what a strong woman
could do alone. But it seemed she respected her grandmother's
choices more.

"Better to be like your mom. She would have said yes to an
adventure."

Allegra rolled her eyes and a moment of awkward silence fell
upon us. It was obvious my daughter disagreed with her theory
but didn't want to say it aloud. Enzo glanced back and forth

between us with a curious look, and I cleared my throat. "Well, I'm sorry I missed lunch and the gelato. Maybe we can walk around and explore. Shop a bit."

"Oh, I'd love to do some shopping. It would be nice to get a new scarf," Mom said.

I decided a good bribe was in order to gain my daughter's forgiveness. "Allegra, I thought it'd be nice to pick up a piece of jewelry. Something that makes you remember our trip," I suggested. "Maybe a bracelet or necklace?"

Allegra shrugged. "I don't need anything."

Oh yeah, she was punishing me. I grabbed at my patience and tried to see her point. I'd have to make it up to her. "I'm sure we'll find something you like."

"I'll point out a few good shops and then I shall leave you ladies to your shopping," Enzo said.

We descended the stairs and I enjoyed the shifting view of the square as I passed each level. I'd almost reached the bottom when my heel began to slide along the slippery pavement, and I floundered to reach the railing in time to keep my balance.

I didn't.

The awful moment happened in a rush. Suddenly, my entire foot caught air, and I fell back. My butt crashed to the ground, I knocked the back of my head, and yet unbelievably that wasn't the end of it. I kept sliding, bumping down a few more steps in a wild, jerky ride, to spill into a collapsed heap at the first landing.

Ah shit.

My body ached from the fall, but my pride stung more. Cheeks burning red, I heard the concerned shouts and caught the pointed gestures toward me right before I tried to scramble to my knees, but I was off-balance and I fell back again. "I'm okay!" I shouted hoarsely to the crowd of onlookers, desperate to get to my feet.

Before I could try again, Enzo reached down and scooped me up in his arms like an old-fashioned lover coming to my rescue.

I was going to die of embarrassment.

Mom and Allegra gathered around me, frantically asking how badly I was hurt, but all I could see was the line of iPhones held up in front of me that had documented every second of my fall. "I'm not hurt at all!" I tried to twist out of his hold so I could convince everyone there was nothing to film here, but Enzo marched with determination through the crowd, cradling me against his chest like I was a bird with a broken wing.

This was so bad. Except the way he held me. For a few stunning seconds, I felt completely protected and safe. The warmth of his shirt, the strength of his lean arms, the delicious scent in my nostrils, all of the sensations swarmed around me until I wished I could shut my eyes and relish the experience.

He reached an empty café table and sat me gently down on the chair, kneeling at my feet. "Fran, where does it hurt?" he asked calmly. "May I feel your head?"

I nodded. People still peered from the edges of the crowd, probably trying to see if I needed an ambulance. Or maybe they just wanted to get a better pic for their Instagram story. Enzo's fingers were firm but gentle as he probed my head, exploring the small, tender lump on the back.

"Oh my God, do you think she has a concussion?" my mother asked, grabbing at my hands like she needed to convince herself I was still alive. "Should we get her to a hospital?"

Enzo remained calm, slowly moving from my head down to my bare legs. "I can definitely take her to the doctor. Fran, can I check your ankle?"

I nodded again, liking that he asked before running his hands over me. He repeated the same actions for both calves and ankles. Shivers ran up and down my spine at the touch of his fingers on my bare skin. "Can you move your toes?"

I wriggled them and they obeyed. Allegra looked distressed, so I forced myself to smile at her. "It's okay, honey. I'm tougher than I look."

"How's your back?" he asked.

I moved from side to side tentatively, but other than basic soreness, there were no sharp flashes of pain. "Fine. It's just some scrapes and bruises."

"We should go to the doctor and make sure," my mother said.

I shook my head. "No. I'm not wasting the rest of the day in a doctor's office for a silly fall. I swear, Mom, I'm okay. I'd tell you if I needed to get checked out. Here, let me try walking and make sure."

I stood up, hobbled a bit, but soon was able to walk at a regular pace. "See? I'm fine. I had a good enough cushion," I said, patting my rear. I noticed Enzo's gaze paused on my ass before quickly jerking back up. Was that a flush on his cheekbones or my imagination? Was it wrong to hope for the former?

Mom still looked doubtful, but I refused to baby myself over a few bumps and bruises. "If I start feeling strange, I'll tell you right away. Now, can we go do some shopping? I want to get away from this crowd, who's still staring at me."

"Mom, you freaked us all out," Allegra said. "You pretty much bounced all the way down the Spanish Steps."

"At least we'll always remember the landmark," I quipped.

Enzo shook his head, but a grin tugged at his lips. "If there is any problem, call me and I'll come get you. I will check on you before dinner tonight."

"*Grazie,*" I said. His gaze probed mine for a few moments, and then he nodded and turned his head. "Enjoy your shopping, ladies."

I watched him walk away and disappear into the square. Mom was still frowning. "I know what our first stop should be," she said.

"What?" I asked.

"New shoes for you. That's why you fell. You need a pair like mine." She stuck out her foot with the god-awful thick sole and ugly leather, and instead of getting mad at her usual "I told you so," I began to laugh. Allegra looked surprised, but then she began to laugh too, and Mom joined in, and we stood by the Spanish Steps, bent over in hysterics, and I realized I hadn't felt this good in a long time. The fall was worth it if Allegra had forgotten all about being mad at me.

"Fine. You win." I linked my arm through my mom's, and we headed to the shops, a pleasant warmth washing through my veins at the physical contact. I'd forgotten how strong her grip was, and the light scent of the lavender soap she still loved, and the scratchy sound of her laugh that erupted from deep in her chest. This time, I noticed the fragility of her arm squeezed through mine and the slowness of her steps, and I swore to do better, because no matter the history between us, there was a love that beat like thread woven in fabric that was part of my very soul. I needed to figure out where the deep well of resentment toward her began, and try to heal the wounds.

But not today. Today was for shopping and fun before dinner. We had plenty of time during the trip for raw honesty.

Later.

CHAPTER FOURTEEN

Allegra

I couldn't believe I was eating in a real Roman palace.

I knew the tour had cool perks, but this was completely lit. After we arrived by bus, a full staff served champagne and let us explore the gardens. Nonni let me have a sip, which tasted like bubbly sparkles in my mouth and was not as harsh as soda. When they called us in, we stepped into the main drawing room, decorated in rich red and gleaming gold. Expensive-looking oil paintings hung on the walls, and plush red carpet cushioned my feet. Tall-backed red chairs were set up around like mini thrones. I felt the rush of royalty and hushed secrets in the air.

But the big moment was the ballroom.

I caught my breath as I stepped onto marble floors and blinked at the massive, glittering chandelier dripping with crystals. For a moment, I felt like Cinderella arriving at the ball, and a girlish twinge of excitement propelled me. I might not be the princess sort, but it was definitely cool to pretend for a bit. A full-size orchestra played soft music on an elevated stage, and tables with crisp linens and sparkly china were scattered around. Crushed burgundy velvet curtains hid the large windows, but there was one toward the back that opened up onto a stone balcony. I caught the gardens in the distance.

The place was this mix of really old with new, and everything had a touch of class and history. I'd never really been to any formal dances or dinners before, other than when Mom won an award for successful businesswoman of the year, and my mom's second cousin's wedding, but I'd been only seven, so that didn't count.

I wanted to sit with Ian and his family, but Mom had already picked out a table, so I ended up with Cherry and Laura, Dana and Steve, and a Japanese family with a young boy I hadn't met yet. I pegged him for about ten years old and wondered if he was already bored with the tour. There was a ton of history and adult stuff in Italy. It wasn't as if he could hit Disney World or a water park, and when I was his age, I was obsessed with eating only pasta or chicken nuggets, as Mom loved to remind me.

I introduced myself and sat next to Nonni, avoiding my mom again. We'd had a good afternoon and she'd bought me a delicate bracelet with tiny gold balls that I loved. I was still pissed, but her fall had scared me, so I'd decided to be nice. She'd seemed different for those few hours—totally dialed in and not once checking her phone. But when we got back to the hotel, she got that distracted look in her eyes again and said she had to work before dinner, and we'd ended up being super late and almost missing the bus. So embarrassing. Then the entire ride she was texting and ignoring us, so it was like she reverted back.

I studied how the bracelet caught the light and watched Mom excuse herself from the table to hurry into the hallway, phone clutched in her hand. Irritation hit me, but I tried to ignore it. If she wanted to ruin dinner in a castle by worrying about work, that was her issue. She'd warned me already about being on my phone during social time, but now I didn't care. If I wanted to call or text David twenty-four seven, she had no right to tell me no.

At least Nonni was having fun. She was swaying to the music—which was all old-fashioned Sinatra and Martin—and chatting with Dana and Steve while we were served our first dish of pasta.

The waiter placed the bowl, which was filled to the brim, in front of me. "This is too much," I said, blinking at the huge portion.

"No too much," he said with a wink. *"Mangia."*

I shook my head, but he'd moved on. He was older, probably in his sixties, with salt-and-pepper hair and a handsome, chiseled face. Dressed in a clean white suit, he looked less like a server and more like the owner, but everything was so elegant here I shouldn't be surprised at the staff outfits.

"I've never seen so much food in my life," the woman to my right said.

I turned and smiled. "Me either. My grandmother taught me to make homemade pasta, but there's something different about this."

"I heard it was the water," she said. "Each region tastes a bit different, from the pasta to the oils to the wine."

"Yes, makes sense. Oh, I'm Allegra. I'm here with my mom and grandmother."

"We've been meaning to introduce ourselves. I'm Hana, this is Dan"—she motioned toward her husband—"and this is our son, Kai."

Hana had beautiful black hair and fair skin. She was petite and dressed in a black cocktail dress with sparkly heels. Her husband was much taller, with broad shoulders and big hands, like a football player. I waved at the boy, who smiled back. "Hi, Kai. How do you like Italy so far?"

"I like it," he said, nodding eagerly. "We've been reading books at home, but it looks so much bigger here. I thought churches were small."

I laughed. I loved that he wasn't shy. His hair was sticking up on the side from a cowlick. He wore blue-framed glasses, a stiff white button-down shirt, and black dress pants. He looked like a mini version of his dad. "Me too. Wait till tomorrow when we see the Colosseum. I can't wait to hear more about it."

His dark eyes widened. "Lions ate people there," he confided. "And real-life gladiators fought."

"I know. I bet when you get home and tell your friends, they'll be impressed."

"Mom said I can buy souvenirs for them, so I hope they have gladiators tomorrow."

Hana beamed and ruffled his hair. "I'm sure they will. Have you graduated high school, Allegra?"

"No, I have one year left. But my grandmother has been wanting to see Italy for a while, and I'll probably be working next summer, so we decided to do it now."

"That's lovely. Kai got all As this year and won first place in the science fair, so we told him he could pick our family vacation. Imagine my surprise when he didn't pick Disney World."

Kai shot her a look filled with half frustration, half humor. "Mom, we've gone there before. I wanted something different. Dad's always telling me to think big and don't be afraid to have a great adventure. Right?"

Hana shot her husband a long-suffering glance and Dan laughed. "Sorry, but he's right," Dan said.

"What grade are you in?" I asked.

"Fifth," he answered. "And my teacher said if I write about my trip this summer, I'll get a free homework pass and extra credit next year!"

"Good for you. Why'd you pick Italy?" I asked Kai curiously.

He began to tick off items in his list. "The Colosseum, Pompeii, the gondolas in Venice, and the Leaning Tower of Pisa. But mostly it was the pizza. Pizza is my favorite and Mom said I could have it every day if I wanted to."

I laughed. He was smart and different from what I'd expected a ten-year-old boy to be like. Dan put his hands up in the air. "That one's on you," he said to Hana.

We ate our pasta and chatted about the tour. I learned they lived in Manhattan near Central Park. Dan was an architect and Hana wrote women's novels. She named a few and I'd actually heard of one, which had been displayed in the Barnes & Noble windows last summer. She said she was taking notes for an upcoming novel about a family traveling through Italy, so I ended up asking her a bunch of questions about writing, which had always fascinated me.

We finished our salads, and Mom returned. I noted she wore a bright smile but her eyes looked stressed, like she was trying to deal with a problem back at the office. She murmured an apology and introduced herself to Hana, Dan, and Kai.

"You missed the first two courses," I said, trying not to make my tone accusatory.

"The time difference is killing me. I needed to be patched into this conference meeting."

Hana looked sympathetic. "It's hard juggling it all, isn't it? Dan's been pulled away a few times also. They can't seem to run any projects without him."

"I used to think it was a good thing, but I'm beginning to want a break," my mom said. I didn't believe her. She thrived on work like people did on food. "I'm free now and looking forward to the main course. Isn't it beautiful here?"

My mother began to chat with Hana and Kai, and I felt my presence being leeched away under the power of her personality. She always knew what to say, even to strangers. It was a miracle I could come up with a few things, and then I usually got nervous and shut down. A rush of envy swept me as I watched her. She wore an apple green dress that flared around the knees and nude designer heels. Her dark blond hair was just a little messy, giving her a sexy type of look. My mother was dynamic, but not classically beautiful. Tonight, though, she came close.

A wave of love washed over me and I wished I was more like her.

And then I hoped I'd never be like her.

"I'm going to check out the balcony," I said. Nonni had gone to the restroom, but I saw her talking with Mary and Ray, so I headed outside alone. A few people filled the alcove, but they made room as I pressed against the stone wall and looked at the darkened city streets. The air was hot and muggy on my face.

I felt a tap on my shoulder and turned. "Hey."

Ian smiled at me. My heart did a tiny leap. "Hey."

"I was hoping to sit next to you but your table was already taken up. What do you think of this place?"

"Pretty fancy. Never partied in a castle before."

"Me either. Had to find my good suit." He straightened his tie with extra exaggeration. Normally, no guy I knew would dare wear a white suit, but on Ian it looked good, especially with his coloring. His lean, lanky height meant he towered over me, and he'd gelled his hair to tame back the cowlick. I wasn't a big fan of freckles, but his deep blue eyes reminded me of one of those Caribbean islands with turquoise, still waters.

"I like it. Reminds me of prom."

He arched a brow and I clapped a hand over my mouth. "I didn't mean that in a bad way!"

He cracked up and relief flooded through me. "It kind of does look like I should be escorting you into a limo. I guess I don't buy a lot of fancy clothes."

"Don't worry, neither do I. Nowhere to go."

His gaze flicked over me, and he didn't try to hide his male appreciation. But it didn't feel icky or sexual, just nice. "I would've assumed you have a date every weekend and were prom queen. You look amazing in that dress."

I blushed. I had a few standard cocktail dresses, but this one was a bit more fancy. I'd found it on clearance and begged Mom to buy it for me, even though I had nowhere to wear it. She surprised me by agreeing, saying a woman always needed a solid backup in her closet for emergencies. The gold slinky fabric clung to my body, but it had a high neckline and a low back and draped to the floor. The fabric shimmered so it looked like light bounced off me when I moved. It was sophisticated but sexy, and I felt really good about myself when I wore it. Even though my boobs were too small and my butt too round, I didn't tear myself apart like I usually did with my clothes.

"Thanks. Nah, I'm not into school dances or formal functions. Not my scene." I thought of my friends showing off at the country club events with their money and fancy clothes, trying to score the hottest boys, who were mostly assholes. Then the image of David flickered in my memory. We'd FaceTimed yesterday after Nonni went to bed. He told me about his night, when Freda and Connor got drunk and passed out in the RV while he played in a dive bar till two a.m. He'd said the crowd was a bit lame but the bartender mentioned he had a cool voice and to keep trying. I wished I was with him to experience a summer with no rules, but I was scared of breaking the law and about getting caught with drugs again.

I was so lame, but I didn't like getting in trouble. I wished there was a way to push boundaries without crossing them completely. "I'll probably skip senior prom too."

Ian nodded with understanding. "I was never with the cool kids either. Had a few close friends in high school, but I sailed under the radar. College was better. Do you know what school you want to go to? Senior, right?"

"Yeah, next year. I'm not sure." Actually, Mom already had an Excel spreadsheet with her top picks, but I had no interest in attending any of them. I still wanted to apply to a few cooking schools like the Culinary Institute of America in Hyde Park. My grades were top rate, and my second scores on the SAT kicked ass, so maybe I had a shot. The words tumbled out of my mouth before I could stop them. "I think I want to be a chef."

His face lit up. "You like to cook? That's awesome. I suck in the kitchen, but I'm good at eating."

I relaxed and laughed. "My grandmother taught me a lot. I'm not sure what direction I want, but a college where I can figure out if I have decent talent is key."

"Your mom must be psyched."

I wrinkled my nose. "Not. She created her own company and eats, breathes, and sleeps work. When I try to mention cooking, she thinks it's beneath me and brushes me off."

"Did you try telling her how important it is to you?"

I let out a breath. "No, because she doesn't care, and she doesn't listen. She's too caught up in her own world." I realized the bitterness ran deep, and my heart ached. I realized she didn't know who I really was. Maybe she never had.

Even worse? Maybe she didn't care.

Ian touched my shoulder. "Parents can be tough. I've had some issues myself to work out. There was a point where I didn't think we'd ever be able to have a decent relationship."

"Really? I figured you seemed so close that things were always good."

"Nope. Things were bad for a long time. But I finally got them to understand what I needed to do, and now we're really close. I meant it when I said I was excited to spend time with them this summer. People change. Maybe this trip is a gift for both of you so she can really get to know you again. Away from work."

I nodded, picking at my thumbnail. I liked the positive way he saw things. I knew there was a four-year difference, but he didn't seem to view me as a kid who was just whining. It was as if he recognized what I was going through. I wanted to hear more, but my grandmother peeked around the wall. "There you are! Honey, dinner just got served. Hi, Ian."

"Hi, Mrs. Ferrari. Did you enjoy the Vatican today?"

His face was genuinely kind and interested as he watched my grandmother. Tons of kids at school asked why I'd want to spend any time with someone so old, but there was a special bond between us that meant everything to me. Nonni's face lit up. "It was magical, wasn't it? All these years I dreamed of seeing such treasures in person but never thought I'd get here."

"My great-grandmother was born in Naples," I explained.

"Any other relatives still living here?" he asked.

Nonni shook her head. "No, my parents both came to America and unfortunately they died young. I remember my mother used to speak Italian in the house and it took a while for her to learn English. When I was growing up, she'd lapse into rapid Italian when she got angry, which made me angry that I couldn't understand what she was yelling at me."

Ian laughed. "You should hear my grandmother curse in Irish. It's a scary thing to behold."

"Now, Ireland is next on my bucket list, so you'll have to give me all the secrets," Nonni said.

"I'd love for you all to come visit." Something flashed in his eyes—it seemed a little bit like regret—but it passed too fast for me to figure it out. "The land gets in your blood so you feel like you can never leave."

His soft, lilting brogue caressed my ears with the dreaminess of his statement. My grandmother glanced back and forth between the two of us, her lips curving in a smile. "That's how a real home should be," she said. "Now, let's get back to the table before our food gets cold."

I followed her back in. "Maybe a dance later?" Ian asked. "If they play something we recognize?"

My nerves tightened. I didn't know how to formally dance, but I shrugged. "Sure."

When I got to my place, the handsome waiter hurried right over and placed my plate in front of me. "I didn't want it to get cold," he said.

Nonni patted his arm in gratitude. "I told her to hurry. Thank you for keeping it warm."

He beamed. *"Prego."*

I stared down at the plate of meat in rich brown gravy. "Is this chicken?"

"Veal, *signorina*. Saltimbocca—medallions in sage with prosciutto. Very delicious." He bowed and hurried off.

My mother leaned over. "Did he say veal? Isn't that baby cows?" She shuddered and looked at her plate in distaste. "Maybe I'll just have salad."

I rolled my eyes. My mother was as much of a control freak over her food as over the rest of her life. Nonni gave her a hard stare. "They worked diligently to prepare this food, Frannie. Try it. You can't subsist on grilled chicken and greens your whole life."

Mom stiffened but glanced down at her plate again. I held back a chuckle at the way Nonni scolded her. "I don't think I like it."

I tried a bite and focused on the taste and textures. She watched me, nervously nibbling on her lower lip, like I'd blow up in front of her from one bite. "It's excellent," I said. "Tender, but thick enough to hold the flavor. Meat cut too thin can fall apart on your tongue and taste flat." My hero was Anthony Bourdain, and I loved the way he was fearless with food. I'd sworn to be like that and cried when he died. The culinary world wasn't as good without him.

Mom stared at me with surprise. "Hmm. Okay, I'll try." She put a piece in her mouth and chewed slowly. "It's pretty good," she finally said.

Nonni nodded in approval, then lowered her head and spoke in a hushed whisper. "I like Ian."

I shot her a warning look. "Nonni, it's not like that. He's very nice but not my type."

One hand waved in the air in her typical fashion. My grandmother always told me if her hands weren't available, no words would be able to pass her lips. "Types? Ridiculous. It is about a boy's soul—not his looks."

I sighed and kept my voice low. "I'm sorry, but I don't find him attractive. Isn't physical chemistry also important?"

"Yes, there are things such as love at first sight, but there are many roads to love. A boy who makes you laugh or looks at you with respect. One who holds your hand when you're scared—those are the things that resonate and the attraction grows. These are the surprises in life that keep us paying attention."

"You said Grandpa had a cute butt," I teased. "Nothing about his sense of humor."

"Oh, shush, you are so bad. I regret telling you my secrets." But her eyes filled with laughter. "You are probably too young. Too caught up in the bad boys who will hurt you. Just never mistake such a thing for passion, Allegra. Are you still texting this boy who smokes weed?"

I avoided her probing gaze. I didn't want to lie. "Yes, but everyone smokes weed, Nonni. Some of my friends have heroin or cocaine parties—it's just more acceptable because they have money."

"But you are too smart to ruin your life for a fake substance. Your mother agreed to come on this trip because she is terrified you will make a mistake you cannot come back from. Drugs ruin you."

I glanced over, but my mother was talking with Hana. "I think Mom came because she almost lost a big account and couldn't handle the failure. This wasn't for me."

"Not true. Your mom is going through some other stuff that maybe she'll share later. This trip is for you, but it won't matter unless you believe it. You are both overdue for a long talk and some honesty. Mothers will never be perfect, my sweet girl. We make many, many mistakes." Her eyes turned sad and a bit haunted, which made my heart hurt. "The only thing we can hope is for our children to forgive us and believe we did our best."

I gently squeezed her hand. The fragile, wrinkled skin was a badge of her age and her wisdom, and it always comforted me. "Mom has nothing to forgive you for. You were always there for her."

"We must forgive our mothers for everything they are not. One day, you'll understand."

Her words struck something deep inside me, but I couldn't figure out what it meant. Instead, I tried to comfort her with the truth. "I'm not into drugs, Nonni. Yeah, I did weed a few times, like most kids do, and I drink at parties, but it's nothing to worry about. And David isn't bad. He just has a different philosophy about things, and he interests me. Okay?"

She squeezed back in reassurance. "Your job is to make many mistakes, and that's okay. Own them proudly. But choose your mistakes carefully."

I shook my head and laughed. "That makes no sense."

"Eat your veal. And have another sip of my champagne. I already feel too drunk to finish it."

Mom leaned over. "What are you guys laughing at?"

"Nothing," we said together. At my mother's hurt look, I felt a flash of sympathy but pushed it away.

Nonni jumped in. "How's your head, honey? I still think you should have gone to the doctor."

"I feel fine, not even a headache. My butt's a bit sore still."

She made a face. "I'm just embarrassed. Did you see everyone staring at me?"

"No one saw," Nonni stated. "You got up really fast."

Mom bit her lower lip at the bald-faced lie. "You can't even fall without being recorded nowadays. I just hope I don't end up on *America's Funniest Home Videos*."

"They give you ten thousand dollars for a winning video," Nonni said. "That would be worth it!"

My mother and I met each other's stares and burst out laughing. It was one of my grandmother's favorite shows along with *Dancing with the Stars* and *Wheel of Fortune*. "It wasn't a funny fall," I pointed out, trying to make her feel better. "A simple slide won't get you any airtime. Now, if Mom did a flip or her pants fell down, we'd be rich."

We finished dinner and the lights dimmed, spotlighting the band as they launched into Dean Martin's "That's Amore." Plates were cleared and my waiter appeared by my side to drop off the dessert—a perfect, plump cannoli spilling out fresh cream, the crust dusted with powdered sugar. The crisp shell crunched and the cannoli filling was stuffed with chocolate chips.

Mom pushed it away. "I better not."

"It's the best cannoli I ever had," I said. "Why are you so stuck on dieting when you've always been thin? Don't you ever want to try anything new?"

She blinked. "I just get used to a routine," she said slowly. "It's easier not to make any mistakes."

"That makes no sense, Mom. Enjoying food or indulging now and then isn't going to blow up your orderly world." Frustration shimmered through me. "Can't you just eat the cannoli and be happy?"

I waited for her to lash back or give me a hurt look and ignore me. Lately, I'd noticed how easy it was for her to shut off from me when I annoyed her. But I watched with surprise as she pulled the plate toward her and took a bite of the dessert.

"You're right. It's really good."

I held back a smile, not willing to give it up for now. At least, not yet.

I ate my pastry while I listened to the music. "Why don't you ask Ian to dance?" Nonni asked, blotting her mouth with a napkin.

I shook my head. "No."

"Why not?" she insisted. "You don't have to marry him to dance with him."

"I know! It's just, well, I don't really know how to slow dance." Embarrassment flowed through me. It wasn't like I had a dad to teach me, or went to dances or on tons of dates. The waiter appeared by my side and began clearing plates.

"Honey, dancing is easy! You just put your arms around the man's shoulders and follow his lead. Do you want me to teach you?"

"Oh my God, no!" The thought of my grandmother showing me in front of our tour group made me want to die. "Forget it. I don't want to know how to dance anyway. Can we please change the subject?"

She sighed. "Okay."

Thankfully, she dropped it. Mom was chatting with Hana, Dan, and Kai, and I just sipped my water as some couples walked onto the dance floor. I watched Mary and Ray sway together. Their feet weaved a simple yet intricate-looking step that made both of their bodies become one. It was romantic, and I sighed a bit dreamily, with the background of a Roman castle and a full-fledged orchestra serenading a room full of beautifully dressed guests. It was fun to be involved in something different from high school parties and drunken beer pong.

Suddenly, a shadow fell over me. The waiter stood before me, his hand held out, bowing slightly. "May I have this dance?"

I blinked. My heartbeat sped up. "Uh, um, oh, thank you so much, but I-I think I'll sit a while."

He didn't move. His dark gaze met mine with a patient affection, his hand still held out in entreaty. Nonni hissed out, "Allegra, dance with the man."

My palms began to sweat and fear pumped through me. I couldn't dance like that! I'd be laughed at and there weren't enough people on the dance floor yet. "Um, see, I can't really, um, I can't dance like that."

"I teach you."

Oh my God, people were starting to stare. Swallowing hard, trapped in a nightmare, I gave him my hand.

He grinned broadly and escorted me to the center of the floor like I was royalty. With an expert flourish, he twirled me into his arms and I automatically reached up to put one hand on his shoulder. "Very good," he said. "Follow my lead. Do not look down. Listen to music."

On cue, the band began to play Frank Sinatra—"I've Got You Under My Skin"—and I gulped in a breath and prayed I wouldn't trip in my heels. With a firm grip, the waiter led me across the floor, slowly at first when I shifted my feet wrong or stumbled slightly, then faster as I began to get the feel of it. When I struggled for control, I messed up because I began overthinking, and as I became more adept at allowing him to guide me, our movements became smoother. I felt as if we were locked into a frame at the top and let loose at the bottom. Most of the dance was too stressful because I was worried, but toward the end of the song, I realized I'd relaxed and actually began enjoying the way my feet were able to match his steps and the graceful glide of movement when I just let go.

Finally, he stopped, took my hand, and led me back to my table.

He stopped at my seat and bowed. "Thank you for the dance, *signorina*. It was a pleasure."

My skin felt flushed, but a bubble of pleasure fizzled in my veins. It was like a natural high. *"Grazie,"* I said, unable to think of something else cleverer.

He winked. *"Prego."*

With a lingering look at my grandmother, he disappeared. I slid into my chair and tried to act cool, but my mother leaned across the table. "Allegra, you looked amazing out there! I had no idea you could dance like that."

"He's too old for you, dear, but now you know what real romance is," my grandmother added. "That's what you deserve."

Mom's eyes flickered with longing. "Don't we all," she murmured.

I tried to brush it off, but everyone at the table was smiling, and I was suddenly struck by a strange joy and grief that twisted within me. I'd never experience a dance with my father, or him walking me down the aisle at my wedding. My kids would have no Pop Pop. I'd never had a chance to love a father because Mom had taken the option away. And, yes, it was probably selfish, because there were never guarantees of getting a decent dad, but I felt strangely bereft, as if the emptiness that was always inside me needing to be filled would never be satisfied. I'd never have a father who'd share in all my firsts, so it'd been with a waiter who was kind, but a stranger.

I excused myself to the bathroom. I desperately needed a few moments alone to process.

This trip was bringing up things I rarely let myself think of, but I had a premonition more was to come.

CHAPTER FIFTEEN

Francesca

THE ICONIC COLOSSEUM rose before me with an arrogance and power that stole my breath. The broken stone and rubbled pathways only added to the mighty glory of a structure that had once been witness to bloody battles, destruction, and death.

The only thing that ruined the experience was the group of fake gladiators lingering around the entrance, urging tourists to take pictures with them. They were the same kind of people as those in Times Square who dressed in tattered Elmo and Batman costumes, luring children to pose with them, only to spring the fee of a ten-dollar bill for the privilege. Enzo waved them away when they approached, but Kai begged for a picture.

Hana and I sighed in motherly commiseration, and I didn't blame her for surrendering. The boy practically shook with excitement as he squeezed in the middle of the fake gladiators and raised two skinny biceps, growling at the camera. Allegra laughed, but we all agreed sometimes you just needed to be a patsy and give in. It was probably worth the ten euros for his joy.

Enzo passed us off to a new tour guide, and we snaked through corridors, which offered brief shade in the choking heat. It was only ten a.m. and my T-shirt was damp with perspiration. When we stepped out into the main center and gazed at the floor that had contained the slaves and lions, a shiver bumped down my spine. The stands would have held only men, rabid for the blood sport of watching men fight for their lives in front of thousands of screaming fans. The soft blue sky and fluffy clouds seemed to mock the past savagery they cloaked from above.

Like my experience in the Vatican, everything was larger in scope and power than I'd imagined, dragging me down into history I'd never experienced before. It struck me again how young America was and how Europe must look at us sometimes—these fierce babes in the woods who believed we were always right even though time had not truly tested our power.

Not yet.

We spent the morning touring the Pantheon, and around lunchtime, the group split up. The three of us decided to roam around the city for our last day in Rome and be off the clock. We sat at a café and sipped cold, fruity Pinot Grigio, splitting a pizza, salad, and a plate of fresh pears and nutty Parmesan drizzled with raw honey.

"Enzo said we'll be visiting a family farm where they make fresh mozzarella," Allegra said, guzzling her soda.

"What do you think of the tour so far?" I asked them. "Aren't you glad we went with the smaller one with more customized outings?"

"It's only our third day, Mom," Allegra pointed out. "But, yeah, I like our group and Enzo. I was afraid they'd make us do a whole bunch of stuff we didn't want to."

"Many tours get kickbacks from the vendors they promise to visit," I said.

Mom mopped her forehead with a napkin. "The only thing I'm regretting is coming in the summer. I had no idea it was this hot."

"Drink water, less wine," I said, pushing away the glass that still held a few more swallows. "We can go back to the room and nap for a bit if you need to."

She snorted. "No way. I'm not missing Rome for a nap. I'll sleep when I'm dead."

I smiled at her familiar saying and a memory sparked. "Remember when Allegra was little and she begged you to take her to the water park?"

"You had to bring that up?"

Allegra glanced back and forth at us. "What happened? I've never heard this story."

"I took you to the Little Squirts Water Park to spend an afternoon and keep us both busy," Mom said. "I had no idea those places were like the *Lord of the Flies.* Kids running and screaming, water fountains blasting out everywhere, and crazy climbing mazes. I lost you within a few minutes and was terrified you'd get hurt. Besides injuries every half hour, all the moms were gathered around the tiki bar drinking."

"Tell her the best part," I urged.

"You had gotten yourself tangled in this rope maze at the top of the slide and couldn't get out. You were screaming and crying for me, so I had to climb the obstacle course to get you out."

A helpless giggle rose from my lips. "Poor Mom got to the top and freed you, but she couldn't climb back down because of the line of kids behind her."

"They were pushing and blocking me from retreat," Mom said, shaking her head. "I tried to get past them but they were like little monsters. I cried out for one of the moms to help me, but they didn't hear."

"No way," Allegra breathed. "Did you get down?"

"Sure, but not the way I wanted. I got pushed down the waterslide. The biggest one in the park. I ended up in a pool of water in my clothes because I hadn't worn a bathing suit. I figured I could just watch you without getting wet."

Allegra gasped. "Where were the supervisors? Didn't they have any?"

"Let's just say no one cared to help. When I landed in the pool, one of them informed me I was too old to go down the slide and to please obey the posted rules next time."

We all burst into laughter. "I never took you to a water park again," Mom declared. "And I still blame your mother. She never warned me it was a terrible idea."

"Yes, I did! I said I'd take her on the weekend and not to give in to her begging."

"Honey, if we had waited, Allegra would never have gone. You worked that weekend again, remember?"

I jerked back at the barb. An awkward silence fell, and Mom cleared her throat, obviously regretting her words. "That's right. I remember now," I said coldly. Nothing like my own mother trying to shame me.

She tried to make peace, but we all knew it was too late. "It was a busy time. You were still building your company and we understood."

Allegra dropped her gaze and concentrated on her pizza.

On cue, my phone buzzed. I glanced at it quickly and read the long text regarding feedback results from the test group and asking for approval on the new print ad. I didn't have to do it. I'd asked to be notified of everything and Kate had agreed to loop me in. Pretending not to stress, I casually tucked my phone back into my purse and decided I'd sneak some work in later. I'd be able to fit it in with the time change.

I drained my wine and motioned for the check. Some things were universal. "Where should we head to? I mapped out all of the plazas we haven't visited, the last two fountains, and high-lighted some highly rated monuments from TripAdvisor."

Mom and Allegra shared a glance. "Let's get lost," Allegra said.

"What do you mean lost? We have phones now and maps that talk to us block by block. We don't have to get lost like in the old days."

Allegra shrugged. "I guess I just want to start walking and see where we end up. It'd be nice to be surprised rather than stick to the textbook."

"Agreed," my mother said.

I nibbled my lip. I preferred planning to chaos. Getting lost just wasn't done anymore, because it was avoidable. But I wanted to indulge them and this was something I could manage. "If that's what you want, I'm in."

"No phones," Allegra warned. "We need to figure things out by ourselves."

"Not even Google Translate?" I asked. I was addicted to technology and not too proud to admit it. "Or a text to Enzo?"

"Nothing. Let's see what happens," Allegra said.

Mom nodded, and I was outvoted. I paid the bill, and we picked a street and set out on foot for an adventure.

It took me a while to settle in and begin to enjoy the sights without worry. We headed over the bridge, crossing the Tiber River, not sure what we'd find. As we navigated narrow cobblestone streets, I was struck by the endless rows of buildings in rich, earthy colors, covered with bright green winding ivy. Wrought-iron balconies spilled over the square filled with pots of red, yellow, and pink geraniums. Savory and sweet scents of bread and sugar drifted in the air, teasing our nostrils. We passed cafés where people lounged at small tables, smoking and drinking aperitifs, and listened to the chatter of lyrical Italian float in the air. Mom bought a leather wallet, and I picked up a bright red Pinocchio ornament with moving legs for our Christmas tree. We guzzled bottled water to combat the heat as the baked pavement seeped right into our flimsy sandals.

"This is so cute," Mom said, her head craning back and forth to take it all in. "Don't you wish we could sell everything and live here?"

"No," I said.

"Yes," Allegra said.

We looked at each other. "Really? You preferred going cross-country in a dilapidated RV with some half-baked musician. How would you deal with simplifying your life to this extent?"

"He's not half-baked," she replied hotly. "He's got a lot of talent and needs to go out there to share his gift."

"As long as he doesn't share his weed."

She blew out an annoyed breath. "You have no idea what would make me happy. I bet I'd do well here with less stress and more focus on living."

"You're eighteen. You need to live big first before you decide to settle down to the simple life, don't you think?"

"My big isn't your big, Mom. It never was."

My mother got in between us and clucked her tongue. "My question was supposed to be fun and hypothetical. No more fighting. Both of you would thrive anywhere because you have strong cores and stubborn determination. Discussion over. Oh, look, a bakery! Let's get some goodies to go."

We followed her into a small shop with assorted baked breads and pastries in the display case. I couldn't afford any further carbs today, so I got an iced coffee and watched Mom and Allegra nibble on mini éclairs and biscotti. As we ventured further into the town, we stumbled upon a gorgeous basilica that dominated a plaza and marveled over the opulent gilded interior, which reminded me of a mosque. We found a beautiful park and sat on benches while we breathed in the lush scent of the plants surrounding us on all sides. Time stretched and flew by until we finally glanced at our watches and realized the late hour.

"Better head back toward the hotel," I said, glancing around. We'd wandered past the main squares into a quieter place that was more isolated. "We need to change and get ready for dinner."

I reached for my phone but Allegra stopped me. "No tech, remember?"

"That's silly. I have no idea where we are."

"Oh, we can figure it out," my mother said, waving her hand in the air. "Let's try this way."

I tamped down a sigh. "Okay, but my feet are starting to kill me."

We took a right and followed a few zigzagging streets that seemed to lead us nowhere. Now there were few people and no restaurants or shops. As we trudged along, my skin felt burnt, sweat dampened my clothes, and blisters were forming on my feet. I began to curse under my breath.

"We're lost," I announced. "And this isn't fun."

"Now who's a complainer?" Allegra taunted. She was known to be a tad of a whiner when things didn't go her way. I hadn't imagined she got it from me. "Nonni's still doing fine."

My mother shrugged. "I told you those Jane Fonda DVDs helped."

This time, I led and headed left. We crested hills, crossed streets, and finally came to an empty square with a few benches. In the distance, a trash can held a raging fire, and two elderly ladies were crowded round the can, looking like they were discussing the latest episode of their favorite show.

"Let's sit down and I'll bring up a map. I want to be found now."

Allegra didn't protest this time, so I knew she was done too. I grabbed my phone and opened the app, tapping a few buttons to get our home location.

"Um, Mom? Those ladies are staring at us."

I turned my head. She was right. They seemed transfixed on us and bent their heads together, pointing wildly. Terrific. I figured they wouldn't be a great source for directions. "Just ignore them, honey. This will take a minute."

I got a home signal and zeroed in on our location.

"Frannie, they're coming over here," Mom hissed.

The two women began to march forward, and I realized they were carrying two large sticks in their hands. Holy crap, what was going on? Even in New York City the homeless left you mostly alone. Were they looking for money?

"Let's go, guys. I'm sure they'll back off."

We rose from the bench and began easing away, but the ladies let out an angry tirade of Italian. As they moved closer, I noticed their dirty clothing, mismatched shoes, and bedraggled hair. But it was their faces that scared the hell out of me. They were pinched in rage.

"Uh, *scusi, mi dispiace*, we go. We go," I muttered. Allegra called out a phrase in Italian I didn't recognize, and I grabbed her hand and Mom's, ready to flee. "We go."

They attacked.

Holding the sticks up high, they raced the next couple of feet, as if we'd done something terrible and they were bent on revenge. I gave a shriek and held tight to Mom's and Allegra's hands, and we ran out of the square as fast we could, our feet pounding on the pavement, heading toward the road we'd passed beforehand.

After a full block, I realized they hadn't followed, and we slowed down to catch our breath. "Are you okay? Mom?"

"I'm fine. What did we do? Oh my goodness, they were mad! Those were the first not-nice people we've met here."

"Do you think they would have hit us?" Allegra asked in shock.

"No, but I'm guessing the bench was their property and we weren't supposed to sit there," I said. "Let's get out of here."

Allegra was ahead of me, her fingers flying over her phone. "Screw this, we're getting an Uber, Mom."

"Good idea."

In a matter of ten minutes, we'd made our way to the curb of some street and saw the magic minicar pull up. We squeezed in and I worshipped the age of technology as the driver drove us directly back to our hotel without worry of translation of language or transfer of cash. It was a beautiful thing.

"We're not cursed or something, are we?" Allegra asked. "You fell down the steps, and now we get attacked."

"There's no such thing as a curse. This is what happens when you get lost. Anyway, you wanted an adventure. Guess we got it."

By the time we stumbled back to safety, the exhaustion of the day had set in, along with a deep satisfaction. I had forgotten the ups and downs that could occur after spending a day with my family. And, yes, we'd annoyed one another, but we ended up sharing an experience we'd be able to laugh at in the days to come. I was just sifting through the realization that this trip had been a good idea after all, when my daughter let out a gasp of shock and stopped still in the lobby. Her gaze was trained on her phone.

"Oh my God."

My heart stopped. "What is it? Did someone you know die?"

She slowly shook her head, eyes wide. "Something tells me you're not going to like technology anymore, Mom."

A strange foreboding washed over me. "What are you talking about? What are you looking at?"

My mother leaned over to peek at her phone. Her hand flew to her mouth. "You taped your mother falling down the stairs?"

"No! But someone must've, and then they uploaded it and—"

She trailed off, biting her lip. Her features screwed up with worry. "It went kind of viral."

A roaring in my ears registered. I stretched out my trembling hand and she placed the phone in my palm. It was opened to Instagram.

FUNNY FALL AT SPANISH STEPS! the caption screamed, with a long line of emojis and hashtags. I watched myself in full, vivid color as my foot slipped and I tumbled down the stairs. My ass bounced, my mouth was open in a wide O, and my face had a weird, horrified expression—kind of like that scary painting *The Scream*. I heard the collective gasps and titters from the crowd, and then I lay in a heap on the bottom step, like a baby giraffe who was just learning to walk. I watched Enzo sweep me up into his arms and carry me away. He was the epitome of the classic Disney prince saving the fallen damsel in distress.

"This is not happening," I whispered. "It's not that funny."

"I think everyone liked Enzo's reaction," Allegra pointed out. "Look at the comments. They think he's very romantic."

She was right. The comments went on about how he tried to whisk me away from danger and that men like him no longer exist. People tagged their friends, and it morphed into a discussion of Italian versus American men. Like a snowball effect, it began to take on a life of its own.

It had already racked up more than ten thousand views.

My chest tightened and I tried not to panic. What if my clients saw this? My employees? I'd already lost the lead on an important account over the panic attack. No one wanted to hire a woman who inspired a ridiculous meme or viral video.

"We need to stop it from spreading," I said, trying to think of a plan. "I can't let anyone from my company see this."

"We can't delete it because we didn't post it," Allegra said.

"Mom, it's not that bad. You're human. The whole thing will probably die down by tomorrow."

Mom jumped in. "It shows the world you may fall down, but you get right back up."

I stared at her in astonishment. "Are you crazy? It shows me falling down and getting carried by a guy! I didn't get up!"

"It was the intended meaning. You would have gotten up. Enzo just happened to be there."

I wanted to scream but didn't want to add to the madness. "How did you find the video?" I asked my daughter.

"Bonnie sent it to me and asked if it was you, but it's also listed in the main search engine."

Which meant it was being shared and commented on and people were finding my fall amusing. I was going to vomit. "I have to go."

"Wait—we need to go to dinner soon," Mom said. "Don't let this ruin our evening. I'm sure no one important even knows it's you."

On cue, my phone buzzed. The text was from Kate.

Holy shit, Fran, did you fall down the Spanish Steps? Are you okay? Who's that hot guy?

A whimper escaped my lips. "Trust me, everyone knows. I have to make some calls to the office. Allegra, don't answer anyone who asks about the video. Pretend it's not me."

Her jaw dropped. "Mom, Bonnie knows it's you."

"Plead the Fifth. Nothing is real on the internet; we'll say it was faked. I'll check on you later." Ignoring my mother's protests, I skipped the elevator and headed up the staircase, my brain clicking through possible options to control the mess I was in.

I didn't come up with many.

CHAPTER SIXTEEN

ALLEGRA

WHEN WE STEPPED onto the grounds of Pompeii, I was struck by a few things. First, it was dusty. I felt as if I was enveloped immediately, a cloud of it blowing into my ears and nose and eyes. Also, everything was brown—a thousand shades of earth surrounded me until even the sky seemed dully tinted. The foreboding outline of Mount Vesuvius shimmered in the distance almost like a mirage, and there was an eerie sort of silence as we made our way through the excavations.

I'd been looking forward to Pompeii, but my bad mood threatened to ruin it. Mom had never gotten to dinner. She'd dumped Nonni and me for the whole night, then come up with a bunch of excuses that she'd been busy "stopping" the video from ruining her career. Like that was even a possibility.

And she called me dramatic?

I was stuck making excuses for her, saying she had a headache, while I made conversation with the rest of the group and kept an eye on Nonni. My mother had been the one who'd forced the trip on me. She'd been the one who'd promised to spend quality time fixing our relationship and who'd said that we both needed a break from the stresses of our daily routine. She'd been the one who swore she wasn't going to work and we'd make Italy an important memory for our family. She'd been the one who warned me about getting off my phone and viewing the world without a lens.

Bullshit.

She wanted to work again and used the video as an excuse. And just like I'd said, the views were already shrinking and had been replaced by another royal family feud splashed all over social media. Even worse? We'd had a great time yesterday. Sure, there were some crazy moments, but I felt as if we'd finally connected a bit. Then she'd gone and ruined it all over again.

I'd refused to talk to her when we got home last night or this morning, even though Nonni tried to play peacemaker. I texted David a few times, but he'd gone MIA so I decided to be cool until he reached out. Mom tried to sit with me on the bus, but I took a seat alone and spent the whole time on my phone. Maybe if I became like her she'd finally see how it felt.

We'd gotten up at six a.m. to be on the bus early in order to see Pompeii, and next we'd have a brief stopover in Naples before heading to Capri for the next few nights. Enzo warned it was a long travel day. I needed to try to focus on enjoying the day and not let her affect me.

Why hadn't I learned? She'd never change. I needed to stop believing she would.

We didn't have any earbuds today. Our guide had a loud, booming voice and a fun, jokey-type personality, even though the site seemed to require a serious, sad attitude because of the tragedy. The sun beat down mercilessly, but I began to forget the discomfort as our guide spun a story of what it was like to live in Pompeii. I couldn't imagine dealing with the awful realization that I'd burn alive, along with the rest of the city's population.

Ian eased beside me. "Is it wrong to be craving a snow cone right now?"

I tamped down a giggle. "Probably, but I wish we'd come around the corner and there'd be a Mr. Frosty truck."

He grinned and jerked his head toward the guy. "He's good. More of a storyteller than a history teacher. I think with large disasters we forget it's personal. We all view things from the worldly scope."

I nodded and we moved as a group down the broken, rubbled road. "Like reading about a school shooting every week. It becomes a new normal until you walk the grounds or know someone who died."

"Exactly." We shared a look and I was surprised at the tiny jolt of recognition my body experienced. It didn't happen a lot. I always figured my hormones were a bit sluggish. My interest was piqued by really hot celebrities, and by Christian Peterson, who was the school god in body if not personality, and definitely by David. But Ian wasn't attractive to me in that way. I studied him more closely, noting his ginger hair and pale skin and freckles. But his eyes were a bolt of hot blue, and his smile made me want to smile back, and he was lanky but sported nice muscles under his T-shirt, which hinted at a good set of abs. I wondered if freckles covered his whole body or if he had red-gold chest hair. I wondered if he'd kissed a lot of girls and if he was good at it, or if he'd been more of a geek and never had a girlfriend.

"Can I hang with you?" he asked.

"Parent irritation?"

"Just a tad. To save money, we're all sharing a room."

Pure horror hit. "Oh, I'm so sorry. I'm pissed at my mom right now, so we're in the same boat."

"Anything serious?"

His interest seemed genuine and not polite. I bet he was a great listener. "Nope, same problem recycled."

"Got it."

We fell silent and refocused on the lecture, our shoulders occasionally brushing.

"Before Mount Vesuvius erupted, Pompeii was a playground for the wealthy," our guide continued. "The resort attracted vacationers, and these streets were lined with villas, shops, bathhouses, and of course, brothels." His gaze surveyed the crowd and focused on Kai. "I'll tell you when to cover his eyes, Mama," he said teasingly to Hana, motioning toward one of the buildings. "There're some pictures you may want to skip."

Kai frowned, obviously not understanding, and Hana nodded in agreement.

"The arena sat twenty thousand people. Imagine crowds gathered in the open-air markets, mothers with children, shopkeepers selling wares, and horses pulling wagons." He pointed to the ground. "This is the original road that was used. Follow me and watch your step."

Our feet sank into the craters of ancient stone as we made our way through the dusty, silent city, which seemed to scream with thousands of unheard voices. He painted an image of the life led in the city until I could almost hear the ancient chatter of Latin drifting in the air. "When the volcano erupted in August 79 AD, there was time for people to flee, but many of them ignored it. Ash, rock, and poisonous gas exploded into the air, and when it came back down, it cut a path of fury that led straight to Pompeii."

"Why didn't everyone just evacuate?" Ian's dad, Patrick, asked.

"Why do we stay when disaster threatens? We don't believe it can happen to us? How can a thriving city such as this be completely destroyed? An estimated two thousand people stayed. By the time the volcano made its final stand, it erupted at a hundred miles per hour and it was too late for anyone left behind. Lava poured into the streets and swallowed the city whole."

The group fell silent, looking around at the remains of a civilization that'd once made a life here. A shiver raced down my spine, and I trembled. As if Ian sensed my reaction, he reached out and touched my arm, offering reassurance. The clean scent of cotton and sunshine seemed to drift from his skin.

"A group of explorers discovered Pompeii in 1748 while digging for artifacts. What they found was shocking—the ash had preserved almost everything. Skeletons were discovered intact, along with everyday objects, paintings, furniture, all of it. It was as if the city had been lifted out of a deep sleep. Now I will show you some of the buildings that contain skeletons and the famous murals that guided tourists who once lived here."

We weaved in and out of the crumbled stone buildings and viewed stone bodies encased in glass. One man was staring up in horror, his hands braced out in front of him as if he'd seen the lava come to swallow him whole. Another showed a woman crouched over, trying to protect her baby, the infant gathered between her arms, forever preserved in a Stephen King–esque show of macabre. Emotion choked my throat. My fingers gently brushed the glass as I gazed at the people who'd fought to live and who had surrendered to Mother Nature's fury.

"Makes you think about how the world is today," Ian said quietly. "Tornados, floods, insect swarms, Arctic melting. We're told there are no global effects and who cares if we kill trees and the bees in order to make more room for condos. Every time we think we can control the earth, we're proven wrong. No one respects God anymore."

I tilted my head, curious at his statement. He spoke like a scholar and not any young, single guy I'd ever met. Almost as if he'd lived a long life and had seen things that made him sad. "Is Ireland like that too?" I asked. "I know we're always fighting for environmental causes in America."

"The world is all alike. We point fingers and say that our country is better, but we're all fighting for the same issues."

"Are you sure you studied psychology and not political science?"

His smile came back and the shadows left his face. "Told you I was a nerd. Forgot to tell you I had a double major. And the environment is one of my hot-button issues."

I respected that. There was too little passion from the kids I knew, who were only focused on their country clubs and new fashion and social cliques. "That's a good one."

"What's yours?"

I stared at him, slowly realizing I was quick to judge others but I had no real passions myself. I'd never supported a particular charity or watched the news with a burning need to make a difference. I flushed hot with embarrassment, not wanting to tell him the truth. "I guess I'm not sure yet," I finally said.

"I have a feeling once you figure it out, you'll be a badass."

We smiled at each other and I relaxed. He wasn't judging me.

Our guide gathered our attention. "Ever hear of the phrase *red-light district*?" he asked.

Everyone nodded.

"The phrase has a long history that continued here. Red lights were set up to mark the open brothels and guide the travelers at night. Pompeii had an underbelly of many, er, interests of the erotic sort. Besides the red light, specific directions were carved into the road to guide men. I will show one to you over here."

He led us to the open door of a building and motioned to the etching in one of the stones.

A penis pointed straight toward the door.

There were titters and giggles as each person took their turn to study the drawing. Ian quirked a brow. "A unique compass," he said with a grin.

"Now, if you enter the building, you will find some paintings. Each of them was used as a catalogue or a type of menu for various offerings. *Signora*, I'd advise your son skip this one."

"Got it."

"Mom, what's that of?" Kai asked loudly, pointing down to the penis.

All the women in the group seemed to hold their breath. I wondered how Hana would get out of this one. Tell him to ignore it? Give him a distraction?

She waved a hand like it meant nothing. "Just a hot dog. It's pointed toward a restaurant so people could eat."

Dan let out a snort.

Kai nodded. "Cool."

"Let's check out this display over here," she said, leading her son deftly away from the brothel.

We smothered our laughter and stepped inside. Immediately, I was struck by the multiple murals on the walls of various couples in sexual positions. A man penetrated a woman from behind, his large penis on display. Two men were entwined together, lying on a bed. Many of the murals were faded and chipped, but the images were clear enough to see detail.

An ancient porn room. How fascinating.

Refusing to feel shy with Ian at my side, I took my time studying the images before going back into the hot sunshine. My mom shot me a look, her brow arched, but I refused to give her any reaction.

"They were a wild bunch," Nonni commented as I walked past. "But talented painters."

I laughed. I adored her sense of humor. "Are you okay in this heat?" I asked.

"Of course. I can barely see anything under this hat," she said, the floppy brim falling in her face. We'd brought extra water for her, but I was impressed with her endurance on the trip so far. Even Mary and Ray, the elderly couple, seemed comfortable on the long walk in thick humidity.

"Did you use enough sunscreen?" I asked her.

She tapped my nose in an affectionate gesture. "Yes, Mom. Just make sure you lather it on too, okay?"

The tour guide clapped his hands. "I will now take you to a beautiful picture site, so get your cameras ready. It's a bit of a walk."

We stood on a high ledge that overlooked the mighty volcano. Everyone posed for pictures, and we boarded the bus again for the next pit stop. Ian made a motion that I should grab an empty seat with him, so I took him up on the offer. Mom and Nonni gave me a look but sat together without protest.

"Thank God," he said in a low voice. "I've been sitting with Mom and she listens to those steamy romance novels on audio. I keep wanting to bleach out the images of what scene she's on."

I laughed and held up my Kindle. "I prefer Dean Koontz and Stephen King. What do you like to read?"

He dove into his backpack and took out a fabric-covered book. "Everything I can get my hands on. This one is Thomas Moore. It's called *Meditations*. He was a monk who ended up leaving the monastery and wrote down his thoughts on life and spirituality."

"Sounds intense. Is it good?"

He nodded thoughtfully. "Yeah. I like that it doesn't apply to a particular time in society, or target a specific generation or problem. It's just various revelations regarding the world and the spirit."

"Do you read a lot of self-help books too?"

"Sometimes. Depends on who's trying to give the help."

I enjoyed his sense of humor—it was clever. "Agreed. I guess you wouldn't consider *The Art of the Deal* a true self-help, then?"

He burst out in laughter. "Damn, you're funny. Are you sure you're still in high school? Or did you skip a grade?"

I tried not to blush. I never thought of myself as witty before, but a guy had never brought out that particular part of my personality. "Nah, I just like joking around. Are you looking forward to Capri?"

"Yeah, heard it's beautiful, especially the Blue Grotto. Not looking forward to the death-cliff drive, though. I'm a bit afraid of heights."

"I'll try to distract you."

"Thanks, but I already brought my rosary beads. Figured I'd go straight to the source for comfort."

I shifted in my seat and gave in to my curiosity. "You're really religious, huh? I mean, I'm just asking, not judging. I saw you in church praying, and the comments you've made and stuff." I hoped my tongue wasn't tangling over itself in ignorance, but he seemed chill and smiled at me.

"No, you can ask me anything you want. It's a part of my life, but some people get weirded out by religion."

I shrugged. "Not me. I think it's nice. My grandmother's Catholic, but Mom didn't raise me to be any religion. She said she wanted me to find my own path. When I took a few yoga classes, they talked a lot about spirituality, and finding your center and your breath, and I thought I'd like to know more about that."

He nodded. "Buddhism, like the Dalai Lama. Many yoga practitioners follow various yogis who they believe have been enlightened. I think belief in something better is necessary to lead a life worth living."

I'd never thought of it like that. I mulled over his words. "Are your parents Christian too?"

"I'm Roman Catholic, and yes. My parents grew up attending church every Sunday and I was in religious school for years to get my sacraments, like communion and confirmation. There are many denominations, like Protestant, Methodist, but many fall under the umbrella of Christianity. Catholic is a bit different—more strict, and we fall under the guidance of the Vatican. We follow the pope."

"I guess visiting St. Peter's was a big deal for you this week."

His blue eyes lit up. "It was a dream come true," he said simply. "Being in St. Peter's was like going home."

He spoke passionately but without judgment. I enjoyed being able to open up and be myself with him. "Maybe you can convert me," I joked. "There's plenty more churches coming up on the tour."

"Is it wrong that I'm just as excited for the mozzarella demonstration? I'm obsessed with the pizza here. What they call pizza in Ireland is a tragedy."

"New York comes in a close second. You'll have to visit me one day so you can compare."

"Deal."

The drive flew by. We chatted nonstop, talking in low voices as a lot of the group slept in their seats, soft snores echoing in the air. Sometimes, our bare thighs would brush when I changed position. The hair on his leg tickled a bit and brought a tiny dip in my belly. I was getting used to his freckles, and the lips I'd once thought too red for his pale skin now looked soft, especially when he smiled. I found myself studying his face more closely, fascinated by the angular lines and his sloping red brows.

Definitely not Prince Harry. But maybe that was okay.

CHAPTER SEVENTEEN

SOPHIA

THE MOMENT MY feet hit the ground, a powerful fist of emotion plowed through my gut. This time, it wasn't the ulcer or the growing source of unease inside my body I was worried about. No, this was the realization that I'd finally reached my destination—one I'd dreamed of since I was young.

The bus took us directly to a well-known travel spot to get the best pictures. I gazed out at the stunning view of my parents' birth city. Dusty brown buildings merged together and set off the calm bay, where various ships docked. Mount Vesuvius hung in a misty shroud in the distance. Enzo kept us entertained with lively stories of the stunning Sophia Loren, the local Napoli heroine, and tempted us with promises of the best pizza in the world. But I craved walking down the same streets my parents had, and steeping myself in the grit and scents of the city that was known for its Mafia crime, garbage, and rough exterior. This was the Naples my parents had told me about, along with the pleasures of a tight-knit community, hearty food, and architectural beauty sprouting from every corner.

We headed straight into the thriving heart of the city—Spaccanapoli, a famous street that split Naples into three sections that housed the old and the new. Enzo called the group together. "You will have two hours to explore and have lunch, so keep your eye on the time. We have a long travel day to Capri and we need to keep a tight schedule." He rattled off a few restaurants and Allegra typed them into her phone. "Those are guaranteed to have the best pizza, but my first choice will always be Sorbillo if there is not a big line. You will also want to hit the bakery and try the *babà*, *zeppole*, or *sfogliatelle*. You can get it to go." He gave his usual charming grin. "Now, get going and have fun. I am here for any questions. This is the Piazza Gesù Nuovo, where you can find me, and then I will guide us back to the bus. If you get lost, please text and I will get you."

"He's such a sweetie," I murmured to Frannie, still wishing she'd indulge in a romance or harmless flirtation. "I'm going to give him the biggest tip known to mankind."

"You do that, Mom," Frannie said with a patient smile. Her brown eyes shone with an emotion I hadn't glimpsed before, but Allegra's question gave me no time to probe.

"Hey, Nonni, is this the section where your mom and dad lived?"

"It is close. My mother lived in Quartieri Spagnoli, which is a working-class neighborhood. My father was from Vomero, which was a bit more for the middle class. They got married here and eventually moved to America, where I was born. There were many Italian families who lived in the neighborhood in Queens with us. We all became close."

"They were madly in love," Allegra said, with a spark in her eyes.

"Yes, they were," I said, patting her shoulder. I loved how my granddaughter was just as fascinated by the story of their love affair as I'd been. My father was extremely handsome, with piercing dark eyes, a trim mustache, and a slim figure. He towered like a giant at six-four, different from the average height of most Italian men. He met my mother in a café and told me about her yellow dress and how it twirled around her legs when she moved, and her dark hair that fell to her waist like a curtain of silk. After they married, they decided to move for something better. It was hard to make a good living in Naples, and they dreamed of America.

Every anniversary, my mother would don the yellow dress, my father a suit, and they'd put on music and dance in the small kitchen together to mark the day they fell in love.

I stopped walking, allowing the grief to pass through me. God, I missed them so much. It had been cruel to lose both of them so young. Fran turned toward me, not realizing I was thinking of an entirely different story. "So, it was like that when you met Daddy, right? You always said you knew very young you were going to marry him."

The past reared up in all its ugly beauty. I'd learned early on that there was no way to remove one piece from your life. Like a puzzle, the missing piece only caused a gaping hole and ended up incomplete. No, you had to take each piece and accept it in order to look at your journey with a clear vision of the whole. I'd made peace with my decisions a long time ago. I wasn't about to question them now.

But maybe it was time Frannie knew the girl I used to be. Before I became a mother and a wife.

"Yes, your father and I both knew we were meant to be married. But our story was different." I forced a thin smile. "You see, my parents died when I was only fifteen years old. They both got very sick with influenza. We called it the Asian flu at the time. It was sweeping fast across the US, and many people in our neighborhood fell ill. My parents died a week apart from each other."

Frannie stared at me with wide eyes. Shock flickered across her face. "Mom, I didn't know that. I knew your parents died, but I thought you were in your midtwenties and already married to Dad."

I shook my head. "It was a terrible time. Of course, I had no other family to go to, and my next-door neighbor was kind enough to take me in. Mrs. Ferrari welcomed me into her home with open arms. I'd already become friends with her son, and when I turned eighteen years old, we began to officially date."

"Daddy," Frannie breathed. "I thought you were friends from school."

"We were. I just never shared the details from before that. The rest is history. We got married, moved to Westchester when he opened up his housing business, and settled down."

The words felt sticky on my tongue, but they were technically the truth. How could I explain to my daughter what it was like to feel trapped? To experience pressure from the woman who'd saved me to marry her son and give him babies? The ripping failure when I was only able to conceive Frannie, so I put my very heart and soul into raising her, making sure I was the perfect mother, only to fail again . . . and again.

The voice drifted to my ears, faint but clear. *You never failed. Not me, or Frannie, or my mother. You were meant to be my wife, and I should have thanked you every day for agreeing. Instead, I took you for granted.*

My thoughts felt like pure betrayal, especially when his words thundered so clearly in my head.

Our roles had always been clear. You took care of the business, and I took care of the household. I loved you too—don't you ever doubt it.

But you never got to choose, did you?

"Nonni, are you okay?"

Allegra's voice jerked me back from my imaginary conversation with my dead husband. "Of course. Goodness, let's get going. We don't have much time to explore," I said, picking up my pace.

They allowed me to lead and asked no further questions. I was glad. There was too much rawness inside and I wanted to let it sit for a while.

We weaved in and out of the narrow cobblestone streets and fought for space in between the scooters shooting madly back and forth amid crowds of people. Tourists seemed to mingle with the residents, and I savored the everyday routine that took place before my eyes: shopping at the local markets and filling baskets with fruit, bread, and salty meats to cook for dinner; children playing ball, laughing and zigzagging in a game of tag, while rows of laundry dried on ropes that were strung up and down the streets like Christmas lights, flapping in the wind. It was alive—the Naples my mother had always described to me—and I savored every footstep and felt my mother's presence sinking into my soul.

We stopped at Sorbillo—one of the most famous pizzerias—and ate the most spectacular thin-crust pizza I've ever experienced. With buffalo mozzarella and only the most special of tomatoes and a light, crisp crust—the flavor and textures exploded in my mouth. Allegra groaned, and we got into a lively discussion of the specific ways the Neapolitans made pizza that could not be matched anywhere else in the world. She swore she'd come back and study the art before returning to dazzle Americans.

This time, Frannie didn't make any mocking comments about her being a chef one day. I was grateful—Allegra didn't need any further excuses to reject her mother's peace offerings.

"I'll be back. I have to go to the toilet," Allegra said, wiping her mouth and disappearing.

I sipped my water, still reeling from the culinary experience. Frannie propped her elbows up on the table and leaned forward. "Mom, I didn't realize you and Daddy kind of grew up together. It must've been hard to live with strangers at only fifteen."

I sighed. "Yes, it was, but I was grateful I had a place to go. Daddy's parents were wonderful to me."

She seemed to struggle with her next question. "Did you—did you ever question your relationship with Dad? Since you were so young? It seems like being in the same household would be hard."

And there was the heart of the problem. Did I tell her the truth or keep the lie to soothe my child? Did I give her a real piece of myself or allow her to believe the tale I'd spun to make things nice?

Right now, in Naples, I wanted to tell the truth.

"It was hard. As the years went by, his mother pushed us into a relationship that was more than friends. She had dreams of us getting married and having children and all of us living close by. Daddy and I fell into dating because it felt like the next natural step. We never dated anyone else and got married at twenty. Back then, women had few choices. We were meant to be mothers and homemakers, and our husbands were the ones to make the money and provide for the family."

Worry skated over her features, but this time, I didn't jump to soothe it. "I know you mentioned you wanted more children. How many miscarriages did you have, Mom?"

Too many. The grief and cut of loss were still brutal. "Four. You were my miracle child."

"I'm sorry," she said softly. Her eyes filled with an empathetic pain I'd never glimpsed before—not with me. "It must've been hard being so lonely with Dad working all the time. I never really thought of it that way. You never wanted to expand into a career? Go back to school? Do something else after I got older?"

My laugh was genuine. "Oh, honey, your father wouldn't have wanted that. He liked a hot meal on the table, a clean house, and knowing the bills were taken care of. His work schedule was too demanding for me to flit off and try to find a job that wouldn't even pay a quarter of his salary. We'd lived too many years with our roles to make a change. And what could I have done? I had no skills. I was afraid of technology. I couldn't even type! No, I made my peace with my choices a long time ago. I had my books and my garden and you. I had friends, and my church and charities. I had enough."

As I said the words, I realized it was the truth. Yes, I'd craved a houseful of children to spoil and pamper, but it wasn't meant to be. I found a way through the years to accept the losses, tucking the crippling wounds down deep in my soul and locking them away. I prayed for my lost babies every day. It may not have been the life I'd planned for, but it was a good one, and God had blessed me in many ways. And though Jack had died much too soon, I'd had Frannie, then Allegra to love.

It was enough.

Allegra came back to the table. We rose, and Frannie shocked me by stepping forward and giving me a big hug. After a second of hesitation, I hugged her back, savoring my child's sweetness and strength and a love that knew no boundaries in this life or beyond.

"I'm so happy we got to see Naples," she murmured in my ear.

"Me too."

And for the first time, I felt seen by my daughter. Woman to woman, standing by our choices and owning our journeys, both the good and the bad. My insides relaxed and my breath came lighter into my lungs. Knowing she understood me soothed the previous raw pain and I hugged her extra tight.

When we finally broke apart, Allegra was beaming. Then we all linked hands and used our last twenty minutes to hit Scaturchio pastry shop and buy a bunch of stuff for the trip to Capri—*babà*, a mushroom-shaped dough soaked in limoncello flavoring; *zeppole* filled with delicious custard and dusted with powdered sugar; *sfogliatelle*, a gorgeous almond pastry with flaky crust and filled with creamy ricotta cheese; and *ministeriale*, a dark chocolate medallion with a cream of ricotta, fruit, and hazelnut filling, and a dash of liqueur.

When we got back on the bus, I stared out the window as we pulled away from Naples and headed to Capri. I said a silent prayer to my parents and to Jack, grateful I was able to visit before I died and make peace with emotions I hadn't been able to face at home.

CHAPTER EIGHTEEN

FRANCESCA

THE MECHANICS OF reaching Capri were exhausting.

By the time my feet hit the top of the hill and entered the cool air of the hotel, I almost wept in relief. My clothes were wrinkled, I smelled, my muscles ached, and I had more blisters on my heels. It was like I was trapped in the movie *Planes, Trains and Automobiles*. After Naples, we'd taken a bus, then a boat, then a funicular up to the top of the mountain.

I'd hoped it was over, but Enzo had declared we needed to walk up one of the biggest, curviest hills I've seen. The group had all turned silent and a bit grumpy, even with the spectacular views and blinding colors of the famous island.

I just wanted my damn room with a big bed and a soft pillow.

I think I let out a whimper when Enzo handed me my key card. He flashed a grin, still looking rested and fresh, in his pressed pants, white cotton shirt, and straw hat tipped over his brow. How did the man do it? Did he ever get cranky? "The hard part is over, *signora*," he said with a twinkle in his eyes. "We're hosting a casual cocktail hour at seven tonight, but you have the entire evening to recover."

I felt ridiculous for complaining. I'd kept a close eye on my mother, who'd needed to rest a few times on the hike up the hill, but she'd made it. "Sorry, it's just been a long day. Why don't you look exhausted?"

"Because you all rely on me and a tired guide is not fun."

I couldn't help teasing him. "Are you fun all the time?"

"My sisters say I am not. When I return home, I shall sleep for a week and allow myself to say no to all favors and requests. But for now, your wish is my command."

"Like the genie in a lamp. Can you get me a clone to answer all my work demands?"

He quirked a brow. "Have you not explained to your partners you are on call for only emergencies?"

Guilt rose. I should have. Kate had insisted, yet I felt too many things would get screwed up without me involved. Was it the reality? Or only my ego? "I don't trust anyone else," I admitted. "I like to be in control."

He nodded in understanding. "So do I. But I have learned through the years on this job, people will always surprise me. I can plan and pretend I'm in charge, but many times, I need to surrender."

"Go with the flow?"

He frowned. "Sorry, I don't know that expression."

"Allow things to happen without fighting it."

"Ah, yes. Perhaps you can take a chance and try to pull back? Just for a few days and see what happens?"

"Maybe. But I have a feeling I'll still require a backup plan."

His grin was all male mischief. "Is it just work, or do you require a backup plan with your relationships too?"

I let out a snort. "More like an escape plan."

He laughed. "Clever girl. We are much alike."

"Afraid of marriage? Commitment? Or even worse?"

"What's worse?" he asked with interest. His cologne drifted around me and I wished I could bury my nose in his neck and sniff. Pheromones, maybe? Something about him just pulled me in.

"When you're not even scared of getting intimate. You just don't want to be bothered."

We both seemed startled by my confession. Why had that type of truth spilled out in the middle of a hotel lobby? I meant to shrug it off and say something funny, but his dark eyes turned serious and he took a step toward me, so we were inches away. My heart slammed against my chest. "Yes, *bella signora*. That is much worse. I find myself wondering too many times if there is a woman out there who could compete with my job—or even want to. I haven't found her yet. But it would be nice, just once, to have a choice." He paused. "Don't you agree?"

We stared at each other as the air shifted between us. I ached to touch him. Run my finger over his rough cheek and blunt nose. Trace the line of his lips. Step into his arms and be held tight. God, it had been so long since a man had held me or I'd experienced an intimate touch.

The question shook me to the core. Was I reading too much into this assumed connection? Was I so rusty I couldn't tell anymore between truth and lies? He probably acted like this with all women. He was charming enough to make me feel special, but I was a paying customer and his tip and review were critical to his job. I shrugged off the faint hurt and confusion, stepping back. My voice came out husky. "I don't know." The silence screamed volumes. "I better go."

The wall slammed between us, and once again, he was a complete professional, his gaze barely revealing any signs of interest. "Of course. I shall see you at seven, then?"

I nodded, and he'd already disappeared, swallowed up by the next group, who joked with him and asked him dozens of questions in a flurry. I walked over to Allegra. "Are you staying with Nonni again?"

I knew she'd been ignoring me and was pissed about my

missing dinner last night. I didn't blame her, but that awful Instagram video had put me into a full-fledged panic, so I'd called my team to have them monitor our social media pages, making sure I didn't get tagged and none of my clients discovered the video. Thank God, my daughter had been right. Within twenty-four hours, the views and shares had declined. I was no longer fresh material. Unfortunately, the damage had been done.

I was grateful she didn't respond with a smart-ass comment. "Yeah."

"Okay. I'll come to your door at seven and we'll have a quick drink, then go for dinner. Do you both need anything?"

Mom shook her head. "No, just a long nap."

I studied her face, which seemed a bit strained. "Mom, we can skip the drinks. I can even bring you some dinner if you want to stay in the room tonight? We did a lot of walking."

"Nonsense, I just need a bit of rest. No need to fuss."

Allegra's gaze was sharp, and she gave me a little nod, as if telling me she would keep an eye on her. Appreciation and a hint of regret warred within me. I'd wanted a child so badly but didn't want to give up my career. I'd been determined to have both and was lucky to have my mother to fill in the gaps to help raise Allegra. Somehow, though, as time passed, it'd been easier to sink back into work mode and let Mom take care of everything. Maybe it'd happened gradually—one missed dinner at a time. One less track meet or tennis match attended in order to meet a deadline. I was grateful to my mother, but if she hadn't been so willing to fill in all the spaces of my life, would I be feeling so distant from Allegra? Were my mother's many miscarriages part of the reason she'd wanted to take over my entire life? And now that I understood her more, did I even blame her? She'd had limited choices. It'd been easier to be angry and resentful when I felt like she'd had alternate paths in her life.

I pushed away my churning thoughts and went to my room. The next few hours passed in a whirlwind. I took a short nap, showered, and worked on my laptop. I'd be hearing back about a new pitch I was hoping to secure, and Kate knew to call ASAP once she got news.

I knocked on their door. "You look better," I told Mom. Her eyes weren't pinched and her skin had better color.

"I told you a nap works wonders."

"Honey, you look so pretty." Allegra was wearing a short yellow dress with white canvas sneakers. Her hair was twisted up and a few gentle waves fell to frame her face. My heart gave a lurch with sheer love. Her acne had cleared up, and her makeup was no longer plastered onto her face in an attempt to look older or more sophisticated. My baby was a young woman going into her senior year. When she went away to college, there'd be less time and less control of her schedule. I made a quick vow that I'd forgo work for the rest of the week. I'd let everyone do their job and focus on my daughter. Enzo was right—it was time to unwind and take advantage of this trip.

"Thanks." She gave me a tentative smile. "You too."

I beamed. I'd donned white capris and a feminine peach lace top. My white sandals had crisscross straps and flattered my calves. "Let's go dazzle some boys."

They laughed and we headed to the lounge on the first floor. Comfortable cream leather chairs and sofas were arranged around a beautiful mahogany bar. Leafy plants and glass tables accented the room, and the patio doors were flung open to a terrace. Most of the tour was already there and held drinks in their hands, gathering in small groups to chat.

I got Allegra a Coca-Cola in a glass bottle, and Mom and I had white wine. Bites of bruschetta and prosciutto-wrapped melon were passed around on platters, along with a selection of cheese and fruit with a variety of crackers. I grabbed a handful of grapes and greeted Dana and Steve.

"Darlin', I didn't know you had to climb Everest to enjoy the island," Dana drawled in her thick accent. "Sophia, how did you end up getting to the top before me?"

"I practiced my Jane Fonda every day," she said proudly. "Fran made fun of me, but it's come in handy."

"I declare, I'm saving money on my gym membership—send me the link to buy one." She fussed over Allegra's outfit and I admired her purple sleeveless jumpsuit and Steve's matching shirt. He was wearing a Stetson again, but this one was white. I wondered how many bags they'd had to pack in order to fit all the hats and jewelry they'd brought. "We're headed to a darling little restaurant that Enzo recommended for dinner. Come with us."

I hesitated, but Allegra and Mom seemed excited, so we agreed. Before long, Cherry and Laura asked to join us, and we all headed out after Enzo called in and managed to get us a revised reservation.

The evening was bright and lively, with crowds of tourists overflowing the shops and restaurants, soaking up the last of the sun. Our table was outside under a bright red awning, the spill of scarlet and fuchsia flowers bursting around us. I breathed in the scents of citrus, ordered a glass of champagne to celebrate my new resolve, and actually enjoyed the light chatter at the table.

We feasted on succulent prawns simmered in a seafood broth and on tender artichokes, and indulged in crusty bread with a light smear of real butter. Cherry entertained us with stories of their rescue farm and animal antics, and Dana battled back with tales of fashionable celebrities gone terribly wrong. Even though Steve was the only male, his droll comments made me laugh out loud. I was just about to order cappuccino when my phone began to vibrate. I ignored it for a while, but my purse kept letting out a low hum, and I began to get nervous.

With an easy smile, I stood up. "Be right back. Restroom."

I got lucky the other women didn't flock to accompany me, and I managed to scurry around to the front and find a sheltered corner to check my phone. Dammit. It was Kate. I quickly returned her call and vowed I'd tell her I was officially on vacation for the next few days and couldn't be disturbed.

"We have a huge problem," she said quickly. "Remember consumers didn't like the social media campaign?"

My heart beat faster. "Yes, but I fixed it before I left. He was happy with the revised ads."

"Not anymore. Now he wants to scrap the entire campaign—not just social media. He's insisting on a new option. Said our direction was too edgy."

I sucked in a breath. "Are you kidding? He told us that's what he wanted. Shocking. Sexy. Vintage Brooke Shields rolling around in front of the camera. We booked that new model who's hot right now."

"I know, but now he's panicking and changed his mind. He wants classy. Less skin and youth—more elegance and movie-star focused. He nixed the hip-hop music."

My brain began clicking furiously for other options. "Okay, get me all the notes and I'll find time to brainstorm in the next few days. Tell Perry we can get him a new plan on Monday."

"Fran, it's too late. He wants it in twenty-four hours. Said he needs to make a decision ASAP."

My breath felt trapped in my lungs. "Did you tell him I'm away?"

"Yes, but I told him you were on call and we'd give him what he needs. Let me pull in a few team members and pull an all-nighter if we need to. Adam and Layla can step up. I have some rough ideas—we can sketch some out and I'll get them to you for approval."

"No." With a growing dread, I realized I had to do it. I couldn't lose this account just because I'd decided to spend a few weeks in Italy. I knew exactly how to deliver a new campaign Perry would love, but I needed hours in a room alone with my laptop. Already, my mind spun with the possibilities now that I had to switch gears. "I'll do it, Kate. You don't know the jeans market and I need you full-time on the Lexi account. I can get it done with the time difference. You'll have it in the morning."

"Fran, this is ridiculous—let me get back to you. Sarah is fabulous with pivoting on a deadline and she's got great ideas."

She was right. Sarah was excellent. But she wasn't me. She didn't know Perry's quirks, or his sense of humor, or that he favored blondes over brunettes and curves over skinniness. The jeans market was cutting-edge and there was no time to get her up to speed when I could do it myself and execute it perfectly. "I'll need you to pitch it for me, Kate. Once I get you the campaign, it's up to you and Layla to sell it. Do you understand?"

She hesitated, but both of us knew the decision had already been made. "Of course. I'm here if you need to shoot any ideas back and forth."

"Thanks, I will."

I hung up and took a deep breath.

I was screwed. Somehow, I needed to get back to my hotel room and work all night, and I didn't want Allegra or Mom to know. It would cause even more tension between us, and I didn't have time to fight or feel guilty. Best to fake a headache and get out of here as quickly as possible.

Mustering my courage, I headed back to the table. Dessert menus had been passed around and hot steam ascended from the coffee mugs. "Mom, do you want to split a tiramisu?" Allegra asked. "Nonni wants the lemon tart, so I'm going to share that with her, but I kind of want both."

I put my fingers to my temple and gave a weary smile. "Sweetheart, I'm so sorry. I have to go back to the room. I've been fighting a headache all day, but it's heading into migraine territory and I don't want to ruin our day tomorrow."

"We can skip dessert and walk back with you," Mom said with concern.

"No, it's a crime to miss dessert. Stay and enjoy. I just need some sleep and Advil—I'll be fine."

Everyone murmured their apologies, offering various solutions from a cold compress to hanging upside down to reverse blood flow to the head, but all I could focus on was my daughter's face.

She knew. Or she suspected. A simmering anger shot from her gaze, but I'd seen her temper many times and that didn't bother me. No, it was the hurt. As if I'd managed to trick her after she gave me a second chance.

If only I had time to make her understand. But I didn't. I would later. Right now, I needed to get to work.

Blowing kisses at the table, I spun around quickly and walked back to the hotel. I settled in front of my laptop, put in my earbuds for some music distraction and to help stir my creativity, and began to outline bullet points for the new proposal.

I'm not sure how long someone was knocking before the sound finally penetrated my music and work trance. I shook my head to clear it and opened the door.

"How's your headache?" Mom asked.

Shit. I blinked and moved to block the entrance to my room so she couldn't see my computer. "Better. I was lying down. How's Allegra?"

"Upset." My mother's steady dark gaze drilled into mine. "I need to talk to you for a minute."

"Um, can we talk in the morning? I really need to—"

"Now." She pushed past and walked in with a maternal authority I knew well. I meekly shut the door behind me. I was too tired and stressed to fight. I'd let her yell and I'd deal with the fallout tomorrow. "I see the Advil worked quickly. Unless work is a cure for migraines?"

I glared at her with frustration. "Fine, I had a huge disaster at work and need to get it straightened out. We spent the whole day together and I only left for dessert. Why can't you understand?"

A sigh escaped her. "Frannie, this isn't about me. It's about Allegra. How do you think she feels knowing you lied to her? You promised this trip would be an opportunity to strengthen your relationship, but so far, you've managed to steadily disappear in our very first week."

"I'm trying. If I don't deliver this new campaign by the morning, I'm going to lose an important client. This is the last time. I'll tell Kate and Layla after this to keep me out of the loop."

"Until the next supposed catastrophe. If you believe that, you're lying to yourself and us."

I paced the room like a caged animal. "Fine, Mom, you win. I'm a terrible mother. An awful daughter. A selfish workaholic who only cares about success. Feel better now?"

I wanted her to yell back at me. I despised my juvenile tirade, but my temper was frayed and I desperately needed an outlet for all this pent-up emotion. I craved a good old-fashioned fight where I could walk away feeling superior and wronged. But she faced me with a calm expression, her hands open and upward in a plea.

"You are none of those things," she said softly. "But I'm watching you slowly fall apart in front of me and I can't take it. I know you were always closest to your father, and we've had our moments, but you're my daughter. You and Allegra are my life. How can I make you understand how badly she needs you right now?"

My heart squeezed from the painful impact of her words. "I'm right here! But she doesn't want to talk to me—not like she talks to you. Whether it's school or boys or friends or college, she blocks me at every turn and shuts me out. Work is the only outlet where I don't feel like a failure, okay?" I continued to pace and let the words bubble out of my mouth. "She's going to leave and live her own life and shut me out. If I let my business fail, I'll be left with nothing."

"Your business will not fail if you take some time off or institute some balance and allow others to help you. I hate to break this to you, my love, but your father found this out too late. He kept pushing for one last deal, one more year before retirement. And then it was too late because time had gotten the last laugh."

I shook my head hard. "Dad loved what he did. I never resented his work. Not like you did."

Pain etched lines on her face. "You don't remember? How angry you were when he couldn't see your school play or your soccer tournament? How about the honor society induction or when you won the first-place ribbon in the science fair? Or the daddy-daughter weekend camping trip?"

The memories were foggy. I'd never questioned his responsibilities and limitations. My mother's role had always been clear. "I didn't blame him."

"What about me, Frannie? Did you blame me?"

I jerked. "Of course not. That makes no sense."

She turned around so I couldn't see her reaction. "Sometimes, children can't make sense of how they feel. You were always angry with me. Resentful that I was the one to show up at all your activities, or sit with you at dinner every night, or tuck you into bed. Your father was a great man, and you revered him. It was easier that way, I think. Easier to blame me for missing him."

I stiffened. There were so many things I disagreed with my

mother about, especially her choice to do nothing on her own beyond staying home to raise me, even when I was in high school. Her life revolved around her family, and when that family was gone, she'd been left alone. I didn't want that for myself. I identified so much better with my father—who was driven by ambition to succeed and work he was passionate about. His identity was more than another person to love. When he came home, he brought a bigger-than-life joy to the house, and even if I only had him for an hour, that hour was pure magic. He played hard and talked about important subjects and made me feel special. He'd take me on car rides for ice cream alone, and we'd discuss any random topic in full detail while he listened raptly and gave me advice that was always spot on. And my mother?

She was the one left behind to deal with the boring day-to-day stuff. The one I argued with and blamed when something went wrong. The one faithfully sitting in the darkened audience alone, to watch me, even though I craved my father's presence. But I reasoned he was doing bigger and better things and that his absence was actually a sacrifice. Mom had no excuses—her entire existence revolved around me.

Had I punished her for such a choice?

She kept speaking as my mind raced in circles. "Allegra pushes you away because she wants more time with you but is unable to express it. It's easier with me. I'm her grandmother."

"You were the one to help raise her. She loves you."

"And she loves you. Mother-daughter relationships are complicated, but this is an important time in her life. She's looking for you to support her even if you don't agree. Or at least listen."

"I try."

"Try harder."

I let out a breath and paced faster. "Like being a chef? Did you put that idea in her mind?"

"No, but she loves cooking and I think it's great she's passionate about something."

"She has straight As and she's bound to get a scholarship and do something important with her life. I don't want her cooking food for people."

A tiny laugh left her lips. "Who cares, if that's what makes her happy? The CIA only accepts top-rated students. That's where she's thinking of going."

I stopped in my tracks. "She told you that?"

"Yes. She also told me she's frustrated about not having a father and that you dodge the subject when she tries to bring it up."

Hurt shattered through me. "That's not true," I practically whispered. "She asked me a bunch of questions when she was younger, and I explained everything."

"That doesn't close the subject forever. She's older now and wants to know more about your choice to have a baby on your own."

"So she can judge me and fault my decision like you did?"

It was too late to take back the words. They'd already been uttered. She gave a tiny jerk, and I knew she remembered that night. I'd announced my plan to get pregnant, and she'd stared at me in horror, then begged me not to go through with it. I'd come to the choice after a long, hard decision, and hearing my mother list all the reasons it was a terrible idea had shaken my foundation. "I had my reservations for a good reason," she said with a lifted chin. "Was it wrong for me to wish you'd fall in love and get married? You set these goals, and if they don't work out on time, you lose patience."

"I didn't want my ticking biological clock to color my idea of a relationship," I shot back hotly. "Too many women want to have a child so badly, they marry the wrong guy because they refuse to wait any longer. I could have ended up divorced and miserable. What's wrong with taking my fate in my own hands?"

"Nothing. Allegra was worth it. I'm just saying your need to control all aspects of your life is difficult on the ones who love you." Her shoulders slumped as if the fight had drained out. "If you keep rushing to douse every fire that happens at the company, you'll never end up with a solid team to back you up."

"And if they fail? I could lose a client and a lot of money."

"There will be other clients and a lesson learned. Sometimes, people have to fail to get stronger. Have you won every account you pitched?"

"Of course not."

"Why should you put these expectations on everyone else? Kate and Layla are capable, but I'm sure you insist on being involved. I wanted us to take this trip so we could be closer. Get a fresh slate and return home strong. Allegra needs you, Frannie. There're some hard choices ahead of her, and a young girl can get lost."

Annoyance flickered. "I will always take care of my daughter. She's going through a tough age and isn't comfortable talking to me. Didn't I go through something like that?"

"Yes, but even if you didn't want to talk, I made sure I was available. Allegra needs you to choose her. Just like you always wished with your dad." I let the words sink in and she walked to the door. "Think about it. I'll see you in the morning."

She left.

I turned around and gazed at the empty room. Memories of my beloved father took hold. Mom had teased the hornet's nest, and I remembered waiting anxiously for him to return home from work trips, or staying up late to catch a good-night kiss. It became harder as I got older, but one of my most treasured images was his face beaming out from the audience during my high school and college graduations. I thought of the simmering resentment toward my mother for her consistent intrusion on my privacy, of her endless questions and constant doting. I had wanted my daughter to have freedom. I wanted to be the mother I dreamed of having, and yet somehow, I'd lost both of those roles along the way.

Exhaustion shook me in its grip. I longed to close my eyes and not think, but I had a job to finish and the hours were ticking away. I needed to work. I'd sort through everything later.

It was five a.m. when I unfolded myself from my desk and took a shower. I'd stolen an hour or two of rest throughout the night, but the revised proposal was complete. We weren't due for breakfast for a few hours, but I was craving coffee, so I threw on yoga pants and a black T-shirt, ran my fingers through my hair, and made my way down to the lobby.

Only a few stragglers sat at the coffee bar, so I ordered a cappuccino and brought it outside. The terrace was empty, and the tables and chairs held a sheen of rainwater. I strolled down the short path and into a small garden. The scents of damp earth and lush blooms filled the air. Birds serenaded in sweet tunes. The sun eased upward into the sky for the start of a new day. I sipped my coffee and thought about my decisions along the way, and what my mother had told me, and if I had made more wrong choices than right. I wondered if my insistence on doing this job myself centered around my fear not only of failure but of not being important enough. I imagined Allegra slipping further away, until the tentative thread that kept us together snapped, leaving me utterly alone.

Like my mother.

This time, the attack came on hard and fast. There was no time to try to regulate my breathing or think happy thoughts. Immediately, my chest seized and drove the breath from my lungs. My heart slammed against my chest in a pounding rhythm, and I began to shake, my vision blurring as pure terror pulsed through me. A sound ripped from my throat. The cup dropped out of my hands and shattered. I bent over, gasping for breath and sanity.

Strong hands wrapped around me. A palm pressed against my racing heart, and a masculine voice whispered in my ear in a low command. "You are okay, Francesca. All you need to do is breathe. I've got you."

I wheezed out some type of answer and clutched at his hand.

"Breathe in to the count of five. One-two-three-four-five. Good, very good. Breathe out to five. One-two-three-four-five. You're doing great, nice and slow. Again."

Over and over, he repeated the count, praising me, his warm strength slowly allowing my chest to loosen and air to rush into my lungs. He never hurried his tone or his pace, and finally, my shaky legs began to hold me. My heartbeat slowed. Eyes closed, I resurfaced and realized his palm cupped my breast, and my fingers were entwined tight with his.

Oh. My. God.

He realized the moment I became aware of our position, and slowly pulled away. But his gaze remained locked on mine, burning with intensity, and my heart began to race again for an entirely different reason. I swallowed hard. "I'm sorry. I-I don't know what happened."

A concerned frown creased his brow. "Have you never had a panic attack?"

"No, I have. I mean, it's only happened a few times before, but I don't know why now. I was just drinking my coffee alone."

He nodded. "Sometimes these attacks happen randomly. Stress or fatigue could be key. Have you slept?"

I shook my head. "Had to work all last night."

"Ah yes, that would do it."

"Do you suffer from them too?" I asked tentatively.

"No, but my sister does. It was difficult for her, but she began to learn her triggers and how to handle them better."

The situation struck me full force and I turned away, embarrassed. I was a mess. This trip was supposed to help me relax and put the attacks behind me. Instead, I'd suffered two of them in the first week, and Enzo had witnessed my breakdown. I couldn't seem to handle anything at the moment—whether it be work or my daughter or even trying to let go and have fun in Italy.

"I'm sorry about the cup," I said, ducking my head. "I'll clean it up. I didn't mean to bother you—I had no idea you were even here."

"Francesca." My name drifted in my ear on a soft whisper. His fingers touched my shoulders and turned me gently around. "Don't worry about the cup. I saw you come into the garden and followed you to say good morning. You could never bother me."

I lifted my head. The air stirred between us. "Thank you for helping me."

"You can talk to me. I hate to see you unhappy during this trip. Is there something bothering you? Work?"

I tried to make a joke. "Don't worry, it's not your fault. I'll still tip big."

He didn't laugh or flash his usual mischievous grin. "I'm asking as a friend, not a guide."

And then I knew there was something more between us, and it wasn't just me. Relief and a sweet rush of happiness filled me at his words. I didn't analyze or try to label what I was experiencing—whether it be a flirtation or crush or something more. I just spilled out the truth.

"I got a call from the office last night and I lied to Allegra. Told her I was sick and left dinner early so I could return to the hotel. She figured it out and got upset. Then my mother came to talk to me, and it became this whole big thing about how I'm going to lose out on a relationship with my daughter because I make the wrong choices. You know the truly awful part?"

"What?"

"I think she's right. I know I use work as a crutch when things get difficult at home. Instead of fighting for Allegra to talk to me, or pushing through the wall, or carving out some time, it's so much easier to fall back on my career. What type of mother does that make me? I always resented my own mother for being there all the time and never wanted to be like her. Now? I'm wondering if I've been wrong the entire time and I screwed up my daughter's life."

Relief swept through me. It felt so good to talk to someone. I rarely opened up, but with his body heat pulling at mine and his gaze trained on my face while he listened, there was a bond that had grown between us.

"You cannot screw up someone's life by loving them," he said. He lifted his hand and cupped my cheek with a natural intimacy. My breath practically sighed through my lips at the contact, and his delicious scent swam around me. "I have watched my sisters rage and cry at my mama many times. There were even days or weeks when they did not speak for a while. But eventually, the bond between them was too strong to break by distance or stubbornness. Allegra is young and finding herself. And, yes, maybe you made some bad decisions, but you are not supposed to be perfect. I think your mama was trying to tell you to use this trip to see if you can mend some of those broken pieces, no?"

"Maybe. I think I have control issues."

His laugh was as warm as his fingers on my bare skin. "*Sì*, this has served you well in the past, especially at work. But maybe you can use the next two weeks to experiment. Italy is your playground, and I am here to guide you. When was the last time you let go and didn't worry?"

"When I was in elementary school," I said.

"Then it is time you give it another try, no? Do these attacks usually center around work problems?"

I thought over the past three attacks. "Yes, they all tied back to something I had to do for the company but worried about delivering on."

"Can you arrange coverage for a few weeks? Get yourself off being on call unless it's a true emergency?"

I hesitated. "Yes, I want to. But I may end up losing a client."

His eyes held a serious glint. "Maybe you need to lose something in order to prove it will all be okay. That is what I tell my sister. She's a top assistant over at Gucci. Ambitious. Smart. Her motto is 'failure is not an option.' She reminds me of you."

I smiled. "Yeah, I know that motto quite well."

"I think we get what we need even though at the time we don't understand. For instance, without those panic attacks, my sister wouldn't have learned to balance things or look after her health. It was a bad thing that led to a good thing. Maybe this is happening to give you a chance to change some things."

"My mom said the same thing. But somehow, you don't make me feel like a screwup."

"Because I'm not your mama." His eyes lit with mischief and he stroked my cheek. The gesture made my breath lock. "I'm a neutral party."

He didn't feel very neutral right now. His gaze dropped to my lips, and I wanted to rise on my tiptoes and kiss him. It had been too long since I kissed a man in a passionate impulse, and he must've caught my intention because his eyes darkened to a deep obsidian and he lowered his head an inch and—

Pulled me into his arms. Tucking my head against his shoulder, he held me tight and pressed his lips to my temple. My mind whirled as it tried to figure out why he'd made the move, but then I sank into the bliss of a man's embrace and let go.

His hard chest cradled my cheek, and he whispered my name softly. My muscles loosened and melted into his muscular body. Seconds ticked by and we didn't move. I just closed my eyes and savored every breath, trying to memorize the imprint of his male figure so I could recall it in my dreams.

Slowly, he peeled himself away, inch by inch. I expected to feel awkward, but he looked at me and smiled, and I smiled back. It was at that moment I realized everything between us had changed.

I was glad.

He walked me back to the hotel lobby. "I'll see you at eight for breakfast," he said. "Try to rest. We have a big day to see the Blue Grotto."

I raised a brow. "Do you realize this is the fourth time you've commanded me to sleep or rest up?"

"Tour guide responsibilities," he said. "I go at a fast pace and I want to make sure you feel good."

The moment the words were uttered, a dark red flushed his cheeks. I laughed, but my body tingled at the idea of him making me feel good in many intimate ways. Most of them didn't revolve around *fast*. "Enzo, I do believe you're blushing."

He shook his head and turned, but I caught his grin. "I knew you'd be trouble the moment we met. Drink plenty of water. Your body needs it."

He walked away. I returned to my room, but rest eluded me.

All I could think about was the sweetness of his embrace, and I wondered when we could do it again.

CHAPTER NINETEEN

ALLEGRA

I DIDN'T GET much sleep last night. Besides Nonni snoring, I kept thinking about Mom and how she lied right to my face. I'm not sure why this was the time that bothered me the most—she'd been ditching me for work my whole life—but I honestly felt betrayed. Like she told me straight up she was going to try harder, and then the moment the office calls her, she jumps.

I shouldn't have believed her in the first place.

I promised myself for the rest of the trip, I'd keep her at a distance. It was the best way. Better not to expect anything and be surprised if it worked out.

David had finally Snapchatted, with Freda and Connor. We messaged back and forth for a while and they sent pics of him playing onstage. I noticed the tons of girls surrounding him, and he'd managed to book another gig at the same place. Freda said they'd found a supplier and were able to get a steady supply of weed, and that the Jersey beach town was kick-ass and cool.

The anger and frustration at what I was missing hit me hard. I'd lost the opportunity to bond with David, and even though I was enjoying Italy more than I thought I would, Mom had managed to dump me again. Maybe I should just concentrate on my grandmother. I'd study the food and art and come home a more well-rounded version of myself.

I was polite at breakfast and refused to let my mom see that

I was hurt. I hated that Nonni looked sad as she studied both of us. Mom was hurting her too; she just didn't realize it. The thought of the three of us staying in Tuscany for a week made me want to scream. I decided then I'd try to bail early, even if I had to fake an illness. The tour was enough. I refused to watch her work while Nonni and I tried to pretend it was okay.

We reached the marina and climbed onto the boat for our tour around the island. I'd hoped Ian would ask to sit with me again, but he spent the morning with his parents. I heard them laughing and joking around. Must be cool to feel so close to both parents. I'd never know.

When the boat cut its way through the water to head toward the Blue Grotto, I was struck by the vivid colors of blue ocean and sky, giant white yachts and earthy rocks spurting out in various twisted shapes. Droplets of water misted my face as we made our way around the island. In my peripheral vision, I spotted Ian whispering something to his mother, and then he was walking over to me with a smile. Dressed in white shorts, a blue polo shirt, and old sneakers, he looked comfortable yet confident. As if he was happy in his own body. His ginger hair was mussed from the wind and his blue eyes sparkled as bright as the sea. The freckles didn't bother me as much anymore. I was getting used to them and they seemed to fit with his face.

He leaned against the rail next to me. "Hey. How was your night? What'd you do?"

"Just went to dinner. How about you?"

"Same, but we stopped at the bakery afterward for some *torta caprese.*"

"What's that?"

"Think dark chocolate tart with almonds. I think Mom cried."

I laughed. "It may make me cry too. I'll have to try it."

"After the grotto I heard we're doing the death drive. Mom

swore to sit by me and hold my hand with a barf bag. I think I may skip it and go back to the hotel."

I stared at him in surprise. "Ian, you can't! We're going to the top of the mountain and it's supposed to be spectacular. You'll regret skipping it."

He wrinkled his nose. "I know. I'm afraid I'll freak out on the bus, though. I was okay on the plane ride and even the funicular, but the idea of hugging the edge of a cliff terrifies me."

"I promise I can get you through it. I'll distract you."

He looked into my face and I caught a flare of emotion that made my stomach clench in a good way. "You don't need to babysit me, Allegra. I don't want to ruin the experience for you."

"You won't." I crossed my arms in front of my chest with determination. "Just trust me. Okay?"

We stared at each other for a while, and then he grinned, reaching out to tug my ponytail. "I can't believe I'm saying this, but okay. I trust you."

Joy burst through me. Funny, it'd only been a few days, but I knew when Ian gave his trust, he meant it. I had an instinct he was honest in everything he did, which made the trust go both ways. I didn't want to be on the top of the mountain without Ian. It wouldn't be the same.

We passed by three towering rock formations off the coast and the boat stopped. Enzo motioned behind us. "This is the Faraglioni rock formations," he said, sweeping his hand in the air. "That one is Stella, the one in the middle is Faraglione di Mezzo, and the smallest is Scopolo. There is a fourth stack down that way called Monacone. Now, our captain will be taking us around and straight through this famous archway. I advise you to find someone you love and give them a kiss as we sail under," he said with a wink. "It is good luck. If you are not with your loved one, pick someone you like—we never want to leave an opportunity for good luck behind."

The boat restarted and sailed around the jagged formations, the clay-colored stone catching the light and giving the rock a glossy sheen. Lavish villas dotted the coastline along with various caves, and I caught a few people sitting on rocks and waving at us.

The boat cut smoothly through the waters, and everyone gave a cheer as we passed under the arch. Nonni turned and gave me a big smack on the cheek, and I laughed and moved the other way and found myself a few inches away from Ian.

I froze. His lips quirked in a half smile, and my heart pounded like crazy as he leaned over and kissed my cheek. His lips were soft and he smelled clean, like soap and lemon. A shiver raced down my spine. "For luck," he whispered close to my ear, and then he pulled away and the moment was over.

The boat sailed farther down the coastline and we passed sleek million-dollar yachts. I craned to see if there were any celebrities or people I recognized, hoping to snap a pic, but Ray mentioned most of them were probably rich CEO types, which was boring.

Enzo called us to attention. "We're about to enter one of the most famous caves of all time. The grotto was originally used as a marine temple during the reign of Tiberius, but then rumors began to spread that demon spirits inhabited it. Sailors avoided the cave until a fisherman, a German author, and a painter visited in 1826 and spread the story about its magical glowing waters, and it became a popular tourist destination."

"What makes the water glow?" Cherry asked.

Enzo cocked his head. "Magic."

Everyone laughed. "If you want the technical answer, sunlight enters the cavern at a precise point under the cave's mouth.

As the light passes through, red reflections are filtered out and only the blue remain. Tiny bubbles cause the light to give it a silvery effect. You will fill up the rowboats four at a time and they will take you into the cave. Watch your step, please."

We transferred to small, narrow rowboats one at a time. I held Nonni's hand while Mom held the other as we got her into the boat. We sat in a line, our legs outstretched and straddling the person in front. The bottom was wet and moisture seeped through my shorts.

We circled around until the other passengers loaded and then headed toward the tiny hole in the cave.

Holy crap, it was small. How were we going to—

"Heads down!" the rowboat operator yelled.

We ducked and the boat shot through the narrow opening. When I straightened up, I caught my breath.

An eerie glow shone and rippled from the blue-green still waters in the cave, lighting up the darkness. The rock walls surrounded us in a tight embrace, and then the utter silence was filled with a rising song as the operators all began to sing together. The beautiful notes of Italian echoed and danced while the boat cut quietly through the water. I put my hand out and touched the water, which was cool and silky. My fingers underneath glowed.

The moment was brief but powerful, and soon we ducked down again and shot back out of the cave into the bright sunlight. I blinked and tapped Nonni on the shoulder. "Are you good?"

She twisted her head around. "Heck yes, I'm good! I almost cried when they started singing. Except my butt is soaked. I'm going to look like I had an accident all day."

I laughed. "It's so hot we'll dry in no time. Or I'll say your Depends leaked."

She gave me a playful swat. "Hold your tongue—I'm not there yet."

I gave her a hug from behind. When we reboarded the boat, everyone was chattering with excitement about the experience. Mom came over, her eyes giving me that pleading look I knew so well. "What did you think, sweetheart? Wasn't it beautiful?"

I nodded. "Yep. Did you check your phone when we were in the cave? Or did it not have Wi-Fi?"

Her face fell, and I hated the guilt that flooded me. "That's not fair," she said softly. "I'm sorry I lied about having a headache. I didn't want you to be angry, and there was a crisis. I already called Kate and told her no more emergencies. It's not going to happen again."

"There's always a crisis, Mom. I wouldn't care except you dragged me on this stupid trip and swore you weren't going to work. It's not just me either. This is Nonni's trip. How much time have you spent with her, huh?"

She flinched, but I didn't want to get into it now. Not on the boat surrounded by people. I moved away and spent the rest of the trip talking to Hana and Kai. When we reached the marina, we transferred to a small bus that would take us to the top of the mountain in Anacapri. I tapped Nonni on the shoulder. "I'm going to sit with Ian."

"Okay, sweetheart." Her eyes danced. "Have fun."

I shot her a warning look and went toward the back, where Ian was waiting for me. His parents sat in front of us and Rosemary swiveled around to hand him a paper bag. "Use this if you're sick. Oh, I have mints! They help with nausea. Just close your eyes and think of a happy place," she counseled, her face worried.

Ian groaned. "Really, Mom? I don't have a happy place. I'm not two. And I'll be fine."

Patrick shook his head. "Rose, give him a break. Nothing's going to happen—they do this tour a hundred times a day and I've never heard a news report of losing a tourist. Allegra will distract him."

I smiled at his dad, loving his thick Irish brogue. "We got this."

Enzo stood at the front of the bus with a broad grin. "Okay, we are headed up Monte Solaro to the top. You will have the option of doing the chairlift when we get there, and have lunch on your own. There are many beautiful shops and cafés, and you will have plenty of time to explore. In order to get there, we will be using the Mamma Mia road. Does anyone know why it's called that?"

"Because we can't use any curse words?" Ray shouted out.

Enzo laughed. "Correct. There are no guardrails, and the road is very narrow, so most people shout out, 'Mamma mia!'— the ultimate curse in Italian. If you are brave enough to look, it is a beautiful sight to behold, but if you are nervous, just remember I've never lost a tourist."

"Told you," Patrick said.

Ian groaned. "I hope you have a plan for talking me off this literal cliff," he said.

"Hey, that was clever."

"Thanks."

His smile was weak, but it was still there. The bus lurched forward, and then we shot off into the road and began the drive. "Tell me about Ireland," I prompted, both from curiosity and to keep him talking. "Where do you live?"

He looked past me through the window as if anticipating the worst. "In Kildare."

"That doesn't help me at all, dude. I've never been to Ireland. Tell me what it's like."

"Oh, sorry. Hmm, okay, it's a beautiful city close to Dublin. Lots of green like you'd expect, but we have a nice village filled with quaint shops and restaurants. We live close to the Curragh racetrack, so we're big racehorse fans."

"That's cool. I've only seen the Triple Crown on TV, so I don't know much about it."

"I like to go out to the farms and watch the young horses train—see the new colts when they're born. Watching a race always gives me goose bumps. There's something wild and free about watching a horse run the track."

"Do you own a horse?"

"No, I wish I did. We have dogs and cats, though."

Rosemary turned around again. "He brings home all the rescues to take care of. My goodness, the boy will pick up any homeless stray with no thought. And that includes people."

"Rose, leave them alone. Here, listen to your Kindle. I thought you were at the good part," his dad said.

"Oh, I am. Beau and Daisy are pretending to be married, but I think they're going to shag tonight."

Ian turned his gaze upward. "Lord, please help me."

I giggled. "Rose, can I borrow that book when you're done?"

"Absolutely, love. Men just don't understand." She winked and put her earbuds in.

The bus turned a sharp curve, and suddenly it felt like we were hanging in a free fall, the cliff drop hugging the wheels. I relished the sight of jagged rocks, blue sea, and tiny dots of houses scattered along the hillside. It was straight from a postcard. Ian's skin tone turned slightly greenish, so I amped up my plan. "Where are your rosary beads?" I asked him.

"Huh?"

I pointed to his backpack. "Your talisman. Rosary beads. Do you have them?"

"Oh, yeah." He reached down and pulled out a simple brown set of beads with a cross hanging at the bottom. "What if another car passes? It could bump us right over."

The idea made my chest tight, but I needed to be the strong one. "The drivers know what they're doing. I'm surprised you don't have roads like this in Ireland."

"None that I've been on." He gripped the beads and rolled his fingers around them. "You must think I'm such a nerd."

"I *know* you're a nerd, silly. And we're all afraid of something. Tell me about your animals at home. I always wanted a dog, but my mom refuses. Says animals are messy and too much work."

"They are, but worth every second. There are a lot of homeless dogs and cats in our area. When I find a stray, instead of bringing it to an overcrowded shelter, I try to give it a home. Most animals are like children—they want to love and trust but they're dependent on good people."

I thought of all the abuse cases I heard about and shuddered. "How can anyone hurt an animal? Don't you think there's too much evil in the world?"

"There is. I just believe the good outweighs the evil. That's my job here—to try and even the playing field one day at a time."

The bus hit a pothole and shook. A quick glance at the window showed we seemed to be at the height of Mount Solaro, looking down on the entire world. "We're almost in the clear. How do you use those things?"

He unclenched his fingers. "Each bead is a prayer. You start with the Our Father right here, and then say ten Hail Marys." His thumb pressed against the break in the string. "Then you start over again until all the beads have been used."

"What does it do?"

"It's a meditative device for a lot of people. A way to calm and clear the mind. For me, I find it a powerful tool. I call it my weapon of prayer."

I fingered the beads, fascinated by the explanation. "Give me an example."

"Well, last year there was a little girl in our town who had an accident. She was in a coma and doctors said she was almost guaranteed not to wake up. If she did, there'd be extensive brain damage. She was only six years old."

"How awful."

"Yeah, it was a hard time for the community. A group of us from church started a prayer chain and did the rosary for her every day for two weeks. She woke up on the fifteenth day. And she had no brain damage—the doctors called it a miracle."

"Do you think the rosary healed her?"

"Yeah, I really do."

"What if she hadn't woken up? Would you say then the rosary didn't work?"

He cocked his head. "Good question. If it didn't work, I would have accepted it was God's plan. But I do believe that prayer is powerful and the more you talk, the more God listens. The more I believe, the more amazing things I witness."

The passion in his words rang clean and pure. "Isn't it hard to believe in something when there's so much bad happening all the time?" I asked.

"We all believe in something. I lean on my faith to navigate through life."

"Then how come you're so scared of this road when you have your beliefs and your rosary?"

He laughed and shook his head. "Damn, you're good at challenging me. You'll set the world on fire one day, Allegra."

"You didn't answer the question," I said teasingly, my cheeks flushed with pleasure at his compliment.

"Because I'm not perfect. I still doubt. And I don't think I could have done this without you, so maybe you're my good-luck charm."

At that moment, a car veered around the blind curve and swooshed past the bus. It seemed like barely an inch of space remained between the vehicles, causing our bus to suddenly swerve closer to the right. Where the cliff was.

Ian made a high noise like a whimper and frantically reached out for my hand. I gripped his tight, our fingers entwining, and a slight vibration tingled up my arm on contact. I glanced at him, expecting anxiety, but his gaze slammed into mine, and suddenly I was breathless and my skin itched over my bones and everything fell away from my vision and thoughts except for Ian.

The bus bumped along and we continued holding hands.

He didn't look scared anymore.

When we safely arrived, he reluctantly broke contact. "Thank you," he said in a low, husky voice.

"Welcome."

"I'm still not going on the chairlift."

I grinned and so did he, and I knew something had shifted between us for good. I just wasn't sure where it would lead.

CHAPTER TWENTY

SOPHIA

THERE WAS SOMETHING magical about Capri, and my heart broke a bit when we left. It was hard on my body with the intense amount of walking, but to sit in the shade of a lemon tree, feast on gelato, and enjoy the hum of the crowds was a memory I'd never forget.

I was proud of completing the famous chairlift, which brought us to the summit of Mount Solaro. The stunning view as the ground fell away under my dangling feet was thrilling. I had one small moment of panic when Allegra fished out her phone to click some pictures and I worried she'd fall out, but even Frannie had laughed at me for my worry. My fingers were so tangled up with arthritis, I doubted I'd be able to hold an object up in the air for too long.

We were heading through Tuscany on our way to Florence and stopping by a family farm in Volterra where they made mozzarella. I'd mastered pasta and bread but never tried to make my own cheese at home. I was looking forward to watching the process.

So far, I'd been able to keep up. I only hoped my determination not to worry my girls would overcome any of my body's deterioration. My stomach hadn't flared up yet, but there was a low burning pain around my middle, and I was horribly bloated.

Sometimes the band tightened and I lost my breath, but it hadn't happened enough for me to worry. Not yet.

I told you to get the tests done before you left, he scolded. *What if you're delaying treatment because of your stubbornness?*

You wrote the book on stubborn. I want to enjoy this trip without anything negative looming over us. How can we have fun if they're worried about me the whole time?

Fine, don't listen to me. You never do. Something is going on with Frannie. You need to get her to open up.

I'm trying. She hasn't been on her phone lately, though, but Allegra hasn't budged. There's some deep hurt between them only some time and talking can heal.

Stubborn. Just like you. Runs in the family.

Oh, shush.

"What'd you say, Mom?" Frannie asked.

Had I spoken out loud again? Oh my. I seemed to be doing that more often. Talking to my dead husband would place me straight on the crazy list. "Nothing. This is beautiful, isn't it?" We climbed up a twisty wooded road and passed sheep, cows, and a variety of other farm animals. The sign read FORMAGGI DI MARIA.

When we got out, we were greeted by a woman a bit younger than me with curly black hair, a plump face, and an exuberant smile. She wore a white apron and a frayed blue dress that reached her ankles. She was flanked by a young man and woman who welcomed us in and explained what the tour involved.

"I am Giovanni, this is Patricia, and this is our master cheese maker, Maria." The older woman nodded and waved at us. "Today we will be showing you our farm and where we make our wonderful cheese. We shall take you behind the scenes. Then Maria will make mozzarella for you with her age-old process she's been doing since she was seven years old. You will make lunch yourselves."

"But I can't cook!" Kai burst out.

Everyone laughed. "Today, you shall cook your own pizza and it will be delicious!" Giovanni told him. "Let's get started. If you will follow me, *grazie*."

The tour took us through the workings of the farm. I watched while a worker milked cows in front of us, and we toured the vegetable and herb gardens, bursting with vine-ripened tomatoes, sweet peppers, basil, and parsley. Olive trees dotted the property, their twisted branches hanging low. Fascinated, we examined the mechanics room, filled with huge metal vaults and industrial ovens pumping out high amounts of liquids for the various cheeses.

We gathered in front of an outdoor kitchen with a large brick oven and long table. Folding chairs were set up, and I took a seat next to Allegra, excited to watch her during the demonstration.

Patricia wore a matching apron and narrated while Maria began to make the mozzarella. "We will show you the most popular form of mozzarella that is sold to stores and local markets—the braided version, which is called the *treccia*."

Pots were set out already with boiling water. "The secret is in the milk, which makes the curds for the cheese. Our cows and sheep are the most important ingredients on our farm," Patricia said. "To make curds, we add citric acid to milk, heat it, and add diluted rennet to complete the coagulation process. These curds will begin to separate, and then she will drain them of the extra liquid."

With expert, precise motions, Maria owned the kitchen like a queen, matching each action to Patricia's narrative. She placed the curds in heated whey and strained the pieces multiple times. "The cheese must cool before we reach the next stage, but we have some over here at the perfect temperature."

"I wish I could take notes," I whispered to Allegra.

She patted my arm. "Nonni, I'm videoing it on my phone. We'll try to duplicate it when we get home."

Wow. I hadn't even noticed because she wasn't holding the phone up in the air. It was just resting on her lap, tilted upward to catch the entire process. I remembered growing up with a color television and soap operas, and when my parents wanted me home for dinner, they'd open the window and scream my name down the block. I shook my head and refocused.

The cheese seemed like a broken lump. I leaned forward with interest for the next step. "The whey will now be heated to one hundred eighty degrees and Maria will work her magic." Maria bowed and we all laughed. With her gloves donned and a white hat on her head, she began to mix the steaming liquid with the cheese, her hands kneading and manipulating the cheese like da Vinci wielding his paintbrush. The lump slowly formed into a shiny, smooth mass. Maria pulled the cheese through her fingers, twisting with varied speeds, and a gorgeous braid emerged, the cheese fresh and glistening when finally laid upon the wooden table.

We burst into applause. A tiny spurt of regret flickered inside me. This was a woman who knew her heritage and her place in life. The only thing I ever prided myself on was my family. I never wanted to work outside the home. Is that why I put my entire heart and soul into raising Frannie? And when she didn't respond to my doting, I only increased it, trying to smother her with enough love so she'd always be mine.

It hadn't worked. She'd drowned under my devoted attention and navigated more naturally to her father. I wondered if Maria had children. I wondered if they'd made it harder for her to concentrate on creating a successful product or if she just naturally balanced making cheese and raising a bunch of children. I wondered if any woman had really figured out the art of balance, or were we all just as confused about what would make us happy? Even worse, I wondered if what made us truly happy was in direct contradiction to what made our family happy.

I pushed away my spinning thoughts and watched as Maria demonstrated how to create the perfect knot, called *nodini*. Patricia came around the table and motioned toward us. "Now we are going to create pizzas with our fresh mozzarella. I need six volunteers to help me up here."

Excited, I raised my hand with a few others. Patricia pointed to me. "Yes, would you come join us? Who is with you?"

"My daughter and granddaughter," I said with pride.

"Wonderful, bring them up!"

I rose, but Allegra tugged at my arm. "Nonni, I don't think I want to go up there."

I remember how unsure I was of myself when I turned eighteen, even though pictures showed a beautiful, confident young woman. Couldn't she see how she lit up a room when she walked in? She radiated a strong presence like Frannie, a woman who was destined to do big things in the world. The tour members adored her, and I wanted her to feel safe to have some silly fun. I gently urged her up. "Sweetheart, we get to make pizza in Italy together! Come on, do this with me."

She bit her lip but followed me to the kitchen. Frannie joined us in the line. Patricia picked out Hana, Dan, and Kai. "How old are you?" she asked the boy.

"Ten."

She nodded and shared a glance with Patricia. "Yes, I think you are old enough to cook. But first, we need to get ourselves in the mood. Cooking is a state of mind. You must be dressed for the part, so everyone will wear special aprons."

Patricia took a stack from Giovanni and went down the line one by one, placing the apron over each of our heads and tying it in the back. Laughter erupted in the crowd and I looked over to see what was going on.

I gasped.

Hana was wearing an apron of a naked woman's body with fig leaves placed over the breasts. Dan cracked up, but then he was presented with a muscled man's chest with a large penis protruding from the front. Fortunately, the penis was also covered by a leaf, but the impression it left urged a shocked humor.

Maria shouted, "You like your aprons, no?"

Dan looked at his wife and raised his brow. "Yes, I most certainly do."

Hana gave him a teasing swat. "Very funny. I'll just call you Adam."

Kai's eyes bulged out, but he glanced back and forth at his mom and dad and grinned. His apron was the body of a goat, which caused him to erupt into giggles. Frannie received a naked Venus with roses covering the private areas, and Allegra and I got two more matching Eves.

One look at Allegra and her flaming cheeks told me she was upset. She was spending more time with Ian and seemed to have formed a connection. I was glad. He was a nice boy, and his parents were fun to speak with. Sure, he was a bit older, but in this case it was a good thing. Even though she denied they were anything more than casual friends, I caught the look in her eye when she stared at him. An undeniable affection and spark of more. It hadn't been there before.

It was there now.

Ian seemed just as interested. He snuck glances at her constantly, seeming to try to come up with excuses to talk to her. A summer romance in Italy was exactly what Allegra needed.

So did Fran.

Unfortunately, I didn't see anything happening on that front.

There were no single men on the tour, and Enzo rushed around with little time to give her one-on-one attention.

I decided to pull the focus to me and help out my cringing granddaughter. I made a show of looking down at the naked body pasted on the apron. "Wow, I haven't looked this good in years! Hello, seventy-five!" I announced loudly.

Our group applauded and whistled, and I took a bow. Allegra smiled and some of the tension dissolved from her face. Maria soon whisked us into the production of making pizza crust, teaching us how to knead and stretch the dough and even showing off a few expert flips. We stood in a line and practiced as Maria made her way to each of us with funny comments and encouragement. She took one peek at Frannie's stretched, broken dough and made a tsking sound, gently removing the shredded crust from her hands. "*Mamma mia*, your enthusiasm is wonderful, but maybe a bit gentler with the kneading?"

I leaned over to my daughter. "All those years I tried to teach you to cook have led up to this moment," I said teasingly. The moment the words popped out of my mouth, I cringed, realizing she might take my comment as an insult. Sure, as a mom, I wanted to teach her to be a good cook like me, but I was proud of her accomplishments and didn't care what she chose not to do. With the tension between us lately, especially after my lecture two nights ago, I braced myself for the chilled look she'd cut me with.

"I'm already an expert, Mom," she threw back at me. "I can dial the pizza delivery phone number with my eyes closed. It's perfect every time."

Everyone burst into laughter, and relief shot through me at her easy tone. Oh, how I wished we'd be able to relax with each other more often. I felt as if every word needed to be carefully analyzed to make sure I wasn't hurting her feelings. When had it begun to fall apart on us? When Allegra began going to school? Or had the broken cracks always been there, slowly eroding through the years because we never tried to repair them?

Maria stopped by Allegra. "*Signorina*, do you cook professionally? You are quite skilled in forming the dough."

Allegra straightened up. "My grandmother taught me," she said proudly, motioning over to me.

"I think the student has surpassed the teacher," I said, noting how her pizza was perfectly shaped and kneaded to the perfect width.

"Very impressive," Maria said again with a smile. We finished with adding the sauce and cheese and stuck them in the brick oven. Maria collected our aprons and stood in front of us. "I have seen many pizza makers in my life, but there is one who has a natural talent. A true artist who I wish lived here in Italy with me to work in our family business."

We waited, and I saw Allegra hold her breath.

Maria walked straight to Kai. "Young man, you are the winner of the pizza-making contest. It would be my honor for you to work with me."

His face lit up, and he looked back and forth between his mother and father. "Thank you, but I'm going to be a firefighter and I can't move to Italy."

I bit my lip to keep from chuckling at his seriousness. "That is a worthy job," Maria said, patting his head with affection. "I guess I can accept your refusal. Now, if you'll follow Patricia into the dining area, we are going to eat these delicious pizzas you all created."

Oversize tables were situated under a big awning surrounded by lush green vines and flowers ripe with sweet nectar. Platters of fresh mozzarella, juicy red tomatoes, and bottles of olive oil were already set up on festive tablecloths. White and red wine flowed, along with fresh-squeezed lemonade. Baskets of crusty pieces of Italian bread were set in the center.

"Allegra, I know you mentioned you liked cooking, but you really did look like a professional out there," Dana said, her many bangles jangling on her wrist. "Maybe you'll go to school and be a chef."

This time, Allegra didn't hesitate. Her features flushed with pride as she answered. "I'm going to apply to the Culinary Institute. And when I get home, I'm going to see if I can get some experience in a restaurant or catering hall."

"How wonderful," Dana squealed. She directed her words to Frannie. "You must be so proud. I can't imagine having a chef in the family."

I held my breath, but I noticed my daughter's gaze focus thoughtfully on Allegra. There was a spark of interest I hadn't seen before. "Yes, I am proud," she said.

I relaxed and we focused on our meal. Maybe this was the beginning of her opening up a dialogue with Allegra on her choices. We ate and drank and laughed under the tent, shielded from the Tuscan sun. The gathering was warm and intimate and felt more like a family gathering than strangers forced to share a meal at the same table. After lunch, we were able to shop at the market, and I picked up a bottle of olive oil and balsamic vinegar and bought each of us a naked apron so we'd always remember this trip.

By the time we reboarded the bus, my girls were smiling together. I'd noticed Frannie check her phone a few times, but she'd never disappeared, seeming to try to focus on being with her daughter.

As we headed into Florence, I prayed it was a new beginning for all of us, and I thanked Maria and her farm for reminding us that even in the midst of hard work, there is always room for fun and laughter.

CHAPTER TWENTY-ONE

FRANCESCA

FLORENCE REMINDED ME of an Italian queen.

The city was regal and shimmering with a sophistication that made its neighboring cities and sights fade from memory. We'd already visited an array of impressive churches, and I figured nothing would come close to St. Peter's.

I was wrong.

The magnificence of Santa Croce church took me by surprise. From the soaring marble frontage to the gilded golden doors, I was swept into an old-world glamour and surrounded by the greatest artists of all time. As I stood before the tombs of Dante, Galileo, and Michelangelo, the vivid, glittering Giotto frescoes demanded my full attention. The detail was extraordinary, from the stained glass to the mural paintings and sculptures lovingly carved from marble. The endless chapels each held an artistic surprise, until we exited the church and blinked in the sun, halfway drunk from the overstimulation of such beauty.

We strolled through the Piazza della Signoria, the main town square, and took in the bustle of crowds carrying designer bags from the luxury shops, passing timeless historical pieces without a second glance. It reminded me a bit of New York and how no one ever looked up at the Empire State Building or paused to view the Statue of Liberty across the Hudson. Enzo was well skilled at delivering factual information mixed with interesting stories to keep us moving and engaged. I actually found him a much better tour guide than the locals he'd set us up with for some of the main sights.

We followed him to the Loggia dei Lanzi, an open-air gallery. The giant archways invited tourists to wander in and enjoy its display of statues. Enzo paused in front of a sculpture that seemed to dominate the whole square. My breath caught as I took in the twisted and entangled bodies carved from a smooth block of solid marble. A man lifted a woman up high in the air, while another man crouched at her feet. The expressions on their faces were filled with ravaged violence. The woman's desperate reach for freedom seemed as if she was about to burst out of the stone and flee their terror.

"This is *The Rape of the Sabine Women* by Giambologna," he explained, motioning us to move closer. "It's based on a famous story of when Romans captured the Sabine women for marriage, because they had been denied many times by the king, who said that the women were not allowed to marry Romans. It is a popular subject for art, and this particular statue was carved from a single block of marble—the largest one ever imported to Florence. It is considered Giambologna's masterpiece. Check out the exquisite detail and emotion. As we wander around the square, I'll give you some brief background on the pieces."

We marveled at the bronze statue of Perseus, holding his sword in one hand and the head of Medusa in the other. Hercules and Nessus shimmered with raw power, and the Medici lions seemed to be guarding the gallery. Enzo's voice wrapped around me as he wove a spell of enchantment and seemed to make the various statues come alive with their rich history. But it wasn't his educational talent that was distracting me this afternoon.

I couldn't stop thinking about our almost kiss.

As if he knew my whirling thoughts, his gaze cut to mine

and dove deep within me. A shiver of awareness bumped down my spine. Since our embrace in Capri, he'd kept his professional distance, but I felt him staring at me throughout the day, his dark eyes brimming with an emotion that he didn't seem to want to hide. I'd been ruthless with my time around Allegra and Mom, choosing not to take work calls while we were out on tour and trying to regain my daughter's trust. Each time I picked up my phone, I saw her expectations for me to flee back to the hotel, but for the past three days I'd surprised all of us by allowing Kate and Layla to make all the final decisions.

I'd managed to please Perry with my changes to the campaign during my all-nighter, so I was hoping the next few weeks would be low-key and I'd hit the ground running when I returned. I hadn't addressed my mother's barbed speech, but I think it was because I sensed she was right. We'd been getting along lately and I didn't want to dredge up any issues. I just wanted Italy to work its magic on us.

Enzo called us to attention. "You have the rest of the afternoon on your own. I'd recommend checking out Giubbe Rosse café—it was the meeting place for famous writers and artists. If you want to indulge in designer shopping, cross the Arno to Piazza della Repubblica. There is plenty to do there. I'd recommend staying away from the Uffizi Gallery today since the lines are quite long, but tomorrow you will have enough time after we see *David* at the Galleria dell'Accademia. Tonight, we shall dine at Buca Mario and you will have the most delicious food. Please be ready at seven p.m. I am here for any questions."

His fans immediately swarmed him, and I couldn't help the smile that curved my lips. Everyone adored him, and somehow, I felt pride at his talent and obvious love of his job. I turned to Allegra and Mom. "Okay, ladies, what shall it be? Shopping, culture, or strolling around to see what catches our eye? We can always get lost again."

Allegra groaned. "No, thanks, that was enough stress for the whole trip. I'm fine to explore. Nonni?"

"I'd love to see the Santa Maria del Fiore," she said. "It has that gorgeous dome and we can shop along the way. As long as you're up for seeing another church."

"I'd love to see that," Allegra said excitedly.

I quirked a brow. "Before we left, you said you'd die before you'd be dragged into lots of boring churches. Have you had an epiphany?"

Did her cheeks turn red or was it just the sun? Or was Ian becoming a bit more important than I'd thought? "I just think we should see all the landmarks while we're here," she said with a primness that was a direct contradiction to the spark in her eyes.

"The church it is."

"I have to use the bathroom first," Mom said. "Enzo said there was a public toilet down the block."

"I have to go too. I know where it is. Mom, we'll meet you back here? We have to head this way to get to the church."

"Sounds good." I quickly checked my phone, sent a few texts, then stuck it back into my pocket.

"Francesca?"

I jumped and spun. Enzo stood behind me, a smile resting on his full lips. My heart slammed against my ribs and I felt like a giddy teenager, honored the star quarterback chose to come talk to me. "H-h-hi. How are you?"

Oh my God, I was stuttering. What was wrong with me?

"Do you have any questions in order to plan your day?"

It seemed like a casual inquiry, but the way he stared told me there was another reason he'd sought me out. I shifted my weight and tried to look unaffected. After all, it wasn't like he'd kissed me. He'd been the one to step back and turn that moment into a hug rather than something . . . more. "We're heading to Santa Maria and doing some shopping. Mom and Allegra made a pit stop first."

He cocked his head. "Pit stop?"

"Sorry, bathroom. Toilet. Umm, what about you? Do you stay in the area or go back to the hotel?"

"I need to make sure some details are arranged, so I'll be at the hotel till dinner." His voice lowered to an intimate pitch. "I wanted to check on you. See if you were okay."

"Oh yes, I'm fine. No more attacks, and I've backed off work. I've really been enjoying the tour so far. I loved Maria's mozzarella farm and all the personal touches you included."

Mischief flickered in his dark eyes. "I wish I could claim credit for the stops, but that's on the tour company. I just make sure the guests are happy."

"Well, I am. I mean, we are."

Silence settled over us, but it pulsed with unspoken words we weren't brave enough to say. At least, I wasn't. He cleared his throat. "I was wondering if you weren't tired after dinner, maybe we could meet for a cocktail? Or coffee? Afterward."

Excitement flickered. He wanted to see me. Alone. The thought of sharing some time with him in private made my belly do a slow flip-flop. "Yes, I'd like that. I'm usually not able to go to sleep too early, so that would be nice."

"Good." His name cut through the air, and he turned, his expression already changing into his professional mode. "I'll talk to you later. We can meet on the upstairs terrace. It's quiet."

I nodded, and he walked away, smiling as Ray pointed to a map and asked questions. Allegra and Mom returned, so we headed out for the afternoon and I swore I wouldn't think about our secret meet-up. It was really nothing. A friendly get-together for him to check on me.

But even I couldn't convince myself it didn't mean anything.

The hours flew by and we were pleasantly tired and happy by the time we arrived at the restaurant that evening. I'd taken a bit more care with my appearance, pairing wide-leg black trousers with an emerald green top that gave a bit of sparkle to my usually dull brown eyes. I fluffed up my hair and added dangly gold earrings, then even spritzed on perfume.

After all, it was a nice restaurant. I had to look decent.

The restaurant held the perfect balance of charm and coziness. The dimly lit room added a touch of intimacy, and the gleaming wood floors, yellow paint, and stone wall added a dimension of Italian character. There was a hallway where an impressive variety of wines were stacked up, and the bar was bustling. A three-person band was setting up, and I noticed another table of about eight tourists next to us. We all waved at them and tried to engage in conversation, but they were all men and seemed super serious, frowning at our friendly attempts and pretty much ignoring us. Odd. I would've figured it was a business meeting, except the guide was talking loudly to them about the next day's itinerary and wore a name badge that declared FLORENCE TOURS DONE *RIGHT*!

The menu was Florentine inspired and held an array of delights. Allegra and Mom convinced me to push my food boundaries again, and I enjoyed most of it, squishing my face up as I tried to decide with each new bite if I liked it or not. We feasted on tagliatelle with wild boar ragù and beef fillets in a rich truffle sauce. Mom chose the sea bass and swooned over our wonderful waiter, Rocco, who treated us like royalty and cleaned her fish tableside. The calamari was crisp yet tender inside, and the red wine was the color of rubies, with a heavy tannin and smooth finish that went perfectly with my beef. I didn't worry about carbs or diets, allowing myself to eat whatever I wanted. The band played and the singer took requests from the guests, launching into familiar old ballads, American favorites, and of course, Frank Sinatra. By the time the berry tarts were served, our table was pretty much drunk and getting rowdier than usual.

Dana refilled her glass, and Rocco promptly brought another bottle. "Have you noticed those guys staring at us, y'all?" she said a bit loudly. "I've never seen people in Italy look unhappy. And they seem to be acting a bit assholery to the waiters. Are they not on vacation?"

Steve forked up a bite of his tart. "Darlin', there are a lot of dissatisfied people in the world. They change their location or their relationships or their job, and hope they'll be happy. But do you think they are? No. Why, you ask? Because happiness comes from within. It's a lesson we all must learn in our own time."

I tamped down a chuckle. Since the beginning of the tour, Steve rarely uttered more than a sentence, so this was like a soliloquy. I also noticed he had a bit of a goofy grin and was bombed along with the rest of the group except me, Allegra, and Kai. I was trying to keep sober for my nighttime chat. Even Mom was swaying back and forth to the music and had proclaimed she was feeling a bit fizzy and warm.

Dana sighed. "You're so deep," she said to her husband, stroking his arm.

The strains of Dean Martin's famous classic, "That's Amore," boomed from the speakers, and everyone let out a cheer. In unison, we began chanting the well-known lyrics, and then Cherry and Laura popped out of their chairs and began dancing together in the small open area by their table.

I waited for the waitstaff to guide them politely back to their seats, but they only cheered them on, and the room became engaged in trying to sing in tune. It was one of those rare moments when strangers came together—like a well-known bar that protected your secrets and stories because you shared a bonding moment over a cocktail. Smiles were plastered on faces, joviality was high, and then I glanced over at the table next to us and saw their obvious disapproval.

Mom leaned over to whisper in my ear. "They're a challenge."

I blinked. "What do you mean?"

She pointed rudely over to them—solidifying her tipsiness. My mother was always ruthlessly polite and kind. "They don't want to have fun. It's our job to push them so they're forced to be happy. We were brought here to give them a bit of joy."

I laughed. "Mom, that sounds quite spiritual, but I think they just want to eat and get away from the crazy tourists."

She shook her head. "I'm telling you, Frannie, I sense we are meant to meet them."

I nodded, allowing her to believe she'd convinced me, and subtly pushed her water glass toward her so she could hydrate. We finished dessert and we finished the song, and Enzo announced we were wrapping up and needed to return to the bus.

Until the chicken dance came on.

The strains hit my ears and I didn't know whether to flinch or laugh. The overplayed, awful wedding song that forced people to flap their arms like wings and stamp their feet was either adored or despised, but I had no idea Italy even knew the song existed.

I stood up to grab my purse, and it all went downhill.

Dana screeched and jumped up, dragging me into a half embrace, and began to shake and cluck. Cherry and Laura made a circle around me, and before I could blink, most of our table had streamed out into the open area and was doing a nightmarish, drunken version of the chicken dance.

Eyes wide with horror, I tried to disengage, but Dana refused to let me go, holding my hand tight. "Allegra, Sophia, get out here!" she yelled, motioning them over. Knowing they'd never get involved in such a public display, I figured I'd sway back and forth and get the episode over with so we could return to the hotel. And then I watched as my mother rose from her seat, grabbed Allegra's wrist, and pulled her into the throng.

No. Way.

Allegra was laughing as Mom began to clap enthusiastically and wiggle her butt back and forth. Within a few more seconds, the entire tour group was stuffed onto the floor of the restaurant, dancing, and then the circle morphed into a line, and everyone fell into a conga line.

I caught Enzo's shocked gaze, but he whizzed by as I was pushed forward around the tables, with Dana's grip firmly around my waist. We passed by the other table of tourists, who were all staring at us, and then Steve reached over with one beefy hand and grabbed one of the men by the arm, lifting him up out of the seat and throwing him with one quick movement into the singing, stomping conga line.

I cringed and prepped for an explosion. I figured the man would start a fight, launch into an outraged lecture, or furiously call for a manager. Maybe even a lawsuit. I stumbled, trying to tell Dana to tell her husband to back off before he got into trouble, but the scene unfolded before my eyes in stunning format.

The man began to dance. The line snaked around the table again, and this time, Steve grabbed another guy. By the third round, the entire table was dancing with us in a giant drunken line of tourists gone wild. Big smiles plastered their faces as they followed the group, bellowing out the last of the lines of the song at the top of their lungs.

When the song ended, the entire restaurant clapped and cheered. I wiped sweat from my brow and watched Steve pat a few guys on the back, chatting away with Dana at his side. Cherry and Laura hugged another guy. Allegra was shaking her head as Mom beamed with delight, telling one of the strangers she was proud of him and she'd pray for him.

Unbelievable.

Enzo finally wrested back control and we reboarded the bus. The entire way home, we sang songs together in sloppy unity, and when my phone began to violently vibrate, I refused to even check it.

It was one of those rare moments I didn't want to miss and I craved to remember. One night in Florence, we'd danced with strangers and become temporary friends. I'd forgotten what surprises felt like. The last few years, my life had followed a ruthless schedule, and though boring, it was familiar and controlled. Tonight, I felt ready to burst out of my shell and take risks.

Big risks.

When we got back to the hotel, I settled Allegra and Mom into their room, making sure Mom took a Tylenol and had a big glass of water. Her face glowed with a joy that warmed my heart. "I had so much fun, Frannie," she said with a bit of a slur, and then she reached out and hugged me hard. I hugged back, comforted by her familiar strength even though her body seemed frail under my touch.

"Me too, Mom," I said, kissing her papery cheek. "Now get some sleep." I walked over to my daughter and stood before her. "Good night, sweetheart. Did you have fun?"

A rare smile crossed her face as she looked at me. "Yeah, it was cool. Everyone was pretty drunk, huh?"

"I think so. But nobody was driving, and I think there should be one night where our group gets funky."

She groaned. "Freaky, Mom, gets freaky."

"Right." I stared at her beloved face and my heart squeezed

with longing. "I love you, Al." I hadn't used the nickname in years, retiring the tag when she hit her teen years and began to complain it was a stupid thing to call her. Not waiting to gauge her reaction, I quickly pulled her in for a hug, desperate to smell her hair and feel my child's body pressed against mine. She relaxed and hugged me back, and those few seconds were pure perfection—a memory of how close we'd once been and a temporary forgiveness.

Emotion choked my throat. She slowly broke the embrace, ducking her head in slight embarrassment, and I stepped away to allow her the space.

"See you in the morning," I said. Then I left.

It took me only a few minutes to brush my teeth, reapply some lipstick, and check my phone. He hadn't texted, but since he'd mentioned the bar upstairs, I'd simply head there. If he didn't show, I'd go back to my room and shrug the whole thing off.

No big deal.

The warm, balmy air caressed my skin like a whisper-soft kiss. I entered the bar area and immediately saw him at a table. It was situated in an intimate corner, overlooking the terrace wall. The sky was studded with stars, and the full moon hung like a ripe fruit before me. I'd tried to keep my interactions with Enzo to a minimum tonight. I didn't want any of the tour group to figure out we were meeting up, and my guilty secret pulsed with a thrill I relished.

I slid into the chair opposite him and smiled. "Hi."

"*Buona sera*, Francesca," he said in his deep, lilting voice. "What can I get you? Vino? Cocktail?"

"Chianti is perfect, *grazie*."

He lifted a finger and gave the waiter my order. He already held a low tumbler of whiskey or cognac in his other hand. The ice rattled against the crystal glass. The lingering scent of smoke drifted to my nostrils.

"Did you have your evening cigarette yet?" I teased. "Or did the chicken dance push you to the edge so you smoked two?"

His chest rumbled with a laugh. He'd stayed in his evening clothes, dressed in sleek, tailored navy pants and a short-sleeve blue striped shirt. He'd discarded the red tie and opened up the first button of his shirt. His hair looked mussed, as if he'd run his fingers through the thick strands too many times. "In all my years of being a guide, tonight was the first time I witnessed a drunken group take over a restaurant and do the chicken dance."

"Pretty badass, huh?" I said with a wink. "Did you see when Steve grabbed that guy? I thought it would be a disaster."

"Me too. I planned to step in, but my presence wasn't needed." The waiter came back with my drink and Enzo inclined his head in thanks. "I see you have some dance moves you've kept hidden."

I choked out a laugh. "I already had a disaster with my fall on the Spanish Steps. If I find another video with me flapping my arms, I'll never recover."

He quirked a brow. "What video?"

Uh-oh. Of course I hadn't told him and was completely relieved when the fervor died down. I checked every day and views were only a trickle with an occasional LOL comment. Thank God I had a business IG account and not a personal one, or I'd have been screwed. I hesitated but figured I'd confess. "Someone must have filmed my tumble, because Allegra found the video blowing up on Instagram. I freaked out."

He shook his head. "That's terrible. They actually posted it? What's wrong with people today?"

I shrugged. "Guess they thought it was funny. You got a lot of fans."

He frowned. "What do you mean?"

I took a sip of my wine. "They filmed you swooping in to my rescue and carrying me away from the steps. You have a new fan club. A ton of comments were posted regarding your swoon-worthiness."

"My what?"

"The public, mostly women, thought you were hot."

It took a few moments for my statement to register, but then he began to laugh. I relished the sound, which woke up my body and sent tingles to my nerve endings. "I had no idea. As honored as I am about my fan club, I'm worried about you. Did that affect your job?"

"I was terrified it would. If a client saw it, who knows if he or she would pull their business? Anything that leaks on social media is an unknown element. Allegra said the fervor would fade away, and the next day views and sharing were way down. But we ended up having a fight anyway. I pretty much locked myself in the room all night to try and do damage control and missed dinner."

He shifted his chair and leaned forward. Up close, I studied the angled curve of his jaw, the hint of stubble hugging his chin. "Are things getting better with Allegra?" he asked. "You seemed more relaxed tonight."

"I backed off of work. It's not fair to my mom or my daughter to be only partially present." I sighed, tapping my finger against my glass. "I don't know when I realized work was getting the lion's share of my attention. I can't go back, but we have two weeks left together. I need to prove to my family they're more important than anything else." I paused, lifting my gaze to meet his. "You helped me see that."

"No, you did that on your own. I just listened. How are the panic attacks?"

"None since that morning."

"Good. I did some research after my sister struggled. I can send you some really good articles."

"Thank you, I'd like that." We fell silent and the connection between us tugged and hummed, pushing me to be a bit reckless. "You mentioned your home was close to the villa we're renting. I was thinking maybe you could give me some tips about the local area. Things to do. Places to go."

"Of course." His hand stretched casually across the table surface. "I could even take a day to drive out there and show you around personally. If you're interested."

My breath caught and I knew there was an undercurrent of meaning in his offer. He was giving me the power right here and now to safely back out and keep him at a distance.

Or not.

"That would be very kind of you," I said.

He stared at me. His jaw clenched, like he was struggling with something. "I'm not doing it to be kind, Francesca. But if I say it aloud, I can't take it back."

I reached out my own hand until our fingers touched. The slight contact made my skin burn. "Maybe I don't want you to take it back. Maybe I need to know if I'm being silly or I'm alone in this."

It was the most I could give him. Vulnerability cut through me. I'd never been the beautiful, most popular woman in the room, and I'd accepted my fate with grace. I was smart and capable and sometimes funny. My partners had been picked by my head rather than my heart, until I was driven to have Allegra on my own and stopped looking for a magical romance that didn't exist. At least, not for me.

Yet, tonight, with my pinky brushing his, I experienced more electricity than I ever had. I wanted more of him. His words, his gaze, his touch. I wasn't comfortable with this version of myself, but if I didn't try, I'd never know what I was missing.

His voice rumbled deep and rough like sandpaper. "Then I'll tell you. It's against the rules to get involved with the tourists. I could lose my job for pursuing anything with you. I've been hit on numerous times before and not once did I have to battle even a passing temptation. Until you."

I trembled but didn't back off. "I tempt you?"

He shuddered. "Yes, Francesca, can't you see it? I'm always trying to get close to you or find excuses to talk, but I keep my distance because I'm afraid it'll be obvious to the group. I don't want to put anyone in a bad position, especially you or your family." A touch of frustration surged, but then his fingers slipped through mine and he was holding my hand, and my entire soul sighed with pleasure. "That morning in Capri, I was crazed to kiss you. I barely managed to hold back in time."

"I wanted you to kiss me," I said simply, past flirting or trying to play games.

A groan escaped him. "I wasn't sure. This is new territory for me. I don't want to disrespect you or the rules of my job. Do you understand?"

"I do. And I don't want to put you in that position either. But—"

"But?"

His eyes practically pleaded for me to finish. "But I can't stop thinking about you either," I whispered. "And I want more, even if it's messy or wrong or crazy."

He muttered in Italian—which sounded like sexy curse words—and gripped my hand hard. "Francesca, I—"

"Hey, guys, is this where the party is?"

Immediately we drew back, as if burned, and turned around. Dana and Steve were walking across the terrace, smiling big and still obviously tipsy. Cherry and Laura trailed behind and waved. I held my breath, waiting to see if they'd caught us holding hands, but they swooped in and dragged chairs over, ordering more drinks and chattering merrily.

"Where's Allegra and Sophia?" Dana asked.

"Oh, they went to bed. I couldn't sleep so I figured I'd have a nightcap and found Enzo with the same idea." I shrugged off his presence like it was nothing and prayed I sounded convincing.

"Best tour guide ever!" Cherry screeched, giving him a high five. "Hey, can I bum a cigarette? I miss smoking so much and I'm on vacay."

Laura gasped. "No! I will not let you slide back into old habits. No offense, Enzo, but you need to quit. It will wreck your body and shorten your life span."

"Oh, he only smokes one per day."

Uh-oh. Everyone turned to look at me curiously, and I realized it sounded weird that I had such knowledge. Enzo coughed, obviously hiding a grin, but that only made Laura warm up to her subject. "Well, that doesn't matter. Research proves one cigarette is just as bad as half a pack."

He glanced at me with amusement. "*Sì*, I remember someone telling me the same exact thing once."

I was tempted to shoot him a warning look but decided acting casual was the best plan. Cherry began to whine a bit, then Laura kissed her, and she seemed to forget she wanted a cigarette. Steve settled next to Enzo and launched into a conversation about the World Cup, and a half hour passed before I was able to finally extricate myself.

I gave a dramatic yawn. "Goodness, I'm tired. I better get to bed. Good night, everyone."

Enzo stood. "Me too. I'll head back with you."

No one questioned our retreat, and after they called out their goodbyes and ordered yet another round of drinks, we escaped to the elevator. The door whooshed closed and we faced each other.

"Well, that was interesting," I said, suddenly shy in the bright glare of lights.

He laughed and rubbed his head. "Their timing is terrible. And they'll be hurting tomorrow."

I smiled back. "Punishment for the crime of interruption."

"Level three, right?"

"Yes."

The light beeped, and too soon, we arrived at my floor.

"I'll walk you to your room," he said gruffly.

"Okay."

My heart raced and my palms had started to sweat, and when we arrived at my door, suddenly I couldn't handle the stress any longer. "What were you going to say before we got cut off?" I asked, turning to him.

He hesitated. Lifted a hand and gently touched my cheek. I fell into his deep, dark gaze and reveled in the warm tenderness of the moment, a complete contradiction to the buzz under my skin and the way my body seemed to ache for him. "I was going to say I'm willing to take a risk if you are. We're both discreet. I don't even know what's between us—but I swear I'll back off if you just say the word. I refuse to ruin your vacation by stressing you out further or distracting you from your family. *Capisce?*"

I half closed my eyes, then leaned into his touch. *"Capisco,"* I said softly.

Blistering words fell from his lips—either a curse or a prayer—and then his head lowered and he was kissing me. I fell into every magical sensation, relishing the soft, firm movement of his mouth over mine, the gentle thrust of his tongue, the delicious, savory taste and scent of him filling up my senses. His body pressed against mine, his hard muscles cradling my soft curves, and my head spun like I'd drunk a cheap bottle of whiskey and had to cling to him for stability.

And then he was stepping back, his gaze locking with mine, and he gave me a smile.

I smiled back.

"*Buona notte*, Francesca."

"*Buona notte.*"

I watched him until he disappeared into the elevator. Then I went inside, changed into my pajamas, and climbed into bed.

I slept deeply and dreamlessly until morning.

CHAPTER TWENTY-TWO

ALLEGRA

"So, what did you think of the statue *David*?" Ian asked.

We were walking back into the hotel after dinner the second night in Florence. The day had been packed, beginning with the Galleria dell'Academia, then the Uffizi Gallery. After standing in front of the towering Michelangelo sculpture and setting my sights on *The Birth of Venus* by Botticelli, I was a little giddy. I honestly felt like I was drunk on art and the nonstop stream of beauty around me on a daily basis. I tried not to act too nerdy, but after spouting off various facts about paintings, I realized Ian enjoyed hearing my thoughts and analysis, even asking further questions until I was comfortable enough to say anything I wanted.

Yeah, it was heady.

We'd had a few hours free before eating at a local café with the most amazing spaghetti and meatballs I'd ever tasted. The tables were small so we'd had to split up, and Ian had been in a different group. I hadn't really seen him one-on-one since that day in Capri. I was glad he finally sought me out.

"I've never been so impressed with a naked guy in my whole life," I said honestly.

He laughed. "Funny, you took the words right out of my mouth."

I laughed with him. "What'd you have for dinner?"

"The spaghetti and meatballs."

"So did I! Wasn't it killer? They put some type of herb in the meat I can't place. Even Nonni couldn't figure it out. She said when we get back home, she's buying every herb to experiment until she finds the match."

"Why didn't she just ask the chef?"

I shook my head in disappointment. "Never. It's a challenge to figure it out yourself. She doesn't believe in sharing recipes."

"Good to know." He turned and glanced at Mom and Nonni, who were a few feet behind talking to Mary and Ray. "Hey, my parents are tired so they're heading to bed early. I don't feel like reading and it's too late to go anywhere. Enzo said it's a full moon tonight and there's this nice sitting area upstairs on the terrace around the corner from the bar. Want to hang out?"

Giddy bubbles of pleasure burst in my veins. I shrugged and tried to be casual. "Yeah, sure. What time?"

"Fifteen minutes? Your mom won't mind?"

"No, I'll tell her where we'll be. I agree—it's too nice of a night to be inside."

"Cool, see you in a bit."

He disappeared, and Mom and Nonni came over. "Are you heading to bed?" I asked.

Mom lifted her brow. "Trying to get rid of us?"

I knew she was teasing but I tried hard not to blush. *Awkward.* "Umm, Ian wants to hang out upstairs on the terrace for a bit. Enzo said it was a full moon, so we thought we'd check it out."

Nonni smiled. "Sounds like fun. I'll be asleep by the time you come back. You have your key?"

I nodded. Mom got this weird look on her face like she'd swallowed a sharp object. "The terrace?" she asked in a high-pitched voice. "Where the bar is?"

I tensed. If she dared to question an innocent hangout, I was going to lose it. I was eighteen years old, we were completely chaperoned, and I hadn't left her sight since the beginning of the tour. One mistake shouldn't erase all the years I managed to stay out of trouble. "It's not like we're drinking. We just want to talk. I'm all packed to head into Venice, so my luggage will be ready in the morning."

"Sure." Was that a gleam of disappointment in her eyes? I didn't understand her. She'd made it a point to tell me Ian seemed nice, and now she was trying to block me from seeing him. The usual frustration shot through me every time I tried to deal with her. It was a miracle she wasn't racing back to her room to dive into her work. I couldn't believe she'd managed not to disappear all day to jump on a conference call. "I guess I'll retire, too. Are you going to freshen up first?"

I rolled my eyes. "No, Mom. It's not a date, and I don't need to paste a bunch of makeup on my face so I can feel better about myself. I have my phone and key and that's enough."

Nonni chuckled and squeezed my shoulder. "Oh, you are so like your mom. She was never into high fashion, cosmetics, or anything too girly. It was one of her best assets. Being comfortable with who she is."

Mom's mouth dropped a bit in surprise, like she had no clue Nonni thought something nice about her. Was she just as insecure with their relationship? Were we all completely fucked up, or were we normal? I knew Mom and Nonni disagreed on a ton of viewpoints like religion, work, and family responsibilities, but I figured Mom didn't care about her approval. Maybe I was wrong.

I headed upstairs to the terrace. The bar was crowded, but around the corner was a high table with two chairs that was deserted. I slid onto one of the seats and studied the view while I waited for Ian.

Up this high, the city of Florence stretched out for miles. I caught the peak of the Duomo, and terra-cotta rooftops filled my sight. Bright flowers spilled from pots that seemed to make the skyline a bit of a garden. The angles and slopes of the buildings gave it a beautiful symmetry that demanded to be captured.

I felt his presence before I even heard his steps. "This is a beautiful spot," he commented, smiling as he slid into the opposite chair. "I can't believe we're already halfway through the tour. It's going so fast."

I agreed, especially since I'd fought coming here. "I know. I'm looking forward to Venice, though. Have there been any places we skipped that you wanted to check out?"

He cocked his head. "We picked this tour because it covered all of our must-sees, but I think I may head to Assisi to stay a few nights. I want to visit the church and the monastery. I also heard that's the place to get the best lasagna in the world. The nuns spend all morning cooking to serve the meal at lunch near the monastery."

"Was the town named after a saint?"

"Yeah, St. Francis of Assisi."

"The one on the medal you wear?"

He reached up and touched the silver disc tucked into his shirt, as if he'd forgotten he regularly wore it. "That's right—he's my patron saint. The one I pray to a lot and who guides me. St. Francis was known for his love of animals. He lived a life of poverty and served others."

"I've heard of him. The pope is named after him, right?"

"Yes, he took his name, which was a great honor."

"What are some of the other saints?"

"St. Anthony is the saint of lost things. His church is in Padua, which also wasn't on the tour, but I figured I should be happy since I've been able to pray in over a dozen amazing churches so far." His blue eyes sparkled and I loved watching his face when he talked. He had a calm, warm energy that made me feel good inside. "St. Christopher protects travelers, so I have one of his statues in my car. My mom bought it the day I got my license."

"I love the idea of feeling watched over." Nonni had tried to get me interested in praying, but it was easier to follow my mom's footsteps and not bother. The few times she dragged me to church had been so boring, I almost fell asleep. But at night, the loneliness struck me a lot. I felt sometimes like I was spinning in a world with no one to tether me.

"Did you ever lose someone close to you? Someone you feel is guiding you?" he asked curiously.

"No. My grandfather died before I was born, so I didn't get a chance to get to know him. Mom and Nonni tell me stories, though."

"You should read about the saints and find who speaks to you."

"Maybe I will." The waiter came over, and we ordered two sodas. "So, you don't need to rush home to look for a job or anything? I know you just graduated. What are you going to do?"

The waiter dropped off our drinks. Ian took a sip, then gazed at me with an odd intensity. "I'm going back to school in the fall. I have the rest of the summer before I begin my next phase of life."

"Cool. What are you getting your master's in?"

A smile touched his lips. "Allegra, I'm going into the seminary. I'm studying to be a priest."

I coughed as the soda spurted down the wrong pipe, and Ian had to pound me on the back. Holy crap! Did he just say what I thought?

"Sorry, I didn't realize that would freak you out so much," he said in amusement. "Did I shock you?"

"Um, yes. I mean, it's great, I mean, I don't know. I've never met anyone who wanted to be a priest. It's kind of a dying profession, right?"

He laughed. "Yeah, it definitely is. I probably should have told you earlier, but it just never really came up."

Disappointment crashed through me. I'd been wrong about the feelings stirring up when I was around him. Sure, he'd kind of held my hand and seemed into me, but I'd been all wrong. Future priests weren't interested in girls or dating. He was just being nice to me and . . . priestly.

"Uh-oh. I can see your thoughts whirling around. What is it?"

I forced a smile and pretended I was thrilled. "Nothing, I'm happy for you. I just don't know too much about it except you can't get married or have a family. You need to dedicate yourself to God, right?"

He nodded. His blue eyes seemed to darken, as if the thought still bothered him. "That's right. It was the hardest part for me to accept. Remember I told you that my parents and I were having a big problem?"

"Yeah."

"Well, my decision to enter the priesthood was the big issue. They flipped out. Tried to talk me out of it. My mom cried, worried I'd be giving up my only opportunity for love and children. Dad yelled at our local priest and told him to stop putting ideas in my head. It was hard for them. I kept trying to explain it was a calling I've had since I was young. When I went into church, I felt at peace. Like I was home. Everything I learned about God not only comforted me, but pushed me to know more." He shook his head. "I just wanted to share my life with the world in order to help. There's so much poverty and violence and unhappiness. If I could do one little thing to make a positive change, it'd be worth it. Sounds ridiculous?"

He was special. There was no one I'd ever met who wanted to sacrifice his future for others. "No, it's not ridiculous at all. It's beautiful. But I still wonder if you could do all that and keep your options open. Like the Peace Corps, or working for a charity? There are tons of jobs that give back."

"You're right, but not one centered completely around God. Following him and doing his work is my calling. No matter where I'm sent in the future, whether it's a small community parish or a big church in a city, I get to be a hands-on messenger. And not in the way of knocking on doors—though I'm not knocking that approach," he said with a laugh, "but in a natural way."

"Can you help the animals if you're a priest?" I asked.

"I intend to. I want to work with local shelters and maybe get a program together with the church. I have a lot of ideas, but I'll need to complete another four years of study in the seminary before being ordained. It's still years of work and training ahead, but I'm excited."

I tried to sift through this new information he'd thrown at me. In a crazy way, I felt like I'd lost the potential to experience something special. Which was stupid, because there was nothing going on between us except a casual friendship based around a tour.

"I'm happy for you. Knowing what you want to do with your life is a big deal. Have your parents accepted your decision?"

"Now they do. We struggled and didn't talk for a long time. Finally, they gave me an ultimatum. Said I needed to go to college and complete a degree first on my own. Then, if I still felt strongly about going into the priesthood, they'd accept my decision."

My eyes widened. "And you did it? Oh man, I would've been so pissed at my parents for trying to force me to do something like that. It's your life, Ian. I want to scream at my mom when she talks down to me about being a chef or tries to manipulate my decisions. They have no right to choose our futures."

He nodded, but he lacked the moral outrage I expected. "I get it, and that's what caused our big fallout. I refused at first, but when I took some time to reflect and pray, I realized they may have been right. I wanted to go straight to the seminary, study theology, and work on my bachelor's degree from there. Now I know it would have been a mistake. I wasn't mature enough, and I didn't realize the sacrifice I was truly going to be making. I'm glad I listened to my parents. I ended up attending a four-year secular college and took a wide variety of classes. I lived in the dorm. I partied. I made tons of friends and dated. And in my senior year, I told them I was still sure I wanted to be a priest after graduation."

"What'd they do?" I asked, breath held.

"They agreed it must be my calling. So now they back me up completely. We planned this trip together, and I remembered how cool my parents really are. We just had to get through a rough patch. I'm even grateful for them pushing me. It helped things become clear."

I stared at him, astonished at his maturity. "You have it all together," I murmured. "I wish I was like you. I'm a walking disaster."

He frowned. "What are you talking about? You are literally the most mature young woman I've ever known."

I let out a bitter laugh and twirled my straw. "Then I really fooled you. Ian, you have no idea how messed up I feel. I'm mad at my mom all the time for ignoring me and trying to push me toward schools that favor math and science. Just because I'm good at those subjects doesn't mean I want to have that career focus. She's been trying to get me to intern at a law firm and says a restaurant is beneath me. I love to cook and really want to study it more. And I love art—I thought of getting a minor in art history. When I mention doing any of those things, she shuts me down and says I need to support myself and make money. Then she trots off to work and forgets all about me until the next fight. Do you know why we're really in Italy?"

He leaned forward, his gaze laser focused on mine. "Tell me."

"Because I got busted for smoking weed. The police picked us up when we were driving, and I got arrested. These were the same friends I planned to join on a cross-country road trip in their RV. One of the guys is a musician, so we were going to hit a bunch of clubs. I was so tired of feeling trapped in this small little existence I had."

"What'd your mom do after the bust?"

"Lost her shit. The next week, we were booked for Italy for the summer. Problem solved by yanking me away from it all."

The bitterness still ran deep. She hadn't even pretended interest in why I was trying weed and had stopped hanging out with my usual friends. Because she didn't know who I really was and didn't care to find out.

"Want to know what's worse?" I asked, unable to stop the dam from breaking open.

"What?"

"In a sick way, I was kind of happy when she first told me we were going to Italy because of the weed. I was actually grateful to have her attention. And then I found out she was working on this huge new account and lost being the lead person to run it, which must've freaked her out. I bet she figured she'd go on a vacation for a while to let things settle before heading back. Once again, it was about her. Not me."

He looked thoughtful and sympathetic at the same time. "Your mom seems to like control."

"She lives for it. That's the reason I don't have a dad."

"What do you mean?"

I'd already dumped way too much stuff on him, but I was incapable of stopping at this point. Why try to hide how fucked-up my family really was? "Mom had me via a sperm donor. She said she wasn't meeting any good guys, and she didn't want to wait for a baby. So she picked out some dude in a catalogue and got pregnant."

He fell back into the chair, brows lifted in surprise. "Wow."

"Yeah, wow. So I don't get a dad because she wants to schedule me into her life with the least amount of mess possible."

He was silent for a while. I waited, expecting him to agree and cite his religious views regarding God's wrath about having babies outside of marriage. I knew the church was strict, with narrow views on conception, sex outside of marriage, and the LGBTQ community. Instead, he managed to shock me with his next words. "I can see how hard it'd be not having a father who can share your life. Even with divorced couples, the child gets a mom and dad. But your mom wanted you so badly, she chose you. Every step she took revolved around bringing you into her life so she could love you."

"But she looked at me like a commodity to purchase! There was no love involved."

His blue eyes burned into mine. "I disagree. There was plenty of love in her intention to have you. I think it's powerful when a parent actually chooses to have a baby with a clear mind and open heart. It may not be the traditional route, but it gives more meaning. My parents chose me, too."

I scoffed. "They were married! They decided to have a baby like a normal couple!"

"They adopted me. My birth mom left me in a basket on the church steps. Just like in the movies."

Another shock barreled through me. "Are you serious?"

"Yeah. I was going into foster care, but my parents heard the story and chose to adopt me. I'm not sure if they were ready for a child. They certainly weren't actively looking to adopt. But it was a small, tight-knit town, and they were well loved, and I ended up being their son." He tapped his chin. "I could have decided to feel like crap because I was dumped by the woman who birthed me. But I like the idea that I was specifically chosen by my parents. It made me feel grateful, not unwanted."

He'd managed to spin something awful into something beautiful. I couldn't quite grasp all the emotions and thoughts flooding my brain, but I knew I'd be looking at things in a different way—through his eyes. I struggled to respond in a way that made sense, but he suddenly gasped and pointed toward the sky. "Look." He jumped up from the table and went to the edge of the terrace. I followed.

A glowing, bright orange sliver of light crept slowly over the horizon. The color emphasized the gorgeous hues of the rooftops and the dusty darkness of the sky. Inch by slow inch, the full moon revealed herself in all her glory. I held my breath at the sheer beauty before me, as if a gift had been bestowed on a limited number of viewers hanging out on a rooftop in Florence. The color intensified and seeped into an almost fiery red as it reached full height and breadth, an angry, moody moon claiming dominance over the stars and sky and sun.

"I've never seen anything so beautiful," I whispered, not wanting to break the quiet hush that overtook us.

Without a word, he took my hand. Slowly, he raised it to his lips and pressed a kiss into my palm. I stilled, afraid to move, afraid to speak, wanting only to be held by a man who was never meant to know more of me. I wanted to study and trace each line of his palm, and his sinewy wrist, and his hair-roughened arm, but I did nothing. And then his gaze crashed into mine, his eyes a dark, intense blue I could drown in. "I have to tell you something, Allegra. It's not fair to keep it from you."

"What is it?"

"I feel things for you. At first, I thought it was just friendship. Now that I've finally committed to the seminary, I figured there were no challenges left to fight. I dated through college, had crushes, kissed girls, but no one got inside of me. To my heart."

I held my breath, waiting for the rest.

"Until now."

I bit my lip, fighting my need to reach for him. "I'm confused. I'm feeling things for you too, but what can happen between us? You're going to be a priest. We only have a week left. Should we even try to figure something out that can never work?"

"I don't know. I should probably stay away from you and keep things simple. But how can I walk away from a gift? That's how I feel about you. I'm happy when we're together. Hey, I'm happy if I can look across the room and see you at the table, laughing, having fun. It fills me up inside."

I groaned, trembling at the intensity, the truth of his words slicing through me. "I never felt this way either," I admitted.

"If you want me to leave you alone, I will. I don't have any answers. We only have a week left, and then I'm off to Assisi."

I indulged myself and stepped into his arms, wanting us to be close. He held me tight, rocking me slightly, our bodies pressed together in perfect symmetry. His clean scent drifted to my nostrils. "After the tour, we're heading to a rental villa in Tuscany for another week. Is Assisi far?"

"No."

"You can come visit, if you want. I'm sure Mom would let you."

"I'd like that. I don't understand why this is happening," he murmured in my ear. "But I want to spend more time with you. We can just take it slow. See what happens. Enjoy Italy together. Okay?"

I sighed. Deep inside, contentment unfurled to relax me. He filled me up. I felt truly seen for the first time. I wouldn't think about the ultimate ending between us. I'd just enjoy the moment and the gift of his company.

We stood in the dark, under the full moon, holding each other. And I knew I'd remember this moment and this moon for the rest of my life.

CHAPTER TWENTY-THREE

Francesca

There were dueling camps of thought regarding Venice. One side swore the city was dirty, smelly, moldy, and sinking. The other cited the gorgeous architecture, elegant gondolas, and timeless beauty of a city built on water.

Thankfully, Mom, Allegra, and I agreed with the latter.

We'd passed the halfway mark of our tour and left a trail of famous places behind us that had stolen our hearts. Even though the bus rides were endless, and we'd packed and repacked a million times, and the heat sank into our skin like a slow burn, bringing a bone-weary exhaustion that staggered me, Italy charmed, seduced, and demanded to be loved back.

And I did.

We were walking to the famous Piazza San Marco to grab lunch after a jam-packed morning tour of the city. Our gondola ride was scheduled for tomorrow, along with a glassblowing visit, and then we'd finish up in Burano before heading to our last stop in Siena.

I watched Allegra practically skip down the cobblestone streets, her face glowing like she had a wonderful secret. And it had to do with Ian.

Since the night they'd escaped to the terrace for their chat, the friendship had definitely veered into romantic territory. I knew the signs well. Secret longing looks shared across the room. Casual excuses to get close—a brush of the shoulders by accident or stolen touches of the hand or arm. They sat together on the bus and their laughter filled the air with the vigor and passion of youthful infatuation. I'd kept my mouth shut, not wanting to cause any undue tension between us. Not when things were going so well. Maybe I was lying to myself by thinking our problems were solved and we'd return home with a new respect for one another. Maybe I was just too happy in this fleeting moment to think about the future and try to control it.

Enzo was slowly teaching me that.

How to relax. How to seize the moment. I was immersed in my own game of hide-and-seek with him during the tour, trying to find ways to sneak in conversations or a private rendezvous. We'd been all set to meet on the terrace again the night Allegra announced she was seeing Ian there. Having nowhere else to go without being spotted, we'd canceled and I'd gone to bed early, just as I'd declared.

But I dreamed of him again.

I'd become a starstruck, giddy teen crushing on my tour guide. It was textbook cliché and I should have been embarrassed, but I felt too good to punish myself so soon. There'd be plenty of time for internal recriminations later.

Once we entered the square, I had to catch my breath. So many movies had been filmed here, showcasing the exquisite detail of Venice and the romanticism of the plaza. Various cafés lined the perimeter, and St. Mark's Basilica dominated the open area, showing off stunning marble lacework. The clock tower held a high archway that led to the shopping streets of the Rialto. We'd put that off until tomorrow so we'd have hours to indulge in shopping. Music rose and fell around us, a rich, soothing Italian melody that matched the otherworldly surroundings. Crowds swarmed the area and squeezed into the open chairs to sip lattes, eat bitter chocolate tarts, and people watch.

"Oh, let's take a picture of us with the pigeons," Allegra said. "It'll look awesome on my IG story."

I looked at the hundreds of fowl walking around, climbing on the body parts of tourists posing for the cameras. They looked like the New York City pigeons but even less afraid of the crowds. If everyone was doing it, the birds must be used to it. And clean. I hoped.

"Sure, do we need someone to take it or are you doing a selfie?"

Mom stepped back and put her hands out. "I'll pass on this one. I don't want them on me."

I tilted my head in surprise. "Why not? You like animals. It's only for a minute. Look—everyone's doing it."

"Come on, Nonni. I want you in the pic!" Allegra urged.

Stubbornness radiated from her figure. "No, sorry. I don't like things crawling on me. I'll take the picture. Stop bullying me."

Allegra laughed and I shrugged. "Fine. Oh, let's get some bird food from that lady over there first. We need a decent amount for a good shot," Allegra said. I gave her some money, and she returned with a small bag of bird food.

Mom frowned. "Do you think that's a good idea? I heard you're not supposed to feed the birds in the square. I read it in an article."

"Mom, look around. There are no signs, and tourists are doing it everywhere. Come on, here's my phone and Allegra's." I loved the idea of having a fun pic with my daughter to post.

We shook out a decent amount of corn and placed it in our open palms. Then we knelt on the ground, close together, and spread our arms wide to wait. Allegra sprinkled some extra around us in a half circle and the birds began to trickle over.

I laughed at the ticklish feeling of a pigeon pecking gently at my hand, and soon a decent group of birds had been tempted over. They perched on our arms and around our legs.

"Mom, take the pictures," I called out.

She began snapping with one phone, then traded off to the other. More pigeons joined the flock. I kept my smile, but then one landed on my head, and more on my shoulders, and in a few moments, all hell broke loose.

"Ugh, Mom, there's too many," Allegra said, shaking the rest of the corn off her and trying to move. "I think we're good."

"Yeah, let's get up."

We began to stand, figuring the pigeons would go away, but another small flock joined the first and had us surrounded. I shook my head, trying to get them off, but kernels must've been stuck in my shirt because one began to dive into my cleavage for his treat.

"Get away!" I shouted, stumbling and trying to wave them off.

This got them more excited. Birds began flying around me in a frenzy to get more corn, and Allegra let out a shriek and started running away.

"Leave them alone!" Mom yelled, launching toward me and holding the phones up like war weapons. She began making shooing noises and flapping her hands like a crazed bird herself, and then I heard shocked gasps and laughter from around us and began to panic about being photographed again. What if it went viral and I was dubbed the bird lady?

Not going to happen.

I grabbed Mom and ducked my head, hiding my face, and we ran to the edge of the square, tearing through the crowds. Allegra was right behind us, the leftover bag of corn dropped where we'd posed, and the flock of pigeons stopped following us and happily munched on the discarded feed.

Breathing heavily, I began patting myself down, checking for bites or poop, then did the same thing with Allegra. "Are you okay?" I asked nervously. "They didn't hurt you?"

"No, it was just freaky," she said, jumping up and down. "They got a little intense."

"You saved me, Mom," I said. "I think they believed you were their leader."

"No pigeons are going to mess with my girls," she said, her expression tight with determination. "I told you posing with birds is bad."

Allegra and I shared a look. Then we began to laugh. We laughed so hard and so long, we bent over and tears seeped down our cheeks. The whole thing reminded me of my fall down the steps and my mother's smug *I told you so* regarding my shoes. Now she'd done it again with the pigeons.

"From now on, we listen to Nonni," Allegra announced.

"Agreed. Let's eat. I'm starving." We walked to the first open café and grabbed a table. I squeezed out a bit of antibacterial gel in both of our hands to sanitize from the birds, then opened the menu. After a few moments, we all agreed on the same things— panini, fries, and frozen hot chocolate sundaes for dessert.

Allegra looked shocked after the waiter left. "Mom, did you actually leave the mozzarella on your sandwich? And skipped the salad? And ordered dessert?"

I wagged my finger at her. "When you're old as dirt and even looking at fries adds pounds, you can apologize for that remark. But, yes, I've decided to relax my stringent calorie intake and live a little."

"I'm glad," Mom said. She stared at me with a gentle affection and approval that made my heart soar. "I think you look wonderful. Life is too short to skip the fries."

"I'll put that on a poster next to my bathroom scale." I sipped my sparkling water, enjoying the dry bubbles that danced in my mouth. Definitely, champagne tonight. "We have dinner on our own. Any special place you want to go?"

"We're eating lunch and planning dinner already? I can't think that far ahead," Allegra complained. "I was going to ask if it would be cool if I skipped out tonight. Ian mentioned doing some exploring. We'd grab a bite on our own. I guess it's his parents' anniversary and he wants them to have a romantic dinner alone."

She faked casual pretty well, but I caught on because I hid my own secrets. I hesitated, not sure if allowing her to traipse through Venice with Ian was a good idea. "He can drink, you can't," I pointed out. "I don't want you going to clubs or bars."

"I won't. Ian isn't a big partier. We just want to see the city at night and catch a meal. Listen, we've all been together nonstop. I just want a break with someone my own age."

"He's four years older," I said.

"I think it's fine," Mom interrupted. "He's a good boy. I've watched him with his parents. She's young and needs a break from us old people."

Annoyance flickered. Had she already forgotten about Allegra being busted with a bunch of delinquents? Why was I always the bad guy? Every time I tried to discipline my daughter, Mom tried to cut in and make excuses for her behavior. "Maybe if she hadn't been arrested for pot I'd be more inclined to let her explore," I said.

Allegra glared across the table. "Maybe if you'd been around more, I wouldn't have gotten in trouble," she shot back, her face flushed with temper. "I made a mistake. I'm sorry. It's not like I've been going to parties every weekend, or drinking in my room, or messing up my grades. I've been perfect, just like you always wanted. Don't I get to make a few mistakes without hearing about it for the rest of my life?"

The waiter delivered our food, cutting off the rest of her tirade. I didn't respond, and we all concentrated on our lunch amid a tense silence. I kept going over her words about me demanding perfection from her. Was I really like that? Yes, I pushed hard because I saw all of her amazing potential. Had she craved more attention from me? Had I believed I was giving her the freedom and space she wanted, but the entire time, she'd just wanted me to be with her?

Was that the reason she was suddenly doing weed and hanging with the wrong crowd? To force me to finally pay attention?

I remember pushing Mom away at her age, desperate to have my own life independent of her. Of course, it was my father I was always chasing after. He was the elusive parent whose approval or attention reinvigorated my drive to be better. But Allegra only had me. Maybe that was why she'd developed such a close relationship with her grandmother. Without a father, she'd needed more from me.

And I'd failed her.

The crushing truth punched me like an uppercut. All this time, Mom had been right. Begging me to give more of myself while I insisted Allegra needed less of me to become her own person. I'd been directing my anger toward Mom for being the chosen one, but maybe it had been crucial to make Allegra feel seen.

My phone rang.

I froze. Casually glanced down at the screen to see Kate's name. The insistent ring practically screamed urgency. It was almost a physical need to pick it up, excuse myself, and make apologies later. But as my daughter didn't even bother to look up at me, I realized she had no expectations that I would keep my word about work. She expected me to break my promises, because I'd believed doing that was less important than losing control over a new account or averting a disaster.

Wasn't it time I really tried to change?

I dropped the ringing phone into my purse and finished my lunch. No one commented, but I caught Allegra's surprised jerk, though she tried to hide it.

It wasn't the time for a big truth talk. Not yet. But a chat was overdue, and I needed to connect with Allegra so we could return home on better footing.

"Okay," I said, catching her gaze. "You can go with Ian. You're right. I have to start trusting you again. I don't expect you to be perfect, sweetheart. God knows, I'm not. But I'm going to talk to his parents so they know you're out with him. And you need to be home by eleven. That's plenty of time for you to hang."

She didn't give me a forgiving smile, but her muscles relaxed. "Cool. Thanks."

"Welcome. Mom, that means it's you and me tonight? How about we go wild together?"

She laughed, but I noticed the deeper lines around her face hinting at a weariness that worried me. She'd been such a trooper and rarely complained, but I knew how difficult these tours were. Was I so wrapped up in my own world I hadn't even noticed she needed more downtime? "I'm not sure I'm up to that tonight. I was actually thinking about going to bed early, but I can rally."

"You know, Mom, I think you're right. We should all take another early night. We have the next two days to explore Venice. Let's grab something at the hotel later on and be asleep by eight. Doesn't that sound good?"

Relief skittered across her features. "Yes, that sounds wonderful. Are you sure?"

"Positive. If I feel beat-up, I can't imagine how this schedule is for you." I reached over and squeezed her hand. "You're amazing, Mom. I'm glad I got my toughness from you."

Surprise widened her eyes. I rarely complimented my mother. Our conversations always revolved around petty arguments or day-to-day discussions that barely scratched the surface. No wonder I hadn't known anything about her childhood or her losses, her true story.

I'd never asked.

She squeezed back and smiled. "Thanks, Frannie."

I felt the vibrations of texts pouring in from my phone, the flicker of the iPhone light going on and off like a pinball machine. My head throbbed. It must be bad. They probably needed me. I could be making a huge mistake by waiting to get back to them until later.

I dragged in a deep breath and focused on Allegra, who began chatting about the crazed pigeons from our dramatic incident, making us laugh all over again.

And I didn't touch my phone.

CHAPTER TWENTY-FOUR

SOPHIA

THERE WAS A faint knock on my door. I left the private balcony where I'd spent the last half hour relaxing and gazing at the busy Venice street and opened it.

"Hi, Mom. How are you doing?"

I smiled at Frannie. She looked nice. The bright yellow shirt she'd picked highlighted the lighter blond streaks in her hair and the spark in her eyes. I'd noticed she'd been taking a bit more time with her appearance lately and I was glad. She was beautiful, but she hid behind her profession, always telling me she needed to dress conservatively, avoiding colors other than black, gray, and navy. Her hair was growing longer, and silky strands clung to her cheeks, accenting her wide dark eyes. She'd changed, but I still wasn't sure if it was the time away from work, Italy itself, or something else I'd missed.

"Good. I took a long nap and I'm going to read for a while. What about you?"

She shifted her weight. "Well, I'm going to stay up until Allegra gets home safely at eleven but figured I'd go out for a little while. Grab a drink with the tour group. Is that okay? Do you want to come?"

"Oh, no, honey, go ahead and have fun. I'm perfectly happy to stare out my window and relax tonight. If you're out, do you want me to text you when Allegra gets home? That way you don't have to rush back."

"Thanks, Mom, that'd be great." She nibbled at her bottom lip. "You think it was a good idea to let her go with Ian, right?"

This was the first time she'd asked for my advice. It felt good. "Yes," I said firmly. "You already spoke with his parents and she's eighteen, honey. She needs a bit of freedom. She made a mistake but we need to allow her time to rebuild the trust. Let her have an adventure in Venice."

Frannie smiled. "Okay, thanks. I'll see you in the morning." She kissed my cheek and disappeared.

I went back out to the balcony, my thoughts ajumble. We still had our fights, but since Naples, there'd been a new understanding between us. I was hoping a week in Tuscany to really bond and talk would help round out the entire vacation. We'd have few distractions and would not be able to avoid one another.

It was time. Time to heal the rifts and be brave enough to say what we felt. My girls needed a new understanding to face the future.

So did I.

My hands pressed against my belly, which had been mercifully quiet lately. But I felt the thing growing inside me, shifting around, and my body trying to compensate. I was sick. I just didn't know the extent yet.

I settled down and read for a while, but restlessness nipped at my bones. I wanted to rest, but the idea of a quiet stroll through Venice called to me. I knew how to get to the piazza from here without getting lost. Maybe I'd sit at a table and listen to the music at night for an hour, and then I'd be tired enough to sleep.

Decision made, I slipped on my shoes, grabbed my purse,

and headed out. Savoring the scents and sounds of the magical floating city, I took my time and chose an empty table at one of the cafés. The sight of the pigeons made me giggle, and I hoped Allegra and Frannie were having a good time tonight.

I ordered a glass of Pinot Grigio, some water, and a pastry to nibble on. The beauty of the plaza at night struck me full force. The orchestra was in full swing, the sweetness of the strings soaring through the summer air, as couples danced on the cobblestones. The lights of the clock tower and shops and stars dazzled my eyes. I sat quietly and took it all in, thinking back over my life and every moment that had led me to right here.

"*Scusi, signora*, are you alone?"

I looked up. A handsome older gentleman with gray hair and smart silver glasses had asked the question. "Oh yes, go ahead and take my chair," I said, gesturing to the one next to me.

His smile showed white, straight teeth. He must've brushed very well. It was hard to keep a smile like that at our age. "Oh, you speak English?"

"Yes."

"Thank goodness. I'm sorry, I was going to ask if you'd like some company. Are you meeting someone?"

I blinked. Huh? "Um, no, I'm alone. Just having a glass of wine." He waited and I realized he wanted to sit at my table. Politeness took over. "Of course you can join me."

He sat down and met my gaze directly from across the table. "Thank you. My name is Milton. I've been touring most of the day and just wanted a place to take in the sights and have a cocktail. When you see a beautiful woman alone, it's silly to sit by yourself. I hope I didn't intrude."

Warmth flowed through me. My goodness, it had been a long time since a man approached me for anything. Except for church. And they were priests so they didn't count. Allegra had teased me about that previous gentleman following me, but I still stuck to my guns in believing that he was really after my granddaughter. "How sweet—thank you for the compliment. I'm Sophia. Are you with a tour group?"

He inclined his head. "We're doing the typical Italian tour and hitting all the highlights. You?"

"The same thing. It's been incredible, but we're winding down. After Venice, we end in Siena. But then I'm staying in Tuscany for a week before heading back home."

"Then Venice is your end and my beginning. I bet we're on a similar tour. We finish in Rome."

I laughed. "Yes, that's where we started. Have you ever been to Italy before?"

"No, this is my first time. How have I missed out for all those years? It's tragic."

"Me too. It'd been my dream for most of my life, but my husband and I kept pushing it out until it was too late."

"You lost him?" I nodded. "My deepest sympathies. I lost my wife five years ago, also. We talked consistently of travel and never went anywhere. Too many children. Too many responsibilities. Then it was also too late."

My heart squeezed in my chest. "We have similar stories. Are you with your children on the tour?"

He shook his head. "They are involved in their busy lives like I once was. I came alone."

I tilted my head and studied him closer. There was a quiet confidence in his demeanor, something only age usually taught, after many successes and even more failures. We were finally comfortable in our own skin, and able to move through the world without comparison or envy or despair that we'd never be enough. Our bodies taught us the lesson of humility, because eventually, we were all the same. The shell is our armor and it slowly disintegrates until it is our time. The clock that used to signal a need for babies now warns us of our limited time.

"I think it's wonderful," I said truthfully. "My daughter and granddaughter are with me on this trip."

"What a blessing. To experience this type of beauty with family is everything. What was your favorite place so far?"

The waiter briefly interrupted, and Milton ordered a Pellegrino and a glass of Pinot Grigio.

"My favorite was Naples. We only stayed a few hours, but it's the place my parents were born and met, so it was special."

"We go there for a few hours also. I had an aunt who came from Florence, so I'm looking forward to the visit. Where else did you go?"

We compared notes on our itineraries and the waiter brought the drinks. Time flowed effortlessly as we chatted with an easy camaraderie, like we'd known each other forever. He spoke of his three grandchildren and his four daughters with a pride I understood. He opened up about his family—how his youngest lost her boyfriend in a car crash and suffered from PTSD; how the middle child took years to conceive before finally adopting newborn twins; and how his wife had been taken by lung cancer even though neither of them had ever smoked.

Something shifted and allowed me to open up with this stranger who felt like a friend. "When I first asked Frannie to go to Italy, she said no. She runs her own advertising agency, and it keeps her busy. I've watched her relationship with Allegra get worse year by year, and I thought a trip would give us the time we needed to bond again. Then Allegra got caught smoking pot and was arrested. Frannie finally agreed to get her away for the summer."

He whistled low. "Tough. The drugs are hard with this

generation—they're everywhere and there's peer pressure. Has the time together worked out?"

"A bit. The first week, Frannie worked nonstop and Allegra refused to speak to her. It felt like the same dynamics as back home. But this past week, something changed. My daughter put her phone away, and I see my granddaughter opening up a bit. Of course, there's also a boy."

"There's always a boy," Milton said with a laugh. "The question is—is he a nice boy?"

"Very. Frannie had Allegra via a sperm donor." I still winced when I said it aloud, even though I'd gotten used to it and thanked that man every day for the gift of my granddaughter. "So Allegra struggles a bit with her place here without a traditional family."

"Makes sense. How old?"

"Eighteen."

He nodded. "Eighteen is such a sensitive age. They're supposed to know what they want to do for a career and suddenly be an adult just because of a number."

"Exactly." I gave another sigh. "I watched Allegra when she was a baby so Frannie could work. I think my daughter resents our close relationship. And growing up, Frannie was much closer to my husband, Jack. Somehow, we lost our way and haven't gotten it back. I don't know, it's kind of a mess between all of us."

"Ah, family drama. Where would we be without it? I know what you mean, though. My youngest, Christy, was horrible to her mother. She was definitely a daddy's girl and I spoiled her, sometimes to the detriment of my wife. They had a long struggle but became very close before my wife passed. I think time and Christy's own experiences made a difference. It sounds to me like you're already making progress here, especially with your daughter. Sometimes, our children forget we're just people like them who make our own mistakes."

It was true. Children seemed to put parents on a pedestal, just so they could knock them off in their teens. As time passed, we'd been ground into the dirt with no idea how we got there. But talking to Milton helped put some things into perspective. It was nice to share with someone who understood.

Soon, our glasses were empty, the moon had risen high in the sky, and a few hours had gone by.

I shook my head when I looked at my watch. "My goodness, I must go soon. Allegra is out, so I need to be back by eleven."

"I've taken up your whole evening. I'm sorry—I'm usually not so bold, but there was something that pulled me toward you. I've enjoyed this."

I smiled. "Me too. I'm glad you asked. Do you have your next adventure planned after this?"

"Yes, I've always wanted to see Paris. Look up at the Eiffel Tower, view the *Mona Lisa*, and put my feet on the ground of Normandy to remember World War II and our soldiers' sacrifice."

I gave a longing sigh. "That would be an amazing trip. I've had Ireland and Paris on my list to visit."

"Then maybe you will join me." His blue eyes sparkled behind his glasses. When the waiter came over with the check, he asked for paper and a pen and quickly began scribbling. "I'm going to give you my email address. I'm planning the trip in eight months. This tour company caters to singles, so it's a nice group to travel with. Oh, I'm also on Facebook, where I post all my pictures of the kids and stuff."

I laughed. "Well, it sounds amazing, but I'm not sure I can go to Paris."

He looked up and our gazes locked. "Sophia, I understand it

sounds crazy. We've just met. My kids couldn't believe I did this tour on my own—they were worried and tried to talk me out of it. I love my children, and I loved my wife. But I don't know what lies before me, or how long I get to be here. It's time to see the sights I've only dreamed about. Make the most of every precious moment. You deserve to go to Paris, or any other place you want. Don't you agree?"

I hesitated, fascinated by the intensity of his words and the truth that struck me full force. He was right. I never imagined doing anything outside of my safe circle anymore. My days were filled with routine and revolved around Allegra and Frannie. Maybe it was time I began branching out and experiencing more. "I don't know."

He nodded with understanding. "Of course—it's damn scary taking off on your own across the world. But already, I feel like I'm hooked."

He was right. I'd figured I'd live on my memories of this trip for the rest of my life. But what if there was more out there for me? I'd cautioned Frannie over and over to step away from work to enjoy the world. Yet my focus was on home and family. Was it really quite different after all? It was just what we both chose as our safe shelter to avoid dealing with the unknown.

"I'll think about it, Milton."

"Good." He pressed the paper into my palm and closed my fingers around it. The touch of his hand brought a solid, comforting warmth my soul recognized and remembered. "Email me. I'd love to know about the rest of your trip and your time in Tuscany."

"Thank you. Enjoy the rest of your tour." He insisted on paying the check, and he stood while I left. For a few seconds, we stared at each other and smiled, acknowledging the incredible evening we'd shared.

When I got back, it was almost eleven. I changed into my pajamas and washed up, and soon Allegra arrived home.

"Hi, Nonni! We had the best time! We walked by the bridge and got dinner at this adorable little place with the best pasta in the world, and guess what! We went on a gondola ride!"

I adored her flushed cheeks and sparkling eyes and the first signs of love sketched on her beautiful face. I sat on the edge of the bed beside her and felt my own heart soar with excitement. "Oh, it sounds amazing! How was it at night?"

"So beautiful." She sighed. "The canal was lit up and people were singing and I felt like I was in a movie. Ian's so nice. We talked and talked nonstop. Do you know he wants to be a priest?"

I blinked. "A priest? No, sweetheart, I didn't know that."

"Yeah, he's heading into the seminary after the summer, but he's going to Assisi after the tour, and when I told him we would be in Tuscany, he asked if maybe he can drive over and stay for a day. Do you think Mom would be okay with that?"

My mind whirled, but I nodded. "I'm sure it will. We can both talk to her."

"Good. Oh, and we found this bakery and I got a coconut gelato with a biscotti and it was sick good."

She chattered on for a while, and I savored every second. A priest? My granddaughter's first big crush and he was off-limits. Of course, he was in Ireland anyway, so nothing could be pursued. It was a sweet summer romance that would change her, even if there was hurt afterward. And though I'd do anything to save her from heartbreak, I knew love and loss needed to be experienced in order to grow. Hopefully, she understood there was only one ending for them both, and it would be bittersweet rather than true heartbreak.

Then again, no one could help whom they loved.

"Honey, text your mom and let her know you're home safe."

She rolled her eyes but didn't give me guff. Her thumbs flew over the tiny screen and I shook my head with amazement at her dexterity. "Done. I'm going to hop in the shower," she said, heading into the bathroom.

I decided to grab my own phone and text Frannie myself, but it took me a much longer time than it did Allegra. Immediately, I saw the three dots.

Did she have a good time?

I decided to wait to tell her about Ian's future occupation until we were face-to-face. **Yes, great time. She'll give you all the details tomorrow.**

So happy. I'll be home later—let me know if you need me.

We're good, heading to bed. Have fun.

Allegra and I talked for a bit longer after her shower, and then she fell asleep with her phone next to her pillow and a smile on her face. I read for a while but then finally got up to get a glass of water. Of course, the water was tepid and I craved it cold. Tamping down a sigh, I pulled on my robe and slippers and grabbed the bucket to get ice. At least it was just down the hallway.

I opened the door quietly and stepped out.

Then froze.

Frannie and Enzo stood a few feet down the hallway, locked in a passionate kiss. Her back was pressed against the door, arms wrapped around his neck, their mouths fused together like lovers who couldn't bear to be parted from each other. I eased slowly back, terrified they'd spot me, and peeked around the corner.

They broke the kiss and stared at each other. I held my breath, afraid to move or shatter the spell.

Her door opened and they both stepped inside.

Then it shut.

Head spinning, I forgot about my water and retreated to my room. How hadn't I seen it? How long had the affair been going on? Finally, Frannie was enjoying a passionate romance, but as much as I'd hoped she'd hook up with Enzo, the reality worried me. It was obvious they needed to hide the relationship— probably to protect his job. Would they be able to easily say goodbye in a few days? Was it serious or just a casual fling?

My daughter rarely broke her stringent rules and I was sure one of them forbade her from engaging in an illicit romance with her tour guide. Which meant she really liked him.

Or more.

I climbed into bed and lay for hours, staring up at the ceiling, thinking of the two women I loved with my heart and soul. Two men had suddenly come into their lives unexpectedly. I was a firm believer that God gave us what we needed, not necessarily what we wanted. It was too big to be a general coincidence that they were both on the same path. I just couldn't see how it would end.

I prayed it would be good for both of them.

But I also knew God had a terrible sense of humor.

It took me a long time to sleep.

CHAPTER TWENTY-FIVE

Francesca

Once I knew Mom was settled in for the night and Allegra was out with Ian, I quickly texted Enzo.

I'm free to meet.

I kept it simple and to the point. Since the night of our stolen kiss, I couldn't stop thinking about the next time we'd be together. My day with Allegra and Mom had been wonderful, but I was grateful I'd have a few hours to steal some alone time. I was finally glad Allegra wasn't sharing my room, or a meet-up wouldn't even be possible. My phone buzzed.

Group is at Harry's for the night. Meet me at the corner across from hotel in five minutes. I know a place.

I didn't hesitate. I'd already dressed in anticipation of his gaze, making me feel beautiful instead of passably pretty. It was rare that I glimpsed true appreciation in a man's stare. I looked on my body as more of a machine than a feminine treasure, grateful to get up every morning and be able to accomplish my goals without pain or disability. But when I caught the hot gleam in his dark eyes, I shivered with pleasure. I wondered if I'd be able to settle for anything less from now on.

He was already waiting at the corner. Afraid to touch in case one of our tour members lingered nearby, we stood close, our gazes locked on each other. "Hi. Where are we going?" I asked, a catch in my breath as his delicious scent rose to my nostrils.

"A cozy place near the Rialto. I left most of our group singing and drinking at Harry's. What about Allegra and your mom?"

"Mom's in bed. Allegra's out with Ian, and Ian's parents had reservations at one of the restaurants near the plaza."

He nodded. "We'll stay away from the tourist spots. Follow me."

Our hands brushed as we walked side by side. He caught me when my foot stumbled on one of the cobblestones, and I felt his fingers burn into my skin. We walked for a while, and I enjoyed his quiet presence and the beautiful sounds of Venice at night. We reached the Rialto bridge, and he led me away from the main street, into a narrow alley with low archways and brick walls. I raised my brow. The buildings seemed like decaying shops that no longer accepted the public. Grabbing my hand, he guided me past two large barrels and through a door. The faded sign read CANTINA DO SPADE.

I caught my breath when we walked in. The place was tiny and packed with people. The high mahogany bar was crammed with displays of food and treats, including a large case that featured an array of desserts, cheeses, and breads. A fully stocked bar took up the wall behind the counter. People squeezed around a few battered wooden tables, drinking and laughing, while small plates crowded every inch of the surface. My knees weakened at the delicious smells. "There's no room," I said, looking around.

He grinned and put up his hand, motioning toward the woman behind the cash register. He engaged in a lively conversation in Italian, and she laughed, pointing to a tiny two-person table in the farthest left corner. He thanked her—I recognized *grazie* and the word *spritz*—and gently led me to our table.

"This is one of the oldest bars in Venice. Casanova used to frequent the place. It's filled with mostly locals, so we should be safe here."

"Wow, I love it," I said in awe, taking in the warmth and charming ambience.

"I ordered us two drinks—try the *spritz*; it's one of their classics. A light type of bubbly wine like Prosecco. Have you eaten?"

I shook my head.

"They have wonderful *cicchetti* here."

"What's that?"

He frowned as if trying to think of how to explain it. "Little portions of food to try. Appetizers."

"Oh, like tapas! So you can get a bigger variety and try different things."

"*Sì!* Are you an adventurous eater?"

I laughed. "No. My daughter is always complaining I don't have a drop of Italian blood in me. I stick with salads, lean meats, and fruit. But I've tried many more things than usual since we got here, including carbs. As you've said, life is too short not to indulge."

He reached over and cupped my cheek, and I leaned into his touch. The table was small and the place was loud and I felt as if I was in a secure bubble that contained only us. "I'm glad you finally took my advice," he teased. "Now we shall test your limits. Will you try the items I order? Even if you don't think you'll like it?"

"Yes. I trust you."

The words fell out of my mouth so easily, I was surprised I didn't gasp with shock. But I didn't. He lifted my fingers to his lips and kissed them, his dark eyes heated. "Thank you, Francesca," he whispered in his deep, husky voice.

I knew right then we were talking about more than food.

I sipped the delicious chilled *spritz* and indulged in a variety of bites that pushed my culinary education. Fried meat-stuffed olives; baked sardines; tuna rissoles—balls filled with shreds of fresh tuna, cheeses, and spices; grilled octopus; and salty cod.

We talked and drank, and he fed me pieces with his fork, watching my face as I registered each new taste on my tongue. It was one of the most intimate experiences, and I realized how food truly was more than nourishment for the body, but more of a story in time that I could remember by closing my eyes and bringing up the flavors lingering in my memory.

We sipped bitter, strong espresso and nibbled on a dark chocolate tart as the crowd began to wind down. My phone buzzed. I checked to see if it was Allegra, but it was the office, which irritated me. I'd checked in yesterday and explained I'd be offline for the next week, citing Wi-Fi issues in Tuscany. Kate seemed surprised by my sudden willingness to let her lead, but I was starting to realize maybe I didn't need to do it all. The more time I experienced away, the better I was beginning to feel. The constant tension thrumming through my body eased. My chest loosened. My breath deepened. For the first time in my life, I had no desire to try to figure out what a client needed or to prove myself.

I slipped my phone back into my purse.

Enzo patiently waited; his lips curved in a smile as he noticed me tuck away my phone. "What was your favorite place you've traveled?" he asked. We couldn't stop touching or asking each other questions, as if we were desperate to close the last inch of space between our bodies and hearts.

"Right here. I never got to travel much. I went straight from school to work and then built my business. After I had Allegra, the only weekend trip I treated us to was Sesame Place in Pennsylvania. My mom used to show her old DVDs of *Sesame Street* and she was obsessed with Big Bird."

"I like him too. You have such a thirst for knowledge, though. Didn't you ever want to burst out of your routine and see more?"

The old Frannie would have taken offense, thinking he was

judging my choices as wrong, but I knew Enzo wasn't like that. He seemed eager to know the truth of who I was, and as he kept digging deeper, I realized I didn't know myself very well. "I never let myself think about it," I said simply. "Maybe I was born practical. I missed out on that magical fantasy gene. Even when I was young, I never imagined myself as a princess or a bride or a celebrity. I wanted to run an important business like my dad."

He smiled. "I love that about you," he said. "That's why you're successful. But maybe you worked so hard for all this time so you can finally take a breath. Enjoy what you created."

"Reap what I sowed?"

He cocked his head. "Yes, if that's what I said."

I laughed and he leaned over and pressed a kiss on my lips. "I love your accent."

"I don't have an accent. You do."

"Mine is more guttersnipe. Yours is sexy."

"*Cara*, you are pretty much one of the sexiest women I've ever met. Want to know why?"

I squirmed, not comfortable with compliments. "Trust me, I'm not sexy."

"That's why you're sexy. Because you don't know it, and you have no ego. Plus, you don't care what anyone thinks."

I blushed. His words embarrassed me, but it was nice to think he was telling the truth. *"Grazie."*

"Prego. Now, pick one place you'd like to see next."

I took my time and analyzed all my options. "Japan."

"A good choice. Why?"

"I read a story that was set in Japan once. The author painted it in such a way I felt like I was there. The traditional customs and beliefs in a culture that reveres smart business fascinates me. You can be in Tokyo—one of the most thriving, exciting cities—and then be in a tiny village witnessing an ancient tea ceremony."

His face softened. "That sounds beautiful. And very you. I like the way you describe things, even in your guttersnipe accent."

I laughed and playfully smacked his arm. "Will you go?" he asked seriously.

"Probably not. It's a long trip and a bit impractical. I'm not sure if Allegra would go with me. She goes to college next year and everything changes."

"You, Francesca Ferrari, deserve an exciting, adventure-filled life. Don't let the details of the day bog you down too much. Now, let's take advantage of the rest of the evening and walk. I will show you the Venezia I know."

We paid the bill and walked out, arms linked. He escorted me deep into the underground of the city, into dark alleyways twisted in a maze that led us by the water, over small bridges, and into shadowed corners. Whispers in the breeze mingled with the dank scents of the water. The light from the stars and moon guided us by the canals and parked gondolas rocking back and forth, creaking gently. He pointed out treasures in shop windows and hidden cafés filled with locals who drank and feasted without the probing gazes of tourists. It was a night of magic and romance, and I savored every precious, fleeting minute.

As the hour grew late, I texted with Mom and Allegra, feeling relief that my daughter was home safe and looking forward to hearing her story. We walked back to the hotel with slow, dragging steps, not wanting to see the evening end.

As we got closer, his hand dropped from mine. My heart mourned his touch.

We rode the elevator to my floor. He walked me down the hallway and stood outside my door.

"Thank you for a perfect night." My throat felt raw with

emotion. Longing. Fear. Desire. All of the mess mixed together in a cocktail that was both potent and tempting.

He moved in, and his mouth covered mine. I pressed against him and looped my arms around his shoulders. The idea of going to bed alone rocked my core, and I knew in that moment, I couldn't let him go.

His lips eased from mine. "Francesca." My name was a whisper. A command. A question.

I didn't pause. "Come inside."

He nodded, his face tight, his eyes burning with heat. *"Sì."*

My hands trembled around my key card as I unlocked the door and he stepped inside with me.

CHAPTER TWENTY-SIX

ALLEGRA

THE REST OF the tour flew by.

The next few days in Venice I'd remember forever, especially the night I spent with Ian. My head was stuffed with memories of us sitting close while we sailed down the Grand Canal in a gondola, the quiet whisper of the boat cutting through the water under a night sky studded with stars. The gondolier was dressed in a striped black-and-white shirt, with a hat and a red scarf wrapped around the brim. He held a long pole and navigated in and out of tight canals. I tried to focus on my surroundings but I kept thinking about how Ian's thigh pressed against mine and the way he kissed me like I was the most important person on earth. He'd finally shyly reached for my hand, and we spent the rest of the gondola ride soaking up each other's presence as we toured Venice.

He made me giddy and hopeful. He listened when I spoke and soothed a loneliness inside I didn't even know I had. It was like being hungry all the time but feeling used to it, and then someone gives you a Michelin-starred four-course meal, and you don't know if you can ever go back to being starved.

Because now you know the difference.

Later, we sat in a small café and ate dinner, talking nonstop about our lives and our dreams. Eleven came too fast, but I'd made a promise, and though Mom had broken many of hers, I didn't want to do the same.

David had stopped checking in. A few days ago, Freda had sent me a video of them partying. She flashed her boobs at the camera—obviously high—and I caught Connor and David in the background with some girls. I made a half-assed funny comment, but then I decided not to check my social media anymore. Would I have been high and drunk all summer if I'd gone with them? Around Ian, I never questioned if I was cool enough or too nerdy or boring. He made me seem perfect just as I was.

My next gondola ride was nice but different. I sat squeezed next to Mom, Nonni, Kai, Dan, and Hana. We took tons of pictures and an opera singer serenaded us as we coasted down the water in the bright sun of the afternoon. Ian floated nearby in another gondola, and we smiled at each other—our own ride a special secret kept between us even though I'd told Nonni. Mom asked a bunch of questions, but I kept it purposely light. I'd spilled so much to Nonni already in my excitement from the date, and I wanted to be more careful with Mom. I needed to convince her to let Ian visit next week after he finished with Assisi.

The thought of saying goodbye in Siena was too much.

The tour ended tomorrow. After spending the morning in Siena, we had a few hours to ourselves, and then a farewell party at a local family vineyard. In the morning, everyone would fly back home, and we'd be left with our pictures, memories, and a Facebook page to share.

Enzo motioned for us to follow, and I shook off my thoughts. We stopped at the edge of the Piazza del Campo, a simple square surrounded by buildings and offset by a clock tower. "This is the piazza where the famous Palio horse race is run. It happens twice in the summer months—once in July and once in

August. Seventeen *contrade*—city neighborhoods—compete for the prize."

"Money?" Dan asked.

Enzo shook his head. "More important than money. A painted banner bearing the image of the Virgin Mother. This banner is the pride and joy of the city and is fought over bitterly by all the *contrade*. The winner must ride his horse three times around the square."

"Doesn't seem too difficult," Dana shouted out.

Enzo laughed. "Oh, *signora*, it is most difficult. There are no rules, so it is quite dangerous. Many jockeys have gotten hurt. Horses have died. Blood has been shed. It is widely known that jockeys can be kidnapped, bribed, or blackmailed to either win or lose. We do not take this race lightly."

I looked at the simple square and shivered. There was so much violence hidden underneath civilized society. Sure, I knew bad things happened. I struggled with my own crap. But I'd been mostly protected. The world was a much bigger place than I thought, because I chose ignorance.

It was easier, wasn't it? Pretending nothing affected me or I had no hope to change things. I thought of the conversations I'd had with Ian about his dream to help people and animals. To be a gentle ear and make a difference here. He had a bigger purpose and wasn't afraid of the work.

Maybe it was time I did the same.

"I'll bring you to the cathedral and you may climb the steps to see a beautiful view of the city. Then I'll give you some time to explore on your own, grab lunch, and we will head to the hotel for our final night. Dinner is at a family vineyard, where we shall celebrate the end of a perfect trip, no?"

Groans rumbled from everyone, and an excited buzz of chatter rose in the air. People had bonded over the last few weeks.

Relationships had formed from not only witnessing great moments of history, but being together through all the boring details of travel. Bus trips, gas station stops, restroom requests. Long lines and long walks in stifling heat. Lost items, including Cherry's passport, which had thankfully been found. And many questions all posed to Enzo, which he'd answered happily, seeming never to get pissed off.

He was definitely cool. And there was something else I'd begun to notice, even though I wondered if I was acting crazy.

He seemed to be into Mom.

If I hadn't been studying him, I would have missed it. But we were on the bus, and everyone was occupied. Nonni slept beside me. I'd been bored and just focused on watching Enzo in the front seat as he talked to the driver, but then he'd swiveled around and seemed to look directly at my mom.

It wasn't a normal glance, like he'd give to one of his tour members. It was the look of a guy hot for someone, with intense eyes and a crazed focus that took my breath. Since Mom was in front of me, I didn't know if she was looking back at him or sleeping, but then he gave this small smile, like he knew a secret that made him happy, and that's when I knew something could be going on.

After that, I watched them carefully. The past two days definitely showed signs. They tried to make excuses to be near each other. He always came to talk after dinner or before we went to our rooms. Mom had even mentioned she was going out briefly to grab something to eat—she had the munchies—and I wondered if they were meeting up secretly.

Had it been going on long? Or was it a new thing that had just happened? And did it matter? The tour was done. We'd be heading to Tuscany and then home. She wouldn't be able to see him even if she wanted to.

Just like Ian and me.

On cue, he fell into step beside me. "Hey."

I smiled. "Hey. Are you excited to see the cathedral?"

"Yes, are you up for the climb so we can check out the view?"

"Of course." We spoke casually, but the connection between us burned so bright, I wondered if everyone knew we'd kind of hooked up. His parents definitely did—Rosemary always smiled at me with a hope in her eyes that I hadn't understood.

Now I did. She hadn't wanted him to be a priest. Was she thinking I could change his mind? That we'd fall for each other and he'd decide not to go through with it?

I hated the excitement that curled in my belly at the idea. I needed to respect his decision. A few kisses and one date in Venice didn't make a relationship.

Cool down, girl.

"I can't believe this is the last church we're going to see," I murmured, staring up at the soaring Gothic cathedral. The front was flat-faced, gleaming white, with perfect pointy spikes stabbing into the air. Intricate carvings along the exterior led up to the angel spires sitting atop a gleaming mural of the Virgin Mary bowing before Jesus. Angels gathered around them, some blowing what looked to be trumpets.

Ian pointed up toward it. "Gorgeous. That's the *Coronation of the Virgin*, painted by Sano di Pietro. I can't wait to go inside and see the dome."

Excitement threaded his voice. We walked up the steps. Three main doors were flung open to welcome sinners. I was getting better at discerning different architecture, appreciating each church's individual flavor. Some were more intimate and simpler, and others dripped with treasures, as if to tempt onlookers to come visit. My eyes took a few seconds to adjust to the dark, cool interior.

I gave a tiny gasp. It was like walking into a palace, from the soaring ceiling and black-and-white-striped pillars to the wide aisle leading up to the magnificent altar. The marble floors were adorned with stunning, detailed mosaics in vivid patterns and colors. I looked up, and rows of busts stared down at me, stoic men who I figured were religious leaders. Statues of angels, heavy gold sculptures, and lots of stained glass dazzled my vision. As I tilted my head farther back, the ceiling mirrored a reflection of gold stars bursting from a brilliant blue background. I didn't know what to study first amid the lavish treasures, but my gaze went straight to Ian.

Joy broke over his face. He stared at the cathedral with a deep hunger that seemed to shimmer from the very depths of his being. Immediately, he bowed his head, his lips whispering in what I deemed a prayer, and my heart squeezed hard in my chest.

With a smile curving his lips, he moved quietly ahead, lost in his own spiritual world I couldn't share. I stood still at the rear of the church and watched him pause at each of the chapels to make the sign of the cross. He moved farther toward the altar, and I took a few steps back, and in that moment I realized the true distance between us that could never be breached.

He'd never be mine.

I know I was only eighteen, and it wasn't like I was looking for happy ever after or anything stupid like that. But it was nice to pretend and dream we could have something big together. Being in the cathedral only reminded me his heart already belonged to God.

Mom drifted over, laying a casual hand on my shoulder. "It's magnificent, isn't it?" she whispered.

I ground my teeth together as helpless tears sprung into my eyes. Then gave a jerky nod, keeping my face turned away.

I figured she'd leave me alone when I didn't answer, but I felt her gaze on me, probing. "Honey? Is something wrong?"

Ah, crap, I couldn't do this right now. For the first time, I wished her cell phone would ring so I could have a few minutes to get myself together. I forced myself to talk. "No, I guess it's just a little overwhelming. It's our last church and it's like they saved the best for last."

She squeezed my shoulder. "Yeah, you're right. Bittersweet. I'm just glad the trip is ending on a high note. And I'm sorry, sweetheart. Truly sorry."

I cranked my head around, curious. "About what?"

Shadows flickered in her eyes. "A lot. Mainly shoving you to the side for work the first week. It was wrong."

She'd apologized in the past. This was nothing new, but it was the way she looked at me when she uttered the words, making eye contact in a way that communicated honest regret I'd never glimpsed before. It didn't mean she wouldn't dump me again for work, but I realized she was finally being real with me. This time, she wanted to change.

Was it enough?

For now.

"Thanks, Mom."

She nodded and we stood in silence for a while, drinking in our surroundings. "Ian seems very comfortable. You mentioned in the Vatican he was religious, huh?"

I let the admission tumble right out. "He's going to be a priest."

She let out a wild cough, and people nearby turned to give her a glare for breaking the hushed silence. "What?" she hissed, leaning close to my ear. "Did you say a priest?"

I almost laughed at her absolute shock. I half figured Nonni had spilled the beans, but I guess not. "Yep. He leaves for the seminary after this trip. It's a long process—he gets another degree before he has to take his vows, so it's not an overnight thing."

"Oh my God!" She covered her mouth with her hand like she'd cursed. "I mean, holy crap! Sorry. I'm just surprised. I thought there was something going on between the two of you."

I ignored my aching heart and shrugged. "Just friends. He's going to Assisi tomorrow for two days. I wondered if he can come visit us? It's only an hour away and he has a rental car. I know we have plenty of room, and it would be fun to hang out before we all return home. What do you think?"

She touched her fingers to her temples as if trying to figure out what to say. Guess I really blew her mind with my announcement. Especially since Mom wasn't the religious type or too approving of standardized religion, no matter how much Nonni tried to bully her back into taking me to church or Bible school.

"Um, I guess. If you want him to stay, we have plenty of room. But just for a day or two, okay? I want us to spend some time together."

"Sure." I'd been excited and nervous about Ian coming, but now, seeing him so peaceful in the cathedral, I began to wonder if I'd made a mistake. I craved more time with him. But was it just dragging out the inevitable and making things worse for when he finally left?

Mom began twisting her fingers in her trademark nervous gesture. "I wanted to tell you something at dinner tonight."

My hackles rose. "You need to work on a project the rest of the week?"

"No! Oh, no, honey, I told you, I'm not working for the rest of the trip. It's just something I wanted to mention, but now's not the time. Do you want to check out the Duomo and climb the staircase? I'm going to stay here with Nonni. Take a picture for me."

She was sure acting weird, but it was probably something lame she thought was important. I floated around, checking out the rest of the chapels, and Ian drifted over. "Ready for the view?" he asked. "Mom and Dad are passing on this one."

"Mom and Nonni too. Which is kind of embarrassing."

"Why?"

I motioned over to Mary and Ray, who were already heading up the steps with enthusiasm. He grinned. "Good, I'll have something to tease the parents about now."

We climbed the spiral staircase, pausing to admire the amazing up-close detail of the rose windows and stained glass. Staring down at the grand marble pulpit made me a bit dizzy—all that gorgeous artwork was almost too much to take in at once.

I had officially gone into an art coma.

Finally, we reached open air and gazed over the spectacular view of Siena. Red-tiled rooftops mixed with dusty brick and terra cotta, a grand jigsaw puzzle with sharp-angled pieces of buildings jamming into one another and creating a picture-perfect scene from above. I heard Ian catch his breath, and I stood still, savoring the spill of colors and textures and an ancient medieval city's secrets.

Low murmurs from the others rose in the air. People wandered and snapped pictures. Ian and I didn't move. Our shoulders were pressed together, the sun warming our naked arms and legs and faces, the scent of him drifting in the hot breeze—freshly washed cotton and clean soap—and the moment was imprinted forever on my memory.

"I could stay here all day," he said quietly. His fingers brushed mine. "When I see the world unveiled like this, it makes me wonder how anyone can not believe in God."

"You're not an evolutionary type of guy, huh?" I teased.

He laughed and bumped my shoulder. "Guess not." He paused, then turned to look at me. "I don't want this to be it."

My heart pounded. "What do you mean?"

"I know I mentioned visiting you later this week. Do you still want me to come?"

I swallowed. "Yeah, I do. Because I don't want today to be it, either."

He nodded. "Did you ask your mom?"

"I just did. She said it's cool. There's a ton of rooms, so you can spend the night. We have the place for six days—she said you can come for two."

"Of course. I'm just glad I can see you again."

The lump in my throat grew bigger. "Ian?"

"Yeah?"

"We're just friends, right?"

His jaw tightened. I watched a mass of emotions flicker over his face before it finally cleared. "We are friends, Allegra. But for me, it's more. I hope that's okay."

My breath eased. And suddenly, everything righted itself. I'd needed to know I wasn't the only one.

I needed to know as much as he loved God, he kind of loved me too.

A smile broke from my lips. "It's more than okay."

He smiled back. We took a few more minutes appreciating the view, then took a selfie of the two of us, with the sprawl of Siena as background. I snapped a few more for Mom, and then we headed back down the stairs.

I was looking forward to the next chapter in our adventure here.

CHAPTER TWENTY-SEVEN

Francesca

THE FAREWELL PARTY took place on the grounds of a family-run vineyard. A large wooden table was set up under a covered alcove, with miles of twisted vines and green landscape in the background. Tiny lights were strung up to cut through the growing darkness. A small band played lively Italian and American songs, and we danced and drank and celebrated the final night of our tour. Multiple courses were served family style, all fresh from the gardens and local farms. Bottles of wine lined the table, and most were now empty.

The evening seemed to unfold like a misty dream. Enzo, Dana, and Cherry gave long, emotional speeches, causing some tears. How had three weeks flown by so fast? Even more important—why did I feel different? Was it finally getting away from my constricted world I'd created, or was it Enzo?

My gaze sought him out at the end of the table, flanked by Dana and Steve. As if he sensed my attention, he lifted his head and lasered right in on me. His eyes crinkled at the corners and his lips lifted in a smile meant just for me.

I couldn't stop thinking of our night together. The natural way we came together in the dark, clothes shed, secrets exposed, mouth on mouth and his fingers over my naked skin. My nails digging into his shoulders as he surged deeply inside me. His lips swallowing my cries. The sheen of sweat and the scent of sex on the sheets.

I'd coveted every precious second, falling into him with an ease that shocked me. I rarely took a man to bed, and over the years, Allegra had never met a man in my life.

Because there'd been none.

Did Enzo think I was pathetic? The lonely workaholic spinster who desperately needed an outlet? Had he been lying when he said I was the only one and that he'd never taken a risk like this before? Were all those late-night confessions uttered in my bed truth or lies?

When he said I was different.

When he said he'd been falling in love with me.

I ducked my head and tried to quiet the mean internal voices that sought to wreck my happiness. No, I wouldn't allow myself to doubt. I wanted to be stronger and braver than that. God knows, I'd been hiding my head in the sand for too many years already, pretending I already had it all and needed nothing else.

Now I knew I was wrong. In my quest for control, I'd cut out physical intimacy. Emotional need. Vulnerability. Being with Enzo made it easier to face the truth.

I heard Allegra laugh and watched as she spun happily around with Ian on the makeshift dance floor. I didn't care what she'd denied today—I knew there was more between them than friendship. But a priest? Lord, what a mess. Were Patrick and Rosemary actually supportive of his decision? I couldn't imagine accepting that Allegra would never get married or have children because she wanted to dedicate her life to God. It seemed like something that happened in the Dark Ages, but then again, what did I know? Other than Mom forcing me into church on

Sundays and getting my sacraments, the moment I was confirmed I refused to go.

He was four years older, but that was a big stretch since Allegra was only eighteen. He'd graduated college, and she was still in high school because she'd been held back a year before entering kindergarten.

Was my daughter playing a dangerous game that would break her heart? Or was I overreacting?

The endless questions whirled through my mind. I had to tell them tonight that Enzo would be joining us in Tuscany for a few days. Like Ian. Worry gnawed at my nerves. Would Allegra get upset and feel like I was ignoring her again? Choosing a man over her? And if she did get upset, was I strong enough to tell him no to please my daughter and keep healing our fragile relationship?

Mom dropped into the chair beside me. "Frannie, why aren't you out there? It's a free-for-all!"

I laughed. "I'm more into watching than dancing tonight. You and Allegra made up for my laziness."

She gave a long sigh. "I can't believe the tour is over. I'm looking forward to Tuscany, but this means we only have a week left. I don't want to go home." She shook her head and waved her hand in the air. "Oh, I'm sure you're dying to go back. Dig into your ad campaigns and return to your routine. But me? This was the highlight of my year. Or years, if I'm lucky."

Normally, I'd agree. I avoided travel because it was easier to keep all the balls in the air if I didn't stray, but when I thought of returning home, no excitement or anticipation reared up. I shook off the strange thought. "Mom, you have a good twenty years left in that body of yours," I teased. "I can't believe you kept up so well."

I caught a glint of grief in her dark eyes, but it passed so quickly I figured I'd imagined it. "We have no control over when God takes us," she recited.

"Speaking of which, did you know Ian's going to be a priest?"

Her guilty expression gave her away. "Well, yes. I was hoping Allegra would tell you herself."

"She did today, in the cathedral. I kind of freaked out."

"I think it's nice. The church is desperate for priests, and Ian seems very down-to-earth. He still has a long road ahead of him, but he's been wanting this since he was young."

I cut her a look. "She's still telling you all her secrets, huh?" I asked. But this time, my remark had no sting.

Mom patted my hand and smiled. "And she'll do the same with you. You just need to rebuild some trust. That's why spending real quality time together is important."

"Did you know she wants Ian to visit us too?" I laughed when I saw her look guilty. "Busted. Well, I told her he could—just for a few days. Do you mind?"

"No. They like each other. At least she's learned how a nice boy treats her. When she gets back home, maybe she won't take any guff from the weed smoker."

"I like your feistiness, Mom," I said with a chuckle. Should I tell her about Enzo? Everyone was involved in their own conversations or dancing, and it was the perfect time. I cleared my throat. "Actually, I was thinking since Ian was coming, maybe we can have another visitor."

"Oh really? Who?"

"Enzo." My voice squeaked a bit. "Funny thing, he actually lives in Lucca, which is close to our villa. We were chatting, and I mentioned where we rented, and he said he could stop by and show us around a bit. Doesn't that sound fun?"

My explanation sounded solid. Casual. I figured she'd say she was thrilled and wave off the whole thing. Instead, her brows slammed into a frown and she leaned closer to me. "I didn't realize you two had struck up a friendship," she said, her gaze shredding mine.

My mouth went dry. I shifted in my seat. "We didn't. I mean, we kind of did, but I figured it was such a coincidence, it'd be silly not to offer."

"So, did you ask him to come over? Or vice versa?"

My palms sweat. "I don't remember. Why is that important? Why are you grilling me like I'm sixteen?"

She sat back and, unbelievably, began to giggle. "I'm sorry, honey, I just couldn't resist teasing you a bit. You look so uncomfortable! I know."

"Know what?"

"I know the two of you are together. I left my room to get some ice and saw you in the hallway."

Oh. My. God. The idea that my mother had watched our passionate kiss unraveled me. I groaned. "Why didn't you tell me?"

"Why should I? You have a right to your privacy. I just got silly tonight. Too much wine, and when you mentioned he'd be stopping by, I couldn't resist."

I relaxed. "Wait till you start seeing someone, Mom. I'll get my revenge."

"Well, I did meet a very nice man in St. Mark's Square that night. He gave me his email address."

My mouth dropped open. "Good for you! Give me all the details."

"Later. For now, I just want to know something important. Does he make you happy?"

The question startled me, but my answer came from deep down. "Yeah. When I'm with him, I'm very happy. But it's a mess. I'm leaving; he lives in Italy; there's no way anything can work."

"You have a week left. Enjoy each other. Push the worry aside and live in the moment." Her eyes darkened and she turned slightly away. "It all goes too fast," she said faintly. "Love is fleeting sometimes, but even for the short time it's here, everything can change."

The words stirred something inside me, but then Allegra bounced over and hugged me from behind. "Mom, you're not dancing!"

I stretched my hands over my head and held her tight. "I'm having too much fun watching you."

"Weren't you the one who said onlookers don't get the prize, you have to be brave enough to participate?"

I twisted my head around so I could gaze at her beautiful, laughing face. "I said that?"

"Someone did, and it fits. We might never see these people again. We should all at least dance together."

"I'm seeing you in Tuscany," I pointed out.

"Mom!"

I savored the whine of my name on her tongue and stood up. When we first started the tour, she would have never danced with the others, but she seemed more open and happier now. "You're right. No one should be sitting. We should be dancing." On impulse, I raised my voice. "Gather around, everyone! It's our final night and we all should show off our boogie skills!"

A shout rose, and everyone flooded the floor. The band launched into some classic pop and I let myself go, shimmying and moving with Dana and Cherry, with my mom and Allegra, and even with Ian and Kai. I caught Enzo leaning against the pillar on the side of the dance floor. I couldn't help giving my hips an extra sway when his eyes darkened, the connection between us crackling with urgency. I was sharing a room with Allegra tonight, so there'd be no secret rendezvous.

But he was coming to stay this week. I just had to make sure my daughter didn't feel like I was ignoring her again. The groundwork we'd built during this trip was precious. I couldn't screw it up.

The music died down, and our family hosts flanked the exit to say goodbye. We filed back onto the bus for the final time to the hotel, a little sad, a little drunk, and a little emotional.

We promised to say our farewells at breakfast in the morning and went up to our rooms. I gave a tiny shake of my head to Enzo, who acknowledged with a nod that we wouldn't be seeing each other later.

We settled in and got into our pj's, and I plumped up the pillows against the headboard, leaning back. Better to clear it with her now instead of waiting until we arrived at the villa. "Can we talk about something?" I asked.

She rolled her eyes. "Mom, go ahead and work. I'm fine."

"No, that's not it. Remember how you asked if Ian can come visit you in Tuscany?"

A tiny crease furrowed her brow. "Mom, he already planned it. Why do you have a problem with this now?"

I blew out a frustrated breath. Having a conversation with her was still like walking through enemy territory, with bombs planted in various places. I never knew what would set her off. "Allegra, I'm not changing my mind, okay? But Enzo and I had a conversation, and I found out he lives in Lucca, which is right by our villa. I invited him to come visit. Maybe stay a night or two. I wanted to check if you felt weird about it, though, because if you do, I'll cancel."

My heart ached at the idea of not being able to see him this week, but I had to begin choosing my daughter.

Her shoulders relaxed. "Oh! Sure, why would I care if he comes and stays? That's pretty cool he lives close. He can probably—"

She stopped, squinting hard at me. "Wait. Mom, are you guys hooking up?"

I tried not to laugh at the simple way teenagers viewed things. It would have been so much easier to engage in a fun hookup, then leave without a backward glance. Instead, he'd managed to crash through the wall I usually had around me, and now my heart was involved. "We're very good friends," I said firmly. "And we like each other a lot."

She gave a delighted giggle. "Deny all you want, Mom, but I know you hooked up! I suspected something going on between you—the way he stared when he didn't think anyone was looking? Very romantic. Why would you think I'd be mad? I've been wanting you to date forever."

I blinked, stunned. "You have? I figured you didn't want anyone to take me away from you."

She shook her head. "No, you don't get it. You live at your office, or on your computer or your phone. You're never *here*. Remember my tennis game at the finals? I made the game-winning point and looked for you, and you were gone because you had to take a call from work? God, I hate tennis! I only did it because you kept pushing me, and you didn't care enough to even stay for the whole game?"

Guilt assaulted me. I remembered well. I'd felt awful, especially when everyone watching congratulated my daughter on her amazing play, and she'd gazed at me with a bit of hate in her eyes. But it wasn't hate. I knew that now. It was disappointment. "I'm sorry, honey. I do remember."

"That's the kind of stuff I can't handle. The way you treat people like they're disposable." Her voice came out soft, filled with layers of tension that had built over the years. I didn't look away from her pain. I was the cause. It was time I dealt with it. "I used to dream that you'd find a cool guy to date and love and get married. We'd be a family. And he'd be able to do what I couldn't."

My throat tightened. "What?"

She shrugged, but I caught the stiffness of her shoulders, as if bracing for a war. "Make you happy."

I couldn't stand it. A cry escaped my lips and I moved to the other bed, pulling her into my arms. The fresh smell of her shampoo filled my nose, and her thin, muscled body fit against mine, notched right by my heart. Tears stung my eyes and I uttered the words in her ear with a fierceness that burned from my soul. "Allegra, you make me happy every day. When I get up and see your face, I realize how beautiful this world is. You are imprinted into my soul. I'm so sorry, sweetheart. I lost my way. I thought you needed plenty of time and space to grow, but instead, it just became easier to leave you alone than fight through. It's not because I don't care. I just made a mistake, and I want to fix it. It's not too late if you give me another chance, and this time, I won't break your trust. I swear to God, I won't."

I hugged her harder, and she pressed her face against my shoulder and shuddered. She let me hold her for a long time, and when she finally pulled away, there was a kernel of hope glowing in her brown eyes. She swiped hard at her nose. "I know I've been a bitch too. It's just hard. All of it. I get so mad at you, and it's like I can't do anything about it because you're not here."

"I know. It's going to change. We're going to fight, probably a lot, but I won't be disappearing. I realized over this tour, it became a habit to just ignore things because I was so afraid to argue. I need to get over that. I'm not perfect, Allegra. This motherhood thing doesn't come with a manual, but I love you more than anything. And I still have a company to run and work that I love, but I won't let it take over my entire world. I learned a few things in these past three weeks also."

She sniffed. "Me too. I think I have real feelings for Ian, Mom. I want to be all cool and pretend it's no big deal that he's going to leave forever, but I'm really sick inside. And I wish he didn't have to be a priest. Isn't that awful?"

"No, it's not. I don't want Enzo to be a tour guide and live in Italy. Why did we have to fall for two men who are completely unobtainable?"

Our eyes met and we began to laugh. Young love and old love. How could they be decades apart yet so similar in the raw emotions? So we used humor to avoid tears, and my daughter finally let me into her heart, and I savored every precious second, hoping this was the beginning of a new understanding between us.

CHAPTER TWENTY-EIGHT

SOPHIA

THE MOMENT OUR villa came into sight, I let out a gasp of delight.

It was just like I'd always dreamed. Casa nella Selva was situated at the top of the hill, overlooking the small town of Borgo a Mozzano. The three-story stone farmhouse was nestled in the valley, with the mighty Appenine Mountains shimmering in the distance. The simplicity of the décor inside contrasted with the stunning views afforded by the terrace and outdoor dining area. I'd done the research and learned it was previously a working chestnut farm and vineyard. I'd haggled with Frannie over which villa to pick, avoiding the too-modern or luxurious residences in favor of the traditional beauty Italy afforded.

It was perfect.

We parked the rental car and did the full tour, chattering and pointing out all the charming nooks and crannies and character the farmhouse provided. The kitchen reminded me of a place my parents would cook, with no fancy appliances and a sturdy pinewood table. Shutters were flung open to allow us to feast on the spectacular views of clustered farmhouses, twisted vines heavy with grapes, and tangles of plants and wildflowers bursting from every space. We each had our own bedroom, and there was room for two more upstairs in the loft, a cute open space with a double bed.

After Allegra and Frannie claimed their rooms, we wandered outside to take stock. "Nonni!" Allegra yelled, racing to the outdoor makeshift kitchen. "They have a pizza oven!"

I clapped my hands with excitement. "We can walk to the market and get our ingredients for dinner. I passed the herb garden too, did you see? Fresh rosemary, basil, sage—everything we need for cooking!"

Frannie laughed. "It's like you two spotted a designer shopping mall right here in Tuscany," she teased.

"This is better," Allegra said solemnly, her eyes lit. "Chefs always say food tastes best with fresh ingredients and good energy. I bet these could be some of the most delicious meals I ever prepare."

Frannie's face softened. "I bet they will. And I can't wait to taste them."

I turned quickly, the stab of emotion cutting deep. She was really listening. There was no mockery about Allegra's love for cooking, or distracted glances as she checked her phone. Gratitude flowed through me. We still had a week together. A week to cook and walk and talk. A week with my two girls before I headed home to face a diagnosis with no idea what to expect.

Even now, the uncomfortable fullness and pressure in my stomach had become a consistent presence. It used to come now and then, but these past few days, I'd noticed bleeding. My body was getting tired. I'd pushed it all I could, but I planned on resting a lot and taking leisurely walks without a schedule or important destination. Maybe this beautiful landscape and fresh air would heal me better than anything else.

And with our male guests heading here this week, if I needed to snatch time to lie down and rest, no one would notice.

"What's our plan for the day?" Frannie asked, leaning against the stone terrace.

"We can unpack and walk into town to investigate," I suggested. "Get things to cook for dinner."

"I'm up for that," Allegra said.

"Agreed. I'll take stock of what we need and we'll start a list. Mom, make sure you wear your hat and your most comfortable shoes. Allegra, you started getting sloppy with your sunscreen— I see the freckles on your nose. Make sure you reapply."

"I don't have freckles—and if you saw the latest news stuff, they said loading up on too much sunscreen isn't good for you."

Frannie lifted her brow. "Oh, I guess skin cancer is, then?"

Allegra rolled her eyes. "They've found some toxins in certain lotions, and if you're caking it on all day, it's just as bad for you as the sun."

"Well, I have the good sunscreen. I think it's organic."

"They don't make organic, Mom. You are so lying."

I watched them enter the house, still bickering. I couldn't help but smile. It sounded so . . . normal.

An hour later, we headed out on the walk. Gravel and dirt kicked up in our wake, but we took it slow and allowed the full magic of the Italian landscape to push us forward. We crossed over the famous stone Devil's Bridge, which lifted us to dizzying heights as if we were perched on top of the world. Alpacas grazed and ran free in the fields, and we passed crumbling stone castles and fortresses brimming with mystery and secrets.

"There's a few things I'd like to see," I said, pausing to sip some water. "The tour books said we must stop by Teatro dei Differenti and Casa Pascoli."

"What's that?" Allegra asked.

"One is a theater, and the other was the home of Giovanni Pascoli, a famous Italian poet. It's a museum now. Oh, and of course, the cathedral."

"Of course—we've only been in a thousand churches," Frannie said.

"But not this one," I retorted. "Each church is unique. It's been the highlight of my trip."

"Hmm, I think my favorite was Venice," Allegra said. "Something about a city on water made it magical."

"I loved Venice too," Frannie said. "But I'm going with Capri. The Blue Grotto, and the views were spectacular."

We reached the town, and I was surprised at the well-maintained look of the houses and buildings—impeccable and bright with colors in mustard, rust, and burgundy. The shops were filled with local delights of all kinds. We crammed bags with hunks of pecorino cheese and crusty bread; ripened tomatoes and pasta; chestnuts, olives, earthy mushrooms, and fresh trout caught right in the nearby lake.

The shopkeepers spoke English and chatted with us, pointing out various places to visit and giving hints to Allegra on good ways to cook the fish. Arms full, we poked around and steeped ourselves in the local atmosphere, then stopped at a café and drank chilled Pellegrino, soda, and iced coffee while we nibbled on the hard edges of the bread.

"These mushrooms are sick," Allegra moaned. "I think we can probably pick them ourselves right outside our villa!"

Frannie choked on her coffee. "Please don't. I can't handle a mistake where I eat a fungus and get sick for the rest of the trip. Also, I think that's a way to get high."

Allegra laughed. "Mom, you know about magic mushrooms? I'm impressed. Did you do any when you were young?"

"No! I didn't do any drugs when I was younger," she said with a huff. "I was too afraid of what the stuff would make me do. Also, I didn't want to get hooked. That's why I freaked out on you."

Allegra looked at her mother with surprise. Sure, she'd yelled and accused and punished, but she'd never spoken from her heart about why Allegra's decision to smoke weed had terrified her. Kids kept many secrets, so I figured Frannie had done her share of experimentation with drugs and alcohol, even though I kept a close eye. Hearing that, though, made me realize she'd always needed control in her life. She'd rarely gotten drunk or done anything that affected her ability to make her own decisions. It must've been hard to always follow such a straight, narrow course without exploring any side roads.

Like Jack. My beloved husband had been content to follow the path ahead without distraction. For me, there'd been no time or opportunity to figure out whether I liked adventure or not. I'd been told exactly what my life was going to be like, and I had accepted it with grace. I'd wanted more for Frannie, yet she'd picked the same exact straightforward lifestyle. How odd that a mother's dream for her daughter can end up taking a detour and leading right back to what you always dreaded.

Her becoming just like you.

"What about smoking a cigarette?" Allegra asked in surprise.

"I think I did a puff once, but I didn't like it."

"Damn, Mom, that's kind of lame. Didn't you ever want to do something really bad?"

Frannie propped her chin in her cupped hands and seemed to think about it. "Yeah. I always wanted to try skinny-dipping."

Allegra and I shared a glance and burst into laughter. "Did you ever try?" she asked curiously.

Frannie shook her head. "Never got an opportunity. I mean, I wouldn't do it with a crowd of people at a pool or anything. But a secluded watering hole or lake, on a beautiful summer night? I could do that."

"Well, I have no desire to swim naked with icky bugs or fish," Allegra announced. "I'm keeping my clothes on."

"Good, let's keep it that way, shall we?"

Allegra stuck out her tongue.

We finished our drinks, took our bags, and headed back home. The sun was beginning to slowly sink in the sky, and the light warmed all the colors of the hillside, blurring them into a misty glow. By the time I got home, my pelvis and feet ached, and I needed desperately to go to the bathroom. My skin had browned from the long days in the sun. My age surprised me sometimes. In my mind, I was forever young and able-bodied, but as I climbed the steps, I realized how easily a deteriorating body can become a prison.

"I'm going to take a bit of a rest," I said cheerfully. "Then we'll make a wonderful dinner and eat it outside on the terrace."

"Okay, Nonni, let me know if you need me."

I smiled at my sweet granddaughter, whom I was so blessed to have fuss over me. She'd eased my loneliness over the years and given my heart a new lease on life. One day, I'd express in words what she means to me. Perhaps a letter she could hold close after I left this earth, and be reminded how she is loved.

I slept for an hour, enjoying the firm mattress and the soft, hand-stitched white blanket. A gentle breeze blew in from the open windows, and the sound of birds floated to my ears. My sleep was disturbed so often, and I'd gotten used to snatching a few hours here and there, so this one short, dreamless slumber was everything.

When I came out of my room, Frannie and Allegra were already on the terrace. "I made lemonade, Nonni. Have some."

She poured from a hand-painted floral pitcher, and I sipped

the cool, tart liquid. "Delicious," I praised. "Are you ready to start dinner?"

"Yes, I'm starving."

While we cooked, I watched with pride as she made her own dough. She rolled and pinched it like an expert, sliced plump, juicy tomatoes, and perfected the balance of herbs to highlight the natural flavors. We sautéed the mushrooms first to take out some of the earthiness, and used a combination of pecorino and mozzarella. There was a bottle of red wine on the shelf, so I grabbed that and poured Frannie and myself a glass. We whipped up some wilted greens and sliced the bread, adding garlic and more herbs for a dipping oil, then laid the platters out on the table. The dishes were a heavy ceramic, and I loved the pots and pans they'd left us: solid skillets that only needed oil to clean them, and hearty pans to hold the large trout.

"I've never deboned a fish, Nonni. Can you teach me?"

"Of course. My mother taught me very young, and it's a delicate process. Come here. This is a fillet knife, and you must be patient. If you begin hacking or get sloppy, you can ruin the integrity of the fish. We start by removing the head."

Frannie groaned. "I think I'm going to be a vegetarian. I don't like to stare my food in the eye."

"Which is why we are beheading it. If you become a vegetarian, you'll break my heart. Think of all the food you'll miss out on in your life."

"Which is why I prefer restaurants. I don't get a behind-the-scenes documentary on where my food comes from."

Allegra laughed. "Mom, it's important to know the origins of your food. Many places pack in preservatives and hormones or abuse the animals. Sustainable sources, freshwater fish, cruelty-free eggs, grass-fed beef, all of it is important to make a difference in the world. I'd like to work with a restaurant that incorporates humane techniques and uses simple, fresh ingredients."

I tilted my head, intrigued. She'd never mentioned those specific passions before. "I think you'd make a great chef one day, sweetheart. And I bet there are many who share your views. You just need to find them."

She nodded, obviously deep in thought as she mulled over my words. "Yeah, you're right. When we get home, I'm going to start researching."

"Good for you," Frannie said. "Now can you dismember the fish? I'm starving."

We laughed, and I took Allegra through the deboning process, until the trout was laid out in the pan. I added lemons, garlic, herbs, and some broth to keep it juicy. Within half an hour, all the food was laid out on the table.

I breathed in the wafting scents of garlic mixed with wildflowers, herbs, and lemon and appreciated the rolling hills and the vines surrounding the villa, listened to the complete silence other than the lazy buzz of a bee or the occasional birdsong. I was in paradise, with my family, and I seized the moment with the ferocity of a woman who knew how fleeting life really was.

"Let's say grace," I announced. We linked hands and bowed our heads. I recited the traditional grace, emotion lumped thick in my throat. "Thank you. I know it took a leap of faith to leave everything behind for a month, but I'll never forget this trip. I love you both."

"Love you too, Nonni," Allegra said, squeezing my hand.

"Love you, Mom."

I blinked back tears and got hold of myself. "Let's do justice to this beautiful food."

We did. I watched with pride as my two girls stuffed themselves like true Italians, appreciating every flavorful morsel. Darkness fell and crickets serenaded us. The wine bottle emptied, and Allegra yawned, stretching at the table. "I'm so tired," she moaned.

"Go to bed," Frannie ordered. "You cooked; I'll do the dishes."

Being the bright young woman she was, Allegra jumped up from the table. "Thanks, Mom! Night, Nonni!"

She disappeared.

I looked at Frannie and we both laughed. "Hmm, that went well. There wasn't even a hesitation," she said.

I raised my brow. "Like mother, like daughter. You hated cleaning. And dishes. And dusting. And making your bed. And—"

"I get it. I was never the domestic type. But I didn't have to be—you always took care of everything."

I nodded, thinking back over the years to the number of hours I spent cooking and tending the house and the garden. I'd made Frannie and Jack my life. I'd prepared for so much more, and it took me a long time to accept I wasn't meant to have it. "Chores were part of my identity," I said simply. "I had nothing else."

My daughter shifted in her chair and leaned over the table. Her gaze locked on mine, those golden brown eyes filled with questions. "Mom, do you have any regrets? Things you wish you could do over?"

I was tempted to wave my hand and say nothing, but it was a night to share truths. "I promised your great-grandmother I'd give your father a big family and take care of him." My voice drifted away, chased by the wind. "I failed everyone, though. I accepted it but will always regret not being able to have more children."

"How could you say that?" Outrage shimmered from her figure. "That's not your fault! No one can blame you for not being able to have a child."

"Childless women get looked at with pity. It was always our

fault, and rarely the men's. When I birthed you, I knew my prayers had finally given me a miracle. I threw myself into being a mother and it gave me the greatest joy I'd ever known." The memories still soothed my soul and helped me sleep at night. My perfect daughter, from her first pull at my breast to her first steps. Her joy and her stubbornness to make something out of her life. Her adoration of her father and her focused ambition to garner the highest grades in the school. I soon became a noose around her neck, chaining her to me and restricting her precious freedom. No wonder we'd battled so hard and so often. I couldn't let her go because she was all I had.

Not her fault. I saw that now. But I was just a woman who made my own mistakes.

"My second regret was the mistakes I made raising you. I know I clung too hard. Tried to direct you in the ways I wanted. I didn't want to lose you, Frannie. It was like you were born to be free, and the time you depended on me was so fleeting. I just kept wanting . . . more."

Suddenly, she got up from her chair and came around to sit beside me, laying her head on my shoulder. I treasured her closeness and stroked back her hair, studying the angles and shadows of her strong, beautiful face.

"There was so much I didn't know about you and Daddy, because I never asked. I was wrapped up in my own world."

"Sweetheart, that's how it always is with a child and parent. It's part of the cycle. We swear we'll never be like our mothers, but after enough time and experience pass, you realize we're all the same. Doing our best. Making mistakes. Pushing forward. Right now, Allegra's struggling to be her own person and force you to listen, but it's difficult to step back and allow her those awful mistakes. Because in the end, you just want her to be like you." I pressed a kiss to the top of her head. "Or not."

She sucked in a breath as if my words stunned her. "I just want to be a good mom," she said softly. "Allegra doesn't have to be like me. But I realized I made a big mistake, Mom. All those years growing up, I thought Daddy was the one really in charge. He made the money and had this big career. He had interesting friends and travel and seemed like this big-time celebrity to me, ready to play and have fun. You seemed boring. Always fussing and getting in my way. Your world was us, and I swore I'd never be that. I wanted so much more."

God, the words shredded like razors, bringing raw pain, but I appreciated that it was the first time she'd told me the truth. All my suspicions had been right. But I despised what my daughter believed of me, when I knew inside I was different. I'd just kept to myself, believing she would never want to know who I really was. What my dreams or fears were. "It's okay. I understand."

"It was another reason I didn't want to have a traditional marriage. I was terrified if I had a child with a man, I'd be the one to give up my career. I'd be the one left behind and end up like you. So I created and controlled my own world, where I was a single mom with all the power and I'd bow to no one. It seemed perfect."

"Was it?"

She gave a tiny shake of her head. "I ended up doing the same thing as Daddy. I let you raise Allegra while I mocked what you were. Meanwhile, you both have this amazing relationship and I have to start over. Because I chose wrong. I failed."

I refused to let her believe she wasn't a good mother, because it wasn't true. "Don't put that on yourself, Francesca," I said firmly. "There's enough maternal guilt in the world to swallow you whole. You'll never win that game because there are only losers. Do you understand me?"

"Yes, but—"

"No buts. You doted on Allegra. She was your life and I was the witness. I may have babysat her during the day, but you were up for every late-night feeding and every nightmare. You grew your business while you juggled sports and teacher meetings and supervised sleepovers with her friends. Don't you dare tell me you failed. You raised a strong, beautiful young woman with dreams. She's not afraid to think big and go after what she wants. That wasn't me, sweetheart. That was all you. It was only when she got older that you believed it was better to pull back, because that's what you always needed from me. But you're brave enough to admit when you're wrong and to try to change. That's what you're doing on this trip and I see it—the trust building between the two of you more every day. It's not about how many times we fail, Frannie. It's how many times we recognize it and change. It's how many times we try to do better."

My body loosened, and it was as if my breath settled deeper into my lungs; a lightness flowed within my muscles and bones that had never been there before. To finally share my inner soul with my daughter was a priceless gift. I'd forgotten how freeing it felt to have the person you loved finally see who you are and accept you truly. Flaws and all.

That was the true power of family. Of love.

"I know I never told you this before, but I realize now, as much as I loved Daddy, he wasn't my rock. It was you, Mom."

My heart stitched and healed as I sat at the table in Tuscany and held my daughter for a long, long time.

CHAPTER TWENTY-NINE

FRANCESCA

THE MOMENT ENZO climbed out of the car and walked over, my entire body hummed with sweet anticipation.

The last two days we'd fallen into an easy rhythm. We all slept late, had a light breakfast, and went for a walk. Exploring the massive grounds had become like a treasure hunt—we discovered something new down each path: a hidden shed filled with dusty bottles of wine, ripened lemon trees heavy with fruit, and a small lake with one lone rowboat floating on the surface. When we came across a small family of bunnies living in the brush, Allegra insisted on leaving carrots for them every afternoon like they'd sprung from a Bugs Bunny cartoon.

Then we went into town for lunch and picked a new sight to see. We'd lingered at the small museum Mom had wanted to check out, and spoke with the locals who knew we were here for the week. Then we'd head back to the villa, take a nap, and spend the evening hours cooking, drinking, and talking late into the night.

But I'd been looking forward to seeing Enzo, who'd agreed to wait till midweek so we could both settle in first. He was dressed in mustard-colored shorts, a cream button-down shirt, and a straw hat tipped low over his brow. His olive skin was dark and tanned, and he walked over with a purposeful male grace that made all my girly parts wake up and sing.

When he reached me, he pressed a full kiss to my lips. "I missed you," he murmured, his lilting voice caressing my ears.

"I missed you too."

"I'm glad your mama and Allegra are okay with me staying."

I gave a small laugh. "They actually seemed thrilled. I think they both realized it had been way too long since I was interested in a man. Plus, they like you already, so we're past the awkward meet-and-greet stage."

His slow grin made my belly flip-flop. "My sisters would love you," he said. "They'd adore your honesty and feistiness."

"I'd love to meet them one day." I meant it. To see Enzo with his family, in his element, created a longing that I couldn't deny. But this week was for me, Allegra, and Mom, and it was important that I keep my focus. "Why do I think our mothers would love each other?"

"Oh, they would. They'd probably arrange our wedding right away." I jerked back a little, but he laughed, running a finger down my cheek. "Just kidding. Well, kind of. You haven't met my mama."

I stole another kiss, lingering a bit and relishing his delicious male scent, which I'd missed. "Come in. I'll show you where you're staying." He quirked a brow. "Where your luggage will be," I corrected, trying not to blush.

For God's sakes, I was in my midforties—I shouldn't be blushing when inviting a man to stay over.

I shook my head at his wink as he grabbed an overnight bag from the car and followed me in. Allegra and Mom were in the kitchen, making more lemonade, and I loved the way they hugged and kissed him hello, like greeting an old friend.

"I heard you were taking us to Lucca on a mini tour," my mother said. "Aren't you getting tired of schlepping us around Italy?"

"Never. You are my all-time favorite tourists," he vowed, placing a hand over his heart. "I love the idea of showing you my home. Lucca is a beautiful medieval city surrounded by walls to protect our secrets. I appreciate your allowing me to crash your family time."

"We're happy to see you," Allegra said. A rush of gratitude shot through me. Her honest welcome helped make his visit more of a celebration.

"I'm going to show Enzo upstairs, and then we can relax for a while before heading out."

I led him to the adorable loft, which had a fabulous view and a decent-size full bed. He dropped the bag at his feet, turned around, and pulled me into his arms, holding me tight against his body.

Then he kissed me. Again and again, his tongue plunging between my lips, hungry for mine. I thrust my fingers into his hair and fell into the embrace, my body recognizing his and opening up in welcome. Slowly, he slid me back down, dragging my breasts against his hard chest until my toes hit the floor.

"Now I can get through the rest of the day," he teased, his thumb sliding over my slick lower lip. "I need my mind clear for the tour."

I tossed him a mischievous grin. "I'll give you a better tour later. In my bedroom."

He groaned, but I was already back out the door, a giggle bursting from my chest. How nice it was to flirt and feel beautiful to the man you were giddy over. I'd forgotten why so many novels and poems and movies were made about love.

It was like a hit of a sweet, wild drug that made you damn happy.

We sat on the terrace, drank lemonade, nibbled on oatmeal

cookies Allegra had made, and chatted. "Your mom said you've been making some amazing meals here," he commented.

Allegra looked surprised, then ducked her head. "Yeah, Nonni's been teaching me since I was young. We've been experimenting with fresh ingredients from the market. Now I even know how to debone a fish."

"My mother said cooking is the most beautiful art you can create in the world. It provides sustenance and nourishment for the body and soul. If you'd like, I know a chef in Lucca who teaches a cooking class. It's just for the day—he takes you to the market, shows you how to pick food, and then you go to the kitchen and cook. I can call him if you're interested."

Her eyes lit up with excitement. "Are you kidding me? I'd love that! Mom, do you think there's time for me to do it?"

I turned to Enzo. "When does he offer the classes?"

"Wednesdays and Thursdays—so if you can take her into Lucca either of those days, I can make sure she gets in."

"I think that's a great idea. When is Ian coming, honey?"

"Tomorrow. But I know he'd love to join me if there's room. We were talking about how wicked cool it'd be to prepare food with a real chef here. Nonni, you want to come too, right?"

My mother waved her hand in the air. "I think I'll pass on that, sweetheart. I've cooked my whole life, and I'd rather take advantage of the grounds. You go ahead with Ian."

"Okay, I'll text him now. Thanks, Enzo."

She grabbed her phone from the table and rushed out. "That was really nice of you," I said quietly. "What an experience for her."

"Not a problem. It's good to take advantage of every opportunity, no? I'm happy to help. It's hard at her age. I was lost for a long time before I realized what career path I wanted to follow."

I sipped at my drink and sighed. "I still want her to go to an Ivy League school. She worked so hard on her grades and test scores. The idea of her leaving it behind to work in a kitchen makes me crazy."

"There are options," Mom said. "The Culinary Institute is an excellent school in Hyde Park and extremely competitive."

"True. I'm trying to be more open."

Enzo smiled. "Whatever she decides to do, she's smart and works hard. She will be okay, *cara*."

Allegra popped back in. "He said yes! Either day is fine— he'll be staying for two nights, Mom. That's okay, right?"

"Yep, perfect."

"Then I'll make the call," Enzo said.

He set up the appointment for the next day. "Eleven a.m. I can take you there."

Allegra jumped up and down with rare girlish excitement. "This is going to be sick."

Enzo lifted a brow. "I hope not. That doesn't sound too good for a cooking class."

We all laughed and decided to head out. "Let me just grab my purse," I said, going into my bedroom. My phone vibrated insistently and I grabbed it.

Kate. I hesitated. I'd pulled way back these past two weeks, even though it'd been hard. Now there was a slight distaste at the idea of spending even a second on work when I had a perfect day planned with Enzo and my family.

I ignored it. Kate was smart. She didn't really need me—she probably just wanted to check in. I tucked my phone in my purse, slicked on some lip gloss, slapped on more deodorant, and met them outside. "Ready."

My phone vibrated again. And again.

Frowning, I fished it back out and checked the screen.

911. Emergency. You need to call me NOW.

Ah, shit.

I bit back a groan, torn. This didn't seem like something I should ignore. Kate didn't panic.

"Guys, I'm so sorry. I just need a few minutes to take care of this, and then I promise we'll go."

Allegra stiffened but shrugged. "Sure. We can hang for a few. Enzo, do you want to see the gardens?"

"Yes, we'll give you some privacy," he said to me with a smile. "Take care of your work so you have no worries for this afternoon."

Relaxing, I nodded. He was right. I'd handle the problem, then enjoy a leisurely trip to Lucca.

I quickly dialed Kate. "It's me. What's going on?"

"Fuck, Frannie. We've got a huge problem here. Our long-term client Anthony Capelli is threatening to walk."

My heart began to race. I gripped the phone with sweaty fingers. "Impossible. He's been satisfied with the results of his campaign—I haven't heard a complaint!"

"I know! But he showed up at the office, demanding to see you, telling us he wants a fresh angle and more punch."

"Sarah said the research numbers were good, though, right?"

"Yes, but he doesn't care. He wants you to call and get a whole new pitch together by Wednesday at five."

"That's tomorrow!"

"I know. Listen, I told him the team can handle it and that you're on vacation, but he said if he doesn't hear back from you personally, he's walking. Layla and I are torn here. What do you want us to do?"

The rush of adrenaline and satisfaction hit me like a familiar buzz. I'd left my prospective partners in charge, and I was still the only one who could keep one of our staple clients. I'd earned his trust and he refused to work with anyone else.

It should have been a sweet victory. A reminder I'd been right all along—there was no way my company could remain the best without me involved in every step.

"I'll call him now."

"Call me right back," Kate urged.

I charged into my bedroom and clicked open my laptop. Thank God the Wi-Fi connection was strong, and in minutes, I'd brought up his original campaign. I bet "more punch" meant he wanted edgier. He believed he could use sex to sell workout clothes, but I knew for a fact that would be a disastrous campaign. I needed to convince him to keep the flirty edge because women bought fitness outfits to feel good about themselves and get the job done—not to pick up guys for some hot sex.

Unbelievable. First, Perry wanting less sex to sell jeans. Now, Anthony wanting more sex to sell athletic wear. Both demanding new campaigns within twenty-four hours.

I needed to work with more damn women.

Groaning, I brought up my contact list and called. He picked right up. "Hi, Anthony, it's Francesca. I heard from my team you've got some concerns about our campaign?"

He did. He laid them out in detail and basically said he wanted more skin, sexier models, and lots of water and sweat. Did he think we were filming a *Flashdance* movie? For God's sakes, why had he suddenly changed his mind?

"Tony," I said, using his nickname for bonding purposes. "I'm on your side. I want to sell your sportswear, but every test and statistic comes back with one result: women buy the clothes and they're offended if it's marketed to them like a pickup line. I've seen the sales numbers and they're solid. Good engagement, steady growth. I'd be happy to freshen up some social media ads, though, if you'd like."

"Well, tell that to Victor over at Sunny Days Marketing," he said with a bit of stiffness. "Victor created an ad for their newest account and it's blowing up everywhere. It shows a naked woman with roses covering her privates. I keep seeing it shared all over social media—it's practically going viral. That's what I want."

"Your product is different. Victor is selling perfume and that's where sex truly does sell."

"Francesca, you're the best. I've always told you that and I want to stay, but if you don't give me what I want, I have to take my business elsewhere. Times are changing and I want to be ahead of the curve, not behind. I'm willing to work right now, all night if we have to, until we come up with a new concept that we like. Are you on board?"

Shock barreled through me. "Tony, I'm in Italy. Can we wait just a few days? That will give me enough time to brainstorm and get you the initial prospectus."

"No. Today. I've got my own vacation to Turks and Caicos, and the wife will kill me if I bother her with this shit. You in?"

I bit my lip hard, trying to contain the slight shakes beginning to seize my body. Crap. This was a nightmare. I couldn't lose this account. It was huge. I couldn't fail. Not like this.

"Sure. Give me a bit to call you back and get my team on conference call."

"Always a pleasure to work with you. I knew you'd never let me down."

I clicked off and bent over. Sweat broke out on my skin. I had to get myself under control and deal with this. Enzo and my family were waiting for me, and somehow I had to find a way to get them to understand how critical this emergency was.

Gritting my teeth, I tried to remain calm even though panic teased my nerve endings. I couldn't have an attack—not now. I'd make Allegra understand. I'd make it up to her. This time, I really meant it.

They were just coming from the gardens when I met them outside. "I didn't realize Enzo loved flowers so much. He knew all the names," Allegra said teasingly.

Enzo shook his head. "It's important that real men know how to cook, clean, and make flowers grow. Or maybe this is because I have four sisters who convinced me of this while I did all their chores."

Allegra giggled. "You ready, Mom?"

I tried to speak but my voice got clogged in my throat. Why were my lungs so tight? "I'm so sorry, honey, I've got a big problem. The office called, and I'm about to lose an important client if I don't revise his campaign. I'll need a few hours, but I'm sure I can do it fast and then meet you in town? Enzo, maybe you can take Mom and Allegra and give them the tour, and I'll knock this out quickly. You'll never even realize I was gone." The words babbled from my mouth, but I knew by her expression that nothing I said mattered. The betrayal was already carved out on her face.

"You've said this before," she said, her eyes hard and flat. "It's never quick."

"This time I'll make sure it is." I shot a pleading look to my mother and Enzo. Enzo inclined his head, his dark eyes full of sympathy. But not my mother. She was solidly behind my daughter, her lips tightened into a thin line of disapproval.

My lungs squeezed further and I tried desperately to remind myself to take long, deep breaths. I couldn't allow them to see me break down. It would only solidify their opinion of my work obsession and how it was unhealthy.

"I'd be happy to accompany these lovely ladies into town," Enzo said, smiling.

My shoulders slumped in gratitude. "Thank you. I swear, I wouldn't do this if it wasn't critical. I can't lose this account, sweetheart. It would be disastrous."

"It's always some important account, Mom. It's always an emergency. I thought maybe you meant it when you promised not to do this to us again, but I was stupid. I believed you! You promised this wouldn't happen in Tuscany, but you can't even do that."

"Allegra, please—"

"Just go. I don't care anymore. I really don't. I'm not going to give you a hard time. I don't even want to fight." She stepped away, but it was so much more than that. The wall between us that I'd worked so hard to take down had shot right back up. And in her gaze was a distrust that almost drove me to my knees.

What had I done?

She turned her back and headed toward Enzo's car. "Let's go, Nonni. I'm sure we'll have a great time."

The words dropped on me like stones and sent shimmers of pain rippling through me. Mom didn't respond, just shook her head and followed Allegra.

Enzo closed the distance between us. "*Cara*, are you okay?"

I gulped back a sob, torn and confused. "No. I can't lose this client, Enzo. It'd be a big hole in my financials and I'd let the entire team down. If he walks, it will be a disaster."

He nodded, cupping my cheek. "You must do what you need to do and hope your family will eventually understand."

"I'm afraid my daughter won't. If I do this to her, she may never trust me again." My hand trembled as I clutched at him, his solid weight reassuring under my shakiness. "I can lose her."

"You cannot lose family, Francesca. She will forgive. But you must know in your gut it's worth the sacrifice."

"But I told you—I can lose the entire account if I don't stay!"

His smile was full of gentleness. "Yes, you may. Would that be the worst thing that can happen to you at this point? Follow both decisions through, and you will come to your answer." He placed a kiss on my mouth, then stepped back. "I'll be waiting in Lucca—text me if you need anything. I'll take care of them."

I watched him climb into the car and slowly drive away.

Clenching my fists, I headed into the house, my mind furiously working on getting alternate plans into place. I texted Kate, ordering the team to drop everything and call me on the conference line in fifteen minutes. I sifted through my notes and began to prep for the upcoming meeting.

But I couldn't stop thinking about Allegra's face. And Enzo's words. And my mother's crushing disapproval.

I'd broken another promise. Yes, this was important. But had I ever considered not responding to any crisis at my company? My work ethic gave me a sense of pride and accomplishment nothing ever had. Knowing I was needed and had a clear role. This moment proved to me everything I'd always craved.

I was needed. I was important. I was somebody.

But wasn't I all those things to my daughter and my mother?

It began with a trickle, then built—the horrifying strangle of air, the trembling seizing my legs, the wriggle of anxiety and fear rushing from my gut to flood my weak body.

No. Not now. Please, not again.

The attack reared and launched, and I dropped my head into my hands, desperately seeking something solid to cling to. But there was nothing but choppy breath and gripping panic, my brain spinning out of control.

Breathe, Francesca. Count to five, pause, then release. Listen to my voice.

I heard Enzo's directions vibrate through my mind, taking me back to Capri when he'd helped guide me through one of the attacks. As my heart thumped like a mad rabbit, I began to concentrate on my breath, counting down each digit, then slowly exhaling.

Eyes closed, I fought my way out with tiny increments of numbers and breaths, until the panic began to slowly recede.

I had no idea how much time had passed when I finally raised my head. Frustrated tears stung my eyes. I stared at the blinking cursor on my computer and the stacks of notes I'd furiously pulled out, and then my phone began to ring with a shrieking demand I'd once revered and now dreaded.

I can't do this anymore.

The truth rose and exploded like a firecracker. I'd created the world I wanted to live in, but now things were changing. There was a man I was falling in love with, and he was waiting for me. My precious daughter had finally let me back in, and I couldn't stand to see her behind that massive wall again. My mother had shared the secrets of her soul and deserved my focus during our final days in Italy.

I can't do this anymore.

The mantra repeated. My heartbeat calmed. I stared at the phone and hit the button.

"Frannie? It's Kate, we're all here, and we have Anthony on hold, ready to conference him in. I've got the last ad pulled up, and I'm here with Layla, Adam, and Sarah. Are you ready?"

Yes. I was.

"Kate, I'm sorry for the inconvenience, but I won't be able to do this conference call. Tell the team to be on standby if Anthony decides to let you take over, but if you don't hear from me, you can stop working on the campaign."

I could practically hear the stunned silence in the room. Kate's voice was threaded with worry. "Um, Fran, I know you have some things going on, but we can do this in about three hours max. We really don't want to lose this account."

"I know. It'll be a hard loss, but there's nothing I can do this time. I'm tied up and don't have three hours. If you can patch Anthony through, I'll talk to him and see what we can do."

"Sure. You can convince him to wait a day or two; you're amazing at negotiations."

She sent the call over.

I spoke with Anthony, who finally made good on his threat and pulled his entire account.

When I finally clicked off, I knew I'd let the team down. We'd worked on the account as a group, and my refusal to put in the extra hours to keep a client would affect my reputation.

Right now, I just didn't care.

I sent out the text to Enzo and jumped in the car.

On my way.

Soon, the three dots appeared. **Already? You fixed it?**

No, I lost the account.

I'm sorry, cara. I know how important this is to you.

I read his words, paused my finger on the button, then went for it.

Yes, but so are you. And my family.

When the heart emoji danced on my screen, I laughed.

Then I drove to Lucca.

CHAPTER THIRTY

Allegra

The high medieval walls surrounding the city of Lucca were beautiful, but I couldn't think of anything but Mom and her stupid broken promises.

I was so pissed.

Anger simmered, but it was the hurt that made it worse. I'd actually done it again. Believed she meant it when she said no work for the rest of the week. She'd managed for a while as long as nothing big happened, but the moment a problem cropped up, she disappeared like a guy after a one-night stand. She'd been getting worse the last few years, but now the truth couldn't be denied anymore.

Mom cared about her career more than me. Yep, a definite slap in the face, but maybe it was time I stopped spinning my wheels and hoping for a change that would never come.

This past week, I felt like we'd gotten closer. Since Enzo, she seemed less of her control-freak self and more open. She smiled and laughed and freely gave affection to both me and Nonni. Honestly, she seemed happy for the first time. Didn't she realize how stressed out work always made her? Her attention constantly on her phone or computer, distracted from the world around her?

I thought having Enzo here would make a difference, but it didn't. None of us meant enough to her. It was a good thing she wasn't involved in a real relationship, because it'd be impossible to maintain. No man would put up with constantly being chosen last.

I was stuck with it. Enzo wasn't.

He must be pissed. Sure, he was acting nice, but I bet inside he was wondering why he'd even come out to visit when he was going to be dumped.

We began the climb upward to walk the various footpaths on the famous walls. Enzo kept up a steady chatter, probably hoping to distract us, checking his phone for a text message now and then.

I tried not to snort. She'd be gone for hours, then offer apologies that were too little, too late. But it was probably best he find that out for himself.

"Ah, she made it. Just in time."

I tilted my head, confused, then saw my mom turn the corner and head toward us. I blinked in shock, and she stopped in front of me, her gaze fastened on mine.

"I made a mistake," she said firmly. "I broke my promise. So I told my team to handle things and I came right back. Because you're more important than any client, Allegra. I need you to know that and forgive me."

Stunned, I needed a few minutes to register that she was not only back, but being completely direct. "Will they be able to handle it?"

She paused. "No, I lost the account. But I needed to put my family first this time."

She lost a client? My eyes bugged out. "Are you sure?" I asked, a bit off-kilter from her announcement. She'd never lost an account. They were her bread and butter, her life and death.

"Yes. He started yelling at me and it felt really good to tell him to walk." A half giggle escaped and she slapped her hand over her mouth. "Unprofessional, I know, but he wanted to use sex to sell gym clothes. Talk about icky."

Enzo laughed and hugged her. "Such work is beneath you, *cara*. We're glad you're back and you didn't miss a thing. You are okay?"

Something passed between them, a connection and understanding I'd never seen before. Mom gave a deep sigh. "Well, I had another panic attack, but I was able to stop this one before it became full-fledged."

My jaw dropped. "What are you talking about? I didn't know you were having panic attacks!"

Nonni grabbed her arm in a worried gesture. "You should have called us—we would have come right back. You must lean on your family, Frannie."

Mom looked directly at me and explained. "I suffered from a panic attack right before we left for Italy. With you being in trouble and my body falling apart, I thought the trip would help. But every time I handled a work crisis, I seemed to have another breakdown. I just didn't want to tell anyone or admit it."

Nonni dragged in a breath. "Frannie, I should have told you before in the hospital, but you seemed determined to ignore it. Your father suffered from the same type of attacks. They got worse over time, and though I begged him to slow down, he just couldn't."

Mom gasped. "Dad had panic attacks?"

Nonni nodded. "It was awful, but he was so stubborn, he kept thinking they'd go away. If I'd known you were having more in Italy, I would have told you sooner."

Mom sighed. "I had no idea. And I'm noticing my attacks also revolve around work. Stress used to give me a killer edge, but lately—well, lately it's having the opposite effect."

"Please, Frannie. I couldn't help your dad, but Allegra and I need you. You have to learn how to balance better." Nonni's face was carved out in stress and worry.

"I'm finally realizing that." She pulled me and Nonni into a quick embrace. "I meant it when I said I wanted things to change. How about we enjoy the day, and I'll try not to keep any more secrets from both of you. Deal?"

Joy leapt inside along with a steady flare of hope. She'd come back. She'd lost a client. Maybe there was a chance for our relationship to be different. God knows, I only had my mom and Nonni. I was beginning to realize how important family really is, since they're the people who know you the best—good and bad—and love you anyway.

I hugged her hard. "Deal. Thanks for coming back, Mom."

"Thanks for not cursing me out or sulking. Now, let's have some fun." I almost gasped when Enzo leaned over and kissed her right in front of us, and Mom didn't flinch. In fact, she glowed.

He snagged her hand and they walked ahead, leading the way.

I shared a glance with Nonni. She grinned and gave me a thumbs-up signal, and I smothered a laugh.

Yeah. Looks like we both fully approved of Mom's summer romance.

CHAPTER THIRTY-ONE

FRANCESCA

"How do you really feel about losing the account?" Enzo asked, his voice low in my ear. I leaned against his chest, with his arms wrapped around my waist. We stood outside in the gardens by the vineyard, enjoying the quiet of the evening and the spill of the shadowy hills in the distance. A firefly lit up and floated around us, then disappeared into the woods.

"It wasn't easy," I admitted, resting into his strength. "It's a habit for me to jump in and fix things. More than a habit. I love feeling like I'm the only one who has the answers—it gives me a rush of power. This was the first time in my life I dropped a client because I couldn't give him what he needed. I've built my reputation on being able to deliver whatever a client asks, no matter what time of day. Twenty-four-hour customer service."

"It's scary to change a habit. Do you regret coming to Lucca and not working?"

"No. Once I made the decision, a weight lifted off my chest, and my panic attack eased. Thank you for the breathing techniques, by the way. They helped a lot."

"I'm glad. But I have no doubt you can tackle the attacks as long as your mind is clear and you remember not to fight your body. You were brave to share the truth with your family. It's hard to open up."

"I feel like we've all been keeping secrets from one another.

Mom told me some truths last night that made me realize I never knew her as a woman—just as a parent. And I had no idea Dad suffered from panic attacks too. It's time I stopped blaming her for things that I misunderstood when I was growing up. And after Allegra got busted for pot, I figured she was just spinning out of control with her whole future at risk. Now I think she desperately needed my attention."

He rocked me gently back and forth. "It's good to share our secrets. Allegra looked so happy when you came back."

"The look on her face was worth everything. We've made such progress this past week, and I knew if I let her down again, I may not get another chance. You were right when you told me to think about the consequences of both actions. It helped make my decision. How'd you get so smart?"

A chuckle reverberated in his chest. "My sisters. They drove me insane, but I learned a lot. Women know more about their inner emotions than men and aren't afraid to dig deep. They forced me to pay attention."

"Your sisters sound amazing, but I still think it's you."

"Me?"

I pressed a kiss to the back of his hand, his strong, tapered fingers entwining with mine. "Yep. You, Enzo Gagliardi, are an extraordinary man. You didn't try to bully or influence my decision. You supported me and took care of my family with a smile. I've never met anyone like you before."

He turned me in his arms and tipped my chin up. I studied the hard angle of his jaw, those gleaming dark eyes, his lower lip quirked in a lazy smirk, his stubble-roughened chin. "I loved spending the day with you, Francesca," he said, his gaze delving deep into mine. "For the first time, I didn't have to worry about someone spotting us or how to get close to you without anyone noticing. I loved holding your hand and kissing you in the sunlight, in front of your daughter and mama."

"I loved it too," I whispered, stroking back his hair.

He'd given us a perfect day. We'd walked on top of the famous walls and gazed down on the town, which reminded me of a hidden jewel in a queen's crown. The Piazza dell'Anfiteatro was once a Roman amphitheater, and we strolled the elliptical shape lined with various shops, bakeries, and cafés, admiring the merging shades of yellow, cream, and white buildings, all with matching green shutters. He'd brought us to lunch at the popular Da Pasquale, which was usually only open for dinner, but Enzo had arranged a special meal for us. We feasted on ravioli and caprese salad and drank tart limoncello from tiny little cups. The day ended with a visit to the Palazzo Mansi National Museum, where we lingered in the lush gardens.

When we got home, Allegra and Mom had retired to their rooms, and we'd spent some time chatting on the terrace, my feet in his lap, his hands stroking my legs, while the sun beat down on us. We'd cooked dinner together—rosemary lamb chops with baby potatoes and arugula salad—and finished our wine while taking a long walk on the grounds.

Now we were left alone, under the star-filled night sky.

Enzo's question pulled me out of my reverie. "They understand about us? They seemed to accept me today as more than your tour guide."

"Oh yeah, I spilled the beans on that one." He quirked his brow and I laughed. "I told them the truth—that we both really, really liked each other."

"Am I sneaking into your room tonight?"

"Definitely. That's why I took the only room on the main floor. But watch the second and third stairs—they creak."

"If I get caught, I'll tell your mama I couldn't sleep."

"Don't do that. She'll make you warm milk and sit up with you all night at the kitchen table, talking your ear off. Just tell her you're sleepwalking and head right into my room."

We laughed together, and I felt silly and giddy, drunk on him and the fresh air and the Italian landscape laid out like a visual gift.

"You are here until Saturday?"

I nodded, not wanting to think about the end of this. Of us. We had three precious days left and I didn't want to waste them worrying about the passage of time. "Yes. But right now, it seems like a lifetime away."

His eyes crinkled at the corners when he smiled, and he kissed me slow and sweet and deep. "You're right. *Quel che sarà sarà.*"

"What will be will be," I repeated.

We slowly made our way inside. Later, he quietly entered my room, and I pulled back the covers to invite him into my bed. His hands tugged off my clothes; his lips burned every inch of my skin; his mouth covered mine when I shook and cried out his name during the long hours of the night. I gave myself to him, body and soul, and finally fell without a safety net, not caring about the future or how he fit into my life or what would happen when I left on Saturday. All I knew was I was happy, and he was with me tonight, and for now, that was enough.

CHAPTER THIRTY-TWO

Allegra

"I can't believe we're doing this together."

I looked up at Ian and my heart did a crazy flip-flop in my chest. From the moment he'd arrived, my body had been acting up. It was like we couldn't stop sneaking in touches here and there, craving a closeness between us that only intensified after our days apart. He'd regaled me with tales of Assisi, eating nun-cooked lasagna by the monastery and spending his time reflecting and praying. He had an innate calmness that intrigued me—it was as if he carried a glow wherever he went, because it came from the inside. The spillover seemed to bring a light to anyone who was in his presence.

Including me.

Now we were cooking in Chef Bernini's restaurant after shopping at the market. There were only four other people in the class, so Chef spent a lot of time with us individually. I learned how to properly handle a knife for chopping, how to use my senses of smell and taste to balance seasonings, and that I needed to use more salt overall. The kitchen was hot with the ovens on, and the work was hard—he pushed us like students rather than a leisurely cooking class, but I loved it. We rolled and pinched ravioli, created an amazing pesto sauce, and learned how to properly braise broccoli rabe to get it to the perfect texture.

By the time we sat down to eat our creations, I was starving. Ian shoveled food into his mouth and groaned. "So. Good."

I shook my head. "This is incredible. I learned so much—I can't wait to go home and try all these new recipes."

"Well, I learned I'm the sloppiest cook in history. Did you see how many times I got yelled at to clean up my space?"

I giggled. "He was trying to teach you to clean as you go. But he said your pesto was impressive."

"Not as good as yours. You were the star pupil." His eyes shone with pride. "You have a gift, Allegra. I had no idea you were a boss behind the stove."

I flushed with pleasure. "Thanks. I've always been interested, but since we came to Italy, I've figured out I definitely want to do more. Take some classes this year. Maybe get a part-time job in a restaurant. We have so many farm stands and organic butchers, I'd love to start prepping more food that's healthy and simple."

"You can even help with the food pantries," he pointed out. "There are many poor people who get fed from a can or box because it's cheap. But they deserve real food to eat also, especially the kids."

I'd never thought of that. "Nonni's church has a food pantry. Maybe I'll look into it."

"How's it going with your mom?"

"Really good. For the first time, she said no to a work emergency. She even lost the client—which has never happened to her."

"That's huge. It seems like you're both finally listening to each other. When my parents accepted my decision to go into the seminary, I felt like we got to rebuild our relationship. I'd been so resentful of them, and they were always pissed at me and my stubbornness. We reached a breaking point, and I didn't even return home for Christmas two years ago." His blue eyes held a gleam of sadness from the memory. "It sucked. It took me a few times to be the one to try and explain why it was important to me. They admitted they were trying to get me to live a life they wanted—which I actually understand. Hell, if I had kids, I'd probably bully them into what I felt was good for them. I'm just glad we broke through and communicated."

"Yeah, same thing with my mom. Every time I brought up cooking, she'd wave it off like I was being silly. Said I hadn't worked so hard to do something beneath me. But she's finally listening to me and seems to really be interested in what I want. Enzo is good for her."

"I had no idea they'd hooked up on the tour. Did you?"

"No! Not until the last leg when I noticed them on the bus. I've never seen my mom even have a date before. It's like she's been a nun since I was born."

He laughed. "Is it weird for you?"

"No, I love it. God knows, I've craved a dad in my life forever. Or even some type of male role model—other than her and Nonni, I had no one else. It got lonely."

"Yeah, me too. I always wanted a sibling, but I do have a bunch of cousins, so that helped. Though one of them was a bully and liked beating me up."

"Did you pray for his soul?"

He winced. "Yeah, but first I gave him a black eye. Then I went to confession."

We laughed and he squeezed my hand in a gesture that gave me goose bumps. How had I ever found him unattractive? His deep blue eyes and his smile and even his red hair seemed charming now. The freckles were just a part of who he was, and I liked to trail my finger across them like tracing a route on a map. And when he kissed me? His lips were so warm and firm, and I just wanted to kiss him for hours.

"I think you better stop looking at me like that."

I jerked back in surprise, blushing. "Sorry."

"No, Allegra, I like it. I'm just letting you know I'm about to kiss you right in Chef Bernini's restaurant and he'll probably yell at me for not concentrating on the food."

Buzzing with female anticipation, I gave him a teasing look. "Then I'll give you a rain check for later."

We finished up our meal and spent some time exchanging contact information with the chef. I explained my desire to go to cooking school, and he wrote down his email and told me he'd help with a recommendation if I needed it. My head spun with excitement and we walked out hand in hand.

"I can't believe he said that. Enzo was so nice to do this for us."

"Yeah, he's perfect for your mom. It's too bad he lives in Italy. Do you think they'll try and continue dating?"

I shrugged. "Not sure. Hope so. I'm not sure how she's going to handle it." I thought of Ian's parents and what they might think. After all, their son planned to be a priest. "What about your parents? Do they think it's weird you stayed to come hang out with me?"

"They loved the idea. Honestly, they loved you. Said you were mature, sweet, and they were happy we got along so well."

"Are they hoping you'll fall madly in love with me and change your mind about being a priest?" I asked.

Holy crap.

I gasped when the words popped out of my mouth, and tried desperately to backtrack. My cheeks burned. "I'm sorry, Ian, I swear I didn't mean that. I was just teasing."

He gave a frown. "Why are you sorry? That's exactly what they're hoping for." He stopped and looked down at me. "Not to freak you out or anything, but I'm already crazy about you, Allegra. I don't have much more before I fall hard."

I gulped, stunned at his honesty. This man didn't believe in games or keeping himself safe. He just put out his emotions and damn the consequences. What would it be like to feel so brave and . . . free?

He noticed my confusion and gave me a quick kiss on the lips. "I'm getting way too serious. Let's have some fun. I'd like to check out the basilica—I read there's a gorgeous mosaic of the ascension of Christ. How about you?"

I pushed away my spinning thoughts and concentrated on the here and now. Plenty of time for serious stuff later. "The Museo del Risorgimento. It's got tons of art I'd love to study."

He grinned. "Done. Let's go so we'll be back in time for dinner."

The rest of the fleeting afternoon we toured. He taught me more about the church and I taught him art history. We wandered the botanical gardens and got dizzy with the scent of fresh flowers wafting in the air. When we finally arrived back at the villa, I was exhausted, still full, and deliriously happy.

"How was it?" Mom asked, giving us both a short hug. "Did you make some wonderful stuff?"

"Chef Bernini is a master," I said. "I can't thank you enough, Enzo, for letting us do this. Besides teaching me so much, he said he'd give me a recommendation if I need it for college!"

Mom looked a bit worried, but she held her tongue. We'd come a long way. "Then you must have impressed him," she said firmly.

Enzo nodded. "He does not give compliments or recs easy. I'm so glad you enjoyed it. Ian, did you get to see some of Lucca?"

"Allegra took me around. We checked out the museum, the cathedral, and the gardens." He shot me a look filled with warm affection. "It was the best day."

Nonni beamed. "Good, that is how it should be. I think you've done enough cooking today, Allegra. Why don't you both freshen up and relax on the terrace? I made more lemonade."

Enzo motioned upstairs. "You're bunking with me, Ian."

"Sounds good. I appreciate you letting me stay, Ms. Ferrari. My parents really loved spending time with you."

"Thanks, Ian. Just call me Frannie. I felt the same way about them, and I think you saved Allegra from mother overkill."

Ian laughed, and we went our separate ways to change.

We were all in a lighthearted mood as we gathered around the table and picked at finger foods Nonni had created. Plump figs and ripened olives lay in small bowls with fragrant oils and herbs to dip. Chunks of crusty bread and sharp Parmesan cheese completed the antipasto.

We stayed up late, listening to Enzo's stories about crazy tourists and the things they'd made him do. Ian spoke of Ireland and sketched out the beauty of green rolling hills, small-town life, and how the pubs were as intimate as living rooms, where everyone gathered. When they asked about Manhattan, Mom and I shared a look and started laughing.

"Do you want to tell them the story?" she asked, leaning back in her chair.

"Sure. Mom and I had gone to see a Broadway play, and—"

"Oh, which one?" Ian asked.

"*Phantom of the Opera*. It was so romantic," I said.

"Hmm, I'd have preferred *Hamilton* or *The Lion King*—I heard they're good."

I pressed my lips together. "I'll take that under consideration if we ever go to a play," I teased.

He grinned. "Sorry, I got caught up. Go ahead."

"So, we're coming out of the play and it's pouring buckets— I mean, we were under the awning and we had pools of water up to our ankles. No one could get a cab, there was barely space to stand, and we were blocks away from the train station."

Mom jumped in, not able to help herself. "We see this

rickshaw—which is basically a bicycle with a small covered seat. He waves us over, and we figured we'd give it a try because we would have missed our train."

I picked up the story. "We get into this tiny seat and squish together, and he starts pedaling like a bat out of hell through these wet city streets. Oh my God, I thought we were dead. He went through yellow lights and skidded in puddles, and the plastic covering began to leak, and we were drenched anyway by the time we got to the train station."

Mom doubled over in laughter at the memory. "We were screaming for him not to kill us and trying to huddle under our jackets as we got drenched. Finally, he skids up to Grand Central and we're both shaking and—"

"He asks Mom for one hundred and fifty dollars!" I finished.

Enzo and Ian gasped. "Are you kidding?" Ian asked. "That's insane."

"I know! So Mom says absolutely not, and he starts screaming in the rain that he'll call the police because by taking the ride we agreed to the terms."

"And he sticks this wet, torn piece of paper into my hand and starts pointing at the fee schedule and how many miles he pedaled. It was a nightmare."

"You didn't pay him?" Enzo asked.

Mom sighed in defeat. "No, I did. I gave him a hundred-dollar bill because I just wanted to get dry, and he was starting to scare me, and I told him take it or leave it. He took it."

Ian groaned. "You got played."

"Big-time, but that happens all the time in the city. Here I was thinking I was a native and too experienced to get played, yet I lost a hundred bucks on the worst ride of my life."

Nonni shook her head. "You two are some pair. Tell them what you did the next time you took your daughter to the city."

Mom winced. "I hired a limo. I couldn't deal with the drive or the train."

Everyone cracked up. A warm glow shot through me. I didn't often get the opportunity to sit around the table and talk like I'd done the past month. It felt like we were a makeshift family, and I realized how important food was to bond people. I wished we'd be able to continue the tradition when I returned home.

Nonni finished her coffee and stood up. "Well, I'm off to bed. These old bones have had enough."

We said good night. Ian and I shared a glance. "Mom, Ian and I are going for a walk. I want to show him the lake."

"Okay, sweetheart. Bring a blanket in case you're cold or want to sit. It's really beautiful at night."

"Thanks."

"Use bug spray, please. Enzo and I are going to head in soon, so we probably won't be up. Text me if you need anything."

I nodded and went inside to get a thick blanket and two bottles of water. Then we headed down the pathway that wound through the vineyards and toward the lake, the flashlight beam lighting the way.

We spread out the blanket on the hill under a twisted old oak tree. Stars studded the sky like diamonds on black velvet. The crickets and night creatures screeched out a song, giving us our own special concert. Ian sat down, spread his knees, and pulled me into his embrace. He wrapped his arms tight around me, and I felt sheltered and safe, his breath against my ear, my head pressed to his chest.

I never wanted to leave.

"I have this need to learn everything about you," he murmured, touching his lips to my shoulder.

"Well, my favorite color is yellow."

He chuckled. "A good start. I guess I still can't believe you don't have a boyfriend. Or someone interested. Are the guys at your school truly stupid?"

"I've never connected romantically with anyone at my school," I said truthfully. "I tried. One of the popular kids tried to hook me up with the school track star, but I found him egotistical."

"Definitely not a good match."

"Definitely not. And I've been focused on my schoolwork, tennis, and track. I'm a big reader and art history buff, so technically I'm a nerd. I like my own company. Sad, huh?"

"Nope, sounds like me. I never connected with anyone at college either. I met a lot of nice girls, but no one I wanted to give up my free time for."

I thought of David and guilt pinged me. After I stopped responding to his and Freda's texts, we'd gone to radio silence. "Right before we left on our trip, I started hanging out with this guy and his friends. That's where I got busted for pot."

I held my breath, awaiting his judgment, but he didn't move away, and his voice sounded steady. "Makes sense. You were mad at your mom and probably looking for something. Did you like smoking weed?"

"I wanted to, but it wasn't my thing." I thought over the encounter with Freda, David, and Connor. "It was the connection I loved. They seemed really tight, and I'd never really felt like I could trust any of my friends with my secrets. I liked how I felt when I was smoking or drinking and part of the crew."

He squeezed my shoulders in reassurance. "Allegra, you're only eighteen and still in high school. You're supposed to experiment and figure out who you are. I get it. Now it makes sense. Your mom freaked and decided to drag you off for an exotic trip to keep you away from them?"

"Bingo. I was pissed. I wanted to travel over the summer in their RV, stopping at different clubs. But now, thinking about it, I don't think it would've been a cool idea. I don't really know them that well, and I had no interest in being high or drunk on a regular basis. The pics they've been sending me kind of confirmed it."

"You're the smartest woman I've met. You have this sense of self that comes right through. There's no need for you to fit in with anyone, Allegra, especially with people who want to change you. Plus, I happen to find nerds extremely sexy."

I laughed and cuddled closer. "Then I guess we're on the same page. By the way, what's your favorite color?"

"Blue."

"Like your eyes."

He stiffened, and suddenly the easy affection between us turned. A spark ignited, and I caught my breath as a raw want shook through me. Slowly, I turned my head and met his gaze.

"Allegra."

My name came out hoarse from his lips in a question I already knew the answer to. I didn't consciously plan it, but there was nothing more I wanted than to belong to Ian tonight. To have him be my first. My heart exploded in my chest and I reached up. "I want you," I whispered against his lips. "Is that okay?"

He shuddered and muttered something under his breath. "Yeah, it's okay. More than okay. I just need you to know I wasn't expecting this tonight, and I didn't come here to—to be with you like this."

"Have you ever done it before?"

He shook his head. "No. I know I needed it to be special. With someone I loved, who I'd never forget. I wanted it to be beautiful."

Emotion choked my throat. "That's what I want. I'm a virgin too."

He clenched his jaw; his blue eyes filled with agony and a hunger that thrilled me. "But I can't give you what you need," he said miserably. "I don't want to hurt you when I leave."

I smiled and pulled his head down, kissing him with a confidence that came from his obvious feelings for me. "Ian, you'd hurt me if you walked away right now without being mine."

His eyes half closed, and then he pulled me in tight, his mouth taking mine in a deep kiss. He lay back on the blanket, and I spilled over his chest, my hands exploring his hard body. We made love under the Tuscan night sky, and when I stopped him as I remembered we didn't have a condom, he sheepishly pulled one from his pocket, his guilty expression making me laugh. He surged between my thighs, and it hurt only for a moment. I concentrated on his face close to mine, the joy and love I found in his gaze, the tenderness of his fingers as he stroked me and owned my body with a grace and humbleness that shook me to the core. Later, we lay together, limbs entangled, his hands in my hair, staring up at the stars.

"I love you," he said.

"I love you too," I said back.

And I knew in that moment, I'd remember tonight forever.

ON THE DAY he left, I wondered if I'd survive the pain.

It was so much worse than physical. No, this type of agony throbbed from the inside out, affecting my entire body. My stomach clenched and I kept wondering what I could do to stop the inevitable from happening.

But I couldn't. I had to go home, and Ian was returning to Ireland.

Ian was going into the priesthood.

Since the night we had made love, it was as if we were in a dreamworld. We spent the day talking nonstop, sharing our dreams and fears and secrets. We walked for hours, hand in hand, and spent the evening with Mom, Nonni, and Enzo around the dinner table. Nonni showed us how to play card games, and we did silly things like charades or Heads Up! from our phones. It was as if the outside world couldn't touch us and we were wrapped in our own special bubble of happy.

Now it'd be broken.

He said goodbye to everyone, and I caught Mom's pained look. We hadn't discussed how serious I felt about Ian, but it was obvious she knew. I caught her watching us with a mixture of happiness and worry, as if she knew well what I'd have to go through when he left.

"Can you text me when you land?" I asked. "Just so I know you're okay."

"It'll probably be hard not to text you every hour," he said, his smile not reaching his eyes this morning. "I know it's only been a few days, but I feel like you're a big part of my life."

I loved the way he didn't hold back. Even now, he opened his arms and I stepped into his embrace, clinging tight, not afraid to show my emotion in case he thought I was silly. I savored the fresh scent of him, and the strength of his arms, and the gentleness as he held me. "Ian?"

"Yeah?"

"Is it wrong for me to wish you didn't want to be a priest? That we could have a long-distance relationship and I could come to Ireland after I graduate and give this a real shot?"

His hands cupped my cheeks and I blinked furiously, hating the tears that stung my eyes when I swore I wouldn't do this. I wouldn't make him feel guilty or beg for something he'd already decided he couldn't give me. I didn't want his last impression to be of a needy girl with tears on her cheeks, begging him to stay.

"No. It's just honest. If you didn't, I may have questioned this whole thing between us. How in a few weeks I could fall so hard for you. If you didn't ask, I would have constantly wondered if it'd been a dream or something I just wanted bad enough to imagine."

"I love you." It was the second time I'd whispered the words. The first had been after we had sex and he held me in his arms, and I knew I'd never feel like this again. "That's real."

"Yes, it is. I love you too. You're a gift, Allegra. You've changed me and you don't even know it. Without you, I'd wonder for the rest of my life what loving someone was like. How can I counsel about love when I never experienced it? Now I understand what it's like to give my body and heart to another. I just didn't realize it hurt so damn much."

I barked out a laugh, pressing my face to his shirt, trying to get myself together. "I don't know how I'm going to do this. Let you leave."

"Me either. All I know is you're already a part of me. I owe you everything. Remember that full moon we saw together in Florence?"

I nodded, too sad to speak.

"When you see a full moon, know that I'll be looking at it and thinking of you. Of what we shared. It'll be our moon, always."

"I like that," I whispered.

He kissed me, then slowly stepped back. "I'll call you."

"Okay."

I watched him climb into the car. He looked through the open window, and his beautiful blue eyes met mine, his lips curved in a heartbreaking smile. I tried to memorize his face and this moment for when I needed it later, but it was already slipping away too soon.

He drove away and disappeared down the path.

I spent a long time staring at the empty drive, wondering if I'd be able to function. We would leave tomorrow, and I had one last day here. I'd promised Ian I wouldn't waste it mourning for him and would take advantage of my final hours here.

It was a promise I planned on keeping.

Taking a deep breath, I walked back inside. "He's gone."

Enzo cleared his throat. "If you'll excuse me, I need to make a call. I'll be in my room."

Mom shot him a grateful glance. I paced the kitchen, already feeling lost. "Are you okay, honey?" Mom asked.

"Sure. I mean, I knew he was going to leave. And, yeah, I really liked him, a lot, but he lives in Ireland and I live in New York, and he's going to be a priest so it's not like we can have this long-distance relationship or anything." My voice kept getting higher, but I couldn't seem to control it. "But I did promise him not to waste the day moping because I miss him, so tell me what the plan is. Maybe drive to Pisa—Enzo said it was close and we only got half a day there. I didn't get to climb to the top of the tower. Or maybe we can go for a hike and get some exercise. It's not that hot, so Nonni should be fine. What do you think?"

Nonni stayed silent, her arms clasped tight to her chest. It was Mom who finally did it. She closed the distance between us and stroked back my hair, the gesture a comfort I rarely experienced with her. "It's okay to feel the hurt, sweetheart," she said gently. "A good cry is the best way to cleanse."

"I'm fine." My lower lip trembled. "It's just—I mean, I think I fell in love with him. Silly, huh?"

I waited for her to dismiss the whole thing as a crush or puppy love and not worthy of me. Instead, she shook her head. "Not silly at all. Ian was special."

"Mom?"

"Yeah, honey?"

"I don't know if I can do this."

And then suddenly she moved and yanked me hard into her arms, and I broke and began to cry. She held me tight and I cried my heart out, and she murmured soothing phrases and promised me I was strong and it would all be okay.

For the first time in a long, long time, I believed her.

CHAPTER THIRTY-THREE

FRANCESCA

I COULDN'T STOP thinking about my daughter.

I sat outside with Enzo on our last night together. We'd spent the day keeping Allegra busy with as much sightseeing as we could handle, distracting her with chatter and pointing out moments of Tuscan beauty. After dinner, she excused herself to go to her room, and I caught the sheer exhaustion and sadness in her eyes.

She'd had her first heartbreak and there was nothing I could do. I felt helpless, but I also sensed this was a turning point for us. She'd opened up and cried in my arms. She'd allowed me to comfort her and try to soothe her pain. For the first time in too long, I was there when she needed me.

"First love is hard," Enzo said, his fingers entwined with mine.

I gave a small sigh. "It is. I can't even rage or be mad at him. He's a wonderful man who made my daughter a better person. He's just not meant to be with her outside of this."

He stared into the night, a thoughtful look on his face. "Some love stories are meant to be temporary," he said, his voice light.

I couldn't help but stiffen at his comment. He seemed so casual, as if he was speaking about us. We hadn't discussed any future or plans after our time in Tuscany. It was too special and precious to ruin with empty promises. But right now, it'd be nice to hear some. "Absolutely," I said. "Nothing wrong with enjoying what it is for the moment. Then you forget."

He quirked a brow and gave me a look. "You never forget, *cara*. Not if it's the right love story."

I gave a sniff. "Whatever."

"Hmm, you seem cranky tonight. Do you have something on your mind?"

I bristled. "No! Just thinking about how badly Allegra is hurting and wishing I could help. After all, I'm leaving tomorrow and so are you. The same thing is going to happen to us. *Será será*, right?"

"You mean, *quel che sarà sarà*?"

"Yeah, that."

Amusement and something else, something deeper, sparked in his dark eyes. "So I guess that means you won't think about me once we leave each other, no?"

"Well, I won't be thinking of you if you're not thinking of me." Oh my God, did I really just utter those childish words? I almost groaned, but I was too far gone to admit defeat. "I mean, we had a great time and all, but now we're moving on. Right?"

"You are going home to New York to run your business. I'm staying in Italy. Unless . . ."

My breath caught. There was nothing logically that could be done, but still I was dying to hear his suggestion. "Unless?"

He seemed to pick his words carefully. "Unless you would like to see me again? I have much vacation. I've been wanting to take a trip to New York."

My heart began to slam against my chest, but this time it was no panic attack. It was hope. "You'd want to come see me?"

"Yes, *cara*. I know it will be hard, and there are many obstacles between us. But the idea of not being with you rips me apart. I'd like to try."

"Do you think we'd even have a chance?" The reality of the situation struck full force. It was crazy. He was an Italian tour guide I'd known for a month. How could we possibly be think-ing about dating? "Or will we just be postponing a necessary heartbreak?"

He leaned in, his hands cupping my cheeks. I fell into that dark, penetrating gaze that was warm and joyous. "I want to try," he said again. "I think you are worth fighting for."

I blinked. How had this man broken through my walls and captured my heart? And did I really want to see what could happen between us? Was it easier to just be strong and break it off now? "Enzo, I need to think about it," I said slowly. "This is hard for me. I have so much to contend with when I get back home. I want to be sure if we do this, we're both all in."

He nodded. "I understand." He kissed me, and I wrapped my arms around his neck and kissed him back. "Will you do one thing for me tonight?"

I laughed. "What?"

"Go skinny-dipping with me."

I blinked. "Excuse me?"

"When we were talking at dinner, Allegra teased you that it's on your bucket list. The lake is beautiful at night. Come with me. Now."

"Skinny-dipping? Me? Right now?"

"Yes, *cara*. The night is still ours. Let's not waste it."

I stared at him for a while before finally making my decision. "I'll do it."

Giggling like teenagers, we hurried outside and down to the lake. It took me a while to work up the courage to strip and dive into the water, but once I did, it was pure heaven. The water was silky smooth against my naked skin, and the crescent moon winked above me amid the stars.

We splashed and swam and floated. Then we climbed back into our clothes, dripping wet, running back to the house and collapsing into bed together to make love all night, feeling like morning might never come.

Eventually, it did.

He left me with a kiss on the lips and a promise lingering in the air. And for the first time, I realized the very controlled, orderly life I'd been so proud of had shattered around me in pieces.

And I'd never felt so alive or hopeful about the future.

CHAPTER THIRTY-FOUR

SOPHIA

MY GIRLS WERE hurting.

We sat at the table for our final breakfast. The luggage was packed and loaded. We'd take the rental car to the airport and make the flight back home. Ian had gone yesterday, and Enzo left in the early morning while we still slept. It was just us again.

Usually, the morning started with excited chatter, lots of coffee, and planning for the day. This morning, there was a deep silence, and Frannie and Allegra seemed lost in their thoughts. The weight of their pain and my unspoken secret lay heavily on my chest.

I'd gotten my wish and experienced the trip of a lifetime. My daughter and granddaughter had fought their way back to each other. There was no cliché happy ending, but they'd laid the groundwork for something better, if they both kept working on it. I'd have to help. But first, I needed to fight my own battle.

There'd been more blood today. The ache and pressure in my stomach had become insistently more painful. I'd been stubborn and wanted to keep this trip on schedule, knowing how important it was to all of us, and not wanting an illness to distract anyone. But it was time to tell them. The moment we got back home, I'd schedule the doctor's appointment and share everything.

I wondered if Frannie would try to keep seeing Enzo. I wondered if Allegra would keep in touch with Ian or if Ian would go through with his plan to enter the seminary. Love did strange things to a person's plan, as did God. Whatever happened, both men had served their purpose well here.

They'd shown my girls they were worthy of love exactly the way they were.

"Are you sad to leave?" I asked them both, needing to disrupt the heartbreaking silence.

Allegra shrugged. "It's time to go home."

Frannie sighed. "I'm sad. I'm a bit reluctant to let real life intrude again. I've enjoyed our trip together."

I noticed Allegra's face soften at her answer. "Yeah, me too," she admitted. "Are you going to see Enzo again, Mom?"

I cocked my head to better listen to her answer. We hadn't had time alone to really discuss her relationship. I just knew Enzo had brought out the best in my daughter. "I don't know. He talked about trying to do the long-distance thing, but it seems crazy. Of course it wouldn't work."

"It could," Allegra said. "If you both wanted it and committed."

"I don't know, sweetheart. I'm sure once I'm out of sight, he'll get on with his life, I'll go back to work, and it'll be just a beautiful memory."

Allegra slammed down her juice cup and glared. "Why does it have to be like that? Because it's easy or reasonable? Or because you want to go back and bury your head in work again, so you don't have to deal with real shit?"

Frannie's mouth fell open. I held my tongue, sensing they needed to sort this out on their own. "Don't talk to me like that! A long-distance relationship is complicated. We're not young kids with big dreams. We already have our lives settled and it's hard to change."

"But you can if you want it bad enough. God, Mom, don't you ever want something for yourself besides a company? I liked the way you were around Enzo. You laughed and got silly, and not once did you pick up your stupid phone. I know you didn't want me to have a father so you could have this uncomplicated, perfect life, but maybe it's time to get a little messy."

Frannie's face flushed and she practically snarled. "You know nothing about my choices or what I want from my life," she shot back. "I'm the mother and you don't get to ask questions!"

"Why not? That's stupid! I told you about Ian—you can tell me how you really feel about Enzo leaving instead of pretending everything's cool."

Frannie grabbed for her coffee, her fingers shaking. "This is a ridiculous conversation. Let's get ready to go."

I spoke up. "Actually, I think this is a very important conversation for you two. I think Allegra has something important to say, and you should listen."

I held my breath, wondering if she'd shut down, but she kept still and stared at Allegra, waiting.

Allegra tipped her chin up. "I hate that I don't have a real father. I hate that I was some type of biology experiment, neatly planned, with no love or passion or romance. Didn't you ever want a relationship? Did you have to control every aspect of your life—even falling in love? Did I just check off one of your boxes along the way to have a kid with no thought as to how I'd feel about your choices?"

Pain for both of them rose up and choked me. I watched my daughter flinch at the words, but I knew it was a wound in Allegra that needed to bleed free in order to heal.

"How could you think that?" Frannie whispered in anguish. "I chose to have you by a donor because I was thirty and had never once been in love. I was terrified to wait for a magical romance that might or might not happen. How could I believe in something I've never experienced? I wanted you so badly, I'd stare up at the ceiling and dream of you. And when I found out I was pregnant, you became my entire world. It was the craziest, most beautiful experience in my life, deciding to have you. You think there wasn't love? Dear God, I was full of love. Every moment from your birth to now is the only perfect thing in my life—don't you understand that? And if you ever doubted you were always wanted, and loved, and worshipped, then I need to beg your forgiveness, sweetheart. You're . . . everything."

They stared at each other for a few earth-shattering moments, and then Allegra swiped at her cheeks, nodding jerkily. "I didn't realize. You never talked about it, and the process seemed so cold."

Frannie rose from the chair and grabbed her, hugging tight. "Never," she said fiercely. "Ask Nonni. I was nuts about you, and every moment of my pregnancy was full of joy and anticipation. I have nothing without you, Allegra. You need to know that, okay?"

"Okay."

"I know I've said it before, but I'm going to make some changes. It's time I give Kate and Layla more accounts and let my team do the heavy lifting. I'll always be passionate about my work, but I don't want this type of overwhelming schedule anymore."

Allegra looked at her warily. "But I thought you loved it. Mom, I don't want you to have these panic attacks anymore, but I want you to be happy."

"Thanks, sweetheart. I think it's way past time I find some other things to make me happy. Just like you and Nonni have been telling me."

"Mother's always right," I chirped, smiling.

Frannie groaned and Allegra laughed. I watched them hug each other tight and swallowed down the lump in my throat.

Now they had a real chance.

Hours later, we boarded the plane and headed back to New York.

And when we got home, I finally told them everything.

I made the appointment immediately, and after the tests, I learned the thing inside me had grown and morphed into the diagnosis I'd dreaded.

Cancer.

CHAPTER THIRTY-FIVE

FRANCESCA

I WALKED INTO the hospital and headed to her room, carrying a bouquet of wildflowers in a mixture of vivid colors, which was her favorite. The door was half open, and I knocked quickly and stepped inside.

"How's our patient this morning?" I asked, smiling as I walked to the bed. I noticed her tray held half of her lunch, so she'd finally eaten. Her color was definitely back, even though the hospital gown and tubes sticking out of her arms made me a bit queasy.

"Better," she said. "But I'll never heal properly without some real food. Can you sneak in some of Allegra's ravioli? Please?"

I laughed, tucking the flowers into one of the extra vases at her bedside table. "No. Besides, you'll be out of here soon. The nurses say you're looking good and they can release you once you poop."

She groaned. "Lord save me from this humiliation."

But I noticed her eyes sparkling again, so she was definitely improving. When we got home, she'd sat Allegra and me down and told us the truth about how she'd been feeling. On the edge of a brand-new panic attack, I'd made myself calm with some deep breathing and quickly got on the case. I got her an appointment with a well-known doctor, who referred her to a gynecologist, who did some tests, then a biopsy.

She had uterine cancer.

The last few weeks of summer passed in a blur as the doctors came up with a plan. We'd all felt lucky to hear it hadn't advanced too far or spread, so she was scheduled for surgery and had a complete hysterectomy. At this point, it looked like they'd caught it all, and she didn't even need radiation.

She'd gotten lucky.

We'd gotten a miracle.

Allegra and I urged her to move in with us, but she was still stubborn, wanting to stay in her home. I hired a nurse and a cleaner, but she'd already thrown a few tantrums, insisting she'd be fine on her own. Allegra mentioned she'd stay at her house for the first week to help out, and we'd made a plan to switch on and off to be with her.

"Shouldn't you be at work?" she asked.

"I'm the boss—I can take a lunch hour," I teased.

"How did you do with the Ackerman account?"

"Still working on him." I smiled, loving her new effort to learn more about my business. She liked to ask pointed questions now about what ads I worked on and occasionally tried to help by jotting down ideas for me. She was actually pretty good and had a creative flair for marketing. Maybe she would've been drawn to the career I'd chosen.

Maybe we were much more alike than I'd originally thought.

I'd made good on my vow. I gave Kate and Layla full partnerships, restructured the team, and gave them more responsibility, announcing my intention to pull back. I was still involved in the bigger accounts and took the lead when I felt it was important, but I was getting better at not needing to run the entire show. I had even tried to get Anthony's account back, but he'd informed me it was too late.

By now I didn't even care. I had things in my life that were more important.

On cue, my phone vibrated, but this time it wasn't work, and I picked up without a pause. "Hey. I'm here with Mom."

"How's she doing?"

"Better. She's feisty and doesn't want to talk about her poop."

"Francesca!" she screeched. "Who are you talking to?"

"Just Enzo. Here, say hello." I pressed the phone to her ear, laughing at her red cheeks.

"I'm going to kill my daughter," she gritted out. "When am I going to see you?"

She nodded, and I enjoyed watching them have a little chat before I pulled the phone back. "When *are* you coming to see me?" I asked.

His laugh was low and sexy, and my whole body sighed with longing. "Christmas, just like we spoke about. I can stay for two weeks if you can stand me."

"I'm sure I can put up with you."

"Good. Did you get the Ackerman account?"

"Not yet, but I'm close. I'm about to dazzle him with an Instagram video to increase his followers and get his views up."

"Did Allegra have her race Thursday? Or was it canceled for rain? She never texted me back."

"No, it rained, and she didn't text you back because her phone dropped and shattered, and we spent half a day at Verizon getting her a new one. I'm sure she'll text tonight."

"Good. I had lunch with my sisters today and they're driving me crazy. They want to FaceTime you, but I'm afraid if you agree, you'll never take my calls again. My family is nuts."

"I'd love that, been dying to meet them. And I happen to love nuts."

"Thank God. I'll let you go spend time with your mama. Love you, *cara*."

Goose bumps shivered on my skin. "Love you too," I said softly.

When I clicked off, Mom was grinning with pride. I groaned. "Don't say it," I grumbled. "I sound ridiculous. Cheesy. Pathetic."

"No, sweetheart. You sound like you're in love. I'm so happy you decided to pursue this with Enzo."

"Me too. I miss him, but I feel good about us. We decided to take it slow and see what works and what doesn't."

My words were casual, but inside, I knew he was worth fighting for. He called on a regular basis and was interested in the day-to-day routine, from my work to gossip to what I was watching on TV. He loved chatting with Allegra and keeping abreast of her athletic meets and schoolwork. We FaceTimed and texted. Even from a distance, I felt close to him, as if our hearts had already recognized each other and didn't want to let go.

"I'm glad—you deserve to be happy and I adore Enzo. How are you feeling? Any further panic attacks?"

"Not lately. But I'm more aware of my triggers, so maybe that helps." I always felt like the monster was close, ready to leap from the darkness and slam my body into crippling anxiety. But just knowing I could control my breathing and get through it soothed me a bit. I'd also been trying some meditation in the morning to calm my mind.

We chatted some more, and a delivery person popped in with a beautiful bouquet of mixed roses. Figuring it was one of Mom's many church friends, I watched her read the card and do something I hadn't seen before.

Blush.

"Mom, who are the flowers from?" I asked.

She turned even pinker, her laugh a touch guilty. "Oh, just someone I met in Italy."

I tilted my head. "Who? Someone from the tour?"

"No, a man I met in Venice." Her eyes gleamed with a spark of excitement. "I'm thinking of joining him on a tour through Paris. He said the group was extremely nice and they catered to senior citizens."

My jaw dropped. "Are you kidding? You can't go off to Paris! You need healing and rest. How come you never told me about this?"

"Oh, Frannie, don't be silly, it's nothing. It wouldn't be until next year anyway, and I'm only considering it. There's no need to make a fuss."

I noticed she gave the roses an appreciative sniff and put them right in her eyeline so they'd be easy to view. "Can I at least know his name?"

She gave a very motherly sigh. "Milton. Now, let's change the subject before the nurse comes in for her rounds."

I did but made a mental note to steal the card and see what Milton had said to my mother.

When I left, we'd made arrangements for her to leave the next day, if she did her business like the nurses demanded.

I hummed under my breath as I got to my car and headed back to work.

It just happened to be Dean Martin.

He was a classic for a reason.

CHAPTER THIRTY-SIX

ALLEGRA

I WAS SO caught up in Mr. Sanderson's lecture, I didn't even hear the bell until the students around me began shutting their Chromebooks. "Quiz on Monday," he shouted over the chaos. "We'll finish up our medieval segment and move on to the Renaissance period. Get ready for nudity, people, and if there are any juvenile snickers, I'll send you to the principal."

I laughed along with the girl beside me and we shared a glance. She was pretty quiet but seemed just as into the history of art class as I was. Too many students said they'd picked it for an easy A, but I couldn't wait to begin delving deeper.

"He's pretty funny," she said. She wore her dark hair caught up in a casual ponytail, and her black-framed glasses gave her a cool, artsy look. "Personally, my dream is to see the statue *David* in person. I heard it's bigger than you think—all parts."

Her wink made me grin. "Actually, I got to see it this summer. I went to Italy."

Her mouth dropped open. "Shut. Up. That's the coolest vacay ever. I got stuck at Sesame Place for my younger sister. Am I right? Is it epic?"

I nodded, the memory sparking something warm inside. "Yeah, it was. And it was really big, and under this amazing golden spotlight so you got to spend as much time as you wanted studying it. The *Pietà* was behind glass but still pretty cool."

She shook her head and stuck her papers and Chromebook in her backpack. "I'm so jealous. Hey, do you paint too, or do you just appreciate art?"

I laughed again. There was something about her that gave off an easy vibe but felt real. I'd backed off from Bonnie and Claire this year, not able to take the fakeness anymore. They couldn't believe I was taking an elective instead of getting out of school early, and they bitched nonstop about their boring summer. I was pretty much over both of them. "I never really tried to paint," I said. "Do you?"

"I try, even though I suck. But it's fun. My friend Tracey and I are doing an art class on Saturday mornings—the new workshops start next week." She hesitated, glancing at me with a bit of wariness, like she was afraid I'd suddenly mock her. "You can join us, if you want. Tracey's really cool. Afterward, we can go for lunch at the café—I'm a vegetarian and they have some really good stuff. If you want. Oh crap, my name's Brianna, by the way. In case you didn't know."

Normally, I'd be nice but make up some excuse. It was easier to stay in my comfort zone. "Yeah, I'd love it," I said. "My name's Allegra."

"I've seen you around school but I don't think we were in any classes together." She grabbed her phone. "What's your number? I can text you the info."

I recited it and she plugged it in. We left each other with a promise to chat, and I enjoyed the hum of excitement when I thought of taking an art class with her. The thought of something new and challenging made me think of this past summer, and I decided to walk instead of take the bus. It seemed to be an afternoon to linger with my thoughts.

I hadn't gone too far off school grounds when I recognized a familiar figure coming toward me. I squinted, then realized it was David. I watched him draw closer, preparing myself for that familiar flare of nerves and anticipation. But when he finally stopped inches away, I realized that sharp reaction had dulled.

"Hey," he said.

"Hey. How are you?"

He shifted his weight and stuffed his hands in his pockets. "I'm cool. Freda ended up having to transfer this year, so she's not around. And Connor got into this new crowd so we haven't been hanging out as much." His gaze raked over me. "You look good."

"Thanks, so do you." He did. He'd cut his wild hair and now it was a bit spiky, making him look less surly, which probably translated to sexy for some girls. He gave off the same chill vibe but didn't seem as distant as before. Today, he seemed to be really looking at me. "I like your hair like that."

"Oh yeah, I got a gig and they asked me to clean up a bit. You never called me back when you got home from Italy."

I winced. It had been awkward. He'd texted a few times, but I didn't know what to say. I kept thinking about Ian, and how David with his weed habit and lifestyle made me feel uncomfortable. I wasn't really wild and rebellious at all. I was still just a nerd. And I liked it. I didn't want to be smoking pot and hanging out late at night. I finally felt interested in parts of my life that had once been flat. "Sorry. My mom wasn't cool with me hanging out with you after the incident."

"Yeah, I figured. Parents are always trying to cut out our freedom. We gotta be brave and do us."

I nodded, taking a step back. "Yeah, but the thing is, I kind of understand where she's coming from. I didn't really like smoking anyway."

"No shit? I hope you didn't think we made you. That's not cool."

I shook my head. "No, it was my choice. I don't blame any-one. I just realized it wasn't me."

He nodded slowly, a slight smile on his lips. "I get it. I'm not really into it anymore either. It's expensive and I'd rather spend my money on doing my music."

He'd sent me a video of a song he'd written, and I was surprised at his talent. His voice was deep and husky and kind of lush. The lyrics were smart too. "You're really good, David. I know it's hard to break in, but you have something important to say. One day, the world will listen."

He jerked back, then narrowed his gaze. "You think?"

I shrugged. "I hope. It's going to be a long road if music is your passion. That's half the battle." I thought of Ian's words and a wave of pain hit me. He'd written me over the past two months, little postcards with a few words scrawled; crisp stationery with Michelangelo's *David* stenciled on the front, his words in a looping scrawl that was elegant and neat; and plain notebook paper with a few lines of poetry he'd read. As much as hearing from him hurt, it also soothed me, knowing he was somewhere out there going after what he believed in, thinking of me.

David shifted his feet. "So, I know you're crazy busy and all, but I wondered if you wanted to go out with me. Get something to eat. A movie. Or just hang and talk somewhere."

I stared at him for a while, wondering how I felt. I didn't know yet. But something had changed, and I was curious to find out who he really was, away from his group of friends, under the defensiveness I sensed prickling beneath.

"We can do that," I said slowly. "Friday night?"

"Yeah, perfect. I'm glad you had a good time in Italy. We ended up cutting our trip short anyway—it was a disaster. Freda and Connor went crazy, and I ended up losing one of the gigs."

I laughed, thinking of her flashing her boobs for the camera. "I figured. Gotta go. See you later."

"Yeah, see ya."

I headed home, a smile on my lips. I had no idea what would happen, but I was open to getting to know David better—on my terms. Mom had called and said Nonni was being released tomorrow, so I could finally stop worrying about her. And I was starting volunteer work at the food pantry. I had spoken with the director about my concerns over the food, and he'd given me a list of what they'd need for donations if I could find any willing sponsors.

I'd hit about six places so far and signed up a local farm to provide fresh eggs and baskets of fruit and vegetables. They were excited to work with the community, and I had an idea it was only the beginning. Even Mom decided to join me, expressing interest in how not-for-profits worked and how to get clean food to people who need it. She called me a clever businessperson, and though I groaned inside, it felt good to know she was proud.

I had big plans.

Later that night, I stared out my window at the full moon and thought of Ian. Thought of our trip, and how Enzo was coming for Christmas, and the way Mom came home for dinner now and seemed happy.

I knew there were a lot of obstacles ahead. Fights, anger, pain, sadness. I felt them so deeply sometimes, I wondered if I'd ever be able to be like my mother and look at the world with a sense of control. It was like I'd become a big open wound, but Italy had taught me not to be scared of it. I didn't want a narrow, closed-off life.

Because there were adventures waiting around every corner.

And I couldn't wait to find out what came next.

NOTE TO READER

I'D LIKE TO share a story with you.

My mother's dream had always been to visit Italy, where her parents were born. But we'd never had the money or opportunity in our family, so we tucked that dream aside for a long, long time.

But one day, we made a decision that changed all of us. I decided I wanted to take her to Italy for her seventieth birthday, along with my niece, who was turning sixteen, and my godmother, my mother's sister. All of us left our lives behind for a glorious fourteen days to experience our homeland and embark on an adventure. With the men taking care of the kids at home, we were free to just be us and bond together.

It was the trip of a lifetime. We celebrated my mother's birthday in Tuscany, under a full moon, in a vineyard. We danced and drank wine and ate pasta. We talked. We learned about each other. We became close with our tour group members and forged friendships that revolved around an amazing shared experience.

As we made our way from Rome to Capri to Siena, I outlined a story about three generations of women who are lost . . . and come to Italy to find themselves and one another.

During the trip, I realized the deep complications and layers in female relationships, especially mothers and daughters. I heard my grandmother's voice whisper to me as I stood on a hilltop overlooking Napoli. I saw the growth in my niece with every piece of art she studied and each glorious church she was lucky enough to enter. I relished the stories from my aunt about her experiences as a career woman and her decision not to have children and the big life she'd embarked on that might be different from what society deems we should do.

We came home changed. And I knew this book would be written one day, containing many of our adventures and discoveries.

There is a bit of truth twisted up with a lot of fiction. Someone may have fallen down the Spanish Steps. There may have been a frantic chase through the deserted parks of Rome by an angry mob. There may have been overenthusiastic pigeons in Venice.

Or maybe not.

Either way, the emotions are all real. I hope you enjoyed the Ferrari women and saw a bit of yourself in their journey. I hope the power of forgiveness and healing and second chances resonates the way I wished it would. And family, of course.

Always family.

Thank you, dear readers, for trusting me enough to come along for the ride.

—Jen

ACKNOWLEDGMENTS

THERE ARE SO many people to thank. I've said many times that a writer may create the story, but it is a savvy team who helps bring it out to the world in the best possible way.

First, to the amazing Berkley team. My editor, Kerry Donovan, thank you for believing in this story when many didn't. You allowed me to accomplish a dream I've had for a while, and I'm forever grateful. Thanks to Mary Geren, to Eileen Chetti for the copyedits, and to a top-notch marketing and publicity team—I'm forever grateful to Jessica Mangicaro, Tara O'Connor, and Craig Burke. To Jeanne-Marie Hudson and Claire Zion, it's been a true pleasure to be able to work with you on this book.

To my agent, Kevan Lyon, who is always at my side—I'm so lucky to have you!

To my assistant, Mandy Lawler, who pushed me hard this year to bump up my branding game and keeps things smoothly running in the background—thank you.

To Nina Grinstead at Valentine PR for helping me with ALL the things behind the curtain that build a successful release.

And, as always, to my readers. Thank you for following me everywhere over the years, to wherever my Muse carries me.

You all rock.

OUR ITALIAN SUMMER

....

JENNIFER PROBST

QUESTIONS FOR DISCUSSION

1.   When we first meet Francesca, we discover she seems to prioritize work over family. Did you feel sympathetic or critical toward her character and her responsibilities? Did she inspire any empathy for her situation, or did you believe she could have made better choices?

2.   The three main characters—Francesca, Allegra, and Sophia—all have individual struggles within the family. Were you able to relate to one of them better than the others? Why?

3.   Do you think it was wrong for Sophia to decide to keep her health problems to herself and not share them with her daughter?

4.   Italy plays an important role in *Our Italian Summer*. As the characters travel, they begin to find out more about themselves. Did you have a favorite town/setting you loved the most? Why? What was it about the scene that resonated with you?

5.   The relationship between Enzo and Francesca grows gradually throughout the book. What kind of future do you envision for them?

6.   Allegra struggles with her resentment of Francesca's workaholic tendencies and with not feeling seen by her mother.

Many of us may experience guilt over our work and careers, and trying to find balance between work and homelife. Discuss the mother-daughter roles represented and the character with whom you identified most closely and why.

7.   Allegra and Sophia share a deep bond, which Francesca seems jealous of. Is there someone you experienced a tight bond with other than your parents? What did you get out of the experience? Looking back, do you see why you bonded with that particular person?

8.   Francesca has always wanted to be the exact opposite of her mother and raise her daughter differently. Yet her daughter ends up feeling more connected to Sophia, embracing her view of life rather than her mother's. What do you think of this dynamic? Do you believe that if Francesca hadn't pushed her so hard, Allegra would have embraced more of her mother's viewpoints?

9.   The overall theme of *Our Italian Summer* is that our relationships to our family develop and change us. Discuss each character's growth arc and how they changed over the course of the book.

10. Allegra and Ian's relationship begins with friendship but morphs into love. Do you think her feelings for Ian change Allegra for the better? How so?

11. Ian wants to become a priest. Do you believe he should have pursued a different path after falling in love with Allegra? What do you think happens to Ian after the close of the book? Do you think Ian and Allegra will always have a relationship?

12. Do you think Allegra and Ian should have had sex if he was intent on pursuing the priesthood? Discuss.

13. The Ferrari women meet many characters during their tour of Italy. Who do you think made the biggest impact on Allegra? Sophia? Francesca?

14. The book includes several descriptive scenes of landscapes and food. What was your favorite? What feelings did it invoke?

15. Have you ever visited Italy? What was your experience there? If you have never been, do you dream of traveling to a specific part of Italy?

Jennifer Probst is the *New York Times* bestselling author of the Sunshine Sisters series, the Stay series, the Billionaire Builders series, the Searching For . . . series, and the Marriage to a Billionaire series. Like some of her characters, Probst, along with her husband and two sons, calls New York's Hudson Valley home. When she isn't traveling to meet readers, she enjoys reading, watching "shameful reality television," and visiting a local Hudson Valley animal shelter.

CONNECT ONLINE

JenniferProbst.com

AuthorJenniferProbst